I0608999

Touchstone Series

Other Books by Beth Barany

Touchstone Series, Romance Novellas, Books 1-4
Touchstone of Love
A Christmas Fling
Parisian Amour
A Labyrinth of Love and Roses

The Five Kingdom Series
Henrietta The Dragon Slayer, Book 1
Henrietta and the Dragon Stone, Book 2

Barany School of Fiction books
Overcome Writer's Block
The Writer's Adventure Guide
Twitter for Authors

Touchstone Series

Romance Novella Books 1-4,

Plus a Bonus Short Story,

"Falling in Love Again"

Beth Barany

Firewolf Books

OAKLAND, CALIFORNIA

TOUCHSTONE SERIES, ROMANCE NOVELLA BOOKS 1-4, PLUS A BONUS SHORT STORY, "FALLING IN LOVE AGAIN"

Copyright © 2015 by Beth Barany

All rights reserved. No part of this publication may be reproduced, distributed or transmitted in any form or by any means, including photocopying, recording, or other electronic or mechanical methods, without the prior written permission of the publisher, except in the case of brief quotations embodied in critical reviews and certain other noncommercial uses permitted by copyright law. For permission requests, write to the publisher, addressed "Attention: Permissions Coordinator," at the address below.

"Touchstone of Love" previously published in the collection, *Gargoyle: Three Enchanting Romance Novellas*, 2013.

"*Falling in Love Again*" previously published in the digital-only collection, *Autumn Magic*, 2014.

Firewolf Books
771 Kingston Ave., #108
Piedmont, California, 94611
www.firewolfbooks.com

Publisher's Note: This is a work of fiction. Names, characters, places, and incidents are a product of the author's imagination. Locales and public names are sometimes used for atmospheric purposes. Any resemblance to actual people, living or dead, or to businesses, companies, events, institutions, or locales is completely coincidental.

Book Layout ©2015 BookDesignTemplates.com
Book Design by Beth Barany
Cover Design by Beth & Ezra Barany
Cover Art by Beth Barany

Quantity sales. Special discounts are available on quantity purchases by corporations, associations and others. For details, contact the "Special Sales Department" at the address above.

Touchstone Series, Novella Books 1-4/ Beth Barany. -- 1st ed.
ISBN 978-0-9895004-5-6

Dedication to Ezra, my touchstone. For our yes.

For everything that is natural,
which is infinite,
which is yes.

−e.e. cummings

Table of Contents

Touchstone of Love

(A Time Travel Romance)

Novella Book 1 of the *Touchstone Series*

for her to finish her analysis for their client. Right after the conference, she had to rush back to her consulting job in San Francisco at one of the top software companies in the country.

She groaned at the thought of the report she had to complete. It was sitting in her tiny travel laptop. She wished she weren't planning to look at it at all during this trip—no matter what the deadlines were—she just wanted a fun, sexy romp and to forget about her normally busy life. She wanted an adventure. She wanted...something more. Rose shouldered her travel bag, sailed through customs, and settled in for the hour-long bus trip to the small Beauvais airport. She didn't mind the transfer; it fit the company budget and allowed her to doze and daydream about Brian's suave smile, generous credit limit and wonderful taste in plying her well with Swiss chocolate and delicious wine. She'd deal with the report once she arrived at the conference hotel.

"WHAT DO YOU MEAN, I missed my flight?" Rose asked in her most polite Parisian-accented French. She wanted to use a few choice swear words, but knew the French attendant would shut down like a trapdoor if she did. Rose wasn't trying to pick a fight, yet.

"Sorry, miss," the attendant said in French. She was dressed in a prim uniform, bright red lipstick, not a hair out of place. She waved Rose to step out of line.

Rose huffed and did as she was asked. She examined her travel itinerary for the hundredth time. All the times were there correctly. How could she have messed up? She dragged her tired body to a hard plastic seat, scrubbed her cheeks and palmed her eyes. That was supposed to calm her, she learned in one of the stress relief and relaxation seminars her boss always had her attending.

She blew out a breath and watched the next flight's passengers queue up in this small but busy airport. Something sparkled out of the corner of her eye, but when she turned to look, it was gone.

Rose re-examined her itinerary. What was going on? There. She spotted it, a transposition of a four for a five. She did that sometimes. Rose was an hour late for her flight. She swore under her breath. Anger faded just as quickly as it came, and she bounced up, satisfied that she'd found her mistake. She was ready for a solution. There had to be a solution to get to Edinburgh on time. Had to be. Brian was waiting. The talk she had to give on the interplay between human social behavior and computer response was waiting. She was missing her talk if she couldn't get to the conference today.

"So sorry to bother you but—" Rose rushed to the Help desk and addressed the attendant, a man in a pressed uniform, in her most polite French. "I need to catch the next flight to Edinburgh—today."

"Sorry, ma'am, but there are no more flights today.

Only one flight a day to Edinburgh."

"*Quoi?*" What? Rose stamped her foot and frowned.

She wanted to kick herself for being so stupid. She sighed. She felt idiotic.

"What are my options?" she asked in French, while the attendant watched her, a bored expression plastered on his pretty face. He probably saw passenger meltdowns twenty times a day. Even so, he rebooked her for the next day. See, there was a solution. She'd just get there a day late.

Rose hopped another bus, her fourth transportation vehicle of the day. She grumbled to herself, a mixture of French and English. Brian would be waiting for her.

She'd have to re-schedule her talk, if that were possible. The organizers would just have to deal, and maybe she wouldn't be invited back. Damn. She hated that, but she was helpless to do anything about it right now. She sighed and settled in for the ride to the nearby town of Beauvais. In the afternoon's fading light, she noticed an arbor in the round reminiscent of the pre-Christian era's rites of harvest. For a moment she thought she saw young women dancing in a circle, dressed in medieval period garb. She blinked. The vision was gone.

As the bus rumbled through the town, neat stone nineteenth-century buildings adorned the wide boulevard. Between two buildings she caught the glimpse of a tall spire that caught the light and sparkled like a beacon. Her heart quickened. She hadn't realized there was a cathedral in Beauvais. Maybe her overnight stay would be enjoyable. A pressure eased in her chest.

ROSE IGNORED THE LOOKS from other pedestrians and continued her walk-jog around Beauvais at dusk. She needed to clear her head. She still felt stupid for making that mistake with her itinerary and missing her flight, but at least she'd been able to get her talk rescheduled and email Brian about her delay. Her watch beeped, signaling the end of her run. She walked along the quiet streets then stretched against a stone fence, finally paying close attention to where she was. She'd made a wide circle of the central part of Beauvais.

Rose was almost where she'd started, a few blocks from her hotel at the center of town, and found herself at the foot of the town's thirteenth-century cathedral. She craned her neck to peer up to the spires, very tall spires, probably the tallest she'd ever seen, and she'd visited all the major cathedrals of northern France.

This cathedral had a funny-looking front door, not grandiose and welcoming as she'd seen at Notre Dame in Paris. The door seemed more like an afterthought, just squat steps leading to the door. She meandered around the closed cathedral in the setting sun and cooled down from her walk-jog. She heard some laughter of young women and men, but saw no one around. That was weird. She brushed off the illusion. She must be really tired.

Beautiful paving stones lay at her feet, huge limestone blocks at eye level, and fine stonework soared far above. She couldn't help it—she put her hands on the stone, feeling the echoes of history under her fingertips. She could swear she heard the sound of a chisel against stone. Her imagination was doing overtime, her jet lag getting to her.

She thought of the men who shaped the stone, cut the stone, quarried the stone, found the vein in the ground, and decided to build a cathedral, all in honor of, in this case, St. Peter. White limestone gleaming in the warm, setting sun, Cathedral St. Pierre looked polished and well cared for at over eight hundred years old.

Rose circled to the back of the cathedral. At least, it appeared to be the back of the grand building because there lay a small, full garden at the foot of steep steps, leading to plain doors. She'd never seen a garden at the back or front door of a cathedral. It seemed as if someone was about to step out of the stone under her fingertips. Just as she reached out, thunder boomed and lightning cracked, and Rose yelped at the stinging on her neck. Then all went black.

Chapter Two

JULIEN OF BEAUVAIS STOMPED through the edge of town, through the fields and the stormy dark. He didn't care about the wet and wind. He needed to find peace, he needed to find inspiration. It was time that he showed Master Stonemason Bernard de Chantilly all of his skill and artistry and present his masterwork to the community and get his approval, even if the master stonemason said Julien could not present his work at Michaelmas in five days.

The master stonemason didn't like him and had not allowed him to present the previous year. But this year would be his. It was time he showed Master Bernard that he was ready to become a master mason and travel as a free man. His training was complete. He'd become a journeyman and done a short trip to Paris with Master Bernard a few years ago. Yet, most men at his age of twenty-six years had already started their own houses and were busy at work on the new cathedrals sprouting all over France.

He wanted to travel to Amiens, or Rennes, and direct his own house, with a woman at his side, and his own apprentices, and a passel of children. The time was now. His time. Oblivious to the cold and the wet, Julien stomped through the field in anger.

Not only was Master Stonemason Bernard a barrier to his dreams, but so was also Marie-Jeanne, his intended. She'd betrayed him with that farm boy from the count's household.

How was he going to create a home when his betrothed was ready to run off with another?

That was why, in his anger, he'd messed up the day's stone carving work and had been relegated to sorting and breaking granite blocks for the other apprentices.

The rain pelted his face as Julien stumbled over something. He lost his footing and slipped to his knees. He put out his hands to brace himself and felt something soft. Soft and warm.

As gently as he could, as if he were handling a new -born lamb back at his parents' farm, he felt for the shape of the soft and warm, and unmistakably touched a breast. A woman fallen in the fields. In the cloudy night with no light of the moon or stars, he reached out to learn more about her. She was alive by the warmth of her, and by the strong pulse at her throat, and not long outdoors, as her skin wasn't completely chilled. He couldn't leave her, so he scooped up her unconscious, naked form and headed for his workshop hidden in a copse of chestnut trees outside the walls of the town.

Once inside his small workshop, he stoked the fire under the cook pot. He rushed to cover her with his blanket and rubbed the hands and feet of the woman, something he'd seen the old midwife do to women who sometimes fainted in the fields. The woman breathed deeply, but remained asleep.

She was naked, curved in all the right places. Clearly well fed, luscious, but quite improperly dressed for a fall night, as if she'd been bathing and wandered off from her task.

Maybe she was under some spell that made her sleep. While he was a god-fearing man, and worshipped Mother Mary, he knew magic was in the land. He felt it when he worked the stone every day, but never talked about it.

The woman appeared calm, even peaceful as she slept. Definitely a woman, not a girl. Her long golden locks had come loose from her tie. She had rosy cheeks, pink lips, an angular nose, and a long column of a throat. Her chest rose and fell with even breaths.

What color were her eyes? He pulled the wool blanket up under her chin, and tucked it around her body to keep her warm. A tiny waist, a warm shapely rump, long legs, strong feet—he noticed all that as he chastely tucked the blanket around her. He'd noticed that her palms were strong, with callused, long fingers, almost as big as his. She must be a farmhand from a neighboring village, but he didn't recognize her.

She was almost angelic in how she slept. His troubles forgotten, he made for his worktable on the other side of the one-room shed and picked up his chisel.

He'd found the inspiration he needed to start his work of art.

Chapter Three

A GENTLE CHING-CHING-CHING woke Rose up, the sound of metal hitting rock in delicate taps.

Rose opened her eyes to a remarkable sight in the warm lamplight. From where she lay on a bed, she could see through a crack in the curtain. A bare-chested man pounded a hammer in utter focus on the back of another tool, over and over again, in careful taps on a huge chunk of whitish stone. He had long, dark lashes, a stern, square jaw line, and lips pursed in concentration. She watched fascinated as he moved his arm in precise movements, his bicep muscles flexing and releasing. He wore faded white pants and leather shoes.

A hands-on man. She smiled and winced. She suddenly felt the pounding headache at her temples. She moaned, holding her head.

The ching-ching stopped. She met his eyes. They were dark brown, and held depth, dreamy.

He put down his tools and approached her, saying something.

"I don't understand," she croaked in French, her throat dry.

He repeated himself, speaking slower. This time she understood, but his French sounded strange. He'd asked her if she was okay, but his words translated to asking if she was of good health.

She answered back in French that she was of good health and only had headache. "Where am I?"

He said something and stepped closer. He was even more good-looking up close. She wanted to reach out and touch his chest. A smattering of dark chest hair was inviting her to brush her hands through it. So she did and practically purred at the warmth of his body and the feel of strength in his firm chest. "You are so beautiful."

He jumped back as if her hand burned him and burst forth in rapid French. She caught the gist of his strange, accented French, which he spoke like a native, so she had to be in some strange man's home. Maybe he was one of those crazy Middle Ages re-enactors who never broke character.

"Loose woman! You are incorrect, *madame,* in your actions toward me. One doesn't do that to a stranger. I'm a god-fearing worshipper of Mary and Christ. You must stop being so forward."

Rose's cheeks heated. Shaming in any language was still a shaming.

She sat up in bed, pulling the wool coverlet with her, and leaned against a wooden wall, ready to retort, when a few things clicked. He was speaking old French, what they spoke in the twelfth and thirteenth century. She recognized some words from her cathedral research and hanging out on those online forums. He must be an avid re-enactor! A nut job. Darn. He was so handsome too.

And the second thing she realized was that she was naked. What had happened to her clothes? She'd deal with that next.

She used her best polite and calming tone and held up a hand to show that she was harmless. "I am so sorry for the misunderstanding. I didn't mean anything by it." She spoke slowly hoping he'd flip into regular French.

He stared at her. She felt his gaze flick to scan her body and then hop back to her face, like he was trying not to stare. He gulped and his pupils dilated.

"Where are your garments, loose—madame?" He gestured at her, his voice full of shock and distaste.

"I don't know." Rose stood on shaky legs, making sure to wrap the blanket around her body, her bare feet sticking out.

She padded around the room, touching things— candlesticks, candles melted down, a bowl with small apples, a sturdy, wooden table, a stool, a block of stone—

She circled the block of stone resting on the ground. It stood a bit higher than waist high. From where she stood a few feet away, the smooth stone looked rounded at its top, like a ball or a head. There was a square pedestal at the foot. In between she could make out an outline of a form, shoulders and perhaps a chest. She wasn't sure. She was sure that what she was looking at was mastery, art. Lovely.

She turned to him, beamed a smile. "What are you make—" she began but he interrupted her.

"Stop where you are. No one is allowed to see my work!"

Chapter Four

JULIEN CLENCHED HIS FISTS. "Women!" he spat on the floor. "Always meddling. Always loose. How dare you!" He sputtered incoherently and stared at this strange harlot of a woman. Maybe Marie-Jeanne had sent a friend of hers from another village to tempt and torment him.

He narrowed his eyes at her. "Who sent you? Was it Marie-Jeanne?"

"What? What do you mean? No one sent me. I flew and then took a bus—" She put her hand out to steady herself on the worktable, a pained look on her face. "How did I get here?" she added softly.

Julien gulped, guilty, his face hot. He'd found her. He'd brought her here. Maybe someone knew his routine, that he roamed the backfields and the town in the middle of the night in search of inspiration. Maybe someone knew he was working on his art in the abandoned shed. He shook his head to clear it. Nonsense.

This time he held out his hand to placate her. "Come, let me help you lie down. The bump of your head must have made you dizzy."

She nodded and let him lead her back to his pallet. Once she lay down, he covered her and went to find a tunic for her to wear until her could figure out what to do about her.

Deus et Maria, she was beautiful under his blanket. Her pert breasts. He flushed again. He was a man, after all. Women weren't to be trusted, he reminded himself. He grit his teeth as he pawed through his jumble of clothes. A clean tunic or nearly clean one would do for now.

"Please wear this." He turned toward her. But she had already fallen asleep.

Chapter Five

THE DAWN SUNSHINE SLANTED onto the meadow and made the dew on the grass and tree branches sparkle like pearls. Rose had slipped on the tunic left by the bedside and tottered on bare feet on the hard packed earth. Birds in the grove of trees behind the cabin twittered their morning joy of the hunt, a vibrant cacophony. The cool morning breeze felt like a caress against her skin. Rose inhaled deeply. She'd never felt so alive. She was sure. Ah, this is why she traveled—to feel deeply, to be steeped in her senses, and to get all those buzzing thoughts out of her head.

"What are you doing? Get back inside!" She froze at his voice, the voice of the man from the night before. It hadn't been a dream.

"What? But it's a beautiful morning—"

He cut her off with a yank of her arm. One look at the man's stern expression had reality crashing down on her. Where were her clothes? Where was she? She really had to get to her presentation.

She tugged her arm out of his grip or tried to. But he held her firmly. That stopped her for a second. She knew a few self-defense moves, and for the first time in her life, finally used them. Without hesitation, she kicked him in the family jewels. He released his hold and bent over, groaning.

Far too soon, he straightened and spat at her, "Harlot!" He glared and pointed to the cabin. "Go inside."

Rose crossed her arms across her chest "What is your problem? I am not a harlot." Was that the best insult he could come up with? So what if she liked men—beautiful, muscular men, like him?

"My problem is it's not safe for you out here— dressed like that."

"What are you talking about?" Rose had put on the soft finely made linen shirt he'd left beside the cot. It came to just above her knees. "What is your problem, buddy?"

She used the French word for buddy, "*copain*," instead of the more intimate "*ami*," or friend.

He stood tall. He had to be still hurting. Man, he was tough. She had to admire his strength, even though he'd used it against her.

He held up his hands to show that he meant no harm. "I am not your buddy. Are you addled? Your head must still ail you."

Rose touched the back of her head, still tender. The pain of getting hit by something sharp flooded back to her. She shivered. "Where are we?"

"The edge of town."

"Which town?"

"Beauvais."

"Okay." But inside she felt frozen.

He looked at her like she had two heads. "Okay? What is this *okay*?"

Panic rose in her throat. "I really need to catch my plane. Where's the downtown? I just need to find my hotel. I have a presentation to give. In Edinburgh."

"I don't know this plane, but there is only one hotel here. And it belongs to the count." He looked at her oddly. "And Edinburgh is in King Alexander the Second's kingdom."

What? Rose shivered. The morning didn't feel so pleasant anymore. She felt dense, her head suddenly filled with cotton. And the day had started so well. She pushed an impossible thought away.

The super clean air. The quiet, aside from the birds. No other sounds. No cars. No horns. No electric hum of the TV.

This over-protective male. The impossible thought wouldn't leave. The mention of king and kingdom.

"What day is it?" She whispered.

He gestured for her to enter the cabin, without touching her. "It's four days to Michaelmas, so that would make it—the twenty-fifth of September, I think, in the reign of King of France, Louis IX."

What? She thought again. So, not a re-enactor. She shivered again, though it wasn't cold, and followed him into the cabin. She stood and watched him build a fire.

She opened her mouth, closed it again. How would she get home?

Courage, Rose said to herself, in French.

"What year is it?"

This couldn't be happening. Was she really in the Middle Ages? What about her friends, her family? She wouldn't see them ever again. Stunned, she rubbed her hands up and down her arms.

"The year of our Lord 1240."

He stood up from poking at the flames. He smiled slightly, as if she was a crazy person. She fixated on the dimple that showed up in one cheek, and noticed his lips— so inviting. He was real.

Rose sat on the cot. "Oh." No, it couldn't be. She wouldn't be getting to her presentation anytime soon, not for another eight hundred plus years. She stared off into the middle distance, unseeing. This was way worse than missing her connecting flight. She gulped and brushed off the tears from her cheeks. It was natural to be so upset when so far away from home, from her friends, job, and espresso machine, with no hope of return. She didn't even know how she got here. She didn't know how long she sat on the little cot in the little cabin, focusing on her breathing. Denial flooded through her. This couldn't be happening to her.

Finally, she popped back up and circled the shed again, touching each object with awe. "The thirteenth century," she breathed. She could always count on her can-do attitude. She wiped her hands over her face. The room was still there.

"What?" he said.

"So we're in the thirteenth century," she said brightly. "How did I get here?"

"I found you in a field behind the city walls."

"Oh. The last thing I remember was that I was standing in front of city hall, admiring—" She sat again. She'd been admiring a statue in front of the modern- day city hall, then there'd been the sound of thunder and a flash of lightning. She didn't remember any rain. "Was I struck by lightning?" she asked him.

"I don't know. You were lying in the rain when I found you, but were barely wet, so must have not been there for long."

"This can't be happening to me. Are you sure this is the thirteenth century?"

He said nothing, just continued to look at her as if she was a bit loony.

Rose popped up and turned in a circle. A bubble of panic threatened to engulf her. She'd never been so poorly prepared or poorly dressed for anything in her life. How would she get home? Would she ever get home? She wanted to throw a tantrum, shout that it wasn't fair. But that didn't really seem like her. She brushed her anger aside. She had to be strong and determined, like the statue in the center of town, in the twenty-first century, and channel her anger into constructive areas. She brushed back a tear and blew out a breath.

Nothing could be done about returning now. She'd just have to wait until the next rainstorm and hope she'd get hit by lightning again, if that was what had brought her here.

She turned to him, smiled, and stuck out her hand. "I'm Rose. What is your name?"

He looked at her hand and back at her face, but didn't take her hand. He frowned and then sighed, as if she were a burden somehow.

She waited. She didn't mind waiting for him. She could have done much worse, landing back in the thirteenth century. He was cute, handsome even, in a rough kind of way, with that dimple and those wide shoulders and tight waist... She gulped and found his face.

He smiled kindly, as if he'd made a decision, and spoke slowly. "My name is Julien." He flickered his gaze down to her feet, scanned up her body, and guiltily landed on her face.

"So very nice to meet you, Julien," she said in her most proper and polite French. "What are you making there?" She resisted the urge to saucily twirl for his inspection. Instead, she waved in the direction of the waist-high stone carving she'd admired the night before.

He took his gaze off her. He smiled with affection toward his stone, as if it were a dear person. He headed toward the stone and worktable. "That is my masterpiece." He spoke quietly, reverently.

"But what is it?"

He smoothed the head, or what she thought of as the head, and picked up a chisel. "A gargoyle. Or a grotesque, to be more specific." He gently tapped on the stone, making changes so small Rose couldn't tell what was different. "A gargoyle usually has a spout for water, but not always."

She followed him and leaned against the table. "It's beautiful."

His cheeks flushed. He glanced sharply at her and covered the gargoyle with a cloth. "I shouldn't tell you—you shouldn't be here—it's not proper—the way you're dressed—" He fumbled over his words. "I don't usually show my work to anyone before it's done."

Rose ignored his awkwardness. "Julien, your work is beautiful. You're an artist, but why do you hide your work away from others?"

Rose knew, based on the date of 1240, that the Cathedral St. Pierre was in progress, though she hadn't studied the plaques carefully when she circled the cathedral and didn't remember exactly when the cathedral was finished. Most cathedrals took over one hundred years to complete.

"If you're at the edge of town, as you say, then something is wrong here. Didn't—don't stonemasons work within a guild, together?"

Chapter Six

JULIEN STOOD THERE, CHISEL in hand. She confounded him. Beautiful, forward, insightful. And she didn't mock him. That above all started to chip away at his heart.

A distant bell chimed. The bells of St. Etienne. The monks were at their morning prayers, surrounding the relics of Saint Vast.

He shook his head to break the spell of her. "I need to go. You stay here. I'll bring you some food. And clothes. Don't go out. At all." He looked at her sternly. "You're my responsibility, until I—" He broke off because she nodded readily. He narrowed his eyes at her suspiciously. What? No fight? She had no strange remark for him. Oddly, he knew her enough to expect the unexpected. But she remained silent. She looked around the room, as if with new eyes. Women. They couldn't be understood. Or trusted. "Don't touch anything."

"What am I supposed to do here then? I have no phone, no laptop."

"I don't know what you're talking about. Just—stay here. I'll be back soon."

He stepped out into the chill morning. He should help her find her home, but—*Deus*—she was beautiful, and she needed him. Julien couldn't turn away from a woman in need.

Chapter Seven

AN HOUR LATER, AFTER Julien returned, Rose had eaten a hearty meal of thick bread and cheese and gulped down a mug of some kind of beer or ale. Delicious. She had to get the recipe for the thick ale. For what? She'd do what with the recipe? She couldn't share it on the social media. She couldn't snap a picture of it to share with her friends. She couldn't gossip about the latest, coolest foodie corner she'd found. She'd never see her fun, foodie friends again. She put the mug down on the tiny side table, which was actually a block of stone. She was stuck in the thirteenth century. She swallowed some tears. What would she do then? Her whole life was gone. In a slow wave, the sadness passed.

All right then.

She stood and clenched her fists. She breathed deep, then relaxed. Another technique she'd learned in one of her stress and relaxation workshops her boss sent her to. She picked up the dress Julien had brought back from wherever he'd gone. "You want me to wear this?"

Julien looked up from his tap, tap, tapping against the white stone hidden behind a white curtain. "*Oui*. Of course." He flushed, ducked his head, and went back to tapping, as if the garment she held in her hand was the most normal thing for a woman to wear. Of course, it was for him. He'd probably helped plenty of women out of a dress like this.

The dress was simple enough. She held it up to her body. The dark green wasn't the best color for her against her pale skin and blond hair, but it was long enough, covering her feet. The sleeves hung long and narrow. The dress had a scooped neckline and ties crisscrossed up the front. The bust was tailored a little, but didn't look too big.

Still wearing Julien's tunic, she slipped the dress over her head, and managed to get her arms in, but the narrow waist caught at her shoulders. The dress covered her face, and her arms were stuck in the sleeves above her head at an uncomfortable angle. She squeaked, "Hey, a little help here!"

"What?!" Julien sounded shocked, but she couldn't see his expression to know for sure.

She heard him set down his tools with a clank.

She felt a tug on her arms as Julien tugged the dress off. He was grumbling, but she couldn't understand his words. He must be using slang she didn't know. But she could smell him. Boy, did he smell good. She leaned in to his warm body and met a hard chest, or what she thought was his chest. She had a dress over her eyes.

"Stop breathing deep," he snapped, his breath warm in her ear. "Stop moving." He gave one more tug on the dress, and then she was free. He'd pulled the dress back off and over her head. For a moment, he was staring at her, only a breath away. She resisted the urge to yank the tunic to cover her legs.

He turned from her with more grumbling, his voice louder. This time she heard more of what he said. "Doesn't she know anything? What's wrong with her?"

"There's nothing wrong with me. What's wrong with you? Help me put this dress on." She huffed. She didn't want to admit it, but she felt naked, even though she still had his tunic on.

He turned back to her and looked at her oddly.

"What?" she said and shrugged. "Maybe I was raised by monkeys!"

"You must be addled. I don't know what you're saying."

Rose held her hands up in a placating gesture. She'd been doing that a lot since she got here. She couldn't believe she was here. How could she never see her friends again? This couldn't be happening to her.

She brushed away the thoughts. She couldn't dwell on what couldn't be. She had to focus on the here and now and find a way to make this work. There had to be a way. Had to be. Grief threatened to bubble up, but her practical nature quashed the sadness. She'd examine it later.

She took a deep breath and gazed up at him because he felt his attention on her from a foot away. His chocolate brown eyes had specks of green in them. Enchanting.

He was watching her, half fascinated, half something else. Was that attraction?

She smiled, her best winning smile, the one she used to get what she wanted. "Julien, will you help me put on this dress?"

He gulped, his pupils dilated.

She smiled inwardly. Time to reel him in. She pouted. "I— where I'm from—we don't wear dresses often. So, I'm sorry, but I need your help."

He started as if coming out of a reverie. "I am here to help," he said. He loosened the ties at the front of the dress, and held it out to her without a word.

Rose stepped toward him, and feeling a little dizzy, put her hand on his shoulder to steady herself. Warm and strong were the words that jumped to mind. And chocolate. She didn't think chocolate yet existed in Europe. She'd miss chocolate. The thing she loved maybe as much as she loved sex. A close toss-up. She would not tear up about chocolate.

"Rose," he said.

She started. She'd gotten lost for a second in the thought of them rolling on the bed on satin sheets in a luxury hotel, licking chocolate off his— "Oh." She smiled and slipped the dress on over her head without a hitch.

"Arms." He said.

"Uh?"

"Hold out your arms."

She did, and he turned the sleeves so the seam was on the underside. His touch was gentle. She shivered involuntarily.

It looked like he was gritting his teeth. She wanted to tease him about how painful it must be to help a woman get into a dress instead of undressing her, but something about the pain in his eyes and the stubborn clench of his jaw stopped her. And she always trusted her read of people, though she didn't know the why of the signals. At least not consciously. She wanted to know his why.

In a moment he turned away, then came back with another layer. "Lift your arms," he commanded.

He slid another shorter dress, more like an apron, over the first layer. "Turn."

She turned away from him and felt him fiddle with something at her back. "How will I get out of this?"

"It's easy." He turned her gently at the shoulders so she faced him again. "You untie the back, then unlace the front." He blushed.

She wanted to caress his face. "You—you are being so kind to me. I—I'm kind of lost."

"I know. You are a woman in need. I am a gentle man, sworn to protect and watch out for those weaker."

She stood close to him. "I am grateful. Thank you." She gulped, not being able to prevent the tears. She felt overwhelmed with her situation and what she had to do—find a way to survive in 1240 Beauvais, France, over eight hundred years from home.

She reached out and touched his cheek. It was rough with stubble. How did men shave in the thirteenth century? She'd love to see that.

He let her then moved his head away. "Come." Julien held out his hand. His broad smile transformed his face with angelic radiance.

Rose took it without hesitation, his grip warm and firm, reassuring her with his strength. "Where to?" She caught his infectious excitement. God, he was beautiful when he smiled. He practically glowed.

"We will find you a place to work."

"Okay. You're a practical thinker, like me." She followed him out the door into the morning sunshine.

He eyed her sidewise but said nothing.

What kind of work, she wanted to ask, but asked instead, "Why are you so excited?"

"Well," Julien smiled broadly as he led her across the field. "So I can get to work. You've inspired me to complete my piece, and...you can't just stay hidden anymore. You're too pretty. I mean—" His blush was so charming.

"You're not so bad yourself," she said, recovering her cool. She smiled at his boyish enthusiasm.

"I can shape the gargoyle now; I know what she looks like and I'll—" He rattled in rapid French using technical terms she didn't understand.

Julien led her toward a waist-high crumbling wall. He let go of her hand, leapt the wall, and turned to her with his arms out. But Rose ignored him, hiked the dress skirt, and hopped the wall in an easy leap. He frowned at her and turned away, without watching if she were following. Rose hurried to catch up. If he didn't like that she could do things for herself, then fine. She hoped not all women were so dependent on men here in 1240 year-of-our-Lord Beauvais. They passed some stands of chestnut trees heavy with fall leaves. Hay was tied in tall, triangular bundles. Soon they were on a small dirt track.

"Are we in the town?" she asked Julien. Huts made of wattle and daub were spaced every fifty feet or so.

"No, not yet. There's the town, and the count's hotel." Julien pointed to a thick, eight-foot-tall stone wall in front of them. She'd seen other French towns that still had their rampart walls. She couldn't see beyond the wall.

She gulped. She could never pass as a true thirteenth-century woman, she was sure. She was too modern, too strong-headed, too—something. Panic surged. She rushed to catch up with Julien and reached for his hand. She felt calmer. It made no sense to mope about hidden in a little artist's hut.

"You're coming with me, right?" she asked.

He looked over to her with an expression of concern as they walked under a stone arch. "I would not leave you to your own devices so newly arrived into my town." He squeezed her hand.

Before she could express more of her fears, they were at a door of a massive house, and Julien was knocking and chattering in rapid French to the aproned, bent old woman who'd answered in just as rapid French.

The woman kept eyeing Rose, a deep frown lining her face. Finally the woman grunted a word, "Enter," and waved Rose into the house.

Rose stepped across the threshold. "Julien! I don't know how to—" she said when he didn't follow her into the house.

"Shh. You'll be in good hands with Ellie here. I'll come get you at sundown." He gave her a kind smile.

Ellie shut the door on Julien. "Come, we have work to do." The round woman hustled off faster than her big frame seemed it could go.

Rose hurried after her, gulping at the panic thumping in her chest.

Chapter Eight

HOURS LATER, ELLIE HUFFED at Rose. "You can't do anything, madame. Wait here. Don't touch anything." The old woman waddled away, leaving Rose in the dark anteroom by the back door.

Rose slumped on a tiny stool. She hadn't been able to even mop properly. How was she to know that converting a broom with a rag to create a makeshift mop would be considered tantamount to witchery, that she was supposed to get down on her knees and scrub her heart out with a brush the size of a toothbrush. And when she finally did that, she was too much of a perfectionist to get much of the grand hall done by the end of the day. She'd only had a five-minute lunch break of cheese, bread and ale. Really? She couldn't mop to their exacting specifications? Last time she'd mopped a floor was—never. She'd always had housekeepers growing up and when she lived on her own after leaving home. She was a thinker, organizer, planner, leader. Not a mopper. But she was sure she could learn such skills if they gave her a chance. How was she ever going to get a job here if she couldn't do the simplest of skills? Hopelessness washed over her.

She jumped up at the knock on the door, heart clanging like a cable car rattling up a San Francisco hill. Ellie was nowhere in sight, so Rose opened the heavy wooden door. "Julien, thank God."

He frowned. "What happened?"

She'd caught a glimpse of his brilliant smile until she'd spoken. "I had a really bad day. I was fired."

"Fired?"

Maybe that word hadn't been invented yet in French. "Let's go. They don't want me."

"Oh. Where's Ellie?" He craned his neck into the empty hallway.

Rose shrugged. "I don't know. She told me to sit here and not touch anything." Rose stepped outside, into the cool evening air, and shut the door. "Come on. Maybe I can work somewhere else, like where you work. With your stonemason."

"You don't do stone work." They walked the path back toward the wall.

"No, I mean in that household."

Julien said nothing.

She couldn't hide the anxiety that made her voice rise. "I need to do something here."

"We all need to work. What did you do where you're from?"

"I—" How could she describe her software job from the twenty-first century to him? "I helped people have a better day." She smiled.

He seemed to think about that for a moment, and then asked, "But where? Where do you come from?"

"Not here."

"I know that." Impatience crept into Julien's voice. "But you're here. Why?"

Rose shrugged and whispered to herself, "I don't know."

"Excuse me? What did you say?" He softened his request with humor in his voice. "Speak up, Rose-from-not-here."

They'd passed the wall and the arch and were now trudging through the fields toward Julien's workshop. The sun was setting.

"I don't know how I got here. I'm from a very different time and place," Rose said louder, opting for honesty.

Julien, frozen in mid-stride, turned to her. He gripped her hands in his, his gaze searching her face.

She felt warmed by his gesture, even though she was at his mercy. Vulnerable. Alone.

"There's something different about you." He peered into her eyes, a slight smile on his lips. "You're... honest."

He dropped his gaze and her hands. Rose felt him pull away from her emotionally, even though she hadn't moved an inch.

"I am." She smiled, feeling sad at how he pulled away. There was so much she didn't know about him, this place, everything. She was overwhelmed.

Julien lifted her chin. "Come. Have you eaten? I have stew, brought from the house. Cook is good."

Rose let that cheer her up when what she really wanted was to throw herself at him. But she relied on him for everything. She didn't want to muck it up. For once, she wasn't sure she could manage on her own. She couldn't just have a fling with him, like she usually did with men, and walk away back into her own busy life.

But not one to dwell on her troubles, she grabbed his hand. "Let's go." She had to find a way to make this work.

Chapter Nine

JULIEN SWUNG THEIR JOINED hands between them. He'd only known her for one day, but already he couldn't bear to be apart for long. The thought of returning to the men's quarters to sleep at Master de Chantilly's manor, as he normally did after working late into the night in his workshop, was not appealing.

Rose inspired him like no other. Her happy can-do attitude, her beauty, her smile, her smooth skin.

He couldn't have fallen for her so quickly. He just couldn't. Even though he'd caught Marie-Jeanne with Jean-Paul, one of the count's stable hands, no one else knew about Marie-Jeanne's indiscretion. As far as Master Bernard and the count knew, Marie-Jeanne and he were still betrothed. The wedding was to be in the spring with the other couples. If he said anything, he'd disgrace Marie-Jeanne and be dishonorable in the eyes of Master Bernard and the count. He was stuck. And now he'd met Rose, a gift from the land.

How could he have fallen for her so quickly? She needed him; she was a stranger here, and a tiny bit addled, what with her talk of being from another time. But maybe she'd been touched by the fey that frolicked in the fields at the light of the moon. He'd heard tales. For some reason it didn't matter. She'd landed in his pathway; she inspired him, opened him to beauty and possibility and a touch of the unknown. His gargoyle was shaping up nicely. He showed his art to no one else before it was complete. But she was special. He couldn't wait to show her his progress. In his artist's studio, her very presence inspired him to work, but that was all there would be between them. Nothing more. He was an honorable man.

As they walked the rest of the way to his workshop, Rose asked smart questions about his art and stonework and kept him talking. He chattered away about his day with his fellow masons at the foot of the growing cathedral as they walked the rest of the way to his workshop.

She was such a good listener. He felt like she really cared and that he was the center of her universe. His heart ached a little. Why couldn't Marie-Jeanne be more like Rose? He was already anticipating the moment when Rose would leave, and Marie-Jeanne would be in her place. He shoved that thought away; it made him too sad.

They stepped into his workshop. Rose turned to him and surprised him with a kiss on the lips. Without thinking he pushed her away. "You cannot do that," he said.

"What is wrong with you? I just wanted to thank you."

"You say '*merci*' to thank someone. You don't make such forward gestures."

"I've never met a man who was such a prude." Rose huffed at him. "It's just a kiss."

"I am a gentleman, an honorable man, not a prude. Besides, I am betrothed."

"You are? So?" She said saucily.

Women! He couldn't understand them, but clearly he needed her—for the inspiration she brought to his art. "Kisses are precious, not to be given lightly."

"What do I need to do to earn one?"

Her eyes sparkled with mischief. God, she was beautiful. His hands itched to pick up his tools. Not that tool. *Vixen.* He rushed to his table and started to chisel away.

Rose said nothing. For that he was grateful.

Chapter Ten

ROSE LET HIM WORK and downed the stew and ale. More ale. Did drinking so much ale increase alcoholism and drunkenness? Not that she'd seen any evidence of that yet. Had they built up a huge alcohol tolerance? Drinking didn't seem to make people happier in general, though, from what she'd seen in her one day in the thirteenth century.

In the count's household, the people she'd seen had seemed unhappy more than not. Ellie was always frowning at her, each time she'd come in to check on her and scold her or point out a flaw in her work; other servants, young and spry, or old and slow moving, seemed to scurry by with hunched shoulders, head down, not making eye contact with her.

A woman in a fur-lined cloak and a finely dressed man strolled by while she was doing her endless mopping and stone cleaning. They didn't acknowledge her in any way. The only person who had been somewhat friendly had been a girl scrubbing clothes at the well in the perfectly manicured courtyard.

The young woman had smiled winningly at Rose and introduced herself as Marie-Jeanne. She was pretty in that youthful way and seemed unaffected by all the hard work that she was surely used to, all that scrubbing of clothes together, wringing out the heavy dresses, and hanging the wet fabric on a clothesline. Very easily and methodically. Marie-Jeanne was strong. But she hadn't seen Marie-Jeanne the second time she'd gone out to the well for a fresh bucket for all that meticulous floor washing.

Rose rolled her shoulders. God, her muscles were sore. A nice massage from Julien's strong hands would be nice, so delicious. Throw in some massage oil, scented candles, and a hot bath and she'd be in heaven.

Except Julien had literally pushed her away. Besides, she was far from the amenities of her time. Maybe Julien was right to do so. He was betrothed after all, and she really shouldn't make any more advances. But when had that stopped her in the past? Her former lovers had sometimes been husbands or boyfriends separated from their wives or lovers. But here, she had only him to rely on.

Hours passed while Julien worked on his gargoyle, only occasionally looking up to stare off into the distance. She sat by the fire and rested, mostly with her eyes closed, daydreaming. Apparently, her presence was enough to get him going. She was happy about that, but...some cuddling would be nice. Rose didn't feel like being rejected, though. There was only so much stimulus she could handle for one day. Time travel was tiring.

After awhile, the fire in the pit died down to embers. Rose crawled into his cot and let the noise of chisel on stone lull her to sleep, wondering where he would sleep.

At some point in the night, Rose awoke. The workshop was silent. In the ember's glow, she could barely make out Julien's slumped form by his gargoyle.

She felt around for another blanket for him. Finding none, she slipped over to his side with the one blanket she had. She tucked the blanket around them both and huddled beside him, nestling her head against his shoulder, and her body against his warm one.

Chapter Eleven

ROSE AWOKE IN JULIEN'S cot, the blanket tucked around her body. Her heart warmed at Julien's gesture. He must have carried her back to his cot. She'd tried to take care of him; he'd taken care of her in return. The workshop was quiet. In the morning light coming through the small windows near the ceiling, she didn't see him anywhere. She quickly donned the dress the best she could and straightened the bed. Without thinking too much about it, she straightened out other things. She found a comb and used it with gusto, braiding her hair. She grabbed the bowls and tankards from the night before and stepped outside to find a well. When she didn't see one, she made for the trees. Just as she thought, a small creek rumbled through the copse. The water looked clear enough. She rinsed out the dishes and washed her face and forearms. She'd have to find out how to take a bath. The privy she'd used yesterday was just a bare closet.

The morning was as bright and beautiful as the day before. She could get used to country living. She headed back to the workshop, serenaded by the happy twittering of birds, the bright blue sky overhead, not a cloud in sight. Today was the day she'd find a job she could do, and start to make her way in the new, strange world. But she didn't feel as certain, as "can-do" as she normally did. Falling back into the thirteenth century could have that effect on a woman. So could not showering, and not knowing how she'd get home. She brushed the thought aside. There was nothing she could do about that.

Julien hadn't shown up by the time her cleaning and straightening was done. She'd have left a note but didn't see any paper or writing implement. So she made her way to the village, butterflies vying for attention in her chest. She'd find her own way to the stonemason's house and get a job there.

She walked through the field, passed the portal unquestioned and made her way down the road, wide enough for a cart or wagon. Men and women hurried down the road. She followed them, wishing to ask them for directions, but she felt shy.

The road opened up into a bustling marketplace. She smiled. She loved marketplaces. This one was bustling with farmers selling out of wagons and makeshift tables. She strolled through the lane. Round farmwives and skinny ones, young men and old were yelling about their ripe apples, healthy greens, and fresh bread and cheeses.

She hurried her steps. A familiar face. Marie-Jeanne was carrying a basket next to the old housekeeper from the count's household.

"Marie-Jeanne," Rose called out when she was near.

Marie-Jeanne greeted her with a friendly *"Bonjour"* and smiled broadly.

"How do I get to the stonemason's house?" Rose asked.

Marie-Jeanne frowned and narrowed her eyes at her. "Why do you want to know?"

Rose gestured toward the old housekeeper who'd nodded at her without a word, frowning. "It didn't work out at the count's."

"Oh." Marie-Jeanne leaned in conspiratorially. "The old bird is just unhappy at home." She burst out laughing.

Rose smiled, a little shocked at how outspoken Marie-Jeanne was, since the old housekeeper was standing right next to her, still frowning, but didn't appear offended. "So, do you know? How to get there?" Rose insisted.

"I do," Marie-Jeanne said a bit smugly. But said no more.

"I need a job, Marie-Jeanne. Please show me how to get to the Mason's house."

"All right, I'll show you once I'm done with old grumpy here."

"Actually, I'd like to go there on my own."

"Why?"

"I know someone there."

"Who?" Marie-Jeanne seemed innocent in her questioning but Rose felt like she was probing and being awfully inquisitive on what should just be a simple matter.

"One of the stonemasons."

"Who?"

"Why do you ask, Marie-Jeanne? Who do you know there?" Rose said casually.

It was just the question it seemed the young woman wanted. Her eyes got dreamy. "His name is Julien, and he has these shoulders, and his arms—"

"Is he your betrothed?" Could it be the same man, her Julien? He wasn't hers, she mentally scolded herself.

"Yes." Marie-Jeanne shrugged. "So? What have you heard?"

"Oh, nothing, nothing at all." Rose fluttered her hand. "Well, I know Michel. His distant cousin, in fact. We're related." Rose held her breath. Wouldn't there be a Michel in every large household? She hoped there would.

Marie-Jeanne frowned. "I don't know Michel well, but he's nice enough, I suppose."

Rose let out her breath and smiled. "Well, then, just point the way, and I can get to work."

Marie-Jeanne narrowed her eyes at Rose. "You're related to Julien? He never mentioned you. But he never talks about his family." She shrugged. "Never mind." Then she smiled, showing off her pretty face. "Sure. It's near the cathedral the bishop is building. So go to rue St. Pierre, go around the back of the pile of stones there. That's the cathedral's foundation, Julien says. The stonemason's manor house is back there. Just ask when you get there because those streets don't have names yet, I don't think."

ROSE'S STOMACH FLUTTERED AS she knocked on the back door. From what she'd read in historical romance novels, servants used back doors; Julien had brought her to a back door at the count's house; ergo, back doors were the way to go. She wasn't dressed as any sort who could manage the front door of the huge manor. Rambling thoughts, she chided herself. No reason to be nervous, just applying for a job in 1240 Beauvais, France, with no chance of going home, and not very good at cleaning stone floors, apparently.

"Good morning to you, dearie, we've been expecting you." An old woman's words startled Rose out of her little pity party.

"You have?"

The old woman's face was lined like a crab apple. "Yes, the portends have foretold it. Come this way."

What portends, Rose wanted to ask, but she was too nervous. With that, Rose entered the stonemason's household. She didn't even need to use her cover story that she was a distant cousin of Julien's as she followed the wizened woman down the narrow hallway. The old woman was small and thin, where the housekeeper in the count's household was large and round; she had her hair in a soft, messy, white bun at the back of her head, whereas the other housekeeper had her jet-black hair pulled back fiercely from her stern face. And this old woman was welcoming, if a bit strange, whereas the other woman had been mean and not so welcoming.

Maybe things would work out here. *Let that be a comfort to you,* she whispered to herself, an echo of something her grandmother had said to her. Rose sniffed at the uninvited tears that threatened. She'd never see her grandmother again, the only family member who hugged her, as if she'd never her let go.

Chapter Twelve

ROSE BENT TO HER task, scrubbing the floors and walls of the main hall, and laying rushes with a shy young girl about ten years old who couldn't speak, according to Madame Delore, the elderly housekeeper who'd greeted her so mysteriously hours ago. As she worked through the grand room in peaceful silence with the younger girl who would smile at her shyly from time to time, Rose watched the stonemason's household bustle around her.

She didn't see Julien. Was he worried about her? Would he come after her? Had he gone to fetch her at the workshop? If he did search her out at the manor, then that would mean that he liked her, she hoped.

Out of line, girl, she scolded herself. The man was taken.

After a small but delicious lunch in the warm kitchen with the girl, Rose was back at it, finishing up of the laying of rushes. She was bent over scattering the sweet smelling hay when a huge voice boomed out a roar of incoherent anger. She froze. Was someone hurt?

A red-faced man was hustling out of a cloak at the front door across the hall and shouting at a young man who was standing there, as a servant waits on a master. The young man said something Rose couldn't hear and caught the red-faced man's cloak as it was practically thrown at him.

"I will not let him display his gargoyle in the competition at Michaelmas," the big man shouted. "I will not!"

"Yes, sir," said the lackey.

The loud red-faced sir must be the stonemason. Who else would act so lordly in such a big house where everyone seemed to have a place?

"I will not. He cannot. Julien is nothing without me. I will not allow it."

"Yes, sir," repeated the servant, following the big red-faced man to the other end of hall to the high table.

"Send for my meal," ordered the stonemason.

The servant bobbed his head and scurried away toward the kitchen.

Rose ducked down but not soon enough.

"Girl, who are you? Come closer. Are you the new housekeeper's help?" The stonemason bellowed.

For a second, Rose was frozen. Should she pretend she didn't hear him? That she was deaf, maybe? No, she had to play it straight. She straightened and walked toward him. He was just a client, like any other, she lied to herself.

"I've never seen you before. Come closer. You're quite a beauty, aren't you?" he chuckled as if it were a private joke.

Rose gulped, and clenched and unclenched her fists. "Hello."

The master stonemason eyed her up and down. Then he smiled. "You'll do. Get back to work."

Rose nodded her head. She didn't think she could manage a curtsey, nor did she know if one was warranted. Instead of heading back to the rushes, she aimed for the kitchen. The man was a pompous ass.

She had to find Julien.

Rose stepped into the kitchen. Madame Delore was nowhere to be found; she'd know where to find Julien. The cook and two servants bustled about quietly, heads bent to their tasks. They ignored Rose.

She'd find him herself. She stepped outside and headed for the chink-chink of metal against stone coming from the back area. She stopped just at the edge of a stone field. It looked as if a giant had smashed granite and limestone with a huge fist. No rhyme or reason seemed to rule the field. Rocks and boulders filled the area. A handful of men, from young to old bent to their tasks. A wagon stood at the far end of the field. A few men were unloading stones, moving them down ramps because the stone was much too large to carry.

Still she didn't see Julien. She circled the yard, eyeing each man carefully. She'd only known Julien for two days. Maybe she wouldn't recognize him from afar, but she didn't think so. She ended up near the back gate. A chest-high stone fence divided the field from a road. Voices raised in argument in rapid French. Julien arguing with a woman.

"What were you doing with him?" Rose heard Julien say.

Rose couldn't hear the answer, but she did recognize the voice. That was Marie-Jeanne, his betrothed.

Rose should go. She shouldn't eavesdrop on a private conversation. She swiveled to turn away, and then heard her name on Marie-Jeanne's lips and stopped.

"That strange girl, Rose, was asking about you."

"Oh?"

"Yes, she was looking for you, wanted to know where you worked."

"What did you tell her?"

"I told her. I sent her here. I'm sure Madame Delore, she's strange too—a witch of the heathers, you know— let her work here. You know how Master Bernard is always scaring away the help with his temper."

"Stop such gossip. If we're to be married in the spring, you're not to speak poorly of Madame Delore or Master Bernard."

"Hey, you're hurting me. Let go of me. We're not married yet. Jean-Paul is not like you. He's gentle."

"You know we have to get married, even though you were with him." Julien spat.

"Why?" Marie-Jeanne whined.

"Because that's the way it is."

"I could run off..."

"You'd disgrace me and the two houses. Both the count and the master stonemason would disown your family and me. I forbid it."

"Julien..." Marie-Jeanne crooned.

The girl was using her seduction wiles on Julien to get what she wanted. Rose had to admire the girl for using what she had. There had to be a way to help these two and get what she wanted.

Rose hurried back to the manor. She couldn't interrupt them. It wouldn't be right. What would she say? "Julien, your boss doesn't want you to present your gargoyle in the competition at Michaelmas."

Yeah, that would make his day. But she had to do right by him somehow and let him know. Michaelmas was two days away, if she had her days straight.

Chapter Thirteen

ROSE WAS EXHAUSTED. MADAME Delore had led her through the entire manor, where Rose had cleaned cobwebs off the ceilings and scrubbed more flagstone than she ever thought possible. But at least Madame Delore was kind.

She lay on a lumpy bed in the servants' quarters; other servants snored in the dark of the night. Despite her fatigue, she hauled her butt up. She had to get back to Julien's cabin and let him know what she learned.

Wrapped in a dark cloak she borrowed from another servant, Rose snuck out of the manor house and hurried down the lane toward what she hoped was the right way. Luckily, the moon was up. With the inner map in her head of modern Beauvais and what she'd seen so far of 1240 Beauvais, she knew the city hall was straight ahead, and that behind city hall she'd find the broken stone wall that Julien had offered to help her over, only the day before.

She hoped no one would stop her as she scurried through the quiet streets. Even the small house of ale she passed was quiet. She made it into the fields without incident. She let out a breath and felt a little shaky.

Julien's cottage sat squat beside some trees. A light twinkled from the high window.

She knocked softly on his door. No answer. She waited a beat and knocked again. When he still didn't answer after a few minutes, she pushed the door open.

He was bent over his stone, chiseling some detail work in the foot region of the white pillar. Instead of the louder ching-ching-chings, his small chisel barely made a scrapping noise as he made tiny changes. His profile faced her. For a moment, she watched. She couldn't bear to interrupt him. He chewed on his bottom lip for a moment, and then leaned back, squatted on his heels. He angled his head, studying his work. Then bent at it again.

She loved his focus, his total absorption. She sighed.

Julien looked up and snapped to standing, surprised. "What are you doing here?"

"What? I can't come here anymore? I came to tell you something."

Julien turned away from her and put down his chisel. He turned back to her, his features smoothed and neutral. "Please, be seated." He gestured at his bed. He folded his arms. His tunic stretched across his broad chest.

Rose sat and mirrored him by crossing her arms over her chest. Her fingers itched to rub against his chest, to have him hold her with his strong arms, up against his firm body. She looked away. He was taken; she was stuck here; she couldn't even play with him. The ways were different here.

"Well? You're here to tell me something?"

"Yes." Rose stood. She needed to be on equal footing with him, needed to look him in the eye as an equal. "I overheard your master stonemason say that he wouldn't let you display your gargoyle in the competition at Michaelmas. I thought you should know. What competition?"

Then she shut up before she blabbed her nerves away.

A display of emotions flashed in quick succession across Julien's face. Shock, anger, sadness, then shuttered to neutral. She caught it all more viscerally than intellectually. She shivered. It was as if his emotions were hers.

She breathed out. "I'm sorry."

"It's not your fault. He's never liked me, not really, and especially not since the count praised my work in front of him and all the other apprentices a few years ago. He didn't let me compete last year, either. But I'm going to compete this year, no matter what."

Rose nodded. She didn't know what to say, so she said the first thing that popped into her mind. "I met Marie-Jeanne today."

Julien frowned and seemed to cross his arms tighter across his body.

"What's the deal with her?"

"Uh?"

"I mean, what is going on between you two? You're together, aren't you? She seems protective of you, but you seem angry with her. She's your betrothed, isn't she?"

"You speak too much that is not for you to say."

"Okay." Rose opened the door. "Goodnight then, Julien."

She stepped out into night. She'd sleep at the manor. Clearly she was not welcome here. She grunted when her toe stubbed something, maybe a clump of grass. She couldn't see much with the tears in her eyes. Why should she care so much about how he treated her? She could leave Beauvais. She didn't have to rely on him; she was a resourceful, modern woman. She could learn the ways of the world. She didn't need him. She could find work in another town.

Something eased in her chest. She was resourceful, after all. Now she just had to find a way to tell Julien.

She turned around and stomped back into Julien's cabin.

He hadn't seemed to move from where she left him. He looked up, stunned, surprised and with a hint of longing in his eyes. Then he masked his emotions like his clean stone.

Rose came right up to him and put her hand on his chest. Before he could voice the protest painted across his face, she leaned in for a kiss.

In the quick kiss, she felt his soft lips welcome her, and she inhaled the scent of male and earth and stone.

She leaned back and smiled.

"What are you so happy about? I thought you were gone for good."

"Soon. Finish your statue. Then I'll go."

"Women..."

"What about us?"

Julien looked at her, eyed her lips, the column of her throat, and back up to her eyes, hungrily.

Rose obliged. She stepped into the circle of his heat. "Julien, kiss me!"

"I cannot. I am promised to another," he whispered. But he didn't push her or step away.

"And...?" Oh, she was bad, but in a few days she'd be gone to Paris on a morning caravan, and he wanted her. She wanted him.

"This is wrong." Julien turned away, a pained expression on his face. "Loose women." He shook his head.

"I am not a loose woman."

"You are—you throw yourself at me. You make me feel appreciated, and you ignore that I am with another."

"But is she with you?"

"What do you know about it?"

"I met her, remember? And, I overheard you two today at the back wall." Rose sat, feeling a little flat for revealing what she knew and poking at Julien's bubble of propriety. "What happened? She cheat on you?"

"I don't understand you, madame."

"Rose. Call me Rose. Did Marie-Jeanne—?"

She waved her hand to fill in the blank, but Julien just glared at her, refusing to fill in the blank and make this any easier. "Did she—how do you say here—play in the barn with another man?"

"She wants us both. I will have none of it. A betrothed must be faithful." Julien picked up his chisel and chipped away at his gargoyle half-heartedly.

"Why stay with her then? She obviously isn't good enough for you. She'll always want the other man."

"I know," Julien said.

Rose padded over to him and put her hand on his arm, stilling his work. "You will be unhappy with her."

"I know." He stood to face her. He searched her face. "But it's the way of it."

She felt that he was drinking her in with his eyes, with his artful way of looking. She felt pulled into his gaze. She caressed his arm up to his shoulder, and held his face in her palm.

He stilled, holding her with his eyes.

"You are an honorable man, Julien of Beauvais. How can I help you?" She stepped back, when she wanted to step forward, offering herself to him with no more words. She couldn't continue to tempt him and pretend he was a modern fling. Her throat clenched with emotion. He meant too much to her.

She had to tell him she was leaving before the competition; she just had to find the right time.

Chapter Fourteen

JULIEN STARED AT ROSE. For a moment, he saw them together, entangled with blankets and each other's heat. He blinked and put his one stool in the center of the cottage.

"Sit. Or don't sit." He motioned. "Just be here, with me. Your presence is what inspires me in my work. Please just stay here. With me."

She smiled at him then eyed the floor. A lovely blush bloomed on her cheeks. She was just his inspiration, his window to open to what was possible. Nothing more. It could never be anything more. He told himself that, but his body wasn't listening.

He turned toward his stone. It seemed to glow in the low candle and firelight. Sparkles mesmerized him. He got to work, tapping, chiseling, and standing this way and that. Looking up at Rose occasionally as she sat examining his room. She gazed to one side, so her profile was to him.

"You're not my model. You can move around if you like," he said.

"And do what?"

"Anything you like. Your presence inspires me. You're so beautiful." That just slipped out. But it was worth it. She smiled and his heart squeezed in his chest. Why couldn't he be with someone he loved, instead of someone chosen for him?

Love was more important than duty; it had to be. He shook his head. No, he was dreaming. He owed the master stonemason and the count his livelihood. He couldn't just dishonor them. Or Marie-Jeanne.

But Rose was so beautiful, and she so inspired him. He'd be known throughout the region as the best gargoyle creator for the best cathedral in all of France.

Now all he had to do was complete the gargoyle in time for the competition only two days away. Julien had a plan to get his gargoyle in the competition, no matter what Master Bernard said or did.

Divine providence and the magic of the land had lined up just right for him to bring love, light, and beauty to his work.

"Julien?"

He looked up from his work to smile at Rose as she circled his room, touching his everyday objects. "What?"

"I need to leave Beauvais."

He stilled. "You can't," he blurted out. *I need you*, he wanted to say, but couldn't get the words past his heart.

"I can't stay here. You're with her, and I can't bear it–" Rose looked away.

Were those tears? Oh no. *Please not tears.* He rushed to her side, a rag in his hand—he didn't even realize he'd grabbed it. He shoved it at her. He didn't know what else to do.

"You can't leave. I need you." There, he said it. His heart fluttered like one of the count's caged birds.

"For that?" she nodded in the direction of his statue.

"Yes."

"It's almost done, isn't it? You'll be fine. You have her."

Julien knew who she meant: the one he was betrothed to, by his master and the count: Marie-Jeanne.

"She isn't the one who inspires me. You are."

Rose shook her head sadly. "And then what? You win the competition, get married, and live happily ever after with Marie-Jeanne?"

Julien sucked his breath. His chest squeezed. All of a sudden, he couldn't bear to never see Rose again. He'd only known her a few days, and yet, and yet—she felt like his whole world.

Tears trickled down Rose's cheeks. He brushed them away.

Rose stood abruptly. "I never—never cared before about the other woman. But now I do. And I don't want to be one. You'll be better off without me. Your life will be less complicated."

Rose turned away from him, as if she was about to bolt like a nervous rabbit in the field.

"My life is mine to decide, Rose." Julien grabbed her arm.

"As is mine." She looked down at his hand and back at his face. "Julien, don't. You don't really need me. I was just a wrong-place-wrong-girl moment."

"Rose, I do need you." Julien pulled her against him. She was soft in all the right places, her breasts pressed up against his chest. She was warm and smelled of lilacs.

Rose didn't resist, just searched his face, a yearning, a sadness in her eyes. Her eyes also held a plea, a desire, smoldering there like a coming storm.

Julien obliged and answered her plea with a kiss. It was just one kiss. But what a kiss. He gave her all the passion she'd awoken in him. He cupped the back of her head, lacing his fingers through her blond tresses that had come loose with his touch.

She returned the passion, fueling his higher. Her arms wrapped around his neck, pulling his body against hers.

A kiss to remember her by. To sear her to him. *Mine, forever,* his heart whispered.

He broke off the kiss. No, this wasn't right.

"Go," he ordered. He turned his back to her and wiped his cheek at the unbidden tears.

He'd just have to finish the gargoyle without her. How would he be able to?

Chapter Fifteen

JULIEN—" ROSE SHOOK HER hands out and bounced on the balls of her feet. He didn't turn to look at her but waved her off. "I didn't mean now. I can stay— until you finish your gargoyle, until Michaelmas. I want to help you—I do."

Julien spun back to her. It looked like he was about to say something harsh, angry, as a way to get her to leave. She'd done much the same thing in the past to push a man out of her life. But he held himself in check. She admired his control.

He just shook his head at her. "This can never work. I am with another."

"Why do you have to marry her?"

He looked at her strangely. "You really aren't from here, are you?"

Rose gulped and shook her head "No. I told you. I'm from another time and place."

"That's just the way things are done."

"But why?"

Julien didn't answer her. Instead, he bent to his work over the stone, tapping away, as if struck by inspiration.

Rose sat. She was glad to help, but felt uncertain of her place. What would happen in two days' time when he won, hopefully, in the competition, and was wed to Marie-Jeanne? He'd forget about her; she'd go somewhere else and find a place for herself. Suddenly, she felt so lost, instead of certain.

She used to think things happened for a reason, but what if she helped Julien and was forgotten in return? She didn't want to be forgotten. She didn't want to be a footnote in his life. She wanted to matter to him. She played out the scenario in which she went to another town, like Amiens, or even Paris, that she knew would be bustling with cathedral building, and found another man to be with. That vision felt empty, felt like wishful thinking. Like a cheap joke.

He was right in front of her. For the first time in her life, Rose wanted a man and couldn't have him. She rubbed her chest. Her heart cracked open. Love hurt.

HOURS LATER, SHE WALKED beside Julien as they crossed the fields damp with early morning dew to the town. Neither of them had slept. She'd tossed and turned on his cot while he'd chipped away feverishly at his gargoyle, not letting her see his progress.

Tears came unbidden down her cheeks. Rose brushed them away angrily. She had to make things work for her. She was stuck here. She may as well accept her fate. Once Julien was done with his gargoyle, she'd leave to find her place in another cathedral town. She'd leave before Michaelmas.

But why had she been thrown back into 1240 Beauvais? There had to be a reason. She had to have a purpose. Many of the time travel stories she'd read revolved around doing a deed, making a difference without upsetting the timeline. In fact, one of her favorite TV shows when she was a kid worked that way.

She glanced at Julien. He watched the field in front of him, a step ahead of her, not looking from side to side. She could feel the energy between them. When they were together something seemed to hum between them.

Rose shook off the mysterious but warm feeling. They passed under the gate and wove their way silently through the town that was coming awake with early risers scurrying along the narrow streets. Julien delivered her to the back door of the stonemason's manor without a word. He nodded at her, not meeting her eyes, and smartly turned on his heel.

Her heart squeezed. She was only his inspiration. No more. *Get yourself together, girl,* Rose chided. All she had to do was find a job in a new town in a few days. No big deal. She'd done it many times back home. Pretending his behavior didn't sting, Rose turned away from Julien and rapped on the wooden door to announce her arrival, then pushed open the door and let herself in as if she'd entered the manor every day of her life. It was time to find out what she was made of in 1240 Beauvais, in the reign of the King of France, Louis IX.

Rose brushed at her cheeks to make sure her tears were dried. The heat of the kitchen warmed her. She hadn't realized how chilly it was outside. Her stomach grumbled.

"Miss Rose, come eat, then we have a house to clean and prepare for Michaelmas." The old crone housekeeper, Madame Delore, held out a wooden bowl to her and smiled kindly.

Rose gratefully wolfed down warm bread and cheese and a fresh cooked egg as the old woman explained how Michaelmas celebrated the feast of Saint Michael the Archangel and marked the equinox, the shortening of the days, and the end of harvest time.

As Rose wiped her mouth, the old crone smiled a toothy grin and winked at her.

"Today, we see what you're made of."

Startled, Rose opened her mouth to ask how she'd read her mind, but the housekeeper hustled off faster than her bent body seemed to support.

Madame Delore led her through the main hall and into a side wing she hadn't seen the day before. Several women were weaving, some were sewing. Without a word, Madame Delore handed her a dress, a tiny needle, and some wispy thread that looked practically invisible in the morning light streaming through the high windows. "Hem this," she ordered.

"What?" Rose squeaked. Her stomach dropped.

But the Madame Delore left, completely ignoring Rose's bewilderment. The old crone was good at that. Both the ignoring and the leaving Rose to her own devices.

The other women, all young, from ages ten to probably twenty, eyed her, the younger ones giggling. Then they looked away and bent to their work, whispering beyond Rose's hearing. She struggled to thread the needle. If she could learn how to do this, then she'd have a decent job and get out of Dodge. Surely, everyone needed seamstresses.

She examined the dress, a plain color-of-wheat affair that covered her lap. The color reminded her of the many conference rooms she'd lectured in. So not helpful. The stitches on the hem were minute and even, as if made by a sewing machine. She gulped and tried a few in the spot where the hem had frayed. Her stitches were huge, uneven, and looked like they were made by a, well, an ignoramus like her. She tried some more stitches, trying as hard as she could to match the tight petite stitches. Her hand cramped. She dropped the needle and shook out her hand. The needle tinkled on the stone floor. She looked up at some whispers and giggles.

"You'll never make it here," frowned one of the young women in a grey, neat frock.

Rose stood up. "Maybe not at sewing." Rose shoved the dress at the girl nearest her and stormed out. It was time to get out of there before she stabbed herself anymore with the damn needle. What was she thinking? These women and girls had probably been sewing since they could walk, probably before.

She stomped to the kitchen. There had to be something she could do.

Madame Delore pointed outside as soon as Rose stormed through the threshold. "Gather eggs." And shoved a basket in her arms.

She could do that.

Maybe she'd see Julien, too. *Shake it off, girl,* Rose thought. *He's not for you.* A sadness fell on her like a heavy cloak. There was only so much enthusiasm she could muster.

Hours later, Rose gobbled up the chicken stew for lunch. "Delicious," she said around a mouthful to the cook who'd just plopped the wooden plate-bowl in front of her. She ate in the kitchen, away from the other help. They sat down at the other end of the table, eyeing her with strange looks, some giggles from the younger girls.

She'd tried her hand at the egg gathering, but had been scolded by cook for dallying. She'd just been chatting with the egg guardian, or whoever the middle-aged man was. She hadn't been able to haul much water. The full bucket was heavy, and she thought she was strong. Then she'd seen Julien and called out to him. He'd waved her off without a word and bent back to chipping away at a big block of stone, half his height.

In the kitchen she wasn't much use either, except to stack wood in the wood box. Again she was scolded for taking her time and dilly-dallying in conversation. But the woodsman breaking apart the larger branches had been more than happy to talk to her about his work.

She'd been able to do the sweeping. That was about it.

Madame Delore tapped her shoulder and slid next to her on the bench. The old woman whispered something Rose couldn't hear. Rose bent in. "What?"

"Take this in your time of need." The old woman passed her a small bundle. Rose palmed it.

"What is it?" she whispered. She felt her face flame with heat. Was it something to do with her time of the month? How did women handle that here? When she'd visited the bathhouse just before dinner for a quick face and arm scrub, she'd been too embarrassed to ask such questions to the several women there.

Madame Delore didn't answer, just patted her hand.

Rose bent her head to hide her red cheeks and to undo the complicated knots of the leather thong. The old woman stilled her hand. She clicked her tongue and shook her head, no.

Madame Delore gestured for Rose to come closer. Then she whispered in rapid French how to use the herbs.

"But why? Does this have to do with the portends?"

"You want your love to survive and prosper, don't you?"

Rose nodded, heat flushing her cheeks anew.

"Good, me too."

Then Madame Delore stood up and left, leaving Rose once again on her own. Why the old woman took an interest in their love and her wellbeing, Rose didn't know. She was grateful for it, though. Rose quickly grabbed the bundle and fumbled with slipping it into her pocket in the dress.

What was going on that she needed a love potion? And would the love potion work?

Chapter Sixteen

THAT EVENING, ROSE STEPPED into Julien's cabin.

"What were you thinking leaving the manor this evening without me?" Julien said to her as soon as she crossed the threshold.

"Well, hello to you, too! I waited for you, but when you didn't arrive, I left without you. Is that what you're so huffy about?" Rose asked. "Or was that 'good bye, no, I won't be needing your help in finishing my statue that's due tomorrow.'" She turned toward the door and was ready to flee when Julien stilled her with his next words.

"I'm sorry," he said so softly she barely heard him.

She pushed out a breath and turned around.

"Come away from the door. Please, sit. Come by the fire. You look cold."

"Well, since you apologized," she sniffed. She wished he'd come over and rub his big hands up and down her arms for the kiss-and-make-up phase. They were already acting like a married couple with their silly argument about nothing. *I wish.* She pushed the irrational thought away.

He looked at her sideways like he didn't understand her tone of voice. "I did apologize." He bent to his work, the gargoyle hidden behind the curtain, the chink-chink-chink of the chisel working at a fast pace.

Rose sat by the fire and relaxed her muscles. They ached in places she didn't even know she had muscles. She wished the soreness wasn't from housework, but instead from a passionate romp with Julien. She bit back a sigh and sat quietly. A tension hung in the air between them.

She was leaving; he wouldn't need her in one day, and she was so very alone in the world after that. And under it all, he was mad at her about something, even though he'd apologized. But he still needed her. She wished he needed her in the way she wanted him to. And they had shared that kiss, warm, intimate, and full of heat. She'd felt a tenderness from him she couldn't deny. Why did it have to take a crazy weird fall back into another century for her to finally fall in love? It so wasn't fair.

"What's wrong?" Julien asked, breaking her out of her reverie.

Rose snapped her attention to him and unclenched her fists. "Nothing." There was compassion in his eyes, not judgment. She let her hands settle in her lap, tried to relax. Then she jumped up to pace and reflect on her new awareness. Love fluttered in her chest like a trapped bird. She didn't like the feeling one bit. Julien was focused on his stone. That was good. She knew her presence inspired him. Her heart warmed. She paced through the cabin, touching objects, like she'd done the first day she'd arrived. Was that only three days ago?

She picked up a small stone carving of a tiny dragon. It was marvelous, delicate and solid, as if it would wake up and scamper away.

"Rose." Julien sounded worried.

"What?" She spun to face him, distracted, nervous. "Did you make this?"

"*Oui*," he nodded and bent to the stone.

"Julien, what's going to happen to us?"

"Us?"

She set down the tiny dragon and was next to him in three steps. He quickly stepped in front of his gargoyle to hide it from her.

"Yes, us." She stood close to him, taking in his singularly male smell, earthy and rich. She breathed deep. "Since I'm go away soon, why can't we be together? Tonight." She pitched her voice low and breathy.

"Rose, you inspire me, and my work, but you are not my lover." He spoke so nonchalantly, brushing her off, and didn't look at her. She was surprised at his casual manner toward her.

"Julien, I want more than to inspire your work. I want— more. I want to know what you're mad at me about, really. Is it because I'm leaving? I want to know what your gargoyle looks like. I want to find a place here, I think. And I want you to kiss me. Now."

He looked at her now. Shock flashed through his eyes. His turn to be shocked. Ha! She was a vixen, as he claimed. She knew. And she wanted her kiss.

After a moment of hesitation, his gaze on her lips, Julien spoke softly, "For art," He leaned in. The kiss was a brush, a whisper. Rose let him give, and then leaned in, and took. She nipped at his lips to entice. He warmed up and gave in to her vixen ways and gave her a kiss that warmed her to her toes. He pulled back and smiled, satisfied as a cat full of a bowl of milk.

"I want more."

"Go over there so I can work, and I'll tell you why I'm mad at you."

JULIEN TURNED HIS BACK to Rose to gain his composure. She was such a tease. And to his surprise, he liked that about her. She was direct. Her tease wasn't a guise, wasn't a ruse to steal and take, but an honest and direct request. He wanted to grant her request. Then he shook his head. That wouldn't be right. He ignored his yearnings and focused on the gargoyle. It was shaping up and was almost done. He got lost in the feel of his work, the smooth stone calling to him, the way Rose did. He glanced at Rose wandering through his studio or sitting beside the fire.

He loved how her waist curved in then flared at her hips. He loved how his simplest touch made her smile and glow with his attention. She was real with him. He loved her questions and her interest in his art. It wasn't so much the shape of her that inspired him—not just that—it was her spirit; it was the sense of possibilities that she carried without even knowing it. He'd never met anyone like her before.

He felt Rose's gaze on him on and off as she paced around his room. She folded his clothes, straightened his bed, and organized the little dragons and other creatures on the small ledge by his bed.

"Is this a griffin?" She'd picked up another one of his stone figurines.

He stepped back from his work, rolled his shoulders, and nodded, smiling tiredly.

"I am finished for the night," he said. "You should head back to the manor house before anyone misses you and get some sleep."

Rose crossed her arms over her chest. She cleared her throat.

Julien moved his eyes from her lovely bosom to her face. She was lovely when she was mad. Really, she was lovely in any mood. He moved back to the gargoyle and smoothed away a small bit.

"You were going to tell me why you were mad at me, the real reason, when I arrived earlier tonight. And by the way, I'm sleeping here."

"You cannot sleep here."

"This is stupid. I slept here before, didn't I? The day you— you found me, and the night after that." Her voice broke on an emotion he noted but couldn't decipher.

He nodded, but kept chiseling. Even the tone of her voice, so strident and strong, and full of emotion inspired him. He tapped away, refining and smoothing the stone. So close. He was almost done.

A warm hand covered his, stilling his chisel. Rose's breath was warm in his ear, her body heating his as she stood next to him. "Let's go to bed."

He should feel offended, or at least uncomfortable by her forward actions, her warm, sultry voice. But he didn't. He only wanted her more, wanted to wrap his limbs around hers, wanted her to himself.

"Rose, I am betrothed to another," he managed to push out. "You know that." He instantly regretted his words. But honor required them.

"Do you love her?" Rose asked as she gently pried the chisel from his grip.

"Love has nothing to do with it." But he let Rose wedge herself between him and his gargoyle and put her arms around him.

"I can see that's true for you," she said quietly, seriously, so unlike her usual bravado. "People do fall in love here, don't they? Isn't this the time of the troubadours, Heloise and Abelard, the Song of Roland, Eleanor of Aquitaine?" She looked up at him and gulped, then laughed a little nervously.

He didn't know who Heloise and Abelard were and what they had to do with anything. His anger dissipated. He wanted to guide her and help her. She looked so lost in that moment. And she was so soft in his arms.

With her he could do anything, be anything, create beautiful masterpieces, live as an artist, make his own way in the world. That's how being with her made him feel. His life could be what he chose it to be.

"Rose—"

"I am leaving in a few days," she whispered. "You'll never see me again."

"I know, and that is what I'm angry about." He gazed into her eyes. "But who I love is my choice. And I choose you."

Her lips beckoned him.

She kissed him and he kissed her back just as fervently, just as passionately, as if he'd never see her again.

He walked backwards to his bed, kissing her, touching her face, holding her. He felt her smile in the kiss. She whispered his name.

He would never let her go.

They fell into bed together, sighing and kissing, and sharing with each other love and passion, and the joy of choosing each other.

Chapter Seventeen

THE NEXT MORNING, ROSE smiled as they swung their hands between them, like children, and crossed the fields. Julien hummed a song. The morning was fresh, sparkly cold dew on every blade of grass. Birds swooped for bugs and warbled. The rich smells of the earth buoyed her. The sky arched above so blue it hurt her teeth. Love was intense; it highlighted everything. It was as if her vision had sharpened. Her hearing was more intense, her taste buds heightened, smell was sharpened, as if she were a wild animal full of knowing of the hidden messages buoyed on the wind.

They made it to the back door of the manor house without seeing anyone from the household. Rose was glad, even though Julien did drop her hand at the city gate. They gazed into each other's eyes. Julien caressed her cheek, and in a blink was gone, lumbering toward the big blocks of stone down the way and around the corner out of view.

They hadn't talked about what would happen the next day. They hadn't talked about the passion they'd shared last night. She knew it was special. The way he touched her—at times wild and passionate, and at other times soft and gentle as a rose petal—he had to feel their time making love was special, too. Was she special enough to change the course of his life? She didn't know.

Rose suddenly felt so very alone. Though they had made love, and it indeed felt like love to her, even though he didn't say the words and neither did she, she knew nothing had changed. She'd have to leave soon or suffer a broken heart.

Without a knock, she slipped into the kitchen.

Chapter Eighteen

J ULIEN POUNDED ON THE wedge and whacked it with his mallet. The limestone split open perfectly. Only twenty more to go, after the fifty he'd cracked, tumbled about him. Other apprentices kept their distances. They knew him well enough to sense the anger rolling off him all morning.

He wiped the sweat off his forehead in the afternoon heat and ground his teeth. Grunt work! Master Bernard knew he was the best, knew his art would win the competition. But Master Bernard purposely banned him from the Michaelmas competition and had relegated him to doing beginner's work two weeks ago. Well, he wasn't going to stand for that. He'd started his gargoyle against his master's wishes. He'd enter it in the competition no matter what the man thought about him. Rose's love had renewed his hope and spurred him to finish.

The competition was tomorrow. His gargoyle would win; he could choose his destination, choose his fate, just as he'd chosen his love. He would go to Amiens with Rose. They could start a new life together, away from Master Bernard and the judgment of the count.

Love made him bold.

He squared his tools and stalked back to the manor house. He had something to say to Master Bernard.

Julien slipped in via the kitchen, carefully wiped his feet, and washed the dust from his face and hands in the corner wash basin. He nodded to the kitchen servants. Rose wasn't around. His heart clenched in his chest when he thought of her and her precarious position in this household. He'd take her away from all this.

He made for the swinging door. Madame Delore made eye contact with him, then spoke.

"Son, he's eating. You really want to go in there?" Her voice quivered with age, but her eyes were clear. He could swear they sparkled with some sort of hidden mischief.

"*Oui*, Madame." He nodded politely. Madame Delore always looked out for him.

"Going to do right by your woman?"

Julien stopped from pushing the door. "What?"

"She is a beauty even if she can't keep house worth a—" Madame Delore smirked, showing off her toothless grin, then she winked. She always did have a salty tongue.

Julien's heart thudded like a mallet on granite. "I thought no one knew," he whispered.

"I know." The old housekeeper tapped her nose in the knowing gesture. "You better do right by her, or—"

"Madame Delore, I'll take care of it." Julien didn't want to know the "or." The master had a way of driving people away. You needed a thick skin to be in the household of the aging stonemason.

"WHAT?" MASTER BERNARD BARKED at him between bites of chicken and thick bread and gulps of ale.

Julien squared his shoulders. "I'm presenting my gargoyle tomorrow at the dinner."

"No, you're not. You're on probation. I'm sure I made that clear."

"I've been here long enough. Became a journeyman two years ago already. It's my time to present for my medallion. You know that." Julien gritted his teeth.

"*Non.* Leave now." Master Bernard didn't even look at him, just waved his hand dismissively.

"Master Bernard, hear me out. I am ready—" The master mason had put him on probation one too many times.

"I decide who is ready or not. You are not. Out!" Master Bernard roared, glaring at him, his bushy eyebrows bunched together.

Julien opened his mouth to fight for his rights, but Master Bernard shook his head and bent his head to eating, effectively dismissing him.

Julien was about to try one more time when Master Bernard threw the worst threat imaginable at him.

"If you say one more word, young man, you will be banned from the entire guild, never to work as a stonemason again. Do you hear me?" Master Bernard's voice boomed, filling the entire hall.

Julien stilled, stunned. A scurrying of fabric rustled behind him, probably one of the servants crossing from one of the wings to another, rushing to escape notice of an angry master. Julien didn't blame them.

Julien closed his open mouth, clenched his fists, and stalked back the way he came.

Chapter Nineteen

ROSE PRACTICALLY RAN UP the steps to the servant's quarters. Thankfully it was empty. Master Bernard really wouldn't let Julien display his gargoyle tomorrow. Bernard was a horrible man. Rose was shaking, and she wasn't even the one Bernard had shouted at. She wanted to run after Julien, comfort him, find a way out of this. She knew how important the competition was to him. She'd heard the other apprentices and servants talking about how the winner would get his choice of work, including traveling to another one of the cathedral towns to set up house. Amiens was the prize everyone wanted, with Paris a fast second.

She had to do something, but what? What power did she have here? None. Leverage—none that she could think of. *Think, girl, think*, she admonished herself.

Rose wiped the tears from her cheeks. She had to get back to work. This time she was trying her hand at the loom. It wasn't so hard. She hurried to finish the errand the others had given her: to bring a pitcher of water back to the weaving room. *Just call me errand girl.* All workers started at the bottom, right?

In the courtyard, Rose carefully brushed off the scum at the top of the water barrel. What would happen to her and to Julien? Their night together was so wonderful. It felt like love. Was it love? Yes, she decided, it was. Rose smiled and felt a warmth in her chest bloom like a rose.

But now if Julien couldn't compete, and even if he did compete, if he didn't win, what would happen to him? And what would happen to her?

"What are you doing?" A shrill voice at her shoulder made her jump.

Rose nearly dropped the pitcher she was dipping into the water barrel, but managed to keep a grip on the porcelain handle. She gulped and spun to face the person with the shrill voice, a voice that she'd heard from afar but never had to confront in this big household: the wife of Master Bernard, Madame Sophie de Chantilly.

"I'm getting water for the weavers, madame."

"No, you're not. You need to get water from the well."

"Where's that?"

The madame pointed in a northerly direction and waved her hand dismissively.

"Will you show me?" Rose asked sweetly, trying to play the dumb servant.

Madame narrowed her eyes at Rose and sniffed. "I will not. That is for another to do."

What did this woman do but issue shrill commands and interrupt her servants' work all day long?

"Okay. I'll ask Madame Delore," Rose said. "It was nice to meet you, Madame Sophie."

The madame sniffed again. "You're the new girl, eh? Be sure you follow the rules and don't dally, young woman." Madame looked her up and down as if she was as horse for sale. Then she turned abruptly and bustled off, her fancy skirts and shawl rustling around her.

"Yes, ma'am," Rose said in English under her breath, full of sarcasm. She finished filling the pitcher at the well and hurried back to the weavers.

Life in the thirteenth century certainly wasn't as easy as it looked in those re-enactment shows on TV. How was she ever going to fit in here? Not specifically this household, but any household, if all she was good for was fetching and sweeping. Such work was probably enough for any woman in this time, but she didn't know if she could ever adapt. Life had to mean more. She wanted to do more. Why did she have to fall back in time to realize that her life was more than a paycheck, prestige of a good job, and hooking up with sexy men once a year?

As she stepped back into the weaver's room, one of the weavers barked at her, "What took you so long?"

"I met Madame Sophie de Chantilly."

"Oh." The weaver nodded in understanding as if that explained Rose's delay. The other women nodded sagely, too. Apparently, Madame Sophie was a terror for the whole household.

"Anything else I can do?" Rose asked.

An older woman smiled at her kindly. "Continue your sweeping, dearie, until dinner, or until Madame Delore comes to find you to clean the main hall. It must be prepared for tomorrow's celebration. We're all looking forward to seeing the fine young men's art!" The older woman winked and turned back to her weaving, the wood pieces clacking together in a complicated syncopated rhythm.

Rose blushed and hustled to grab her broom, and get back to work. They couldn't know about her and Julien, could they?

ROSE HURRIED TO FINISH the last corners of the great hall, sweeping away dust and laying rushes. She was on a ladder, stretching up and sideways to polish the frame edges of the sparkly glass windows. She was just about to hop down and follow Madame Delore back into the kitchen for a bite to eat when she froze at a high, shrill voice chattering in rapid French; it sounded like Madame Sophie. She peeked around the heavy curtain she was behind.

Madame wasn't nearby, but stationed at the other end of the hall, hands on her hips, yelling at Master Bernard about how things were such a mess in the household, how everyone worked too slowly, that things were not ready for the grand presentations the next night. Master Bernard's voice was too low for her to distinguish his words, but his tone was clear, full of annoyance and anger.

Rose kept to the walls and scurried into the kitchen. With the swinging door between them and the shouting, Rose calmed down.

She smoothed her dress and searched for Madame Delore. The old woman sat at the long table, bent over a bowl of something, slurping, her back to Rose. Rose wove her way through the busy servants and cooks, ignoring looks of irritation, and mutterings against her person in a slang she didn't specifically know, but could guess.

Rose slipped in next to Madame Delore, who slid her a bowl without looking at her.

Rose gratefully spooned the soup. Barley and carrots, flavored with chicken. Delicious.

"You still have the pouch?" Madame Delore said.

"Oui."

"You must use it tomorrow night."

"How?" *Why*, was really what Rose wanted to ask. But that seemed to convey mistrust of Madame Delore, who had been nothing but kind and welcoming to her, if a bit mysterious.

When the old housekeeper didn't answer right away, Rose chanced a glance at her. For some reason, the old woman was being cagey, as if they were not to be seen speaking to each other. Madame Delore shook her head sharply once and eyed the door.

"I'll go get more water." Rose stood up, hoping that was what the old housekeeper was meaning—wanting her to step outside so the two of them could have some privacy. Rose grabbed a bucket hung on a nail near the back door and stepped out into the courtyard, expecting Madame Delore to follow.

It was dusk. Thankfully, the back windows of the manor were lit, so Rose could navigate the path to the rain barrels beside the hen house. Where was Madame Delore? She was turning back with the bucket, heavy with water, when there was the old woman, as if conjured by Rose's thoughts.

"Listen well, young woman," Madame Delore said.

Rose nodded, walked slowly, and listened to Madame Delore relay complicated instructions, repeated twice slowly, with mounting confusion.

"Understand?" Madame Delore asked, when she was finished.

Rose nodded again, then shook her head. They were at the kitchen door. Rose felt the pressure to go in and keep up appearances before anyone wondered what she was doing out late in the coming dark.

Madame Delore lay her hand on Rose's arm. "You must follow my instructions, exactly, or your love will be threatened."

"Julien?" Rose whispered. Her heart pounded in her throat.

Madame Delore placed her hand on Rose's chest, and shook her head in the No direction. With that, the old woman let herself into the kitchen without a backward glance.

More confused than ever, Rose blew out a breath. Would she ever understand? If not her love for Julien, than whose love?

Chapter Twenty

ROSE WOKE TO THE moonlight on her face. Thank goodness for her internal alarm clock that allowed her to take catnaps and wake up at her decided-upon hour.

All the servants around her were breathing heavily, asleep. She slipped on the outer dress, wrapped herself in her cloak, slipped on the boots she'd borrowed from another servant, and tiptoed down the stairs and out the kitchen door.

Would this be her last night making her way past the cathedral foundation stones and its low protective wall, through the village and fields to Julien's studio? This time tomorrow night they could be proudly celebrated, or at least Julien would be. She'd be by his side, proudly beaming, she hoped. She didn't want to leave him, like she'd said before. She wanted for them to make a life together.

Who was she fooling? As far as anyone else knew, he was still betrothed to Marie-Jeanne, banned from presenting his gargoyle, and relegated to grunt work breaking apart limestone.

Well, she wouldn't give up on Julien. She'd be there for him while he finished his gargoyle. She believed in him. There had to be a way for them to have happiness together. There had to be.

Rose was at his cabin door before she'd registered her quiet nighttime surroundings, as if her feet knew the way of her heart. She let herself in without knocking, without thinking, so she didn't notice at first that there was another person in the cabin, besides Julien.

"What are you doing here?" Marie-Jeanne asked, her hands on her hips.

"What?" Rose stopped at the threshold.

"Close the door. It's cold in here," Julien barked. "Marie-Jeanne was just leaving." Julien was glaring at Marie-Jeanne and not even looking at Rose.

Rose slammed the door. "Great, just great. What are you doing here, Marie-Jeanne?"

"How dare you?" Marie-Jeanne spat. "And I thought you were so sweet. But instead you're a foreigner with no manners."

"Yes, I am a foreigner with no manners." Rose spun on Julien. "Speaking of no manners, you've told her, haven't you?"

"Told me what?" Marie-Jeanne said with a whine in her voice, sounding so young. Then she probably was; the young woman looked all of eighteen years old.

"Nothing," Julien said.

"What?!" Rose fluttered her hands to encompass the cabin. But she wasn't going to say it, about their night together, their shared kisses. That was private. She stilled her hands by balling them into fists on her hips.

"What is going on here?" Marie-Jeanne narrowed her eyes at Julien and examined Rose up and down. "I thought you were his relative."

Rose pursed her lips to prevent more explosive words from shooting out. How could Julien say "Nothing"? She crossed her arms over her chest and waited. The gargoyle was hidden from view. Julien had covered it with a drop cloth. That made her happy, that he'd hidden it from Marie-Jeanne. The small statue was their special connection.

Julien cleared his throat. "Marie-Jeanne, we cannot marry."

"What?" Now it was Marie-Jeanne's turn to say that.

Rose shrugged and said nothing when Marie-Jeanne raised an inquiring eyebrow at her.

"You can't do that," Marie-Jeanne said shrilly. "It's been arranged. We're to be married as soon as you get your master mason badge in the spring."

"That's not going to happen," Julien said.

"Why not?" Marie-Jeanne pouted.

Rose opened the door.

"Where are you going?" Julien said to her back.

"I shouldn't be here for this," Rose said.

"Please stay," Julien said.

Rose turned at the sound of his voice. Though he'd never said the words, his voice carried warmth, and his eyes conveyed love. At least she thought it was love. She wanted to touch him, hold his hand, and feel his strength at her side. "Okay." She closed the door and stepped to the fire pot, warming her hands that were suddenly chilled, her back to Marie-Jeanne.

"What is going on?" Marie-Jeanne said. "Are you two..."

"And if we were?" Julien said.

"But—"

"Marie-Jeanne, I know about you and Jean-Paul," Julien said.

Rose turned to watch, as if glued to a car wreck.

"Oh." Marie-Jeanne's cheeks were bright red.

"There is no love between us. I've known you since I was sixteen and you were six."

"But love is for the courtly types," Marie-Jeanne said and moved to reach out to Julien. "And we have been promised under the guild and the court and God."

"They have nothing to do with it. Love is for all of us," Julien said. But he didn't take Marie-Jeanne's outstretched hand. "But just not you and me."

Marie-Jeanne dropped her hand and spun toward Rose. Her cheeks were still red.

"You—you—it's all your fault."

Rose turned to her. "Marie-Jeanne, your Jean-Paul, he's another one of the apprentice stonemasons, the one with the round face, and strong right hammer arm."

"How did you know?"

"I talk to people." Rose shrugged.

"So?" The young woman narrowed her eyes at Rose, distrustful.

"You love him, right?"

"Well..."

"He does have those big muscles and a dimple on his cheek when he smiles."

"Why you? If you make a move on him, I will—"

Rose laughed. " 'Love comes through the eyes.'" Rose quoted from a troubadour's song she'd heard at the mason's dinner table the night before when she'd been serving.

As if it were possible, Marie-Jeanne turned a brighter red.

Rose left her spot by the warm fire pot and before the other two knew what she was doing, she grabbed both their hands and tugged them into the center of the cabin.

Julien sputtered in protest, a hurt look in his eyes. Marie-Jeanne looked confused, but said nothing.

"Now," Rose said. "Look at each other."

"You can't—we—you and I—" Julien started.

"Shhh. Trust me?" Rose asked.

After half a second, Julien nodded, warmth shining from his eyes.

Marie-Jeanne watched their exchange still looking confused, with a pouty mouth.

"Okay—"

"What's this 'okay'?" Marie-Jeanne asked.

Rose ignored her and barreled ahead. She put their hands atop each other's, her own on top, and gulped. Such a risk she was taking, messing about with local customs. But people deserved to be happy, didn't they? She also ignored the tears starting to leak. "You both deserve love. And it's just turned out that it's not with each other, right?"

Marie-Jeanne nodded.

Julien just watched her, wariness in his eyes now.

"So, just agree to allow each other to pursue love, and let go of your bonds to each other."

Marie-Jeanne smiled shyly. "We can do that?"

"Why not?" said Julien gruffly and dropped his hands.

Marie-Jeanne kissed Julien on the cheek and then glanced at Rose and back to Julien. She smiled sweetly.

"Good luck, my friend. May love give you as much sweet pain and joy as it's given me."

With that, she rushed out the cabin.

In the silence that followed, Rose held her breath.

Julien gathered her in his strong arms. "Rose," he breathed into her hair. "My fair and bold, Rose!"

Rose relaxed into his embrace and let the tears fall. She didn't know where she'd be a day from now. But being in his arms now was good enough.

And then Julien surprised her with his next words. "Stay with me forever as my dear wife. I choose love. I choose you."

Rose pulled back to examine his face. "For real."

"Yes, it is real."

"But the master mason, the count, the rules..."

Julien shushed her with a sweet kiss that melted her insides. "For you, my love, I would defy them all. 'Love rules them all,'" he whispered a quote from the troubadour's song and kissed her again.

Chapter Twenty-One

THE NEXT EVENING, THE feast was in full swing. Rose bustled between the kitchen and dining room, pushing her way past the kitchen door with her hands full of platters of steaming, fragrant meat and hustling back with empty platters and jugs. Her feet ached; her back ached; she'd never worked so hard in her life. Julien was sitting at one of the tables grim-faced, not acknowledging her.

The Master Mason Bernard was talking loudly, laughing loudly, yelling loudly, everything loudly, dominating the whole room full of his two dozen apprentices, selected members of the count's household, and some priests.

Beside Master Bernard at the high table was the count and his haughty wife wrapped in furs. That must be a fox around her throat. On the other side of the master mason was his wife, Sophie. Her mouth was pinched. She seemed to spend more time barking at Rose and the other servants than she did participating in the meal and the raucous behavior. On the other side of Sophie was a pale-faced young priest. Rose had not seen him before in her short time in Beauvais.

Lined up alongside a far wall on a stage that she'd seen young men build earlier that day were piles covered in cloth. Those must be the apprentices' projects.

Rose had been so busy during the day helping with odd chores, lots of carrying and fetching, that she didn't see Julien sneak in with his gargoyle. She would have loved to see it finished in the privacy of his studio, but last night he wouldn't let her see it. "Later, my love. Later, we'll enjoy it together," he'd said. When he won, Rose understood him to mean. Last night they'd spent the night together again. Rose sighed. She'd woken up early to his chink-chink-chinking on the gargoyle, his back to her.

"*Attention*, miss. They'll be wanting this." A servant brought Rose out of her reverie with a nudge. Rose was sure her cheeks were flaming red. They sure felt hot. She took the platter the young woman handed her. The young woman winked at her shyly. Rose fumbled the tray, but caught it before it tipped too much.

"Careful, miss. I'm hoping Julien wins it tonight. Don't you? He's so strong and handsome." The young woman smiled, winked again, and turned to fill another platter.

Rose didn't know that everyone had the hots for Julien. Or did the young woman know her business? Regardless, Rose was a lucky woman that he'd ended up with her.

The wall of noise accosted her as she stepped into the main hall. But one voice in particular. A shrill female voice. Sophie. She was yelling at the servants to hurry, that they were too slow. Rose luckily was serving at the other end of the room, near Julien, so she wasn't the target of Sophie's wrath this time.

She smiled at him, but he looked away. Rose felt her heart sink. Why couldn't he acknowledge her among everyone? He wanted to marry her, for goodness sake.

Rose felt a warm hand on her arm.

"Patience, dearie." It was the housekeeper, Madame Delore, who'd been busy directing all the servants for the dinner from the back of the hall or from just beside the kitchen door. The old woman leaned in close. "Did you use it?"

Rose gulped and bent to whisper in Madame Delore's ear. "I forgot. When I saw him last night—I forgot."

"Well, it's not too late. I'll distract them soon. Wait for it."

Rose grabbed the nearest empty platter and rushed back to the kitchen.

On her return trip back to the hall, she made sure to carry something smaller than a heavy meat-filled platter, so snagged a pitcher of cider. There it was—the sign. Had to be. Everyone was standing, singing, and swinging their tankards in time to the rousing song, their backs to her, hiding her from everyone's view. She set down the pitcher in the corner.

As quickly as she could, Rose slipped behind the tall curtains and peeked under each cloth to find Julien's gargoyle. Luckily, most of the carvings were of the traditional gargoyles made to be water spouts, well-carved most of them, but not Julien's. So far she'd seen only one other standing gargoyle, and she knew instantly it wasn't Julien's—the stone was too dark and it had no pedestal like Julien's had. Finally two thirds of the way through waist-high stones, she found his.

She was supposed to rub the herbs on the four directions of the gargoyle and chant the phrase Madame Delore had her memorize. But she couldn't reach the far side of the statue without possibly revealing her position. So, with her hands smudged with the pungent herbs—a mix of sage, lavender, rose, and other scents she didn't recognize but reminded her somehow of the quiet brook behind Julien's studio, she touched three sides of the pedestal base and rubbed them on the gargoyle's head to compensate. She quickly whispered the short poem Madame Delore had her memorize, ancient words she didn't recognize. Under the cloth covering, her only illumination was the chandelier full of candles high above and flickering wall sconces. Under the shadows, she couldn't get a clear view of Julien's statue.

The song was ending. People were clapping, cheering and laughing. Then Master Mason Bernard's voice boomed, "Silence! The moment has come."

Rose heart pounded like a cable car bell. She had to get out of there before she was caught. She scurried back toward the kitchen, full pitcher in hand, the clattering noises of everyone settling back into their seats covering her retreat. She hoped the magic worked, binding their love and prosperity. She hoped with all her heart.

Chapter Twenty-Two

JULIEN SEARCHED FOR ROSE But didn't see her.

"You there!" Madame Sophie's voice cut through the noise.

Julien cringed internally. He would not miss Madame Sophie's voice. He'd thought that after all these years in the de Chantilly household he'd be used to her behavior, disrupting the calm he needed to work. At least, Rose wasn't like that. When she was mad, her cheeks got an attractive red and she glared at him like a she-cat. His she-cat.

There she was. Rose was hurrying toward the kitchen, a pitcher in her hand. Madame Delore had her working hard. But Rose never complained, never had a pinched sour look like some of the servants. *Soon.* Soon it would be time to stand up.

Rose turned her head at the Madame's voice and saw she wasn't the target. Another poor servant girl near the head table was. Rose pushed her way into the kitchen.

As soon as she came back out—he told himself. His heart beat like a hammer against a wedge.

Master Bernard boomed over his wife's voice, "Apprentices, step up."

In a tangle of limbs and legs, the young men on either side of Julien pushed back the bench and stood. Julien moved along with them. The men lined up in front of the stage of covered stones.

Julien had to time it just right.

He glanced toward the kitchen door. All the servants including Rose stood against the far wall to watch the presentation.

Julien stepped forward and waited for the room to quiet down.

"What are you about?" Master Bernard boomed. "I didn't give you permission to present or to speak."

"If I may be so bold," Julien started. "Brother Vincent and Count de Cressonsacq." Julien nodded in greeting and bowed. "I am here to present for my master mason badge. The time has come for me to advance—"

"You do not have my permission," Master Bernard cut him off.

"Let him speak," the count said.

Julien let out a breath. "Thank you, sir."

Without delay, Julien nodded to two younger apprentices, and together the three of them moved the covered statue to the front of the stage. The other two younger apprentices backed away into line. Julien whisked the cloth off his gargoyle and turned toward the front table. Clapping and oohing and aahing from the crowd. His heart swelled in pride.

A quick glance at Rose sent a frisson of joy through him. She smiled and had her hands clasped in front of heart. *His everything.* He flashed her a quick smile.

"Enough!" Master Bernard shouted. "I forbid this."

"I request my master mason badge and to marry!" Julien shouted above him.

Some apprentices gasped. They knew the consequences of crossing the master. Well, consequences be damned. "I will no longer wait. You know it is my time."

"I am the one to decide." Master Bernard stood, his face red from drink or from anger, probably from both. "Your fate is in my hands."

"Hear the man out," the priest said. "He does God's work, after all, Bernard."

"It is time for the marriage to take place," the count said. "Where is the young woman? Step forward, girl, and face us."

The room fell silent. Julien scanned the room, knowing who the count meant. Among the servants, Marie-Jeanne wouldn't meet his gaze. Rose watched him and gave him a quick nod. He trusted her to move on his signal.

Julien stepped forward. "I name as my bride, Rose, newly arrived at Beauvais."

People gasped.

Rose moved forward. Julien motioned her with his hand to stay.

"But she's not from here!" Madame Sophie said.

"The new girl? Who is she?" Master Bernard added.

"I don't know who she is, but she is not the one to whom you are betrothed, young apprentice," the count said. "You would defy all of us tonight. You walk a dangerous territory. What is the meaning of this?"

"It's time I take a stand for love."

"Love has nothing to do with marriage," said the priest.

"Love is everything," Julien said. "I want to embrace love to live life fully, otherwise I live a life half-lived."

"Clearly, love has made you foolish," Master Bernard said. "You defy me. You defy the elders of the town, and the edicts of the Church—"

"I am willing to give up everything for the love of one good woman." Julien stood tall.

The room buzzed with talk.

"Life is not a troubadour's song," the priest said in his soft voice as soon as the room had grown quiet.

"Bernard, you must do something—" Madame Sophie tugged on her husband's arm.

Master Bernard shook her off and wagged a finger at Julien. His voice boomed, filling the great hall. "Julien de Beauvais, you are hereby banished from the guild and will never find work again. You have defied me one too many times."

The apprentices behind him gasped. Rose paled. Even Marie-Jeanne looked sad for him.

"So be it," Julien said and held out his hand toward Rose. She walked to him. She looked afraid, but firm, her spine straight, head held high. Brave, brave woman, to be with a man like him.

Cacophony erupted in the hall, but Julien only had eyes for Rose.

"What do we do now?" she whispered when she'd gripped his hand and stood by him side by side.

"Get married," Julien whispered, giddy and as afraid as he'd ever been in his life. In a loud voice, he said, "Madame Delore, you're the closest thing to a mother to Rose in her short time here. Will you give us your blessing?"

"How dare you!" boomed Master Bernard.

"I cannot bless this union," the priest said sternly.

"Love is from God. He blesses us," Julien said. Gasps in the hall. "Blasphemy" whispered in ripples throughout the hall.

"Out!" Master Bernard pointed to the door of the hall. "Out! You will never work again."

"I heard you the first time," Julien said softly.

Madame Delore nodded her head solemnly and motioned them out.

Head held high, Rose tightly at his side, Julien left the hall where he'd spent over ten years of his life.

What would happen to his gargoyle?

Chapter Twenty-Three

AN HOUR LATER, ROSE clasped Julien's hands in his studio.

"You know, I can't go back," Julien said looking into her eyes.

"I know," Rose said. *Neither can I,* she thought. She squeezed his hand and smiled.

"Let's get on with it, dearies," Madame Delore said. "The stars are aligned for only so long. New lives await you and your love together."

Rose felt her heart would burst with love. In the little time they had, she managed to wash her face, smooth her dress, and even weave a few ribbons in her hair.

"By the power invested in me by Mother Earth, Sister Moon, Brother Wind, and Father Sky, I hereby pronounce you husband and wife," Madame Delore said and wrapped a ribbon around her wrist, and another around Julien's wrist. "So that you remember each other as individuals." She wrapped another ribbon around their wrist together. "So that you will always be together. No matter where." She smiled at Julien. "No matter when." She winked at Rose.

Rose jumped a little. How could the woman know her secret? Well, if magic lived here like science reigned in her day, who was she to judge?

"You may kiss," announced Madame Delore.

She kissed Julien, long, and passionate. And never wanted to let him go.

Chapter Twenty-Four

LATE THAT NIGHT, AFTER the world had fallen asleep, Rose slipped out of the studio, cut across the fields, and tiptoed back into the hall. She wanted to see the gargoyle before they left town. Julien was snoring in his cot, exhausted from staying up two nights with her and finishing his statue. The time for the honeymoon would be later, she imagined.

In the great hall, the servants lay snoring in between the tables. The gargoyles and other statues had been left on the low stage, all revealed in the full moon light peeking through the long windows.

Rose felt blessed. All was right in her new world, despite the challenges ahead.

Like a moth drawn to the light, Rose found her way to Julien's gargoyle. It was beautiful. White limestone, a wide open smile on the beast's face, big ears like a lion, a scaly upper body, big front paws, and back legs like a lizard. What a beautiful beast wrought from Julien's imagination! It was so beautiful, much more stunning up close.

She had seen his gargoyle before. She only now connected the dots. Rose had admired Julien's gargoyle when she'd circled the cathedral back in her own time. But her life was here now.

Rose smiled and reached out to touch its head just as she noticed a small creature between its legs in some sort of shell, as if it were protecting a little one. The limestone was cool to the touch, but a shiver went through her anyway.

Thunder cracked. A pain shot through her head. *Oh no!* she thought as the world went black. *Not again.*

Chapter Twenty-Five

"MISS? MISS?"

Rose jolted up, her heart in her throat. It was night and she lay on the cold stone pavement outside the cathedral. The night air smelled damp, as if it had rained recently. She shivered. She was in her jogging shorts, top, and running shoes. Only her thin jacket added a layer against the elements. A couple hovered over her.

"What? Where am I?" She felt awful. Her head ached as if it had been run over by a train. Like in the cartoons. But it wasn't funny.

Something was off. Then it clicked. The people hovering above her spoke in modern French.

"What day is it?"

The woman gave her the date she'd arrived in modern-day Beauvais. How could she have checked in to the hotel only a few hours ago when she'd been in thirteenth-century Beauvais for days? She must have traveled through time again. Her heart squeezed when she thought of whom she'd left behind.

"Julien!" She couldn't help the sob that broke through. God, she hated time travel.

"Looks like you hit your head when you fainted. Are you all right, miss?"

"Please stop calling me miss. Can't you see I'm married?" Rose stuck out her hand. The ribbon was still there, wrapped around her wrist.

They looked confused.

Ignoring them, she stood and gazed at the cathedral. She recognized where she was: at the back of the Cathedral St. Pierre. She looked up to the roof where Julien's gargoyle perched when she'd first seen it. It wasn't there.

She bit back a sob. "It can't be!"

The kind couple fussed over her, urging her to go to the hospital. She must have interrupted their romantic night walk.

"*Non.*" Rose wrapped her arms around her body to try to stop the shivering, gazing at the spot where Julien's gargoyle should be, had been. Had she changed history by meeting him? What else had she affected?

Tears streamed down her cheeks. What was there to do but carry on? She should go to her hotel, sleep, catch the plane, and go to the conference tomorrow. But she couldn't move. Frozen, she stared at empty spot once graced by Julien's gargoyle.

Arms around each other, the couple stood beside the vegetable garden that had been here the last time she'd visited. But now there was a gargoyle in the center of the small patch of vegetables, a small fountain atop its head. Lit by spotlights from the surrounding buildings, the gargoyle grinned at her, mocking her. It was Julien's gargoyle.

At the edge of the garden stood a plaque with its own small spotlight. Rose rushed to it. She had changed history. She'd somehow helped bring the gargoyle from the roof to the garden and to the center of attention, no less. She read the plaque, practically holding her breath. It described the gargoyle in the complicated French way, how this gargoyle was unique and unusual, and how it was the only one the archaeologists and cathedral restorers had discovered that had a saying on its base. The gargoyle was also unusual because the statue had been signed.

Rose held her breath as she read the saying again, slower this time: *"Ses cor viu, car ab me no l'ai, Qu'ilh l'a en bailia!"*

She released her breath as she translated it carefully, using her immediate knowledge of thirteenth-century French and from all those hours poring over medieval French as her hobby. The words translated to "I've no heart with which to live, for my love possesses it."

The signature was a rose carved in full bloom with a fancy J woven through it, as if the rose was nestled in its stem.

"Non!" She rushed to the gargoyle and couldn't hold back more sobs.

The couple tried to comfort her and to get her to come with them, or at least go back to her own hotel. She refused. Eventually, they left, maybe to get the cops or someone to commit her to a hospital. She didn't care. She wasn't moving from this spot.

She didn't know how much time passed, only that it was still night, and late enough that all the spotlights had been turned off. The city probably decided that no more tourists would be coming by. She guessed it was around 4am. The witching hour, her grandmother always called it.

What was she going to do with her life? She fingered the ribbon around her wrist. She couldn't have dreamt it all, could she have? She should have asked the couple—what? They'd think she was crazy for asking about world events to make sure the modern world was as she remembered it.

Rose moaned and hoped she wasn't going crazy. Grief and a broken heart could do that to a body.

Suddenly, a boom loud like thunder sounded and lighting flashed, charging the air around her. Her skin tingled. For a split second, the garden, gargoyle, and fountain were highlighted. Then the light was gone and the night was dark as ever.

Rose reached for the gargoyle. It was still there. She patted herself. She was still in her jogging clothes. *Good.* That meant she hadn't transported anywhere.

Still, she sensed something had changed. She held her breath, listening hard. Maybe she'd seen something. She couldn't be sure, but whatever it was could be to her right. Could it be possible? Could the thunder and lightning have transported another time traveler? Maybe even Julien? She stepped carefully and held out her hands, blinking to get her eyes to adjust to night.

She took a small step, and something crunched underfoot. Must be the kale, or maybe the lettuce.

"Julien?" She took another step, then another. "Is that you?"

No one answered. Her eyes adjusted a bit more to the dark. There was a darker shape amongst the vegetables.

In two steps she was there. She knelt slowly, her leg muscles shaking with the cold and nerves. She reached out and touched a warm body. She closed her eyes to listen better and heard faint breathing. Without thinking, Rose bent to inhale his scent. That more than anything confirmed for her that it was Julien who lay unconscious before her. She patted what turned out to be a leg, then a hip. And oh my, he was naked. She caressed his abs and chest, placing her hand on his chest. His heart beat strong and regular.

Her heart burst in her chest, full of joy and amazement. Some force had brought Julien to her. She wanted to hug him and never let him go.

"My love, Julien!" She shook his shoulder. "Wake up!"

He didn't make a sound.

"Julien! Wake up," she repeated.

Still no response from him.

"Julien!" she yelled.

He groaned. Rose shook his shoulder, kissed his lips, wanted to pound his chest, but instead just yelled his name again.

"What?" he said at last then groaned and grabbed his head.

Rose pulled his arm. "Please sit up!"

Julien let her pull him up.

"Come on! Stand up, *mon amour*."

"Rose?"

"*Oui?*"

"I finally found you. Don't leave again."

Rose choked back a sob of happy tears and hugged him. He squeezed her back in a strong hug.

"Rose?"

"Hmmm?" She didn't want to let him go, ever.

"Where are my clothes?"

She let go and laughed through her tears. "Gone. Come on."

He got to his feet, leaning on her unsteadily. "Where?"

"My hotel room." Rose led him out of the vegetable garden and down the cobblestone path past the cathedral.

Julien stopped her when they got to the sidewalk and his feet hit the pavement. He sucked in a breath. From the streetlights, the modern town of Beauvais spread out in front of them. He turned and gasped. "Where am I?"

"Beauvais."

"But—" He didn't complete his thought, just stared at the cathedral clothed mostly in shadows. He gestured at it. "It—looks odd."

"It is. It never was finished." Rose felt him shiver. "Let's get you to the hotel and warmed up."

He said nothing, but leaned on her a little as they made their way through the empty streets at the dead of night. Thankfully, they saw no one. Rose got Julien into her little hotel room without incident. Julien had said nothing, and now just stared wide-eyed at the light fixtures as she flipped on the lights.

She helped him into bed and covered him with the thin hotel blankets, wishing for the homespun wool covers in Julien's artist studio.

She was about to explain the bathroom, but Julien was already asleep. Time travel was exhausting. Rose kissed him on the lips. For whatever magic had brought him here—she guessed probably provided by Madame Delore, the old witch—Rose was thankful.

She switched off the light and felt her way to the small bathroom and indulged in a long shower. She slipped into the double hotel bed beside Julien's warm body, snuggling against him.

"My Rose," Julien whispered.

"*Oui*, my love." She squeezed him hard.

"You really do come from another time and place."

"I do."

"I don't understand it, but now we've found each other for eternity. I'm so thankful. I choose you. Wherever you are is home enough for me."

A Christmas Fling

(A Christmas Elf Paranormal Romance)

Novella Book 2 of the *Touchstone Series*

SUMMARY:

What if falling in love put the life you cherished in jeopardy?

Dahlia, a Santa's Elf, has 21 days left before Christmas to create the best toy in the world without using magic or revealing her true identity. Stuck on how to complete the prototype, and working as a temp in San Francisco's financial district with no time for love, will her Christmas fling get her unstuck, or will she turn her back on her beloved career for her heart?

Liam, an up-and-coming financial analyst, swore off women after getting dumped by the love of his life. He just found out his ex is going to the company Christmas party with his rival Michael Hendricks. Up for promotion against Hendricks, Liam has to win the favor of his boss. His best bet is to invite the vivacious secretary Dahlia to the party. Will Dahlia be a welcome distraction, or will she turn his life upside down?

Chapter One

DAHLIA STROLLED THROUGH THE small neighborhood park. It was great fun to think about how the children would enjoy her toy once she was done with it, but she had to complete it first. She only had twenty-two days to fix whatever was wrong with it before returning home. She'd gone over her designs and schematics and taken it apart and put it back together a dozen times, but it still wouldn't work.

Dahlia left the park and headed down the street toward the detached studio she rented on Miles Avenue.

A dog bark had her look up just in time to almost but not quite avoid getting tangled up in a long leash. A man with the warmest brown eyes she'd ever seen gazed down at her, a half smile on his face.

She smiled back startled out of her daydreaming, but not before she noticed his endearing dimple on one side of his mouth.

She said, "Sorry, I didn't see you. Thank goodness for your dog. Oh, she looks like a Husky."

Dahlia shifted her bag to one hip, so she could bend down and pet the dog.

The dog wagged her tail.

Dahlia said, "You must feed her really well. Her coat is so soft and luscious."

"She's a Bernese Mountain Dog. Sally. My roommate's."

His voice was deep. She had to look up to smile into his deep brown eyes. He was a whole head taller than she was. Almost two meters. She translated into American measurements. Six foot three or something.

"My uncle, well one of my uncles has one—that he uses for work. But I hardly see him because he lives—" She paused. "I'm prattling, aren't I?"

"Yes, you are, but I like listening to your accent. Scottish?"

"Yes, wow, you guessed correctly. Most people here can't do that. Yeah, we're from Scotland, but it's been a few generations." She couldn't very well tell him how Santa's elves lived a very long time. It had only been her grandparents that had immigrated with Uncle, known as Santa to most, and some neighbors to set up the North Pole.

"So, you're in school here?" He waved off toward what she knew was the art college a few blocks away.

"No. I'm here on an independent research project for a few more weeks."

"So you're from—"

"Alaska. Well, near Alaska, anyway. I—I best be going," she interrupted and gestured to her bag of goodies. She shifted from foot to foot on the corner of Miles and Clifton Streets, still tangled up in the Bernese's leash. "Gifts to wrap. For the kids. Big project." She gulped and held out her hand. "I'm Dahlia, by the way. Dahlia MacMillian."

With a half-smile, he shook her offered hand. His grip was firm and strong. "Liam. Nice to meet you, Dahlia MacMillian." He led the dog around her, slowly untangling the leash.

How he moved with grace and power, even in his simple gestures. He was tall, lean and muscular, broad shoulders identifiable even in his sweatshirt with the UC Berkeley name and logo on it.

"There we go, Sally," Liam said, his voice a rumbling, soothing cascade.

Sally licked Dahlia's hand, bringing her out of her staring. She gulped and felt the heat of a blush creep up her neck and onto her cheeks. Dahlia stroked the soft fur to cover her embarrassment. It had been a long time since she'd felt attracted to anyone. Everyone she'd dated at the Pole was so familiar to her, and mostly related. She didn't have time for a distraction.

She looked up when she heard Liam chuckling. He was shaking his head.

"What?" She couldn't help but ask.

He shrugged. "I guess I should run into girls more often with my roommate's dog. I didn't realize it could be such a pleasant experience."

"You must not walk her very often then." Oh my, she was flirting. The Elf boys back home never brought that out of her. She felt her pale skin flush. *Och, yes, this was a man,* she thought. "Thank you, then. For the pleasant experience. And the untangling."

"You're welcome." Liam said to her, smiling, that one dimple showing again. Then he spoke to the dog. "Come on Sally. Let's finish your walk, so we can go watch the game."

Dahlia waved good-bye and turned to go down the street and headed for her apartment. But first she had to watch Liam walk away. He fit nicely into his jeans. For a moment, a pang of wistfulness washed through her. She shook her herself. She had other things to focus on, like completing her toy on time so she could get her Master Elf badge, and even win the Grand Prize.

She was sure she'd be able to make progress on her toy tonight. Maybe it was something about meeting a happy dog and tall brown-eyed man that made her feel hopeful. Yes, she would get her toy done in time.

LIAM TUGGED ON SALLY'S leash. It had all happened so fast. She'd practically run into him. He'd had to yank on Sally's leash to prevent the girl from running into him, which had made the normally quiet Sally bark.

The girl, well, actually more like a very nice looking woman—all that wild hair and those sparkly eyes that seemed to practically twinkle when she spoke. Must have been a trick of the afternoon light. She seemed so light-hearted. Dahlia MacMillian, with the soft lilt in her voice. Her mess of red hair part frizzy, part curl that turned golden red as the winter light touched it. A winter jacket covering tantalizing curves. Strong legs in hugging jeans. He almost wanted to make her do a pirouette so he could check out her ass. But he hadn't.

She was so unlike the highly polished co-workers and high-rise office colleagues he worked with. He loved that environment. He loved his eclectic neighborhood, too. They were right next to an art school. By now he should expect to run into the artsy design type of people in this neighborhood in

Oakland. So different from the financial district where he spent over sixty hours a week in downtown San Francisco.

He realized he'd been standing on the corner with Sally when she tugged on the leash, done with her business with sniffing every fifth bush. She needed to get walking. His roommate Josh Kleine, one of his best buddies from college, was away in Paris at a conference and had made him promise to walk Sally himself at least once a day. He did, even though a dog walker helped out during the week, while he was at work. But on the weekends, Liam thought he should walk Sally himself for her twice-daily walks, as he promised Josh.

"Okay, girl. Let's go." He picked up the pace and jogged with her up the quiet street.

Dahlia had been so friendly to the dog. She'd made him smile. God. He couldn't remember the last time a woman made him smile like that. Maybe he could ask her out. No, he'd sworn off dating, even casually, since the fiasco with Christine back in February, seven months ago.

He turned up Clifton, crossed College Avenue, jogged up it a little more until he got to Broadway, then he crossed Broadway and took the dogleg turn and hiked up Broadway Terrace at a good clip to the golf course. On his way back down the hill, his cell phone rang. It was Josh, no doubt checking up on him to see how well he was treating Sally.

"Hey," Liam answered.

"So?" Josh asked.

"She's fine. We're just heading back from our walk. We went as far as the golf course today. She's got her miles in. Don't worry. Second walk today, too."

"And she got her food?"

"Of course. Who do you think I am?"

"It's just the responsibility—"

"Seriously? We're going to have this discussion again? I manage crazy-ass databases with hundreds of millions of dollars on the line for Cooper, Andrews & Sons. And you don't trust me to feed your dog—"

"Cool your jets, Liam. Numbers don't require regular feeding and—"

"Sally is your baby, I know, Josh. You'll be back in a week, and you can look after her yourself. How's the Transportation conference going? Meet any hot Parisian chicks yet?"

"It's good. No, on the Parisian chicks. Just—no, never mind. Hey, I ran into one of your colleagues here. Michael Hendricks. He's in your department, right?"

"Yeah, he handles the transportation portfolio analysis. Right. I forgot he was going." Liam frowned.

"He told me he's bringing his fiancée to the company Christmas party. And implied that you were going to lose out big time. Something about gaming you out of the corner office. MacAuley, that guy has it in for you."

"Yeah, always does. He always wants what I have. Now he wants the same promotion I'm after." He stole his girlfriend, ex-girlfriend from him. And Christine let it happen. "What's this about bringing his fiancée to the party? What fiancée? Is it Christine?" He really didn't want to see Christine ever again. He ground his teeth.

The promotion was a straight shot to a corner office, weekly golf with the shareholders, and a seat at the C-level table.

"I don't know who," Josh said. "Not surprised he plays the field. He's a jerk. I heard his talk was poorly attended. Don't worry, man. I didn't go."

"Thanks."

"Anytime. Hey, how's Brett? You guys do your weekly squash game last week?"

"Yeah. Like always. What? You're homesick or something?"

"I don't know. Yeah. Whatever. Something happened in our behind-the-scenes tour of the Paris Metro that shook me a little. I'm fine. We're fine. It's nothing. Just miss home, and my buds—"

"And your dog."

"Yeah. I miss Sally. Put her on the phone."

"Dude."

"Come on."

"I'm on the street."

"So? It's a crazy town, so just do it, okay? Hey, the French wouldn't think it's weird. They love their dogs."

Liam huffed, but put his cell phone to Sally's ear, so Josh could coo or whisper or whatever he did when he talked to Sally through the phone. Sally paused from her sniffing the millionth bush and lifted her ear a little, as if listening. He gave Josh a minute tops, then put the phone to his ear.

"Okay?"

"Yeah. Gotta go get some shut eye to get up early for the conference tomorrow. I'll call you tomorrow."

"Sure. Take care. And go meet some French women, will you? Sounds like you need to get laid."

"Where did that come from? Speak for yourself."

Liam barked a laugh and clicked off the cell phone.

Josh was worse than Liam's own mother for the way he checked up on him. At least his mother only expected to talk to him once a week. Tonight. He groaned inwardly. First he'd watch the football game. Then he'd call his mom. She'd still be up in New York, testing out new pastry recipes for her boutique Italian pastry company.

In five minutes he reached the bottom of the hill and crossed Broadway, turned right on College. A few minutes later, he turned at Forest Street, passing the toy store. He'd never really noticed it before, though he must have passed it hundreds of times on his runs, and certainly seven times in the last seven days he'd been walking Sally for Josh. This store must have been where Dahlia had done her toy shopping, though he hadn't seen the bag logo clearly. She'd had stuffed animals and some tubes of sparkles sticking out of the top of the bag.

Perhaps she had kids. A wistful pang washed through him. He thought he'd start a family with Christine, but she killed that dream before it had a chance to blossom when he caught her cheating on him with Hendricks. He hadn't had a serious girlfriend since he ended it with Christine seven months ago. Thank goodness he hadn't proposed to her. He'd been thinking about it. Since then, he'd sworn off all dating. And he'd sworn off love.

Love was for losers. He had to bring someone to the party and show up Hendricks, and Christine, if it was Christine that Hendricks was bringing. Show them he was fine. Have a great time. Live it up, and all the while beat Hendricks out by getting his analysis in on time and under budget, so he would get the promotion over Hendricks.

His stomach grumbled, tearing him away from the past.

"Time for an early dinner, eh, Sally?" he said.

She gave a soft woof. He picked up the pace and jogged back home to the house on Locksley he shared with Josh. Sally kept pace with him the whole way, the perfect running companion. She didn't talk and could keep up with him. He'd take her out for their morning run tomorrow at 5 a.m. before he left for work.

It wasn't until he put the key in the front door that he realized what Michael's jab about bringing his fiancée to the Christmas party was all about.

"Damn," he muttered under his breath. Hendricks *was* bringing Christine. The guy was trying to psych him out, acting like having Christine at his side was his ace in the hole, his secret weapon. Hendricks wanted to push Liam's buttons and have him lose focus on the big job. He wanted Liam to crash and burn so that he would get the promotion.

Liam slammed the door and felt like throwing his keys down the entry hall. His buttons were pushed all right. But throwing the keys would startle Sally and leave marks in the hardwood that he didn't want to have to deal with or explain to Josh. So he dropped his keys in the ceramic bowl his grandmother had made for him eons ago. He slipped off his shoes, lined them up next to the entry mat, and unhooked Sally's leash. She trotted off probably to find her favorite chew toy and settle down for a nap by the fireplace.

He tromped to the kitchen, opened the fridge, and grabbed the celery and Parmesan. He knew how to handle his anger. He'd focus it into something creative. He chopped some onions and celery, hammering the knife against the cutting board. Got the water going. Heated up some homemade tomato sauce. Grated some cheese.

What the hell was he going to do? He really wanted this promotion. It was what he'd been striving toward for the last eight years, through grad school and propelling his way up the ranks in the financial companies he'd been employed at across the country, until he'd landed at Cooper, Andrews & Sons three years ago.

He pictured contacting the vivacious Dahlia, the girl he'd just met, but brushed that thought aside. He didn't even know where she lived, or how to contact her.

His cell phone rang. "Hi Mom. I was going to call you after the game. It's about to start."

"Liam, dear, have you married and made me a grandmother yet?" His mom's favorite question of the day.

"Mom, not tonight."

"What? Bad day? Did your team lose?"

"Ma, the game hasn't started yet. Just got back from the dog walk."

"Then what?"

"Nothing, Ma."

"You're cooking, aren't you?"

"Yeah."

"You always cook when you're upset. What's the matter?"

"I don't want to talk about it."

"Then at least tell me what you're cooking."

Liam sighed and relented, telling her what meal he had in mind. That took them both off his problems. For the time being.

Chapter Two

DAHLIA EYED THE COMPLICATED phone system Mary had just pointed out to her. "I got it," she told Mary. "You should see ours back home. You would not believe how many lines we have to manage. The twenty-five you have will be fine."

"Really?"

"Yes." Dahlia flashed her what she hoped was a reassuring smile. She couldn't very well tell Mary that the phone system at the North Pole had thousands of lines ringing year-round, twenty-four-seven. That when she subbed there as part of the Elf Foundations training, she handled at least one hundred switchboard lines at a time.

"Good. The temp agency said you were good in a pinch. Thanks, Dahlia. We didn't expect Sherry to go on maternity so soon. I guess her baby will be a pre-Christmas baby instead of a post-Christmas one."

"Early gifts are great. Not to worry, Mary. Go ahead. I'll be fine."

Mary hovered halfway between the receptionist area and her back office for the last fifteen minutes after explaining the phone system, the message system, the filing system, and the expected schedule for coffee and lunch breaks.

Dahlia waved her off again and settled in her chair, slipping her headset on. It was almost 8 a.m., time for the office workers to start streaming in. Every corporate front office was the same. She didn't mind. She was a good front desk person. She liked the controlled chaos of the day, but was just as happy to leave it all behind to hustle home or to her volunteer job, and then work on her toy at home.

Phones started ringing right on time, eight o'clock sharp, when the weekend service went offline. Dahlia went to work. Between calls and sometimes during, she glanced up and smiled at the women and men in suits as they strolled in, with heads down examining their smart phones. Some stopped and asked for any messages the weekend service had collected for them, and any mail brought in earlier by courier. She imagined these people would be at their desks by 6 a.m. if it made a difference. Some of them had to work in synch with the east coast New York Stock Exchange.

"Hello, Cooper, Andrews & Sons. How may I help you?" She smiled into the phone. She nodded at the request, even though the caller couldn't see her. "I'll patch you through to his voice mail." She scanned the office list, hit the right buttons, and got that woman on the line to the right extension.

She heard the door open and automatically smiled. Then smiled brighter. "Hello there. I met you yesterday, didn't I?" Dahlia stood up and held out her hand. "You were with Sally, the Bernese. Liam, right?"

From frowning at his phone, he glanced up, surprised, his brown eyes widening. He seemed to falter in his stride. "Uh, hi. Yes. Liam." He shook her hand.

His large palm, warm and rough, surrounded her smaller hand, his grip firm and steady. Not at all what she imagined an office worker's hands would feel. His hands felt more like a wood workers.

A little shiver of anticipation washed unbidden through her. Her last sweetheart at the Pole had been a woodworker. He'd done nice things with her, with those hands.

She released Liam's hand. "I'm sure you have mail or messages or something like that." The pounding of her heart was probably just nerves. She scanned the little vertical slots, but then realized something. "What's your last name, Liam?"

"Where's Sherry?" He scanned the receptionist area, ignoring her question.

"She had to leave for maternity early. At least that's what Mary told me."

She waited but he was considering his phone, distracted.

"Liam?"

"It's MacAuley."

"You're Irish."

"On my dad's side."

She checked the message cubbies. "Sorry. There's nothing here for you."

"Okay, thanks," he said without looking at her and strode away down one of the hallways snaking off from the lobby.

She rallied the calls and greeted more people as they came in smiling and nodding. She felt strangely deflated. Liam was a lovely surprise, someone she met in her neighborhood. But his cool reception of her, after being so friendly the day before, threw her. No matter. She was just here for a few more weeks then she was going home. What mattered was completing her toy—if she could just determine what the flaw in her design was and fix it. Time was running out. Her day job was just a way to earn a living, sock some dollars away for future vacations—Elves got to come back to the Human world for occasional vacations—and to get to know the local customs so that she could be a better toymaker and inventor. That was all. She just needed to have the toy working by December 22. Ack! She only had twenty more days.

"DUDE, YOU'RE OFF YOUR game," Brett Barnaby huffed out at him.

Liam swung but missed the racquetball zooming by at a million miles an hour and missed his chance for a corner shot. "Am not."

"Really?" Brett smashed another one and made him dive for it. "You're thinking about the job offer I gave you."

"No. Stop it. Cheap. Tricks." Liam faltered then got his groove back. But game success was not to be. He soundly lost the round, fifteen to nine.

He picked up his towel, wiped the sweat off his forehead, and guzzled his power drink.

"Hah!" Brett snapped him with his towel. "If it's not you coming to work for my awesome killer startup, then it's got to be a girl, isn't it? About time. Dude, when was the last time you got laid? Forget Christine already, will you? She's not worth it."

Liam shrugged. "I know. Want to play three out of five?"

"Liam, I just beat you, all three sets, and you want more punishment? You must have it bad."

"No, there's no one. That's the problem."

"If we're going to talk girl problems for real, I need a beer."

Liam shrugged. "Sure. Whatever."

"I hear you. See you at the bar in ten?"

"Yeah, sure."

Liam headed for the locker rooms, quickly showered, and dressed. He met Brett at the long sports bar next to the gym. Happy Hour was loud. His team wasn't on the big screen so he turned his back to it and ordered his favorite on-tap beer, the local Anchor Steam. He nursed it while Brett settled on the stool next to him. They sipped in silence for a while.

"Okay, what gives?" Brett knocked him in the shoulder.

"I have to bring a date to the company Christmas party in a little over two weeks."

"Just someone? Anyone? Why?"

"No, a girlfriend—" Liam put "a girlfriend" in air quotes.

"Why?" Brett asked again. "You don't have a girlfriend."

"Exactly." He gulped the beer, hoping for inspiration.

"MacAuley, spill."

"Hendricks is taking Christine."

"No. That dog. Yeah, that's not cool. On both their parts." Brett swore.

"Thanks for the support," Liam said.

"Of course."

They sipped their beer. Then Brett slapped him on the back and laughed. "Hire a girlfriend."

Liam sputtered his beer. "What? No. Besides where am I going to find a girlfriend for hire?" Liam punched Brett on the shoulder. Hard. Brett deserved it and Liam owed him one. "I don't want just anyone. I want—I want someone who is cool, fun—"

An image of Dahlia's bright smile and infectious cheer came to mind, not to mention her shapely, well, everything. Hell, it had been a long time. He was daydreaming about a girl he met once. No, actually, twice. And she was all woman.

After Brett recovered his balance from nearly falling off his stool, he said, "Well, there's always my kid sister. She just got out of college…"

"No." Liam shook his head. "But you gave me an idea."

"What? Call up Girlfriends-R-Us? One of those fancy escort services? Hah! You? Mr. Straight-laced, by-the-book Liam MacAuley? That'll be the day."

"Stop being so dramatic, Mr. I'll-do-anything-once Brett Harper."

"Whatever." Brett grinned. "Maybe I'll hire one of those hot escorts for my company's launch party next spring."

"You don't need to. You have all the women you could ever want falling all over you night and day."

Brett shrugged, and frowned for a split second, then his trademark gap-toothed grin was in place. "I gotta try everything once. You said it. I didn't."

Liam grunted and stared off in the middle distance. Maybe he could pull it off. With some special planning.

"Spill it," Brett said.

"Once I've executed it successfully, I will. Promise. Thanks, man." Liam clapped a hand on Brett's shoulder. "I gotta go. Early day tomorrow."

"As usual."

"Yep."

"Go get your millions, bro."

"As always." They fist-bumped and Liam walked the three blocks to the train and headed for home across the bay, scheming. His plan just might work. No, it would work. Everything Liam set his mind to he accomplished. Everything in his work life anyway.

Chapter Three

DAHLIA SETTLED INTO HER second day at the corporate headquarters of Cooper, Andrews & Sons office, greeting and welcoming each employee from her post on the front desk. Even though it was a busy welcome desk, she managed it solo. She didn't mind. Elves learned from a young age how to master speed and detail. Besides, working the front desk was fun. But soon the fun would be over and she'd be going home. She wanted to go home, but her toy wasn't complete.

Far from it. Maybe she should bring magic into it. Then whatever wasn't working would be fixed, theoretically. At least that was how the Master Elves did it. Santa's Elves had to study from a young age how to make things by hand, and only then were they allowed to use their magic. You had to both visualize and create what you would later use magic for. It was the rule. Dahlia always followed the rules. Well, mostly.

No, she couldn't use magic again. Mom had warned against using any magic whatsoever in the Human world. "You never know what will happen. It's too dangerous. The Human world and Elf world don't mix well. You can't control the consequences of your magic there," Mom had said before Dahlia left the Pole.

{ 134 }

She had to figure out what was wrong with her toy, and soon. She couldn't arrive back home with an incomplete project. She'd be a failure, relegated to grunt work under another Master Elf, or worse asked to work for Custodial Services. Not that she had anything against Old Mac and his team. They did important clean up work. It's just that—that wasn't what she wanted for her life. She wanted her very long life to be full of toy making, and love, and family, and celebratory parties that went with being a celebrated Master Elf, like her parents were.

As the morning rush picked up, Dahlia shoved aside her wandering thoughts and focused on the tasks at hand, punching phone buttons, flashing smiles to employees strolling in. She was in the groove. Until he walked in. Then she ratcheted it up a notch.

"Good morning, Liam." She flashed him her biggest smile of the morning yet. "How's Sally? She's such a lovely dog." She handed him his overnight messages.

"She's fine."

Wow. He smiled back. He looked so very handsome when he did that. He stood there at the high counter separating them. Their fingers hadn't touched. She wished they had. For a moment, she regretted not dating during her year abroad in the Human world. What had prompted that decision? Oh, yeah. Her life was back at the Pole. This important year was just a required stepping stone to becoming a Master Elf.

A few more employees came in. Dahlia nodded and said hello and handed out messages. Liam stood there, flipping through the messages she'd handed him, his brown hair cut short, but curling just a little over his ears. So cute.

Suddenly he spoke. "How's your project coming?"

Dahlia felt her good cheer falter and warmth flood her cheeks. "Uh, not so well. You remembered that?" She squared some papers on the desk. "And it's been months working on my project... I'm so close to finishing."

She only had nineteen days. Panic rose up in her throat. She didn't want to remain here like her Aunt Holly, who turned away from becoming a Master Elf, even though she'd created a fabulous toy, and could have won the prize. Instead Aunt Holly had fallen in love with a human and stayed in San Francisco, giving up forever the wonderful life of a Santa's Elf at the Pole. It was rare, but they could have made it work with Uncle John leaving his life with the Coast Guard to move forever to the Pole. But John hadn't wanted to do that, apparently.

How had it come to this? She thought she'd been so diligent, yet the toy wasn't finished.

"Are you okay, Dahlia?"

She nodded and smiled, not meeting his eyes. She waved her hand as if to brush aside a pesky fly. "Yep. Yeah. Yes. I'm fine."

Liam was lingering. He clearly wanted to say something more, but she didn't know what. So she went about her business. She greeted more employees coming in and handed out messages without forgetting their names. Elves had better memories than humans. She knew everyone's name. She learned them on the first day and took pride in that personal touch.

He cleared his throat, and she had to look up. She smiled. Humans were so exotic, rounder faces, more muscular. This human sure was. His wavy brown hair, those intense brown eyes. Caramel or chocolate? She couldn't tell from a few feet away. She liked how his brows arched upward as if he were intrigued by, well, everything. He came across as smart, energetic, and keen. His long, lean form wasn't so bad either, those wide shoulders...

"Would you like to go to lunch with me today?" he asked.

She blinked. "I don't do dates with co-workers."

He smiled and seemed to suppress a chuckle. "Okay. Then it's not a date. Just a friendly co-worker thing, eating lunch together." He was standing right in front of her. She was sitting, so she stood.

"Okay. Then you can't buy me lunch either. Besides, I brought my own."

"I brought my own too. Let's eat by the water at the Ferry Building."

"I'll meet you there." She clenched her hands behind her back to stop them from fiddling with papers.

"Actually, let's meet in the lobby."

"Uh, sure." Dahlia shrugged. She wiggled her fingers behind her. She couldn't help it. The nervous energy had to go somewhere. "I look forward to our non-date lunch—thing."

"Me, too." He looked so serious when he said that. Then he smiled, and it was like the Northern Lights illuminating the mid-winter sky.

A FEW MINUTES BEFORE meeting Liam in the building's lobby, Dahlia rushed to the lobby bathroom. Hair, check. Lipstick, check. Clothes, so-so. Her top and skirt and striped knee highs just seemed a tiny bit drab, even though this morning they'd looked fine before she left the house. She wanted something more cheery, more sparkly.

She wanted a little excitement before going home. What harm could it do? But the consequences... She brushed the thought aside. She wanted to feel—special.

To summon her magic, she took a deep breath, closed her eyes, and found that calm place inside that she hadn't visited since she'd had her mess up with magic when she'd first arrived in the Human world nearly a year ago. This time she'd use less. It would work. As her magic coursed through her, her solar plexus jumped with giddiness. Her hands tingled.

In her mind's eye, she pictured exactly what she wanted, down to the last detail. She envisioned pretty iridescent sparkles, like the kind she played with in her art studio. She visualized them all over her clothes, artfully of course. Vision done, magic tingled throughout her body. She heard a ringing in her ears and a low hum thrummed through her. The magic was done. She opened her eyes. She clapped her hands and giggled at her reflection in the mirror. Sparkles were sprinkled lightly on her blouse and skirt. So what if a few sparkles got in her hair?

"Wow!" She twirled. Perfect. It worked.

She grabbed her lunch bag and rushed out to the lobby right on time, and there was Liam. Her heart pounded. It was ridiculous, but she was super excited to go on this non-date.

He smiled at her. "Ready?"

"Yep."

He held the heavy glass door for her, a whisper of a touch on her lower back, and then they were out on the busy San Francisco street. What a gentleman. She sighed.

They walked toward the Ferry Building. A block away, he paused on the street corner. "This way." He gestured toward the Hyatt Regency hotel.

"A surprise. I love surprises." Her stomach grumbled with hunger. She giggled, from nerves, she was sure.

He smiled down at her. Goodness, he was tall. Her head would fit neatly on his chest, tucked in. She had a vision of her mother, petite with flaming red hair, leaning against her father, tall, robust, sturdy. She fluttered her hand to erase the memory and suppressed a sigh. She missed them.

Liam was speaking but she'd missed his meaning. "Sorry, what was that?" she asked.

"I said that where we're going is a good spot. I thought since you were from out of town that you may not have been here."

"Where? The hotel? I don't usually play tourist inside hotels." She smiled.

"This is more than just a hotel." He guided her through the revolving door and up an escalator to a hallway with rooms winging off on either side.

She felt so special, and this wasn't even a real date. It was a non-date. She didn't date co-workers, and besides she was going home soon. In nineteen days. But for a split second she wished she did date, especially this co-worker. *Let loose more. Be more whimsical,* she thought. She'd been working so hard.

"What about eating lunch?" she asked as they walked down the hallway.

"Are you hungry?" he asked.

"Yes."

"Me too. Let's eat here." Liam said.

They'd left the hallway and stepped into a brightened room, the hotel lobby, she guessed. He took a few more steps and turned to wait for her.

Dahlia followed. The light changed, lighter, softer from the bright LED lights of the enclosed hallway. She gasped in awe. The open space shimmered in the filtered sunlight beaming in from somewhere. The lobby was dotted with comfortable couches scattered throughout with a bar to one side and an exhibit to the other. The lobby curved so she couldn't see what was at the other end.

"Look up," he said, his voice close to her ear.

She turned to peer at him, and his lips were right there, parted slightly. She gulped and looked up as he requested. And gasped again.

Plants cascaded down from what looked to be ten or fifteen levels above. From this far away, the plants looked like indoor ivy. Low maintenance. Worked well in this lighting. The ceiling appeared to come together at a point far above, the walls coming together as if they were inside a pyramid.

She sighed. "So lovely."

"Isn't it?" His voice was a little farther away so he must not have been right behind her. She stopped herself from checking, though she wanted to. Wanted to feel his warmth at her back.

The thought came unbidden, like a sudden spring melt waterfall: *Why couldn't she have a fling? Why not?* She couldn't think of a good reason why not. He was handsome, kind, and smart.

LIAM GESTURED TO A couch nearby. "Let's eat our lunches here. I thought the wind might be too cold to eat outside at the

Ferry Building." It wasn't the right time or place for his question.

"Sure, but I don't mind the cold," Dahlia said and sat on the couch. She crossed her legs under her and opened up the tiny backpack she'd brought with her.

After they ate their lunches sitting on the lobby's soft benches—he had his homemade risotto, and she had a colorful vegetarian sandwich with sprouts—he led her to the elevator.

As they stood waiting for the elevator, Liam snuck a sideways glance at her. Lovely sparkles across her cheeks, and some in her hair. Must be some kind of artistic make-up. He admired her vivaciousness, and she made him smile. The realization hit him in the chest.

"Close your eyes," he said as they stepped into the empty elevator. It was perfect. They were the only ones in the elevator. He could set the stage.

She widened her eyes and made an O with her mouth. Then she smiled mischievously and scrunched up her eyes and covered them with her palms for good measure. She was such a good sport. Something fluttered in his chest. He couldn't acknowledge what it was. But he could acknowledge that he was having fun.

As the elevator rushed them to the restaurant on the top floor, Liam buzzed with anticipation. That must be it. Anticipation. She was funny, pretty, wore colorful socks, and seemed ready to play. Hopefully she'd be a great fit and wouldn't turn down his proposal.

As the elevator pinged its arrival at the top floor, his chest twinged. This time he could identify it as an awareness of guilt. *It was just a business arrangement,* he reminded himself.

They were having fun. She seemed to like him. She was good company, and not actually a co-worker, since she was a temp—he listed the reasons why it had to work. But maybe that wasn't fair to her. He swatted that thought aside. He'd be upfront with her. It had to go well. Had to. His job advancement depended on it.

A few moments later, the maître d' led Liam and Dahlia to their table right away for their drinks and dessert.

"A window seat, as requested," the maître d' said and left them alone.

Liam had made a reservation right after Dahlia had said yes this morning. Thankfully the Equinox Restaurant wasn't that full for lunch. The business diners in their suits and few tourists in thick sweaters were seated here and there throughout the large round restaurant. He liked the idea of having the space practically all to themselves. It made their time together more intimate and set the mood for the request he had in mind. He quashed his romantic notions.

"What a view!" Dahlia sat, her petite frame slipping into her chair gracefully. Her bright blue-green eyes sparkled with pleasure. For a moment, he wished they sparkled that way for him, and not the view.

Liam tore his gaze away from her and admired the Bay Bridge for a moment. Ferries powered across the bay toward and away from San Francisco. Of all the high-rise views he'd seen around the world in his business travels—New York, London, Paris, Hong Kong, Perth, and Buenos Aires—he had to say that he liked San Francisco's views the best. There was something refreshing about the sparkling bay and its bridges, from any vantage point.

A waitress came and took their drink and dessert orders and left.

Moments later, he was nursing a Perrier, and Dahlia a root beer and a toffee chocolate crème brûlée, which she seemed to take inordinate pleasure in, sipping and sighing, nibbling and smiling.

"You must not drink root beer often. Or eat dessert," he said, feeling a smile bubble up at the way she took pleasure in her soda and fancy pudding.

"No. All that sugar. But I love them. Did I tell you about how I was considering using a color like root beer in my toy? In my market research, I found out that boys responded differently to different shades of brown."

Liam listened to Dahlia share about chatting with moms and their kids at a local playground for her research for a toy of some kind.

Should he ask her now or after they finished their drinks and dessert? What if she said "No"? He usually had a Plan B, but he'd felt so confident as he schemed up his plan last night. His only fallback plan was Brett's kid sister. No, she wouldn't work. She was too much like his own kid sister. He needed someone who could play and look the part, and here she was. Sparkles and all.

Her playfulness was good for him. He'd been working so hard. It was time to have more fun. Take a few risks outside of the office. For the good of his career and his sanity. And to show up Hendricks and Christine.

"Dahlia?" he said when she'd paused to admire the view, her blue-green eyes wide with delight.

"Yes?"

"I have an interesting proposition for you. I know we've only just met, but you're fun and—"

For a second he lost his nerve. But then she turned her bright blue-green eyes on him that seemed to glitter along with her actual sparkles.

"I am, I guess. Fun, that is." She nodded encouragingly, her mouth quirked in a half-smile. Her lips suddenly captivated him, red and kissable. He pulled his gaze away from them and back to her sparkly eyes. This was business. He dove ahead.

"Would you like to go to the company Christmas Party with me? It's on the twenty-first."

"I told you that I don't date co-workers." She fiddled with her straw paper, folding it into an accordion and flattening it out again.

"Well, we're not exactly co-workers. You're a temp. And it's not a date."

"You sure tell it straight." She chuckled and crumpled up the straw paper into a tiny ball. "You don't have anyone else to ask?" She stilled and watched him.

"I work—a lot." He held her gaze and shrugged and gave her his best charming smile.

"I see. That's Solstice... " She broke their gaze and turned to regard the view. She sighed and peered around the room. "I do have so much work to do..."

He waited. He had to play this right, relaxed.

She straightened and peered straight into his eyes. "Will there be dancing?" She wasn't smiling.

"Pretty sure." He sipped his Perrier, breaking her gaze for just a moment.

"A big decorated Christmas tree?" She waved her hands in the air signifying garlands strung gracefully around a tree.

"Probably."

"Hmmm. I see."

She seemed to want to say more, but instead glanced away and bit the side of her nail, and then rushed her hands to her lap.

"Will Santa be there?" she finally said without looking at him, her gaze on the view again.

"No."

"Mmmm."

Liam took this chance to study her. Her gaze unfocused, she seemed lost in thought, as if she was having an internal debate with herself. He could tell because she mumbled, nodding, and then shook her head, as if disagreeing.

He held his breathe, and then released it to calm his nerves.

She turned to him, a broad grin on her face. "I'm in."

He smiled at her exuberance. "Great!" *Thank goodness*, he said to himself. Yes, she was good for him. She had him smiling so much it gave his face muscles a workout. Maybe she'd give other parts of him a workout too. He swatted away that stray thought. This was just business, he reminded himself. "That's a relief." He chuckled. "I thought I'd have to ask my best friend's kid sister."

"What's wrong with her?"

"Nothing. She's like my kid sister. She's barely out of college... and new to—Doesn't matter. You're in."

She laughed full and loud.

He wanted to join in. The desire startled him. But he stopped himself and leaned toward her, a nervous flutter in his chest like before an important game. "I didn't tell you the other part."

"What?" She narrowed her eyes at him, but still had that half-smile quirked on those kissable lips.

"We have to act like boyfriend and girlfriend. Like 'play acting.' Pretend."

"So, no Christmas fling, huh?"

He didn't know what to say to that.

She laughed. "You should see your face. You look shocked."

"Do not."

"Do too." She gave another laugh. He couldn't help but smile.

When she was done laughing, she leaned toward him conspiratorially. "So, I see. Like a game, right?"

"Like that." *Where was she going with this?* he thought. "You're going to back out because it's not a fling?" he said keeping his voice pitched low.

She smiled and looked like she was holding in a laugh. "You really have no one else to ask, do you?"

"I just realized I needed to bring someone."

"Corporate. They like to keep you on your toes. The same the world over." She leaned back and smiled knowingly.

"Yep." He practically held his breath. He really should have had a Plan B.

"Well..." She bit her lip and eyed the view. "I did say I was in...but this new condition...I don't know."

Breathe, he coached himself. His whole career hinged on her answer. How did he come to this, again?

He'd vowed to never rely on a woman again for his happiness after Christine dumped him seven months ago. In the space of a heartbeat Christine had beat his heart to a pulp. Now Dahlia held his career in her capable, yet dainty-looking hands.

"Okay," she said finally. She smiled at him, her glitter on her cheeks and blouse picking up the light and shimmering like crystals. "Why not?" Then her smile slipped. "I'm going back home soon, so..." She looked away. "Pretend works for me." She turned back, her smile bright again. "Shall we shake on it?"

"Sure." Liam held out his hand and took her petite one. Her handshake was firm, and they shook once, European style. "So, where are you from?" His heart pounded with relief like he'd just played a whole set of racquetball.

"Up north. This is my year abroad." She then said a word that sounded like "she-burr." She added, "It means 'travel year' in a Celtic dialect."

"Then this should work. It'll be fun. God knows, I need more of that in my life."

"Me too." Dahlia turned toward the view. "Oh!"

Liam smiled and waited for her to say it.

"The restaurant is turning." She clapped her hands in delight.

A pang of guilt stabbed Liam's chest. They were adults, walking into this open-eyed. He was misleading her. He would just have to underscore the pretend aspect of their arrangement. It should be fun, light. But the thought hit him like a loose ball on the court: It was going to be hard, for him. What had he just stepped into?

DAHLIA LOVED THAT THE RESTAURANT TURNED. There was Alcatraz Island, the notorious prison island in the middle of the jewel of a bay. Beyond that was Angel Island and beyond that the rolling green hills of Marin County that she'd explored only a little during her stay in the Human world.

They sipped their drinks in silence. Her heart thudded like one of those fancy programmable toy drums one of her older siblings had invented. He'd become a Master Elf with his invention. She wanted her toy to succeed so bad she could taste it.

She sighed.

"A penny for your thoughts?" Liam asked.

He was sweet. She really liked his attention and wanted to make him smile more. So she smiled back at him. "I'm stuck. So close to finishing my toy..."

"Is this like a final project, or something?"

"Yeah, or something." She sipped her drink. "It'll stay an 'or something' until I get it working."

"What's wrong with it?"

"That's just it. I can't tell. I've taken it apart and put it back together a bazillion times."

"A bazillion, uh? That the scientific term?"

"Yeah." She smiled. "That's the problem right there."

"Maybe it's not as complicated as all that. Maybe you need to think of it in terms of food groups, categories. Analyze it in larger chunks. Like when you cook a meal—"

"You cook?"

"Yes, of course." He shrugged like cooking was the most natural thing in the world. "Men in your family don't cook?"

She shook her head. She couldn't very well tell him how nobody cooked at the Pole, at least not in most of the households. Meals were served at the Commissary and very good ones at that. Cooks specialized in their craft and created culinary delights three hundred sixty-five days of the year. Who had time to cook when you created delightful toys for the boys and girls of the world?

Liam nodded. "I get it. Not everyone cooks. Well, we all cook in my family. We're Italian, at least on my mother's side. Southern Italian," he said as if that explained it.

She nodded to keep him talking. He had a nice voice, warm and melodious. She never noticed how a man's voice could be that musical, at once soothing and engaging. Elves voices were pretty, but not as deep as Liam's.

"If you want to cook a meal, you get out all of your ingredients, and divide them by type. The grains, the vegetables, the sauce, the spices. In the categories, you may have a few choices, depending on your resources, but a good pasta dish will usually have something in each category." He smiled, his dimple showing, clearly enjoying talking about cooking.

"So I should think of my toy as a pasta dish?"

He chuckled. "Boys would like a toy that tastes like pasta, especially if it has tomato sauce and lots of cheese."

Dahlia laughed. "Not a bad idea, but my toy isn't for toddlers."

"Darn. Then you'd have a winner." He swatted at something glittery falling from the high ceiling.

Suddenly the whole restaurant rained down glitter from the ceiling. Some people laughed. Some screeched, maybe out of surprise. The restaurant guests hustled out of their seats and headed for the elevators, where there was a low ceiling and no glitter falling.

The glitter was harmless, she wanted to say. But she couldn't be sure, and she couldn't say anything that might reveal her suspicion—that this crazy little stunt was caused by her using magic. Guilt panged in her gut. She'd messed up.

Glitter fell like quiet rain, catching the light and sparkling like diamond rainbow specks. Dahlia glanced at Liam. He looked puzzled, but reached for Dahlia's hand and guided her to the low-ceilinged area where no glitter fell.

A couple that had been seated a few tables away from Dahlia stood laughing and holding each other tight, the woman gazing up into the man's eyes like there was nowhere else she'd rather be. For a moment, the woman broke her gaze and smiled at Dahlia, noticing her attention. The woman's smile was open, happy, delighted in the moment. She wore a bright pink rose pin on her lapel, the silk folded intricately. The man sported a short-brimmed sailor's cap with a compass and chisel pin on the band, the symbols of a stonemason. The woman winked at her.

In the next moment, Liam guided her toward the elevator, breaking Dahlia's silent communication with the happy woman. Would she ever have that kind of happiness, in the moment and in love?

"Must be left over from some party," he said puzzled, still holding her hand.

"It—" She clapped her hands over her mouth. *It wasn't*, she had almost said. A stab of guilt pierced her solar plexus again. The magic had backfired. She was in trouble now. She glanced around the lobby by the elevators. Most people were smiling. The only people frowning and grumbling were the restaurant employees losing their lunch crowd. At least no one had been hurt.

A Christmas Fling

LATER THAT NIGHT, DAHLIA FROWNED at her work table, actually her dining table, but who was going to know she didn't have an actual workshop?

Nothing she tried so far seemed to diagnose and fix her toy—something to do with the wire connections or the electrical circuits. She was so close, yet she'd been here eleven months and her toy still wasn't complete. Most elves bragged that they'd finished their toy early and took time off to travel and sightsee while in the Human world.

She'd arrive home with an incomplete project in hand. Great. Big Uncle and Father would laugh at her, the rest of the clan would frown, and she'd be relegated to the honorable, but behind the scenes, task of Janitorial Service, minus her Master Elf badge and all the privileges, rights, duties, and honors that that status entailed. She wanted to create special and unique gifts, not clean up after the creatives.

The phone rang, saving her from her depressing vision and dangerous urges that had haunted her in the last few months. She'd already messed up today with magic.

She answered. Her Aunt Holly. Uh-oh. But Dahlia was still happy to hear the voice of the one family member she had regular contact with since she'd been in the Human world.

"Dahlia, your mother called me today—"

"Oh no!"

"Oh yes. You know the rules. You've been so good up to now. No magic."

Dahlia hated the disapproval she heard in Holly's voice. Usually Holly was so upbeat and happy, more like an older sister than her aunt.

"I know."

"Why did you then? Was it a boy? You've been so good up to now," she said again. "No, I don't want to know. Just behave, will you? I don't want to get another call from your mother."

"Why did she call you and not me?"

"I don't know... Maybe because you don't have an answering machine and—"

"I do have an answering machine. My home phone wasn't turned on?"

"That must have been it... Are you any closer to completing your toy?"

"No... What am I going to do, Holly?"

"You'll figure it out. I know how much you want this. It's always darkest before the dawn."

"How did you figure it out?"

"I had help."

Dahlia could hear the smile in her voice.

"Uncle John?"

"Yes," Aunt Holly said with warmth.

Dahlia thought of Liam's advice as they'd walked back to the office after their drinks at the restaurant. Maybe she would try it. After all, she'd tried everything else it seemed. "I gotta go. Just got an idea."

"Good luck, *grá*." Love.

"Thank you," Dahlia said and hung up.

She took a deep breath, pushed all the parts and spare parts aside, and opened a page in her sketch book. As she and Liam had walked back to the office, he'd suggested she list all the categories of her toy's parts and then list the components that could be faulty or out of place. Then he recommended she analyze them piece by piece.

Time to get to work. She set the egg timer shaped like a rooster to twenty minutes—because she knew she could get something done in that time frame—and jumped in, listing, doodling, sketching, and listing some more. When the musical buzzer rang, she lifted her royal blue Sharpie and examined her list. The next step, Liam had said, was to focus on the first thing on her list. And if that didn't work, move down to the next thing. Be methodical, and analytical, he'd said, observing what was working and just focusing on that.

Dahlia got to work with renewed focus and hope.

Chapter Four

DECEMBER 4

LIAM RUSHED OFF THE elevator to the offices of Cooper, Anderson & Sons on the twentieth floor of the San Francisco downtown high-rise. He was excited to get his "project" started with Dahlia. He had only seventeen days to get to know her and have them appear as real boyfriend and girlfriend. He was surprised to feel excitement at the prospect. It's just for work, he reminded himself. Once he got his promotion he'd—he didn't know—say thank you very much and offer her a nice gift. As she said, she was returning home anyway. A little fun for them both. He shoved away the niggling of guilt that maybe what he was doing wasn't right. He wasn't hurting anyone, both of them would benefit, have some fun in the process, so it was all good. He was good at giving himself pep talks.

He strode into the lobby and faltered in his step. Dahlia answered phones and greeted his co-workers with grace and a smile. Her reddish hair swirled atop her head in some kind of exotic bun. She was gorgeous.

Dahlia smiled and worked the front desk, answering phones, greeting co-workers. When she saw him, she gave him a big smile.

Ignoring the sunburst in his chest, he spoke, "Would you like to meet for coffee Saturday morning at the Rockridge Bakery?"

Dahlia held up one finger as she shouldered a ringing phone and handed a co-worker his messages.

He stood there patiently when what he really wanted to do—an image of her ripe lips close to his, running his fingers through her luscious riot of curls, inhaling her vivacious scent of woman. His blood rushed down to his crotch. He swore, shifting from foot to foot, startled at his vision. A little fun, yeah right.

Dahlia stood and smiled back at him. "Sure, that would be nice. What time? Oh, hold on." She greeted another co-worker, and then turned back to him, her smile gone. "What time did you say? Oh, right. You didn't say." She peered at him, waiting. Then scribbled something down, tapping her pen against the desk.

Distracted from his plan by her faded smile, he asked, "I know you're busy at the front desk. But is everything okay?"

She shrugged. "It's my toy—I tried what you suggested but still couldn't solve my problem..." She laughed, not a happy laugh, then frowned.

"We can talk about it more. Maybe I can take a look at it. How's 10 a.m.?"

A stray red curl had escaped her fancy bun. He couldn't help it. He brushed it back behind her ear. Her skin felt soft, like silk. He'd wanted to show everyone, anyone who was watching their connection. But he didn't expect to feel the zing of electricity from his fingertips, up his arm, all the way to his pounding heart.

Dahlia blushed a pretty pink and her eyes widened. "Sure."

The phone rang and broke the moment. She stared at him wide-eyed for a moment longer then shifted to answer the phone.

Liam rushed off to his office, his suit jacket folded over his arm to cover his reaction to her.

Chapter Five

SATURDAY MORNING, DAHLIA DREW in her sketch book, her colored pencils spread out in front of her on her café table. Coffee and morning bun at her elbow. She needed a break from worrying about her toy and how she only had fifteen days to get it working properly.

So she felt inspired to do something creative, something different. She drew a mom with her infant hugged against her chest in one of those wraps, sitting at a back table. There also was an older man with his dog, standing at a tall table on the sidewalk. The dog wore a red bandana around its neck, and the man wore one on his leather rainproof bush hat. Next her eye was pulled to a hipster couple with their two dogs, two kids, and lots of tattoos on both the woman and the man. They sipped hot beverages while the two school-age children munched on muffins and croissants. The family scenes made her smile. Maybe she'd have a family one day. But that felt far away. Elves aged slowly and most didn't usually get married until well into their thirties.

Dahlia had been at the café since it opened at 7 a.m., drawing for an hour already. She hadn't been able to sleep much. Well, she didn't really need to sleep much this far south of the sixty-fifth parallel at Fairbanks, Alaska. She was a night person when she worked in her studio at home, but this early morning café meeting should be fun, and maybe she was a morning person. She couldn't tell.

She examined her pencil sketches. They were pretty good, true to life, capturing smiles and looks of tenderness. This pretend "dating" was great for her creativity, all that sweet flirting in stolen moments at the front desk two to three times a day for the last two days. Excitement thrummed through her chest. Now she only needed to take the next step and channel her energy into finding a solution.

TEN MINUTES TO 10 A.M. on a crisp, cold Saturday morning, Liam hustled toward the café on College Avenue, Sally tugging the leash in front of him in her fast walk, her nails clicking against the sidewalk. He hadn't planned to bring her to the café meeting, but he'd skipped the dog's morning walk to work off some sexual frustration, energy, call it what you will. He'd gone to the gym and played a few pickup basketball games with some high school kids instead of Brett. Brett hadn't answered his cell. Probably had partied late into the night with some pretty young thing.

He'd rushed home, jumped into the shower, and quickly changed. He made it down the three blocks to the café in record time with Sally in the lead. The whole front wall window was slid open, so he saw Dahlia before she noticed him. Her head was bent over her drawing book. Her hand flowed over the page, her red curly hair half-covered her rosy cheeks. Her kissable lips were pursed in concentration. God, she was beautiful. He needed a cold shower.

What was he going to do? He wanted this pseudo-date, getting-to-know-you morning to be light and fun. No pressure. But his body wanted to run the show. No. He had to take charge. He didn't want to get carried away and be foolish, again. Like he'd almost done with Christine. He'd been planning to propose to her on Valentine's Day after they'd only been dating two months, when he'd caught her bed with Hendricks.

Love was for immature suckers. He just wanted a fun fling with Dahlia, and to beat out Hendricks for the promotion.

Then she peered up at him. Her eyes brightened in welcome and her lips curled up in a lovely smile. His heart leaped. Without his say so.

Dahlia jumped up and hustled toward him. For a split second he thought she was going to throw herself in his arms, and he welcomed the vision and the act. But instead she threw her arms around Sally, who obligingly woofed and whacked her big tail on the ground, and generally made a big fool of herself.

For a split second there Liam wanted that unconditional love, both to receive and to give. But then he brushed the desire aside. It was about business, only business. And light fun, he reminded himself. Love was for fools.

"YOU HAVE A WHAT?" Dahlia said. Her heart pounded with excitement.

"A list. Of questions. For us to get to know each other." He sat across the table from her and looked at her sideways over his coffee.

"Sorry." She covered her mouth, then gave up, and let out her laugh. "You're so organized and practical."

"I'm glad you're taking it well." He smiled. "Yes, I'm organized. It's good you already know that about me."

"I do. That was easy to spot. Are there deep dark secrets we have to reveal to each other?" Dahlia gulped down some coffee and broke eye contact. She had secrets, not so little things, like who she really was that she didn't want to, couldn't, reveal. In fact, it was forbidden to, unless she wanted to forfeit her life as an elf. And she really didn't want to give up her elf life.

"I don't think so... We just need to know the important things about each other." He paused, so she lifted her gaze to his.

He leaned toward her. "You want to get out of here? Sally could go for some more walking, and so could I."

Sally perked up her head and wagged her bushy tail at the mention of her name.

"Sure. May as well make this whole getting-to-know-each-other thing practical by combining it with some light cardio and a dog walk." Dahlia chuckled.

"Are you making fun of me?" Liam stood.

" 'Course not. Why?" She stood, too.

"I can't always tell."

"Well, I could make fun of you in a nice way, if that's what 'girlfriends' do." She made air quotes with her fingers at the mention of the word "girlfriends."

"I suppose some do." He tilted his head, as if he were about to say something, but seemed to think better of it.

"Are you teasing me? I can't always tell either."

"Well, that makes two of us." He untied Sally's leash from the table leg. "Where to? Walk toward the lake, downtown, the university, or farther, like to a marina...?"

"Choices. So many... I don't know. You pick. I've visited all those places briefly, but don't really know." Dahlia gestured to the street and shops around them. "Be my tour guide. Let's go somewhere fun."

"I like the lake. Lake Merritt. So does Sally."

"Let's do it," Dahlia said.

"But it's a forty-five minute walk just to get there. I could drive?"

"Think I can't handle it?" She smiled.

"I don't know. Can you?"

"You mean, can I keep up with you?" She glanced at him.

"Why do you say that?

"You're in trainers, I mean running shoes, well-worn and lived in. You probably work out often and like it. And, sure, I can keep up with you."

"I didn't know you were so observant, like a detective in training." He shook his head and led her down the busy sidewalk.

Lots of people strolled down the sidewalk, out and about on a Saturday morning. She was usually holed up working on her toy. Look at what she missed out on a winter Saturday morning.

"Did I say something wrong?" Liam asked after a moment.

She knew he meant no insult so kept her tone light when she said, "Well, I am an artist and a researcher. You sound surprised at my—" She waved her hand in the air, searching for the word. "My ability to observe."

"I guess I am. I don't really know what I thought." A light flush crept up his neck and the side of his face. Kind of cute how he embarrassed easily like that.

She touched his arm to reassure him. "Hey, that's okay. We're getting to know each other." *And I've really never done this*, she realized. All her previous boyfriends had been guys she'd known her whole life. She'd never experienced the whole getting-to-know-you phase. And she hadn't dated at all since she'd been in the Human world. What had been the point? She was going home again at the end of the year, and her life was at the Pole. So why had she said yes to Liam? Maybe it had been his brown eyes. Maybe it had been because he'd asked. She was curious. She wanted some excitement, a change. She had to shake things up, do something, anything, to finish her toy.

"Right, so the first item on my list is 'Favorite Hobbies.' I'll start," Liam said.

"Sure."

So as they walked through the busy Rockridge neighborhood and up a steep hill near a tiny reservoir, Dahlia listened to Liam talk about squash, wing chun, karate, kendo, and more martial arts that she'd never heard of. Liam guided them through hilly neighborhoods and down the wide Grand Avenue to Lake Merritt. They'd passed through a lovely tiny rose garden in a canyon, all the rose bushes trimmed back and dormant in the winter. Even the fountain was empty. She imagined it running and livening up the garden in the spring.

At the foot of Grand Avenue stood a majestic art deco movie theatre. She stopped on the corner. Dahlia's fingers itched to sketch it. Something about the curly cues and colorful marquee captured her imagination.

"Have I said too much? Am I boring?"

"No. Why?"

"You've been standing there staring at the theatre for the last few minutes."

"Oh, it's just so lovely. I have to draw it."

Liam smiled. "Sally could use a jaunt around the little park across the street. Let's hang out there. They have benches." He waved in the direction of the park filled with vendors. "We can also check out the farmer's market. Then you can share with me about your hobbies."

Dahlia nodded, crossed the street with Liam, and sat on a bench while he walked Sally around the little park.

What had she gotten herself into? She needed to be in her studio working. She only had fourteen days to have her project ready before she flew home.

A half hour later, Dahlia sat perched at the edge of Lake Merritt sketching a pelican that had just skimmed the water and landed with a plop. Liam sat beside her quietly. She couldn't stop sketching. It was something about being with Liam. She liked all his questions. She felt jittery. She liked sharing about herself and listening to him. While she drew, she'd shared with him about her love of music, music boxes, and singing songs from old Broadway musicals. He nodded encouragingly and asked her where her love of music came from.

She shrugged. "I'm not sure. Music and singing has always been a big part of our family."

"I'd love to hear more about your family. But I'm hungry. Let's head back for lunch," Liam said.

"Sure." Dahlia stuffed her journal in her purse slung across her body. For a second she felt awkward. Like she'd said too much about herself already. She was glad he didn't ask her any more questions about her family. She hated lying to him.

"We did Favorite Hobbies." He glanced at a small piece of paper.

"That your list?" Dahlia asked.

"Yeah, how about family?"

Oh dear. "Family..." Dahlia shrugged. "I have a big family. It'll take a while. You first."

"Again?"

"Yeah." Dahlia bent to pet Sally.

As they walked back the way they came, Liam shared about his parents, how his mother had a pastry business inspired by her love of her home in southern Italy, and about his father, always traveling to Ireland for business, where he was originally from, and about his two younger siblings, twins, currently in college.

"That's where you got your cooking bug from? From your mom?" Dahlia asked.

"Yeah." Liam smiled. "In fact, we could have some lunch at my place. Do you like fava bean soup?"

"Don't know. Never had it." Something about his thoughtfulness warmed her. "You prepared for us to have lunch together?"

"Yep. Ready for an adventure?"

"Sure am!" Dahlia said.

In another forty-five minutes they were back in the Rockridge neighborhood, at the corner of Miles and Clifton Street.

"This is where we first met," Liam said.

"You're right," Dahlia said. She couldn't look him in the eyes. Standing on this corner near her studio made her deadline sit up and yell at her. "Sorry, Liam, I need to get back to work."

"Oh, I thought we'd spend the whole day together."

"I—I just need to get to work. Deadlines, you know." She wasn't going to apologize again.

"Oh, I know deadlines. But, we all need to eat. How about you stop by for a quick lunch, and we'll call it a day."

Dahlia felt a flutter in her lower belly. She liked Liam. They had their pretend relationship together. And she did need to eat. "Okay. How can I say no to a home cooked meal?"

And that was how she found herself ten minutes later at the bachelor pad that was Liam's and Josh's home, standing in the front hallway. Let off the leash inside the house, Sally ran off and came back with a toy between her teeth.

Dahlia laughed.

"That's the first time you've laughed all morning," Liam said. "What's up?"

Dahlia sighed for what felt like the millionth time. "Haven't I bored you to tears with my project?"

"No." He smiled kindly and he shrugged. "I want to help."

"You're sweet."

"Thanks," Liam said, shucking off his jacket and hanging it on the peg. "I'll get lunch together."

You could be my lunch, thought Dahlia. Oh dear! She had it bad.

LIAM BUSIED HIMSELF IN the kitchen, heating up the oven for the bruschetta and getting bowls out for the soup.

When he looked over at Dahlia, she was still staring off into space, sitting on his living room couch.

He wiped his hands on a dishtowel and called over to Dahlia. "Something wrong?"

"No. Yes. I don't know."

"Maybe this isn't such a good idea." He'd have to ask Brett's kid sister after all.

"What?"

He could only see her profile, a half-frown on her face.

"This pretend thing—we're doing."

"Why? What?" Dahlia stood and turned back to him, confusion in her gaze.

"I mean I like you, but if it's making you uncomfortable..." He stood feeling off balanced, Dahlia standing behind his couch, as if it were a protective barrier. "We don't have to do this." He waved between them.

She darted her gaze around nervously, fiddling with her purse strap. "No, no, that's not it." She finally met his gaze and smiled brightly. He got the distinct impression there was a lot happening inside that she didn't want to share. He wanted to know what was going on inside her. She intrigued him.

"Then sit and let me serve you," he said and smiled.

DAHLIA SAT AT LIAM'S counter on a high stool, enjoying his fava bean soup. Delicious and hearty for a cold winter afternoon. She sipped the sparkling water he'd offered her. They ate in silence for a while. She enjoyed the silence, but then it stretched longer and longer. The need to speak bubbled up in her throat.

"Delicious, Liam. Thank you," she said. "I'm sorry... I'm just distracted..."

"Hey, this is supposed to be fun, right? So, if you want to talk about your project. A toy, right? I'm interested, curious actually..."

"Thanks." Dahlia studied him. Even in his casual clothes he radiated confidence, mastery, and a vibrant energy, like he was ready for anything. His brown hair hung in a wave across his forehead like the classic Superman from the 1950s. "I know I keep saying it, but you're so sweet."

He flushed pink at her compliment, sipped his water, and chuckled. "You are too."

"We chatted about sports and my music boxes. What else is on your list?"

"You sure?"

Dahlia nodded. His kitchen was cozy. She didn't want to leave it. All she had waiting for her was her mess of the toy in a million pieces and maybe a voice mail from her aunt.

Liam popped off his stool. "I'll make us some coffee and you tell me what you like about the San Francisco Bay Area. That work for you?"

"Sure."

Dahlia shared with him how she loved the soaring redwoods in Marin County, the cold moody ocean, and the view from San Francisco's Coit Tower.

"I scored when I took you to the restaurant yesterday."

"You sure did." She laughed.

He leaned against the stove casual-like, one foot crossed over his ankle, his hands tucked into his pockets. What if his hands caressed more of her, like he'd caressed her cheek a few days ago at the office? Her heart sped up a notch. Was that only three days ago? And their day felt quite full already. Enough for two or three days worth of socializing and getting to know each other, right? Maybe she should go home soon after all.

"Dahlia—"

The way he said her name all gentle and smooth startled her. She shivered as the image arose of them entwined in an embrace. "Hmm? What?"

Liam held a question in his gaze, seemed to be about to say something, shook his head, then finally spoke his voice rumbling over her, drawing her in. "You went away? Where'd you go?"

"My, you're perceptive."

He gazed at her seriously and nodded. "I am, with you."

"Not everybody?" She gulped in some air. Heat shot up her cheeks. She stayed where she was and gripped the counter edge to prevent the very strong impulse to vault herself over the counter and into his arms. Her overactive imagination was overreacting.

"No." His brown eyes held her captive.

Her fingers tingled to capture the strong jaw and cheekbones, the half-day stubble. Did he have to shave twice a day with only a towel wrapped tight around his waist?

"You're doing it again," he said.

"I am? Oh, I'm just—" She waved her hand in the air, "Daydreaming. Overactive imagination. Do it all the time. Does it bug you?"

He laughed. "Are you trying to please me now?"

"Isn't that what people do in relationships?"

"I guess... I don't know. I'm no expert." He shoved his hands into his jeans' pockets, calling her attention to his muscular frame.

Something gurgled on the stove, breaking her daydream. She stood.

Liam turned away to tend to it. "Coffee will be ready in just a second." He turned back and placed a silver pot on the counter between them. The strong aroma of coffee wafted up between them. "Sugar and milk?"

His words drew her attention to his intense gaze. She fiddled with the napkin. Her toy called to her, but this dance of getting to know each other hung between them, pulling her toward him, as a magnet to its opposite. "Yes, please. But I gotta go in.—" She checked her watch. "In twenty minutes."

"I'm sure we can find out all there is to know about each other in that amount of time," Liam said with a straight face.

Dahlia chuckled. "I'm sure." She sipped the strong brew. "Delicious, just like the lunch. You have a gift, Liam MacAuley."

"Liam Giovanni MacAuley."

"Giovanni? I didn't see that on the company roster." She smiled, trying to keep her gaze on his face, when all she wanted to do was roam his jawline, his strong column of a neck, broad muscular shoulders—

"My mother's great-uncle's name. He was a mischievous pirate captain, according to the family legends."

"Really? I think I have a few pirate ancestors too."

"Oh?"

"Yes." Dahlia sipped her coffee. Her heart pounded like the cannons of yore. She shoved aside her overactive imagination and snuck a peek at Liam.

He sipped his coffee too, staring off in the middle distance. His strong-looking fingers were long and tapered and seemed so at home holding an espresso cup. His muscled wrists peeked out of his long-sleeved polo shirt, sinews and veins showing. He set his cup down with a clink.

"I know you've been here a year, and that you're going home soon. And you're doing me a huge favor going to this party with me." He toyed with his coffee cup, keeping his gaze on her. "I want to do something for you. To return the favor. Let me help you get your project done."

Dahlia stared at him, at his lips held in a firm line. He was waiting for an answer. She steadied her gaze on his eyes. "I hadn't thought of getting any help. In fact, we're supposed to make it entirely on our own. Requirement and all that."

"I don't mean to work on it. Just problem-solve it. Or help you get through the blocks you mention."

"I don't think so. That's fine. I'm just blowing off steam, blathering. Overactive imagination searching for a place to go, and all that."

He considered her seriously. "Whenever I need to blow off steam when a work project is bugging me, I play squash, or cook. You know, something completely different."

Dahlia nodded, but she didn't know what to say. A frozen part of her heart rose from her chest and into her throat, like a piece of ice that desperately needed to melt. He saw her. He actually saw her. So unexpected, and so desired, but she hadn't known she'd needed to be seen for herself. Not consciously anyway. Not until this moment.

Gently he said, "Do you have something like that? Something different to do?"

"No." She gripped the spoon, not being able to meet his gaze. An image of how she spent her free time popped into her mind's eye. When she sat in front of the TV, she adjusted pieces of music box metal and its prongs. "Wait. I do. I watch TV shows and fiddle with—things."

"What shows?"

" 'Dancing With the Stars' and 'So You Think You Can Dance' and 'American Idol' and 'America's Got Talent.' "

"Okay. That can be inspiring." He nodded.

"But playing with music boxes may be too close to what I'm trying to create."

"If you're doing a music box as your final project."

"Not really."

"Watching those shows is a break from what you're working on," he stated.

"I guess."

"Maybe we should take it up a notch."

"What do you mean?"

Liam said nothing. He slipped off his stool, padded over to a white box with an iPod in it, and fiddled with it. In a moment, blues belted out of the little machine. He turned to her with a smile and lifted an eyebrow, as if challenging her.

She could play along. " 'Baby, Please Don't Go' by Muddy Waters."

"Wow, nice." He held out his hand. "May I have this dance?"

"Hmmm," she hesitated. "Too slow."

He nodded gamely and returned to the iPod. Next, rock and roll burst out of the speakers.

"That's easy. 'Born in the USA' by Springsteen. It's good but too jumpy."

"Okay, Madame. As you wish."

Next came a Celtic rock band.

" 'Dreams' by The Coors." She laughed and felt her feet tapping the floor.

"Yes, you certainly know your music."

"I do indeed." She couldn't help it. The music moved her. She hopped and skipped a little, twirled and took his outstretched hand.

"I love this song," she said, breathless. *This is different*, she thought. *Maybe just what I need.*

They danced, hopped, twirled together. Liam had great rhythm. He spun her around, he pulled her close at just the right moment as the song stopped. She was pressed against his body.

He gazed down at her, serious and probing, and eyed her lips. Before her mind knew what she was doing, she was parting her lips, ready, and accepted his intention. Enough flirting.

When the kiss came it was light, and sweet. He tasted delicious. But she wanted more. So much more than light and sweet. She wanted hot and heavy, and in an instant, opened her lips to him, inviting him in.

By the time she broke away, she was panting, vibrating, and shaking. She wanted him so much more, and down that path, she could not travel.

"I have to go." She stepped back.

His eyes widened. "Dahlia, wait."

"No—I can't do this. Sorry."

He reached for her, but she was already scurrying away toward the front door. In under a minute, she'd grabbed her coat and bag and hurried out the door. She froze on the sidewalk shivering in the dusk. She wasn't shivering from the cold. The night air felt good against her heated skin. She was shivering from the passion she felt for Liam.

She hustled home, three blocks away. "I barely know him," she said under her breath. "I can't—you can't—" she scolded herself.

Oh, but she wanted to, wanted to throw caution and rules and edicts to the wind. And the consequences be damned. And for once in her life, the good girl reputation she'd happily carried all these years suddenly felt like a yoke around her neck. She couldn't fall for a Human man. Her life was back at the Pole.

LIAM RUSHED OUT THE door after Dahlia and caught up with her halfway down the block.

"You walk fast."

"Go away."

"No." He kept his hands in his pockets otherwise he'd reach out for her. It wasn't the time for that yet.

"You're the stubborn sort."

"Yes."

"I'll add it to the list," she said in a huff.

"I'm glad you're keeping one. That means you don't completely hate me and never want to see me again."

She stopped and glared at him. Her mouth opened and closed. She spun forward and continued her fast walk.

In one stride he caught up to her. "Dahlia—"

"I said Go away. "

"I want to apologize—"

"Don't you dare."

"You're the fiery temper type, too."

"Add it to your list."

"I will." He walked along side her, glancing at her every few minutes.

Her jaw worked. She nodded then shook her head as if she were having a debate with herself.

He blew out his frustration. "We need to set things right. I need to know what scared you away."

"I can't tell you that."

"Can't or won't."

She grumbled.

"Which is it?"

"I don't know, Liam. I'm all mixed up and feel pulled in a million different directions."

"I know how you feel..."

She stopped and rounded on him. "How could you know how I feel? You don't know anything about me."

"Well, that's because you can't, or won't, tell me. But Dahlia, I know enough. And what I see I like. You're fiery, tempestuous, creative, and passionate. What is so wrong about that? I think you wanted to kiss me as much as I wanted to kiss you."

She wouldn't meet his eye. "Can we not talk about this in the middle of the street, at dusk? My place is just at the end of the block."

"Okay."

They kept walking. He let himself relax. At least she was inviting him in. He liked his chances. He liked her. A lot. He warned his libido to behave. An invitation to her place didn't mean he was going to sleep with her. But by all that was holy and good, he wanted to now more than ever. That way lay madness, he reminded himself, because if he did, he feared the worst. His heart would melt all over the floor. Then he'd gather the jelloed mass and serve it to her on a pretty platter. When it came to love he was an all or nothing guy. Up to now, after his terrible mistake with Christine, he was just a nothing guy.

He followed her down a narrow path alongside a large house, and they soon stood at her front door. In the surrounding ambient light and her front stoop lamp, her place looked like a small one-floor granny unit behind a two-story Victorian house. Two tall flower pots presided on each side of the door, deep purple petals hugging green wide leaves.

She unlocked the door and stepped in. He followed without a word. He waited to see what she'd serve back to him.

Dahlia flipped the lights, and like she said, things were everywhere, whimsical and curious art supplies and projects and wires, wheels, and gadgets in a state of becoming something. Craft materials were strewn all over—on the table, the couch, a small coffee table, a kitchen counter, and on another table in the far corner by a small TV. He wanted to examine each one and guess what she was working on.

She shucked off her coat and shoved her bag on the table atop some papers full of blueprints and sketches. "This is it." She waved her hand around.

"Where do you sleep?"

She blushed and pointed toward a Georgia O'Keefe flower print cloth panel that hung on the wall. "Beyond there. A nook. It's just a studio."

She moved into the open kitchen and opened a few cupboards, closing them again with a clack.

Liam just waited. She invited him in, but he didn't want to upset her creations. Every available sitting surface had something on it.

She pulled some boxes out of a cupboard. "Want some tea?"

"No, thanks."

"I need some. It's part of my ritual. I make tea. I get to work. Or fiddle. Or..."

She turned her back to him at the sink, her shoulders shaking.

Oh no. Was she crying? What brought that on? He wanted simple, he wanted fun, but he couldn't turn away from her, even if she was crying. *Not ever*, a voice whispered in his mind.

He rushed to her and touched her shoulder. In an instant, she plunked the teakettle into the sink, the water still running, and folded herself in his arms, mumbling into his shirt. God, she felt so right in his arms. She was just the right fit, warm, snug, and all curves.

"We can't do this, Liam," he heard her say.

"Okay." He smoothed her hair, feeling the silky curls bouncing around his fingers. "We won't. We're just having fun, remember? Just until the twenty-first. Then we can get serious."

She shoved him away, her hands on his chest. He wanted more of her hands on his chest. Not less.

"You don't understand."

"Explain it to me."

"I can't."

"Okay. I'll have some of that tea now. Where shall I sit?" He turned off the running water and stepped from her. She had enough to think about.

She spun around, eyes wide, as if seeing her tiny place for the first time. "Wait here. Don't move."

She scurried around her apartment, rushing like a little pixie, moving something that looked like a mobile to the top of the counter, and moving other items, clearing the couch and small table in a whirlwind in no order he could spot. Things just seemed juggled around.

"Sit on the couch," she motioned. "Tea's coming right up."

"I can do that." He smiled at her but she'd already spun back to the kitchenette and left him to his own devices.

Could he entice her to a Christmas fling and would he survive it intact?

DAHLIA WAS FACED WITH a choice. Submit or die. No, no, that wasn't it. Again, her imagination was running away from her, and not even leaving a memo, or breadcrumbs. Dahlia's hands shook as she ripped open the tea bags packet and plunked them into mismatched mugs she'd found at a neighborhood garage sale. She hoped Liam liked mint. She loved all kinds of mint. That was all she had in her cupboard, peppermint, spearmint, the mix of spearmint and peppermint, and mint from North Africa, and from her own garden. Jitters of excitement, or was it dread, flew through her. Jeez, she hoped it wasn't dread. Did she have to feel all of her feelings *all* the time? Liam. So close. Sitting in her little cluttered creative home. His tall length folded into her tiny couch.

Heat flooded the pit of her belly, up her chest, and spilled out onto her cheeks. In her body, it felt like rockets going off for Chinese New Year. Oh dear.

She managed to fill the mugs from her whistling tea kettle and hardly spilled any hot water. She took a comforting inhale of the spicy mint and carried their mugs over to the tiny couch and to the chest that served as a coffee table. She placed them on the flat surface with nary a big spill. Only a tiny one. Nerves. It had to be nerves.

Liam rested his big palm on the back of her hand. She gasped at the tingling heat that zoomed up her arm and straight to her center.

"Dahlia, you okay?"

"Um, yes." She straightened and smoothed her hands down the sides of her shirt.

Liam's gaze followed her movements.

She stilled her hands. "Why wouldn't I be? You're only the first guest I've had over at all, and you're a man."

"I noticed."

She fluttered away to straighten things, not really paying attention to what she was shifting, but it felt good to move. "Maybe this was a bad idea. I don't know. I just—"

Liam was beside her in an instant, offering his warmth, his certainty, his firmness, oh boy. "It doesn't have to be so complicated, does it?"

"What is it with you guys? Everything is just so easy for you—"

He placed his hands on her shoulders. "It's not."

"What?" That stilled her movements. She peered up at him, his gaze serious, his mouth not frowning, but not smiling either.

"I haven't felt this way in a long time," he said and placed his hands on her shoulders, caressing up and down her arms, his body only inches away. His meaning was clear to her.

"No," she whispered and put up her hands in protest and met his warm chest, muscled and firm under her palms. "You're not supposed to fall for me."

"I'm not." He smiled. "It's just a Christmas fling."

"It is?" she said, eyeing his mouth.

"Mmmm." He didn't wait for a royal invitation but bent his head and angled it just right so she could kiss him, and crawl all over him, hands on his back, firm butt, arms, shoulders, all muscle, warm, and hard in all the right places.

"Curtain," she mumbled when she was finally able to gasp for air a million years later.

Still kissing him, she walked backwards with Liam across the room. She managed to guide them to the curtain. With a flick of her wrist, she shoved aside the curtain and fell into her double bed, Liam beside her. They fit, surprisingly.

"You sure?" he said softly, pushing off the bed to hover over her, his arms framing her head.

"What could be better than a Christmas fling, Liam?" she smiled. Her heart pounded.

"You deserve so much more."

"I want this." She didn't want to be a good girl anymore. "I want you."

He smiled, wide and open. And then he kissed her. And she kissed him back with all her heart.

Chapter Six

L IAM AWOKE. HIS INTERNAL clock said it was sometime after midnight, early Sunday morning. He must have been quite tired to fall asleep. But what a time! Dahlia was so sweet, so luscious, that part of his body shot to standing immediately.

But Dahlia wasn't in bed. He slipped on his jeans and padded a few paces to the main room. Dahlia was seated at her dining table, bent over a small gadget that looked like a circuit board connected to a motor.

"Coming back to bed?" he asked softly.

She started. "No." She practically jumped out of her chair, her painter's smock slipping off of one creamy enchanting shoulder. She threw a cloth over her contraption. "You should go. I gotta—I gotta work." A curl bounced out of her ponytail.

"You sure? What are you working on?" He swept the curl out of her eyes and kissed her lightly on the lips.

She kissed him back, then turned toward the table, her gaze looking inward.

He waited.

She shrugged and said softly, "I can't get it to work. And I've tried everything I know."

"Show me."

"Really?"

"Yes."

She gazed at him and brushed his cheek. "Okay."

He knelt beside her and she explained how the circuit board connected to the moving parts.

"There seems to be a faulty connection somewhere because the circuit doesn't function." She pointed to two small parts of the inner workings of the toy.

He examined where she was pointing. "Hmmm."

She said nothing, just stared at the parts, a small frown on her face.

He stood.

"Sorry," she said.

"For what?" He slipped his hand into his pocket and drew out his Leatherman Wingman Multi-tool attached to his keys.

She shrugged but said nothing.

"This might help." He opened the tool.

"How?"

He pointed to the circuit. "It looks like the wires weren't stripped properly. Too much maybe." He indicated the wire stripper on his Leatherman. "Try using this."

Dahlia peered at her circuit board and hummed. "If I cut and re-strip this wire and try again, maybe it'll work," she said with excitement in her voice. She bounced out of her seat and kissed him on the lips. "May I?" She gestured to the Leatherman.

"Of course." He slipped it off his key chain.

She flashed a radiant smile at him and took the Leatherman. "This may work. Finally." She sat and bent to her toy, expertly handling his tool.

He smiled at that thought and kissed her on the cheek.

She hummed again, her deep-in-thought noise.

"I'll just let myself out, *cara mia.*" *My dear.* Liam rushed to gather his shirt, shoes, and coat, something fluttering in his chest. "I have a phone appointment I have to keep, anyway. In the morning, Sunday morning." He was babbling uncharacteristically so he shut up.

Dahlia hummed some more without looking up. He'd just have to find out later if his help was useful.

He had himself together in two minutes flat.

Dahlia tinkered with a tiny screwdriver. He bent over and kissed her on the cheek. "I'll see you tomorrow."

"Mmm." She made a noncommittal sound.

Liam let himself out quietly. So that was a fling with the most beautiful girl he'd ever met.

In a short ten-minute walk he was home. He had just set his much lighter keys down in Grandma's bowl when his cell rang.

"Hi, Ma. It's not Sunday. It's the middle of the night, Saturday night." He rubbed his face. His mother's timing was uncanny. Maybe he should have let the phone call just go to voicemail. But that would only make things worse. It always did.

"Well, hello to you, too. Can't a mother call whenever she wants? You sound different, Liam. What is it?"

"Nothing, Ma."

He must have sighed in some kind of mother Morse code because she said, "You've met her, the One! I bet you've invited her to the Christmas Party. I know it! I'm going to be a grandmother soon. When's the wedding? I have some wonderful news. I'm coming out to San Francisco."

"What? No, yes, Ma—" How did giving birth entitle mothers to have some secret radar to know what was going on in their children's lives? It was damn annoying. "Stop that!"

"Don't you sass me, young man. I really am coming. I have business in North Beach, research, talk with vendors. Is she the One? Tell me, Liam. And you need to take some time off from work. You work too hard. You need to enjoy life more." His mother rattled on full speed.

And this from a woman who worked all the time, even into the wee hours of the night, or morning, and made sure she looked just right doing it.

"No, Ma. Yes."

His mother continued on about her travel plans, in detail, the taxi from the Upper West Side apartment, the airplane she was on, the length of her flight, her layover for lunch in Houston, her arrival at the San Francisco International airport. He listened with half an ear.

His mother drove him nuts sometimes. He wished Dahlia was the One. But he couldn't tell her that, not his mother, not Dahlia. No one. Them's the breaks. No love for him. *Just when he finds the One, she's leaving.* He brushed that thought aside. Besides, he promised her only a fling. And he kept his promises.

"Bye, dear. I'll call you when I land."

"Okay, Ma."

Liam hung up and headed for the shower. He'd stripped off his shirt, thinking of how Dahlia had slowly pulled it over his head, when his cell phone rang again.

It was Josh.

"Dude, your flight leaving soon?" he asked his best friend.

"No, man. That's why I was calling. I—I'm going to be delayed."

"Until when? Sally misses you." Liam kicked off his shoes and then placed them in his closet.

At the sound of her name, Sally woofed from the living room, where she'd been quietly gnawing one of her chew toys.

"Did you hear that?" Liam added.

"No. She okay?" Josh asked.

"Oh yeah. She's been getting a lot of walking. Yesterday she went with me and Dahlia around Lake Merritt and back home—

"Oh, the girl you met last week?"

"Woman," Liam corrected. "The very same."

"You like her, eh?"

Liam said nothing.

"You have it bad, man. Don't you? Don't let her do what Christine did."

"I won't. And no, I don't have it bad. Besides it's just a fling. She's going back soon. We're having fun." Liam felt punched in the gut by his own words.

"Right," Josh said. "Well, take it easy, man. You work too hard."

"Hey, not you too. I just got off the phone with my mom." Liam padded to his bedroom for his bathrobe.

"What was she doing calling so late?"

"I don't know. What are you doing calling so late?"

"I was just going to leave a voice mail. Why did you answer? It's late there, isn't it?"

"Yep."

"Okay, I can tell you don't want to talk about it. But you'll tell me everything when I get back."

"Which is when?"

"I—I'm not sure. Soon. You okay with that? Watching Sally and all?"

"Yeah, sure man. What's up?"

"Not sure."

Liam waited for more, but Josh didn't speak. "Okay, you'll let me know more when you can. Yeah?"

"Yeah."

Liam hung up on his good friend from college. He hoped Josh could work things out. His life seemed as complicated as his own had suddenly become.

DAHLIA FELT HER HEART PATTER in her chest as she worked on the toy. His fancy tool just might do the trick. She stripped the wires and reconnected them. She really liked him, really, really liked him. Being with him invigorated her, got her moving, got her focused. She had to kick him out though. She needed to concentrate, especially after his suggestion and right tool for the job. His scent lingered on her skin, spicy and male. She smiled and got back to reconnecting the rest of the toy. This version might just work.

ON SUNDAY AFTERNOON, he called her just as she was finishing the last connector switch. She stood to admire her handiwork. Her heart thudded in her chest. She was about to turn it on.

"Want to go for a walk with me and Sally?" Liam asked.

She laughed. "I get you *and* Sally?"

"Of course."

"All the better then."

"I'll swing by your place."

"No. I'll meet you in front of yours. My place is a mess."

"More than last night?"

She blushed. "Yes." She laughed again.

When she didn't say anything, he cleared his throat, then spoke. "Are you okay?"

"Yes. I've been up all night. I'm about to click the On button."

"And...?"

"I have to hang up. I'll tell you when I see you." She clicked the cell phone off and clapped her hands with adrenaline. She paced her apartment, made herself a cup of mint tea, and was considering taking a shower, when she realized she was delaying the inevitable. Either it would work or it wouldn't.

She clicked the On button and all the parts whirred, then started to move as designed, like a well-oiled fifty-piece symphony. She shouted, "Yes."

She skipped the shower and rushed the few blocks to Liam's place. When he answered the door, she threw herself into his arms. "It worked."

Chapter Seven

ONDAY MORNING, HE GAVE her a big smile when he stepped into the front office. He reached for her to give her a kiss, but Dahlia turned away to answer the phone. He managed a light peck on the cheek. She didn't know why but she seemed suddenly embarrassed, even though Sunday night they'd spent half the night together in her bed.

For the rest of the week, Dahlia had lunch with Liam when he could get away from the office. Dinners too. Nights were spent in his bed or hers. She either kicked him out of her place, or rushed back home, her focus on putting the final touches on her toy. He was all easy going with it, she was pretty sure.

Chapter Eight

FRIDAY EVENING, THEY WERE on his couch at his place, Sally resting at their feet, and after a particularly lovely make out session, Liam was gazing at her, with an all adoring look in his eyes.

She squirmed in his embrace.

"What is it?" he asked softly.

"Well, you know I have to go home soon." She picked at the nubs on the throw blanket across their laps.

"Yeah, I know." He smiled and his dimple showed. He was so cute, and handsome, and an all-around good person.

"I'm almost done putting the final touches on my toy and... I want to go to the party, but I have nothing to wear." She laughed, nervously, her heart aching. She pushed the feeling aside.

"Okay." He searched her face. "There's something else..."

"I can't get anything past you." She tried to say it cheerily, but it sounded a little sad to her ears. A wave of missing him already crashed on her. She gulped. He was right here.

"Nope." He squeezed her hand and waited. He was so patient with her. So kind. So steadfast.

She shook her head to clear the sadness. "I—I just feel that we're getting too close, too fast." There, she'd said it.

"Really?" He pulled back to better study her. "I have no idea why you would think that. I've only spent all my free time with you, minus work and racquetball."

"And breakfast." She smiled at the memories.

"Sometimes." He nipped her on the lips with a little kiss.

This time she pulled back. "But, still, Liam, I'm going home soon, and—and—I don't know when I'm coming back."

"Whose heart are you trying to protect?" he said softly.

Her chest hurt. She slipped out of his embrace and stood, upsetting Sally. "Why do you have to be so perceptive?" She paced the living room, from one wall to the opposite one, passing the banked fireplace on each pass. Why did love have to be so complicated?

He said nothing. He was probably waiting for her to speak. She paced some more, sneaking glances at him every few minutes. Liam stared off into space, his expression thoughtful, like he was calculating things. God, and all the angels, he was so handsome. She couldn't lie to herself anymore, she'd fallen in love with him, and hard.

"I have to go." She hurried to the front door and slipped on her coat, hat, and scarf. It was cold and rainy out.

"Dahlia." Liam had padded to her in his socks without her hearing.

She spun. He was right there and put his hands gently on her cheeks. He bent to kiss her, but she turned, so he missed her lips and landed one on her ear.

"Maybe I need a few nights off," she said, without looking at him.

"Okay." He squeezed her shoulders.

"You're not mad?" She peered up at him now. His chocolate brown eyes were soft and warm, full of warmth, for her.

"No. I've been having fun. I want this to be fun. I want to have fun with you at the party, and I want to have fun with you for every moment I get to be in your presence."

"No fighting?"

"Only if it's fun."

She smiled, feeling the strain across her face.

She caressed his cheek. "I'll see you Monday. I need the weekend off from—us." She waved between them and fled before she broke down into a flood of tears in front of him.

A GUST OF COLD wind slipped in as Dahlia slipped out. He didn't even offer to walk her home, he realized. Uncharacteristic of him. And he hadn't even made her dinner. Very uncharacteristic of him. But he couldn't run after her this time, like he was some lovesick puppy. *Why not?* a niggling voice asked him.

Because this was only a fling, he reminded himself.

What was he going to do tonight? What did he do when he wasn't with her? He couldn't remember. She had changed him much in just a short amount of time. What was he going to do when she left? He'd adapt, he was sure.

But—he rubbed his breastbone—but did he want to? Dahlia had brightened his whole world.

A pang of guilt had him rubbing his temples. What had started out as a connection of convenience to help his career and show up his ex and rival had blossomed into so much more.

He sat down at his desk and opened his email, and groaned. There was a snarky email from Michael Hendricks, said rival. He couldn't deal with him right now, and didn't have to.

He meandered into the kitchen and fixed himself a light meal of leftover pasta and salad. His house felt empty.

Chapter Nine

D AHLIA SWIRLED IN THE dress she'd picked out at a funky dress shop on a tiny street in the North Beach neighborhood in San Francisco. Holly clapped her hands. It felt good to be out of her tiny studio.

"Lovely. If only your mother could see you now. Oh, I'll take a picture." Holly bounced around Dahlia snapping photos with her smart phone.

"It is lovely, isn't it?" Dahlia swirled again in her bare feet. She couldn't help it. It was a darling dress. The dress hugged her body, then fanned out just above the knees. When she twirled, the gossamer bright lime green fabric flared out like the blossoms of an upside down Icelandic poppy. She sighed with delight. "Yes, I'll take it."

"Finally. Wait, are you sure? It's only like the fiftieth dress you've tried on. Usually we have to get to number one hundred for you to be sure." Holly flopped back in the waiting room plush chair.

"Yes, I'm sure. And I promise you a luscious dessert for your troubles." She was a little surprised she was so sure, so soon in her hunt for the perfect party dress for the company Christmas party with Liam.

"I'll believe it when we're at the register." Holly smirked.

"Ha! You'll see." Dahlia called out as she stepped into the dressing room and switched back into her jeans. "I'll be right out at the register before you can say snicker doodle with punch,"

"I love snicker doodle with punch," Holly said. "And I'll take that dessert for my trouble."

Dahlia laughed, then gazed at the dress and sighed. She was looking forward to the party with Liam. Dancing, libations, more dancing in Liam's strong and capable and sexy arms, up against his body, smiling into his dark brown eyes that reminded her of toffee, warm and inviting. She shook herself mentally. She shouldn't get too carried away, she scolded herself.

She really *was* going home in twelve days. She couldn't wait until she saw her family again. She missed the crazy bunch. That made these last few days all the more poignant, and her time with Liam more special in a lovely yet painful way.

Why did she feel torn now about going home and never leaving? Maybe that was why she'd fled his place on Friday and needed a few days away from him. It was all getting too intense.

She brushed the thoughts aside. She was going home. Her project was done. That definitely was one excellent thing about being with him. Who knew that sex and affection would help her get focused? If she'd known that, she should have hooked up with someone much, much earlier in her year. But then she would have missed meeting Liam, being with Liam, kissing Liam...

"Hey, you there, starry-eyed lover girl, get your butt out here. I'm ready for that dessert you promised," Holly called out.

"Yeah. Yeah." Dahlia smirked at herself in the mirror and grabbed her purse, stepping out of the dressing room, lovely silky dress draped over her arm. "I spotted a nice dessert place across from Washington Park. Hope you haven't been there before."

"Nope," Holly said.

"Let's go." Dahlia paid for her purchase, wincing a little at the price. It was worth it, though.

Ten minutes later Dahlia and Holly were sipping cappuccinos and nibbling puffy, creamy, chocolaty, luscious desserts in a tiny boutique dessert shop. In the European style café, a few other women sipped and munched. Their purchased items from the neighborhood trendy shops surrounded them in shopping bags like little chicks around the mama hen.

Dahlia sighed as she bit into the puffy dessert. "This reminds me of—Oh!"

"You're blushing. Do tell. Tell me about your beau. You naughty girl."

"He's not my beau. And I'm not naughty," Dahlia said. Then she leaned forward to Holly, waved toward her ears, and whispered, "I didn't say anything about—Promise."

Holly grabbed her hands. "Stop that."

"What? I just said he's not my beau." Dahlia felt a flush creep up her cheeks. "Is there alcohol in these pastries? I feel slightly tipsy."

From across the small room, a woman laughed heartily and boomed with a strong foreign accent. "Oh, yes there is. That's amaretto you're eating, or drinking, I suppose I should say." She smiled broadly, showing all her teeth that Dahlia couldn't help but return the smile.

"It's lovely," Dahlia said, feeling the heat creep up her cheeks again, and blurted, "They remind me of the ones I had with my—boyfriend. He said his mother made them. So good." She giggled and slapped her hand over her mouth in surprise at her tipsy behavior. She never drank. And now she knew why. Elves were sensitive. Alcohol was pretty much a no-no.

The older woman, probably around her mother's age, was dressed to the nines in an all-black brocade suit, skirt and jacket, with a bright fuchsia scarf, probably Hermès, knotted Parisian style around her neck, and matching fuchsia shoes, lipstick and handbag. Quite stylish. She squinted at Dahlia and scanned her from head to toe and back again. Then she jumped to her feet and practically sprinted toward Dahlia with her hand outstretched. "*O Dio mio, O Madonna*, you must be Her. How wonderful, *bella*, you're beautiful."

Dahlia stood and politely shook the older woman's hand. "Her who?" Her whole body heated, like a big flame ball.

"Oh my dear, *cara mia*!" The woman pumped Holly's hand, then turned back to Dahlia, grabbing Dahlia's hand in both of her strong palms. "I'm your boyfriend's mother. I make these desserts."

"Liam's mother? Nice to meet you..." Dahlia said and gulped. She fanned her face. She still felt hot.

"Ms. Giovanna Rosa Leone MacAuley. But you can call me Giovanna."

"Won't you join us at our table, Mrs. MacAuley—Giovanna?"

She glanced at Holly. Holly smirked back and winked. Dahlia wanted to swat her, but pulled a third chair to the table instead.

"Likewise," Giovanna said and crossed her legs at the knee, showing off her elegant calves and pumps.

"I thought you lived in New York City. What brings you to San Francisco?" Dahlia asked, her poise mostly recovered.

"These." Giovanna waved at the pastries in front of them. "They're mine."

"Yours?" Dahlia felt thick, dots not connecting.

Giovanna laughed loudly. "My company's. Mine. My recipes. How do you say, 'Secret proprietary recipe.' Like a good love affair, eh?" she said and winked at Dahlia. "Ah, *amore*."

"Oh!" Dahlia glanced away, sure her cheeks were flaming red again, like her hair. More blushing. Oh dear.

"He really likes you," Giovanna said, quieter.

"What did he tell you?" Dahlia recovered, again, and leaned in, her heart pumping into high gear.

Holly elbowed her and smiled. *Stop it*, Dahlia mouthed to her.

Giovanna smiled kindly. "He didn't, but I can tell. He's my son." She leaned closer, too, conspiratorially. "And he's delighted to be able to bring you to the party. He adores you. Bringing you will really help him show you off to make his horrible ex-girlfriend jealous. She's going with that terrible Hendricks. *Orrible. Terribile.*"

"What?" Dahlia froze, her hands and feet suddenly numb. "An ex-girlfriend. Make her jealous? He didn't say anything about that—"

Giovanna opened her mouth into a perfect "O."

"I thought he just needed a date... some kind of job promotion thing..." Dahlia said, choking past the shock lodged in her throat. She had lies, too. Yet they'd shared so much, gotten so close. He'd helped her fix and finish her toy.

She jumped to her feet, grabbed her purse, and jetted out of the café, her heart breaking, and she hadn't wanted to acknowledge her heart was invested. Traitorous heart.

"Dahlia, wait." Holly called after her. "Your dress."

"I don't care about the damn dress." she called out over her shoulder. She ran to Columbus Avenue and whistled for a taxi. How could he have lied to her?

Chapter Ten

D AHLIA KEPT HER HEAD down when employees strolled
in. She didn't want to be friendly. First time she'd felt
that way. Ever. Having a disappointed heart did that
to a girl. She shoved that thought aside. She couldn't have a disappointed heart. No, she wasn't in love. But she knew that was a
lie. She had fallen for Liam. And it hadn't worked out. Maybe
that was for the best.

She pasted on a fake smile and pretended like she'd never
met Liam. Employees didn't seem to notice. The world didn't
seem to notice her mood. Just as well.

She was rerouting a call when she felt him on the other side
of the tall counter, standing beside the pretty red azaleas on it.
Could she just hide behind them? No. She'd face what was
coming. And make him face it too.

He stood there with his mouth open, about to ask her for his
messages, no doubt. She handed them to him without a smile.

He leaned forward to kiss her on the cheek, as he had the
entire week before. But she just stood there, frozen, not leaning
in, staring at him.

He quickly righted his spine, like nothing had happened,
flipped through his messages, and peered back up at her.
"Dahlia." He cleared his throat. "Is everything okay?"

"Just fine, thank you."

"You seem different." He squinted at her.

The phone rang. "I am," she said and picked up the phone, "Good morning. Cooper, Anderson & Sons. How may I direct your call?"

She rotated her body so she no longer faced Liam. He could stand there if he wanted, but she didn't have to make googly eyes at him. She wasn't a schoolgirl anymore. *Go away,* she thought.

Maybe he walked away. She didn't know. She didn't care. But she didn't hear his footfalls retreat.

She turned back to the counter when she felt someone else approach. She was about to snap at Liam that she never wanted to see him again. But that wouldn't be very professional, especially since it was Susan in HR reaching for a piece of paper on the counter. Dahlia grabbed it, before Susan could snatch it up. She crumpled the paper, then thought better of it. She smoothed open the rectangular sheet. In Liam's neat block handwriting was a note. For her. "Dahlia, We need to talk. Meet me in the lobby at noon." It was signed just with the letter "L."

"You okay, Dahlia?" Susan asked.

"Yeah, sure." Dahlia shrugged.

"We're still on for 12:30 p.m. today for the exit prep." She smiled sympathetically.

"Of course."

Susan nodded once and clipped away to her office.

Dahlia crumpled up the slip of paper again and chucked it into the wastebasket. Every day last week, the lobby was where Dahlia and Liam had met for lunch. She wanted to blow him off. For good. But she owed him an explanation for her behavior this morning. And he very much owed her one. What the hell had he been thinking—not telling her his true reasons for inviting her to the Christmas party? A game, my ass. According to his mother, he wanted her as trophy on his arm.

She'd call it off. Her Christmas fling over before it had barely began.

She hadn't told him the truth, either. She couldn't. There was nothing that could be done about that. Maybe she was a little relieved, and a little sad.

LIAM HAD BEEN MULLING it over all weekend, after Dahlia stormed out demanding space. He needed to come clean with her about the real reason for him asking her. But could he do it? He was being a coward, he knew. He almost picked up the phone all day Saturday and Sunday. But he wanted to respect her space, as she put it.

Even a few games of racquetball at the gym with Brett hadn't set his head right. There was no way around it. He had to tell her.

Then when he walked into the office bright and early Monday morning, and she was there all officious and wouldn't even look at him, he knew he had to come clean. They were too attached to each other, anyway, or had been. If he came clean, was that it with them? No party. Did he completely blow it? His chances for the promotion and for showing up Christine were over. That didn't matter anymore. Perhaps for this year, he'd be passed over for Hendricks, and would have to deal with the humiliation of Hendricks and Christine laughing in his face. So what? His job wasn't important anymore, not if it turned him into a status-hungry person.

He took the stairs from the twentieth floor to the lobby. Dahlia deserved more than someone like him who had put work ahead of true commitment to someone. But he didn't want to be that guy. At the tenth floor down, however, he wondered if maybe he'd be better off if he were that guy, for Dahlia, and for himself. Perhaps he could put love first, instead of work. What had he been working hard for all these years, but a way to provide for the family he dearly desired?

DAHLIA TOOK A FEW minutes to refresh her lipstick in the woman's bathroom in the lobby. She remembered being here for her first lunch meeting slash non-date with Liam, and how excited she'd been, right before he'd taken her to the revolving restaurant in the sky and asked her to the Christmas party. Now she only wanted to rip his eyes out. She stared at herself in the mirror, shocked at her level of violent desires. Well, her parents did say she'd learn a lot about herself while away on her *Suibhal*, her year abroad.

They also said to go after what she truly wanted.

She strode out into the lobby. Liam was tapping away on his smart phone. As soon as he looked up and saw her, he slipped it into his pocket. He was frowning. He crossed his arms then let them hang loose, like he didn't know what to do with them.

For a split milli-milli-second Dahlia wanted to kiss and make up and throw herself onto his tall strong body, and have him hold her and peer deep into her eyes in that serious way of his. *Och* jeez, get a grip, she scolded herself.

She just stood there gazing up at him, not smiling.

Liam cleared his throat like he'd done at the desk that morning. He shifted from foot to foot, but maintained his gaze on her, inscrutable, serious. "Hi, Dahlia. Shall we walk for a bit?"

"I have to be back in thirty minutes. Got a meeting with Susan to prepare for my leaving at the end of the week."

He nodded and glanced away for a split second, his expression unreadable. "Just to the sandwich stand then." His deep voice vibrated in her chest, sending shivers to the bottom of her stomach.

She held his gaze. "Okay. What did you want to talk to me about?"

"You and me."

She headed for the revolving doors. "There's no you and me, Liam. Not anymore."

THERE WAS NO HER and him? His heart lurched with pain. Liam had gone and done it. Fallen in love. Again. But this time was different. Had to be. He hadn't gone in with stars in his eyes, his heart on his sleeve. And he thought he'd protected his heart against this type of thing. Had it all locked down, thrown away the key.

He glanced at Dahlia. She stole his breath with her zest for life, even when she was mad at him she vibrated with energy and purpose. Even when she kept pace with him as they strode down the busy street toward the specialty sandwich stand on the corner. She looked straight ahead and not at him, frowning, yet maddeningly attractive with her red curls flying into her eyes with the bay breeze.

How could there not be a them?

DAHLIA FELT WASHED IN sadness, swimming in it, like a little fish pushing upstream against some vast horrible current. The anger had passed and now she only felt sad. She didn't want to care so much about Liam but she did. And soon she would be gone. Maybe it was for the best, she reminded herself.

When they got to the sandwich stand, she ordered her favorite and quickly paid before Liam could, as he'd done all last week.

Liam ordered and paid for his usual. They stood waiting for their orders, without speaking. She didn't want to look at him, her sadness pulling her down and away from him. Then realized that was silly. And not courageous. She promised herself she'd be more courageous this year, to step into professional life, create her toy, and take her place in the Elf community as a Master Elf.

"Liam—"

"Dahlia—"

They spoke at the same time.

Dahlia smiled, just a little.

"Go ahead," Liam said.

Dahlia nodded and blew out her breath. "You lied to me." She dove right in.

"I did. I'm sorry."

"You don't even—what?" She shook her head. "You're making this too easy."

"I am?"

Her number for her sandwich was called, so she stepped away to grab her thick sandwich. Then his was called, and they strolled to their spot at Sue Bierman Park to sit on the bench and eat their sandwiches. Luckily it was only a grey day, not rainy at all. Mild compared to the winters she grew up with at the Pole.

Liam finally spoke after they'd both had a few bites. "Would you like me to make things harder for us?" He spoke softly, his warm brown gaze held no judgment or anger.

"No." Dahlia tugged at her napkin. "Of course not. It's just that—" She stared off in the distance. "Sitting with you here, being with you—I don't want to be mad at you." Or sad, she thought. "But you lied to me about the real reason for inviting me to the party."

"I did. I—I have no good excuse. Only horrible ones."

She said nothing.

He asked, "How did you find out?"

"Your mother. Weird. When I was buying my dress for the party. She figured out who I was by something I said about the pastries we were eating in a café." She nibbled her sandwich and stared off into the middle distance.

"I'm so sorry," Liam said softly.

She peered at him. "I want to hear some of them."

"What?"

"Your excuses."

"You do?"

She nodded.

"My job—I've been working at the company for eight years, and thought that's what I wanted. A good career. Promotions, prestige. I learned at the last minute that my ex-girlfriend was going to be at the Christmas party with Hendricks. Hendricks is the guy two doors down from me at the office."

"I know who Hendricks is."

"He and I are competing for the same promotion."

"I didn't know that."

"And my ex-girlfriend, Christine, cheated on me with him."

"That sucks."

"Yeah." He gazed at her, not smiling. What was he thinking?

"Liam? Why?"

"Why what?"

"Why the drive for promotions and prestige? And the need to bring someone to the party."

"Because my work is—my life. And I need to show up Hendricks, and Christine. They can't walk all over me like that. I have to show that I got this job, that I'm promotion-ready. Hendricks likes to play mind games."

"Why couldn't you have told me the truth from the start?" she frowned and set down her sandwich. "I mean—this thing about it being a game, pretend—"

"I just wanted to keep it light—"

"I get that, but it hurt that you couldn't be up-front with me." Dahlia gulped. Tears sprang to her eyes. "Liam—"

In an instant, he set his sandwich down and gripped her hands in his. "Dahlia, I'm sorry."

She shook her head, no words coming past the feelings welling up in her heart and her throat. She almost told him the truth just then.

"I really am. I ruined what we had."

She finally found her voice. "If you hadn't asked me, we wouldn't have found it. What we had." She let go of his hands to check her watch.

"Your meeting."

She nodded and gazed at him. "Liam, what *do* we have here?"

"It's not a fling."

"It's not?"

"No, it's much more." He leaned in and kissed her, just a whisper of a kiss.

Dahlia felt tears trickle down her cheeks at the connection, and at the sadness of soon leaving this warmth and sweetness they had. She pulled back, breaking the kiss. "I have to go."

"I know. I'll walk you back."

"No, it's fine. Call me when you get home tonight. Okay?"

He flashed her a broad smile. "Okay."

Dahlia squeezed his hand then hurried off. Had they solved anything? He'd come clean, but she hadn't. It didn't matter. Their much-more-than-a-fling was going to end soon anyway. And that made her very, very sad.

Why did claiming her rightful place in her community mean stepping away from love? If there was a way to have both, she couldn't see it. Holly had to leave the Pole to be with her sweetie. They couldn't bring Humans into the Pole. Unless... No, a human coming to the Pole hadn't happened in her lifetime. And no Elf could still be a practicing Elf and live in the Human world. She loved her Elf life more than anything. Her year abroad hadn't changed that one bit.

What was she going to do?

LIAM STROLLED BACK TO HIS OFFICE after he finished his mondo sandwich. Dahlia hadn't finished hers but had wrapped it up tightly and stuffed it in her bag.

They hadn't settled things, the details. Was she still coming with him to the party? Was the party still important to him? She definitely was, but that clearly wasn't enough for him. And she was leaving. What a mess.

He entered the glass building and headed for the elevator. The door slid open and Hendricks hopped in just as the door was sliding shut.

"Ha, I made it. Hey, MacAuley, I haven't seen you around much. Working hard for the promotion, eh?" Hendricks tried to elbow him.

Liam side-stepped out of his reach.

"Going to the party Saturday night?" Hendricks continued.

"You know I am." Liam crossed his arms. He really didn't like Hendricks. If Liam got the promotion, Hendricks would be under him. Maybe he could transfer him, give him a different boss. If Hendricks got the promotion instead, Liam would ask for a transfer, maybe to the London office. Liam clenched his teeth together. He didn't want to be pushed out by Hendricks.

The elevator dinged as it reached their floor. Hendricks bounced out with a cheeky wave to Liam. Liam wanted to sock him, but calmed himself as he crossed the threshold into the company's lobby. Dahlia wasn't at the front desk. Wouldn't do to walk in with a scowl, not part of the company values of family wholesomeness and leaving a legacy for your family and community.

But maybe he didn't want to work for a company where every emotion had to be locked down. Liam shoved the thought aside. He had work to do.

Later that evening after work, Liam strode into the Fairmount Hotel on San Francisco's famed Nob Hill. Past the opulent lobby, down a wide gold-accented hallway, he slipped into the low-lit Tiki Bar. As his eyes adjusted to the mood lighting, he heard his mother's voice.

"Yoohoo, *caro*, dear *figlio*, my son, over here."

His mother was quite dramatic, always mixing English and Italian, especially when she was excited and in a public place. It was part of her persona.

He approached the bar. She was already nursing a colorful martini. He kissed her on both cheeks. "Hi, Mama. Why couldn't we have just chatted over the phone?"

"I'm in town. I wanted to see you. You wouldn't deny your dear mother. I came all this way..."

"Save the dramatics, Ma. I'm here."

"I know, dear. Sit."

Liam did and ordered a soda.

"What, no drink?"

Liam shook his head and waited.

Mama sipped and then sighed.

"I met your girl yesterday and I think I upset her terribly."

"I know. She told me."

"She did?" She looked thoughtful. "Good girl. She's a keeper."

I know, he thought, but said, "She's returning home."

Before he could take a drink of his soda, she put her hand on his arm. "Oh dear. I am sorry. But you will go after her, dear, won't you?"

"I don't know. My job—"

"Stuff your job, don't you know love is the most important thing?"

"Mother, you and Dad—"

"We have always done right by each other. Now you go do right by her. Do the right thing. You always have."

"You and Dad don't even live together half the year."

"I know." She smiled, quite pleased with herself. "And we love each other dearly. Now, go do what's right—for love—for you."

LATER THAT NIGHT, LIAM stood at Dahlia's door. He'd knocked twice already and still no reply. He'd texted that he was coming, but hadn't gotten a reply back. The bright flowers in his hand felt heavy with expectation. Would she like them? Would she even accept them, him?

He lifted his fist to knock a third time, but the door swung open. There she was, a dab of what looked like white paint on her cheek and her hair up in a messy and oh-so-sexy bun. She looked at him wide-eyed and a little dazed. Her sweater sloped off one shoulder and her jeans had paint smudges too.

He cleared his throat. "Going to invite me in?"

"Yeah." She spoke in a distracted voice and stepped aside.

He brushed past her. She smelled good, like cinnamon and floral something.

Dahlia closed the door. It was then that he noticed she had a small painter's palette in her hand and a tiny brush in the other.

"Now's not a good time, Liam. I'm—the last little finishing touches—" She waved in the direction of her table.

Liam stepped closer to her, ignoring the toy parts all around. He wanted to reach out to her and hold her close. She gazed up at him. A flush rose in her cheeks. She turned away.

"Sorry, I—can't—not right now."

Liam leaned down to kiss her on the lips, but she turned away. He ended up kissing her cheek instead. "Dahlia—"

But she wouldn't look him in the eye. "You should have called first."

He stepped back to the door. "I wanted to see you."

She nodded absently.

"Dahlia."

She looked up. Her gaze focused on him, finally.

"We're on for Saturday night?" Liam asked.

"Yes." She smiled.

"See you tomorrow, then."

She made a humming sound.

He found a jar for the flowers, filled the jar, and left the colorful flowers on her counter. He kissed her on the cheek on purpose. "*Cara mia*," he whispered.

"Thank you," she whispered and turned back to her painting.

He let himself out.

Chapter Eleven

AHLIA DIDN'T GO INTO work the next day, Tuesday, or for the rest of the week. She'd arranged it ahead of time. She needed to finish her project, and now that she was so close, she really took advantage of the time, working on the final touches of her toy and packing too. She didn't have much she wanted to bring back, except her finished project. She didn't answer Liam's calls. She just let them go straight to voicemail. He texted her a few times, but she didn't reply to those either. And he didn't come to her door again—thank goodness.

She just wanted to be ready to go home, she told herself, and find a way to say a proper good bye to him. That was all. She'd have a good time at the party then fly home the very next day.

She put all her energy into finishing her toy, thankfully functional due to Liam's help.

Saturday arrived, and she was exhausted, having stayed up nearly the whole night to finish packing. When the knock came at the door she hopped out of bed, threw on her sweatpants and tank top and rushed to open the door.

Her heart sped up. It was Liam, looking all serious. Sally gave a little yip drawing Dahlia's attention to the sweet huge dog, her tail whomping against Liam's leg.

She knelt to give Sally a pat and a hug. Sally gave her a wet kiss against her cheek.

"So we're back to that now, are we?" he said. His deep voice held a hint of humor.

But when she straightened to look at him, he was still serious. She stood there feeling awkward in the threshold, not rushing into Liam's arms. She rubbed her breastbone and stepped backward. "Come in. I'll be right back."

She turned and fled for the bathroom. She didn't care if he had to wait. She hopped in the shower, hopped back out after the shortest shower on record, and changed into jeans and a long sleeve shirt. Nearly everything else was packed.

She stepped into the one-room studio and stopped, inhaling the mint steam filling the small space. She sighed with pleasure. Couldn't help it. Liam had made himself a cup of mint tea and it looked like a second mug for her. The feelings of awkwardness fled. She smiled at his sweet gesture.

"Thank you," she said softly and sipped, standing across the small kitchenette counter from him, not looking at him.

She turned to lean against the counter and gazed around her near empty apartment instead. She'd given away much of the furniture she'd collected and what was left didn't include any chairs.

"You're really going," he said finally.

"Yes."

"I guess I didn't want to think about it. When do you leave?" He sipped his tea.

"Tomorrow."

He sputtered out his tea and set down his mug. "Dahlia—"

The way he said her name, all soft and low, like they were entangled in each other's arms in bed, had her turning to face him. He peered at her without smiling. After a moment, he held out his hands to her. He still didn't smile.

She hesitated for only a second and set her mug down to take his hands. Tears threatened to spill. She wanted to brush them away, but he wouldn't let go of her hands when she tugged.

"Dahlia, there's nothing I can do or say to make you stay?" He spoke softly she had to look up to read his sincerity. It was there, in his deep brown eyes, in his soft lips, parted just a little. He was waiting for her response.

"I—no—there isn't." *I'm sorry*, she wanted to say, but couldn't speak past the lump in her throat.

"Then I guess tonight is our goodbye."

She spoke past the tears that threatened to spill. "Why does it feel like we're saying good-bye just as we got to the good part?"

"The good part?" He wasn't smiling, but there was a mischievous glint in his eyes.

"Yes." She nodded. "Hey, want to get lunch or breakfast, or something? It's lunchtime, right?"

"This is the good part?"

"Indeed." She needed to move, to walk, and maybe to spend a casual afternoon with the man she'd fallen in love with, but couldn't have.

They spent a companionable walk down 51st Street to a sandwich shop on Telegraph Avenue. Sally trotted ahead of them wagging her tail.

"Is this why you avoided me all week? To finish your toy and pack?"

"Yes." She nodded without looking at him.

"What will you miss about the lovely San Francisco Bay Area?" Liam asked.

You, she wanted to say. "The weather." She laughed.

"Yes, we have great weather here. Even the fog is lovely."

He stayed away from talking about them—thank goodness. And she wasn't about to bring it up either.

In fifteen minutes, they'd arrived at her favorite sandwich shop in the neighborhood. She'd stopped by for lunch often over the last year. They stood in line for the best chicken sandwiches she'd ever had. She was going to take the recipe back to the Pole. She especially liked the caraway seeds inside the sandwich and the way the fat sandwich was stuffed with whole pieces of chicken, not processed meat.

Liam stopped with his questions as they moved forward in the line that wrapped around the corner.

Dahlia was fine with the silence. She petted Sally's head and rubbed behind her ears where the dog liked it best.

Without preamble, Liam said, "Tell me about your family, Dahlia. All you've said is that you're from a big family."

Dahlia stilled, then stepped forward as the line moved. She was silent for a while. Then the silence stretched into awkwardness, but Liam didn't press her. Maybe he thought she hadn't heard him. He tied Sally's leash to a post.

Then they were at the front of the line. They ordered. They sat to eat at refurbished ironing boards perched on the sidewalk.

Dahlia sighed as she bit into the huge sandwich. "I'm going to miss these."

"No sandwiches back home?" Liam asked, not looking at her and enjoying his own sandwich.

"We do. Just not this kind."

"Are you going to answer my question?"

"Hmmm?"

"I asked you to tell me about your family."

"Didn't sound like a question to me."

"Are we actually having an argument?"

Dahlia nodded. "It's fun."

Liam smiled. "It is." After a moment he said, "I'm going to miss you."

"You'll get over me." She said over the sudden lump of emotion rising in her chest.

"Not likely," he said seriously.

"You're going to make me cry, and I haven't even finished my sandwich yet."

"Sally doesn't mind."

"What? The crying or the sandwich?"

"Either."

She smiled and managed to finish the sandwich on her own. Then she started in. "I have nine brothers and sisters, two older sisters, and two older brothers. I'm the fifth, and I have five younger brothers. We're an industrious family, all grown, all working for my uncle's business."

"And what's that? Toys? Like the amazing gizmo you made."

Close enough. "Yes, like that."

"Thanks for sharing that with me. I'm guessing you don't want to talk about them because that only reminds you how much you miss them."

"Yes..." Dahlia wanted to say more. She really did. Wanted to tell him the truth. But if she did that she would forfeit her life as an elf.

"Earth to Dahlia."

"Uh?"

"Day dreaming again."

"Yeah." She stood. "Let's walk back. I have a few more things I need to do before you pick me up later." She pasted a cheery smile on her face, at least she hoped it was cheery.

Liam walked her back to her tiny studio, this time they didn't speak. She didn't trust herself not to cry, and didn't want to put on a false cheery front anymore. Liam seemed okay with not talking. She liked him even more for that.

"I'll pick you up at eight," he said, leaving her at her door.

She nodded and watched him head down the sidewalk for home. She knew leaving Liam would be hard, but didn't think it would be nearly as painful as this was.

Chapter Twelve

D AHLIA WAS A VISION of silk and ribbons the color of new spring leaves, the light green dress highlighting her red curls and creamy skin. Dahlia was staring up at him, her lipsticked pink lips pursed in puzzlement. He realized his mouth was open. He snapped it shut.

"You are beauty incarnate, Ms. MacMillian," he breathed.

She blushed prettily. "Thank you."

"Are you ready?"

She nodded and grabbed a wrap that matched her dress and her tiny handbag and stepped out into the night.

For a moment they stood under the door lamp, gazing at each other. Then she took a step ahead of him and coyly looked over her shoulder. "You clean up real nice, MacAuley."

"Thank you." He smoothed his hands down his jacket and followed her down the pathway to the street. "A man must have a tux, my mother always said."

"She raised you well."

"Yes, she did."

"But she's meddlesome."

"I know. Aren't all mothers?"

"True." She stood on the sidewalk beside his car, silent. He opened the door for her and she slipped in.

The drive into San Francisco was quiet. She didn't try to make small talk and for that he was grateful. Traffic was light as they crossed the Bay Bridge. He wound his way expertly to the Mark Hopkins Hotel at the top of Nob Hill, across from its cousin, the posh Fairmount Hotel.

He pulled up to the front door, put the car in park, and hurried around the hood to help Dahlia out of the car. A valet took his keys to park the car.

She oohed and aahed at the fancy decor of the hotel lobby. The party was on the top floor. He grabbed her hand and guided her to the elevator.

As the doors glided shut, he turned to her, his hand still in hers. "Thank you for coming with me tonight." He breathed out. "I have a big request."

"What is it?" She squeezed his hand.

He didn't deserve her, he thought. Well, it didn't matter anyway. She was leaving. Their charade was for one more night only.

"I need for us to act like we're in love and happy together." He breathed out to calm his nerves. Her answer meant more than he'd realized.

She gazed up at him, her gaze serious and deep. "No need to act," she whispered, and pulled her body flush with his.

He blinked, aroused, and his heart breaking all at once.

"And we're sad that we're parting," she continued in a low voice.

"That's the part I don't want them to know. Okay?"

"Okay." She nodded solemnly. "Happy and in love. I can do that." She smiled brightly to show him she could.

He bent down and kissed her on the lips. And pulled back too soon for his own liking but he didn't want to mess up her lipstick, he told himself. She stayed snug against him. He couldn't let her go, his arms tight around her. She felt so right against him.

"Thank you. And I mean that," he said.

"I know." She glanced away and wiped her eyes. "Okay, let's get this party started."

As if on cue, the elevator door whooshed open and a barrage of voices and big band music enveloped them.

"I love live music." Dahlia laughed, stepping away from him, leaving coolness where her body had been.

Liam smiled, relieved. They'd enjoy themselves immensely, he'd introduce his charming girlfriend to the bosses, show everyone, especially Hendricks and Christine, how awesome they were together, and he'd get his promotion.

But that plan didn't feel as exciting as it had when he'd first dreamt it up nearly three weeks ago. A promotion without Dahlia to celebrate with him was...empty.

"PLEASED TO MEET YOU," Dahlia said. "Lovely Christmas tree. Tall ones are my favorite kinds. And the lovely angel you have on top, what a beauty. She looks like a cross between a Black Madonna and a Hula dancer." She shook Mr. Cooper's hand, *the* Mr. Cooper. "It is an honor to meet you, sir."

The older white haired gentleman smiled at her kindly. "And I you. And thank you. We pride ourselves on inclusion and diversity. And she's a beauty, just as you are." He patted her hand, still held captive in his. "You are a delight, my dear. I saw you on the dance floor with our Liam, cutting up the rug, as we like to say in my generation. You two make a lovely couple. You will have to come out to the cabin in Sonoma Valley for some wine and horseback riding this spring. Won't you dear?" He winked at her.

"Why, of course, we'd be delighted to." she replied and glanced at Liam by her side.

Liam nodded his agreement and gave her a gentle smile that seemed a tiny bit wistful, as if they could continue this charade into next year and beyond. She smiled back, but inside she was crying. She didn't think this playacting would be so hard when she agreed to play this game with Liam three plus weeks ago. A part of her wondered what it would be like to extend their fling into next year, but then she brushed that thought aside. Her life was being an Elf, a prestigious Santa's Elf, something she'd worked hard for her entire life.

She held out her hand to him. "Let's dance, my love. You promised me lots of dances, so let's go."

Liam winked at Mr. Cooper. "Anything for you, my dear." And grabbed her hand.

Five dances later, Dahlia was still nestled in Liam's arms. "You'd think they're playing all these slow songs for us." She smiled up at him.

"Not only us." Liam indicated with his chin.

Other couples hung on to each other in the dance floor four times the size of her studio apartment.

A couple sidled up to them as the next slow song started.

"MacAuley," the man said.

"Hendricks," Liam acknowledged.

The woman in Hendricks's arms smiled and nodded in greeting to her, a twinkle of pride in her eyes. She was a raven-haired, long-legged woman in a skintight fire-engine red dress that showed plenty of cleavage, leg, and back. Dahlia couldn't tell her age, but she was probably a few years older than she was.

"I'm Dahlia MacMillian," Dahlia said and held out her hand to the new couple. Hendricks was in a tuxedo with a bright red cummerbund, matching his date's dress.

"Christine Blackburn. Nice to meet you." Christine shook her hand.

"Michael Hendricks, but I'm sure you've heard all about me." Michael said, and held onto Dahlia's hands a little too long.

"Uh..." Dahlia didn't know what to say. This was *the* Hendricks and ex-girlfriend.

"Hendricks, you can let go of my girlfriend now," Liam said with steel in his voice.

"Don't you dare tell me what to do," Hendricks said. "You will never be the VP. I'm getting the promotion, and don't you forget it."

"Hendricks, what are you, five? Grow up. We're still colleagues."

The music picked up and Liam led Dahlia away before Hendricks could say anything more.

"So that's your rival, and your ex," she said as they danced.

"Forget about them. He's a jackass. And she's—"

"I can see that he's a jackass. And she's a social climber."

Liam laughed, his eyes wide with surprise. "You can tell, eh?" He chuckled. "You see what I've had to endure."

"We don't get to choose our co-workers, or ex-girlfriends' behavior."

"No, but we do get to choose the ones we love." He bent down to kiss her. She responded automatically, brushing her lips against his.

No, we don't always get to choose who we fall in love with, she thought, breaking a little more inside.

DAHLIA WAS A BEAUTY in her body-hugging dress that he couldn't wait to strip off her. She could be his, Liam thought, as he led her in another slow dance. He didn't mind that the live orchestra kept playing ballads and waltzes from his parents' and grandparents' eras. All the better for holding her close, and pretending that this was his life.

But she was leaving and there was nothing he could do to stop her.

A wild idea came to him. He blurted it out before he could censor it. "What if I quit my job and came with you?"

"Where?" Her eyes widened and she stopped dancing.

He nudged her into a turn. "Wherever you're going."

She looked away. "I can't Liam. I just can't... give up my life for..."

"For what?"

"For you." She broke out of his arms and ran toward the French doors.

He couldn't have her. He'd have to go forward with his plans of working hard ten to fifteen hour days, play hard, work hard, and no love. Suddenly, the life he'd built up so carefully around him after Christine had dumped him seven months ago seemed fake, just a facade. What good was a successful career and prestige and money if he had no one to share it with? No one to

Beth Barany

come home to. A roommate who was rarely there and a sweet dog who was always there didn't count.

He hurried to follow her, but the crowd of his colleagues and co-workers slowed him down with hellos and congrats on a good year. He finally made it to French doors that led out to the balcony. He stood there feeling foolish. A few women stepped out that he recognized but didn't know well. Finally Mary from HR stepped out. People must be smoking out there in the chilly air, admiring the view of the city.

"Is she out there?" he asked without preamble.

"Who?"

"Dahlia."

"I didn't see her. It's kind of dark."

"Okay. Thanks."

"I can check for you," Mary offered and examined him shrewdly. "You have it bad, don't you?"

"That's what they tell me."

"Who?"

"Well, apparently everyone, including you."

"It's true, though, isn't it?"

"Yeah, so what? There's nothing I can do about it. She's— she's leaving." Liam stormed back toward the bar. Halfway there, he turned around and came back. He pushed open the French doors. A gust of frigid damp air hit him.

Christine was stepping back into the hall, her hand on the door handle. "Well, hello to you, Liam." she said. "You're looking quite handsome tonight."

"Is Dahlia out there?" He ignored her come hither tone and how her gaze swept him from head to toe and back up again. What had he ever seen in her?

"Jeez, give a lady some privacy, buddy. You upset her. She's crying all over the place. What did you do? You—"

He brushed past her, letting her unspoken insult roll off him. He didn't want to waste breath. He stepped out into the cold night. Couples were clustered at the balcony, arms around each other. Some people were smoking, also in pairs.

In the far corner, in the shadows, there she was, arms wrapped around herself.

"Dahlia," he called to her as he approached.

She said nothing.

He stood beside her. "Did I say something that upset you?"

She sighed. "Yes, but not for the reasons you think."

"Let's go inside and you can tell me the reasons, okay?"

"I can't."

"Okay. Then I'll go inside and you'll join me and not tell me the reasons, but we'll still have a good time. Deal?"

"Okay." She turned to him, her face upturned. In the shadows, she looked different.

"Your ears." Shock rippled through his body.

"What about them?" she said quietly.

He blinked. Maybe the light on the balcony was playing tricks on him. "They're pointy. Like the Vulcans or the elves in Lord of the Rings."

"No, nothing like that." She slapped her hands over her ears and ran for the doors.

Hendricks was stepping out onto the balcony with two glasses of wine in one hand. Dahlia rushed passed him, Liam a few steps behind.

"Women, right?" Hendricks said.

"What do you want, Hendricks?"

Beth Barany

"I'm going to get that promotion. You messed up big time. What with that big fight on the dance floor. And soon you'll be working for me." Hendricks said.

Liam said nothing and moved to open the French doors and step into the hall. But Hendricks got up in his face. "You're going down." He poked Liam once in the chest and headed for the balcony, before he did even more foolish things.

"Whatever." Liam sighed and slipped into the hall. Dealing with Hendricks used to make him angry, now it just made him feel tired.

Just then Dahlia hurried over. She took his hands. "Sorry about that. I guess I lost it."

"What did you lose?" He stepped closer to her, to feel her heat. Her nervous energy emanated from her in waves. He pulled her into his arms, hoping he could lend some calm to her.

She gazed up at him without speaking. She stood on tiptoes and kissed him on the lips. "I'm going to miss you," she whispered. Then she swirled out of his arms in a fancy dance move, tugging him along with her. "Let's dance."

And just like that they swayed together close, and Liam kept his mouth shut. Having ears that looked pointy in the cold didn't bother him. It was endearing, actually. And he would enjoy their last moments together, and pretend it was forever.

DAHLIA FELT SNUG AND WARM in Liam's arms, protected, supported, and admired. She never wanted to leave the circle of his love.

She choked back a quiet sob and held him close, her head on his strong chest, right above the chuga-chuga beat of Liam's heart.

He'd seen her ears and still held her tight, as if he knew the depths of her feelings.

Maybe she could use her magic to—to—she didn't know what she could do to make things any different than they were. Elves' magic didn't extend to going back in time. And only Uncle could bend time. But if she'd met Liam earlier, if she didn't want her dream job so much, if—if. As her mother always said, "Wishing doesn't make it so."

"Penny for your thoughts?" Liam said softly, brushing a kiss on her cheek, and another on her lips.

"Is there anyone else we need to meet and greet?"

"Why?"

"Well, I wanted to get out of here, and have you all to myself." She smiled in what she hoped was a coy and sexy manner, but it was no act. She squeezed him.

He smiled back, his brown eyes warm with love.

She brushed away her tears.

"None of that," Liam said.

"I know. It's just that tonight is our last—"

"Shh. I know." He bent to kiss her, deeply, passionately. She leaned into him and gave him all she had, all her love, her desires, her wishes that could never be. She never regretted turning away from all the flirts she'd had back home, not that there were many, but she didn't want to turn away from Liam. How could she be of two minds and hearts, so divided?

"Get a room," someone shouted.

She heard laughter. It sounded good-natured.

She pulled away from the kiss and smiled, wiping her wet cheeks.

Just then a waiter glided by, his platter full of champagne flutes. He handed one to her and one to Liam. Everyone was getting a glass.

The music ended, the crowd clapped, and one of the board members Dahlia had met stepped up to the stage.

"Thank you all for coming and celebrating with us and your loved ones," the elderly man boomed, his voice strong and warm. "Let us give a toast to all the wonderful couples dancing and showing off their moves." He winked. People chuckled at his innuendo. "I'd like us to raise our glasses to why we're here, why we exist as a company." He lifted his champagne flute. Everyone followed suit. "To love and family. To our future generations."

"Hear, hear!" the crowd around them shouted.

Dahlia lifted her glass, but could only mouth the words. No sound could get passed the lump in her throat. She wanted love and family, and a future generation. She wanted it with Liam.

More board members got on stage, but Dahlia didn't want to hear more toasts. She stood on tiptoes to whisper in Liam's ear. "Let's go."

He nodded, grabbing her hand. They snaked through his colleagues and tumbled into the elevator after she gathered her wrap at the coat check.

They rode the elevator down in silence, hand in hand, Dahlia tucked into his side. They slipped through the opulent hotel lobby and waited on the curb for the valet to bring the car around.

In twenty minutes, they were at her door. She couldn't wait any longer, but pulled him to her and kissed him under the lintel. "Liam," she sighed. He kissed her harder and followed her into her now empty apartment.

"DAHLIA..." HE GAZED INTO HER eyes as they disrobed each other.

"Mmm?"

"This isn't a game anymore."

"I know. It stopped being one pretty quick."

He kissed her with all the love he had in his heart. Why would fate hand him love, only to have love leave to parts unknown?

Chapter Thirteen

A FTER A SWEET AND tearful goodbye with Liam at the San Francisco International Airport, Dahlia cried her eyes red and puffy aboard the plane. At least the early morning flight had few passengers so she could have the window seat and the rest of the aisle to herself. At a layover in Portland, she cleaned herself up and had a lunch with cousins. Luckily, they didn't ask questions and she was back on the airplane pretending that she was only going home for a happy homecoming and the next stage in her life as a Santa's Elf.

Nearly eight hours later, with everything she took back home in her carryon, including her precious toy, she finally disembarked late at night at Fairbanks Alaska Airport into the welcoming embrace of her mother.

She couldn't help it. She burst into tears. "Momma, I found him. I found the One, but he's human." She cried some more. She ignored the looks of her younger siblings.

"Oh, dearie. You'll work it out. Your aunt did."

"But I want to be an Elf, Momma. She didn't—she wasn't— she didn't present her toy. I want to be home. Have a life here." She sniffled. "What am I going to do?"

"You have your toy?"

Dahlia patted her carryon and smiled through her tears. "I do."

Momma hugged her. "It'll work out. It always does. Look at your father and me."

AFTER LIAM HAD DROPPED off Dahlia at the San Francisco International Airport, he stopped by the office, mostly out of habit. It was Sunday, he felt aimless, and he had an extra gym bag there. He suddenly needed to blow off some steam, and bad. Maybe after five hard and sweaty games with whoever was at the gym, he'd get his mind off Dahlia. Not likely, but a guy had to try.

He stepped off the elevator into the empty lobby. He glanced at the reception desk. His heart ached. The office would be a dimmer place without her and certainly less sparkly. His life would be a duller place without her, too.

"Hey, there you are. You got my message," Mr. Cooper said.

Liam opened his mouth to answer, but Mr. Cooper interrupted him.

"Glad you got here first so I could tell you the good news."

First? Liam thought.

Mr. Cooper held out his right hand to shake Liam's. And in his left he held an envelope in the company stationery. "Congratulations, son. Go ahead. Open it. You're one hell of an analyst. Management can't wait to get you on the team."

Without thinking Liam shook his hand and said, "Thank you." He took the envelope and opened in.

The offer for the promotion, a raise, great benefits. Everything he'd worked for.

"You're the best man for the job." Mr. Cooper slapped him on the back.

The fine print on the page blurred. "Thank you, sir."

Mr. Cooper chuckled and then fell silent. Finally he spoke. "Well, I'll leave you to it. We'll get you set up in your new office come New Year."

"No, thanks." Liam blew out a breath. Nerves jumped in his chest.

"What?" Mr. Cooper eyed him with confusion.

"No, this is not the job I want after all. Give it to Cole, not Hendricks."

"What? Hmm. We hadn't considered Cole. But you're the one we want," the older man said.

"It's not for me. But thank you anyway." Liam shook a stunned Mr. Cooper's hand, moved toward the elevator and punched the button.

"Wait, young man, where are you going?" Mr. Cooper called out.

"I have a plane to catch," Liam said and stepped onto the elevator.

Chapter Fourteen

FOURTEEN HOURS AND TWO layovers later, Liam landed in the Fairbanks Alaska airport. He'd sent a message via Skype on his cell to Dahlia because she'd said that was the best way to communicate with her. Regular cell phone calls didn't work. But she hadn't replied. Would she be waiting for him? Would she say yes?

DAHLIA HAD RECEIVED LIAM'S Skype message as she was settling in, greeting her large family. Not only her nine other siblings, but her cousins, aunts and uncles. But not *the* Uncle. She had until tomorrow night, Christmas Eve, to present her Gift to Santa. She couldn't very well give Liam directions on how to move through to the Northern Lights, so she hurried toward the Gate of Worlds. She'd use the magic of the Gate to dash from the Pole to the Fairbanks airport and greet him. Then she'd decide what to do.

LIAM WAS SCANNING THE crowd. He was at the Arrivals gate and didn't want to leave. He'd Skype-texted her where he was and didn't want to stray from the spot. Something bright and twinkling distracted him out of the corner of his eye. He turned to look but nothing was there. His heart thudded in his chest.

He checked his cell phone. No message from her. He'd already sent her two texts since he'd arrived. He had to move. He paced the corridor keeping the Arrivals portal in view. The whomp-whomp of a helicopter distracted him for a moment, pulling his attention to the tarmac where the planes were gliding into their slots, or taxing slowly toward the runways. But he didn't see a helicopter. Something kept his gaze there. He moved to the glass separating him from the tarmac.

Then he saw Dahlia stepping down some stairs toward him, exiting some sort of dark hallway full of sparkles in blues and greens and pinks, like the Northern Lights. Exactly like she was stepping through the Northern Lights.

He rushed toward her, a pathway at his feet, the glass gone. He had only a moment to wonder about that when Dahlia threw herself into his arms.

"You made it," she breathed out and kissed him. "You're one in a million, Liam. You found me."

"Dahlia, I'd go anywhere for you."

In reply, she kissed him again.

IN AN INSTANT, LIAM was on one knee. She shook her head.

"Let me speak, my love, please. I've come all this way."

Dahlia dared not look behind her, so she gripped Liam's outstretched hands. "This is sudden. Are you sure?"

"Yes, it is. And yes, I am." He gazed up at her. "Dahlia, my dear sweet and wonderful Dahlia. You have brought so much joy and laughter to my life, where before there was only seriousness and work. I know it's sudden. But I've never been more sure of anything in my life. Will you marry me and be the light of my life forever?"

Dahlia gulped. "Oh, Liam."

"Is that a yes?"

He'd made it through the portal on his own. That must be the Gate's magic blessing him. She hadn't revealed her true identity, but he loved her, even after seeing her ears, even not knowing what she was. But he knew *who* she was.

"Yes," she said.

He stood, his arms wrapped around her.

"I don't have a ring. I was kind of in a hurry."

"That's okay," she whispered.

He gazed down at her with love in his eyes, all for her. Never in her wildest dreams did she think he would really come.

"Kiss her already," Dad shouted from behind her. Or was that Uncle?

Liam's eyes went wide with surprise, but he did as commanded and bent his head to hers and kissed her long and deep.

The family hooted and hollered.

"Uh, Dahlia?"

"Yeah?"

"Is this your family?"

"Liam, yes, this is my family."

"Where are we?"

"We're at the North Pole. And I'm one of Santa's Elves."

Liam chuckled and shook his head, as if he was part surprised, part happy. He hooked her hair over her ears. "I love you."

"But...your job, your life in San Francisco... You're really ready to leave all that behind? For me?"

"Yes. And I want to meet your family." Liam smiled and kissed her.

Hours later, Dahlia waited in the wings with her fellow Suibhal elves. The fiddles and horns soared and reached their crescendo of joy. The Commencement song ended on a triumphant rise.

"Announcing our winner for this year's Master Elf Grand Prize—" the Master of Ceremonies boomed.

The curtain rustled. Dahlia held her breath. A wave of jittery excitement flooded her belly. She breathed out and pulled her shoulders back. She stilled and peeked onto the stage. Liam sat between her father and one of her older brothers, his gaze rapt on the stage.

"Drum roll, please," the Master of Ceremonies called.

The rumble of snare and tom drums filled her body.

Over the drums, a deeper voice spoke, "For the right to have his or her toy featured in next year's Christmas—" It was Uncle speaking. As was customary, Santa would give the prize. "We are proud to bestow the title of Master Elf to Grand Prize winner...Dahlia Rose Blue MacMillian."

Dahlia squealed and jumped and hugged her fellow elves. They whispered their congratulations and shoved her out of the wings and onto center stage. She stopped at the designated spot, just left of Santa's massive chair. He was holding up her toy for all to see, and the crowd was on their feet applauding.

Santa nodded and grinned to the crowd. They finally sat and quieted. Dahlia held herself still, but surely beaming from ear to ear.

Santa continued. "Based on the latest on-the-ground research, I am honored to present to you the Hovercraft Car

3000 with next generation stabilizers, remote control, and video camera."

The crowd applauded again. Liam nodded to her and mouthed, "I knew it." He grinned.

She felt her cheeks heat with a blush and let the applause and joy wash over her. She'd done it. This was what she'd worked so hard for.

Santa set the toy on the table on the other side of the chair. He turned to her and opened his arms. She stepped into his arms.

He breathed in her ear, "Congratulations my dear Dahlia. I am so proud of you."

She soaked up his warmth and love, then stepped out of his hug.

Santa picked up the golden medal, "Best Toy of the Year" engraved in the center, and looped it over her head. She smiled to the audience as they applauded. A wave of joy washed over her from head to toe and back again. She took her place beside her toy, and the other elves were called to the stage. She and her peers received their badges as Master Elf.

Deep into the night, after much festivities, dancing, and delicious food, Dahlia finally had Liam to herself in her room. She'd finally kicked out her loud older brother and sisters and nosy younger brothers. She'd forgotten how annoying they all could be. Dahlia stood with Liam in the center of her dorm room, part of a huge, hive-like dormitory system, and hugged him, head on his chest. They swayed, like they'd done at the company's Christmas Party. Hard to believe that was only two days ago. So much had happened.

She pulled back to gaze at him. "You do realize what you've done."

"What have I done?"

"You renounced your regular Human life and basically have to live here."

"I know. Your father took me aside and explained it to me in great detail. Is he a lawyer?"

"Yeah."

"Didn't know elves had lawyers."

"There's a lot you don't know about us," she said quietly. "You really want to do this?"

"Yes. Your father said that I can only go back sometimes, and that an exception is made for people like me only once in awhile. Special factors and circumstances. And benefits." He kissed her, a sweet peck on the lips, and pulled back.

"You'll have to tell me about those benefits."

He kissed her again. "I certainly will." His dimple winked at her.

"Is Sally being looked after?" she asked.

"Brett is looking after her. Another friend. You didn't meet him. Josh isn't back yet. Not sure what's up with him. I think he's having too good a time to leave Paris."

"I didn't get to meet any of your friends."

"Well, they know all about you and will love you like a sister when we meet."

"We can't—"

"We can. I checked with your father. We can have our wedding somewhere warm where elves and humans can come together, discreetly."

"Like a tropical island?" She smiled. "Lovely." Then she frowned. "What about your job?"

Liam shook his head. "I told them, 'no.' "

"So Hendricks will get it?"

"No, probably not. I recommend Cole."

Dahlia nodded. "Cole was always a nice guy when he greeted me at the front desk." She squeezed Liam. "Like you."

Liam hugged her back and nipped her lips in another kiss. "How's Maui in March? For the wedding." He nuzzled her neck.

"Hmmm." She shivered and walked backwards toward her bed.

"Is that a yes?"

"Yes," She tumbled with him on her bed. "A thousand times, yes."

Parisian Amour

(A Fairytale Paranormal Romance)

Novella Book 3 of the *Touchstone Series*

Summary:

Sarah Redman, a bank project manager, wants adventure in her life. Trainer extraordinaire, Josh Kleine, needs to pull off a successful presentation at a Paris conference to land more clients and save his company. Together they may hold the key to the strange disasters striking the City of Lights. Can Sarah unravel the secrets of the city and of her heart in time to save them all?

S ARAH REDMAN STROLLED ACROSS the pedestrian-only bridge, Pont des Arts, in the middle of Paris, wrapped in a raincoat, hat, and scarf. Her breath puffed out white before her. The night winter air chilled her cheeks. The light rain helped her feel refreshed from her long red-eye flight from San Francisco. Seeing the City of Lights grounded her for the big interview tomorrow morning.

This job could be the chance of a lifetime. She was glad for the impulse that had had her looking for it and acting upon the sudden request for a face-to-face interview. The change of pace was just what she needed to shake up the doldrums she'd been experiencing at her job as a project manager at a conservative bank in downtown San Francisco. She wanted some adventure in her life.

A man walked by her, cell phone to his ear, speaking too low for her to hear. His double-breasted navy coat collar was turned up against the cold. With his white scarf tied in an aviator's knot around his neck, a seaman's cap low over his forehead, he seemed so French, almost like a character out of one of the Tintin stories. For a second, he glanced up at her and then did a double take. In the streetlight, his hazel eyes sparkled like he knew a naughty secret about her. Her heart sped up and her cheeks heated.

In the next instant, he passed by before he could see her blush. Thank goodness. But it was good to feel the surge of attraction.

And it was good to be doing something other than working and being alone in her apartment with her cactus and her books, or working and going out with the girls to the newest local restaurant. Or working and going on one of her camping trips with the all-women survivalist team. As exciting as those social activities were, they'd become routine.

A car horn blast blared from across the pedestrian bridge on the Left Bank, the opposite direction of her hotel. Just more snarling Parisian traffic, dealing with the rain and the late night. But it was new and different. She smiled. The start of a new chapter in her life, she hoped.

She yawned. But first she needed a decent night's sleep. She'd slept a little on her flight, but not nearly enough. She turned around before she got to the end of the bridge and headed back toward her cute hotel, tucked behind the church St. Eustache and next to Les Halles, where the famous central market used to be.

Halfway across the bridge, that was when she saw them. The locks, large and small, gym locks and safety locks, old-fashioned and new, decorated the entire iron siding of both sides of the walking bridge. In the lamplight, words were scribbled on the locks in what looked like indelible ink. She paused and knelt to examine one. Scrawled on the small space was a heart with the letters "S & J" inside the heart and the date of November 30, just the day before.

The "S" could have been her. She didn't have a "J" in her life, but maybe if she'd made room for a relationship, she could have.

Yesterday had been her thirtieth birthday.

Tears welled in her throat unbidden and unwelcome. She was now thirty and had no one to love. Love wasn't for her and relationships never lasted.

She stood and rubbed the pebble in her coat pocket. The small stone kept her grounded and reminded her of the Tehachapi Canyon where she liked to camp.

A flash of a dream came to her, one she'd had in the days leading up to her trip to Paris. In her dream, someone or something was weeping in a huge cavern, its cries echoing off the high ceiling and far walls—a creature crying with all its heart, as if it were tragically broken.

Sarah's heart ached for the creature.

Then a gust of cold air brought a sheet of rain into her face, snapping her out of the dream.

She hurried across the bridge back to her hotel.

Dreams were just dreams.

Dragons just existed in fairy tales.

She had her own adventure to create.

COLLAR UP AGAINST THE rain, cap low on his forehead, Josh Kleine strode across the bridge and cooed to his Bernese Mountain dog, Sally, at the other end of the phone line, back in Oakland, California. Then without warning, his best friend and housemate Liam took the phone away from his dog and teased Josh about his habit of talking to his dog, especially long distance.

"Whatever, man. You know I love Sally more than you. I gotta get some shut eye to get up early for the conference tomorrow," Josh said. "I'll call you later."

"Sure. Take care. And go meet some French women, will you? Sounds like you need to get laid."

"Hey, where did that come from? Speak for yourself." Josh shook his head.

Liam barked a laugh and clicked off the cell phone.

Josh slipped the phone back into his coat pocket and passed a beautiful woman strolling on the bridge. Under her hat, she had long brown hair flowing over her shoulders, seemingly not minding that her hair was getting wet. She had a faraway look in her eyes. In that moment, passing only a few feet away from her, he could swear that he smelled the hot air of roasting chestnuts. A whoosh of hot air surrounded him. He'd smelled and felt that the day before in the behind-the-scenes tour of the Paris Metro. Strange.

He wasn't underground in the Metro. He was on the bridge. With her.

He caught himself staring at the woman and glanced away. And sighed. Too bad. She was so his type—tall and gorgeous. He saw them—his arms around her, holding her close to him, those long legs that could wrap around his body... He did a double take.

Their gazes locked. His heart sped up.

She strode by, her boots clicking against the pavement.

The rain gusted.

It had been a long time since he'd been with a woman.

But that was on purpose. He always fell too hard, too fast, and the relationships always crashed and burned.

The last relationship had nearly ruined his business too. No. Relationships were bad news to his heart and his career. He didn't trust himself to make the right choices as far as relationships went. He'd let Melanie into his life and his apartment and his business. Then only months ago, she'd stolen his biggest client and dumped him, all on the same day.

He turned around toward the Left Bank. Time to get back to his affordable room he was renting in an apartment, located up the street from the conference near the Saint-Germain Boulevard.

He had to get up early to meet with his prospective clients and prepare his presentation for the transportation conference. He needed to get those clients to keep his consulting and training business afloat. He was still recovering from the Melanie disaster.

He had no time for women, French or otherwise.

THE NEXT MORNING, SARAH sipped her espresso at the famous café Les Deux Magots on Saint-Germain Boulevard and tried to soothe her nerves. The croissant she'd had back at the hotel was churning in her stomach in reaction to the man sitting across from her.

A French businessman from Credit Paris, one of the largest banks in France, looked conservative enough in his expensive grey suit, short-cropped beard and salt and pepper hair. But the way he was looking her up and down, like she was a pony for sale, grated on her.

"Monsieur Montefort, I thought you asked me here for some espresso before we toured the office and had our interview," Sarah said in English. Her French was rudimentary at best.

He waved a hand. "No. This is our interview. Much better, yes?" He leaned a little too close. His rich cologne assailed her.

She coughed, but restrained herself from waving her hand in front of her. "This may be how you do business in France, but— She raised her voice.

"Oh my dear, don't get so excited. There's a time and a place for that you know." Then he winked at her, actually winked at her. "I have an offer for you."

She swallowed and let her expression go neutral, she hoped.

"I have a special proposition for you. How shall I say in English? A two for one."

"I'm listening." Though she wasn't sure why.

"You would be perfect as the special project manager in our western Paris branch in the sixteenth arrondissement. You're well qualified."

"Thank you."

He nodded. "And I want to offer you an all-expenses paid apartment in the quarter, I mean, neighborhood, too."

"I see."

"So we can be together when you're not working. I'll take you out, show you all the beautiful sights, wonderful restaurants, special secret delights of the city—"

"What are you offering me?" She huffed. She knew what he wanted.

He smirked at her.

"How dare you!" She spoke maybe a little too loudly, but she didn't care.

"Don't be such a prude. This is France, after all."

Sarah frowned. "I came all this way for a job interview, not to be propositioned by my prospective employer."

"You Americans." He clicked his tongue in a sign of disapproval. Then he shrugged and smirked again. "You do have spirit."

"That's it." She stood, her chair scraping the polished wood floor, and held out her hand, wanting to be civilized. "Monsieur—"

"Yes?" He had a grin on his face and held out his hand.

She shook it. "No, thank you," she said loudly.

He stood too and dabbed his mouth with a napkin. "Ah."

Without waiting for his reaction, Sarah grabbed her coat and hat. She pivoted and ran smack dab into a hard chest. "Pardonnez-moi," she mumbled and wobbled on her high heel boots.

The man put a hand on her shoulder to steady her.

She glanced up and flushed. It was the man from the bridge last night. She was sure. Those hazel eyes drew her in. Maybe it was the guarded yet commanding look in his gaze.

"Are you all right?" he asked in American English.

She nodded automatically and rushed for the exit.

JOSH HAD BEEN SIPPING HIS espresso at the zinc bar, saving a few euros. When he'd turned to leave the cafe, he'd seen the leering man, and the woman frowning, her voice raised in English.

Josh frowned at the woman's hasty retreat. Something about the set of her shoulders, and her profile, quite unhappy, had drawn him. Plus she was clearly a fellow American.

He stepped toward her just as she'd stood to leave. He rubbed his nose where she'd knocked into him. The woman from the bridge. Had to be. The smell of chestnuts. Strange. Just like on the bridge. And that long hair and long legs. Up close, she had a look of panic and a determined set of her jaw.

But now she was gone. A too strong attraction and concern for her had him stepping back to lean against the bar.

He glanced up.

The older man was glaring at him. That made Josh's blood boil.

He snapped out of whatever had overtaken him and strode to the cafe table. "Monsieur, I'm sorry to bother you," he asked in formal French. "But what did you do?"

"Whatever are you talking about, young man? This is not your business. Stop playing the jealous lover."

"What do you mean? I don't know her. I'm just defending a fellow American."

"That cannot be true. You interrupted a very important job interview."

Now who was lying? Before Josh could say that, the older man stood, grabbed his coat and hat and left the cafe. At least the older man had left some euros on the table.

Josh didn't know what got into him. He couldn't solve someone else's problems. He had his own to attend to—namely landing new clients. He had to get to the conference.

"WAIT," SARAH HEARD MONSIEUR Montefort yell. Boots scuffled against pavement behind her. She thought she heard the man pursuing her, calling her name. First "Mademoiselle Redman" then louder, "Sarah." But she didn't even look over her shoulder to see how close Monsieur Montefort was.

She clipped faster down the broad sidewalk. There had to be somewhere she could disappear from view.

There, a block ahead she spotted the metro sign. Perfect. She wove in and out of the other pedestrians and pounded down the stairs into the Saint-Germain-des-Prés metro station.

Sarah had bought a weeklong metro pass at the airport when she'd arrived so she was prepared, as always. Mid-morning the metro was still crowded with the morning commute. She pressed her pass against the gate and it slid open with a whoosh.

She rushed through it and took the first turn and stairwell she came to. She only had two directions to go—the station had only one metro line running through it, the number four. She could go south to Montparnasse station and probably could lose him there, if he somehow managed to follow her. Montparnasse was a big station. A train station connected to the metro, from what she remembered from a previous business trip. But it might be better to head toward the center of the city. More choices for her that way.

So she chose the opposite direction, north toward the destination Porte de Clignancourt. She was grateful that a train was waiting at the platform. She hopped it just as the buzzer sounded, signaling the doors were about to close. Then the doors snapped shut, right in her face, because the train car was crowded with morning commuters. All the seats were taken, so she clung to the overhead metal bar.

The train pulled out of the station and swayed a little as it picked up speed. She glanced over her shoulders, both ways. No Monsieur Montefort. Just quiet Parisians with their heads down reading *Le Monde,* or the free daily paper with a big picture of the weather forecast that could be read in any language—rain and thunderstorms predicted. Or the commuters were gazing at their smart phones, headphones in.

The train rumbled, then turned into a curve, and moments later slid to a stop. Without thinking, she opened the door and jumped off. The metro train trundled off. A rush of relief flooded her.

Then the quiet pressed in. And she noticed something strange.

There was no one around her—no commuters, no people bundled in their coats and scarves waiting for the train, no one. Not even disheveled old men who seemed to occupy many of the stations to stay warm.

The station was empty.

Where was she? She pulled out her small Paris Streets book and studied the metro map in the back of the book. It was the latest edition, just purchased at the airport the day before. She traced her route. She'd started at Saint-Germain-des-Prés, had been heading north, and had gotten off at the next stop. She should have been at the next stop on the map, which is Odéon. But that was not what the wall said in big blue tiles, art deco style. It said Marronniers.

She stared at her map, tracing the Line 4 with her fingertips. She'd landed at a station that didn't exist according to her map. How was that possible?

She'd heard about stations like this, called ghost stations. They should have been all blocked off to the public. She knew this because...she wasn't quite sure, but thought she may have read it in a magazine... something about using ghost stations to film famous French films, like Amélie. And people being able to take tours to see them.

These details though wouldn't help her get out of here. She listened for more trains, but didn't hear any rumbling or feel the wave of heat that seemed to be pushed before each train as it barreled into a station.

Logically the only way out was up. At least she wasn't being followed any more. She searched for the nearest staircase, but didn't see one going up or down, just a curving hallway at either end of the platform. She checked her smartphone for the compass app. But the compass couldn't detect any direction. She waved it around to get it to orient and find true north. But after a few minutes of that, and no change to her phone, she gave up. She must be too far underground to get a cell signal. She may as well flip a coin. For a second, she panicked. Then she blew out a breath and followed her gut as to which way to go.

When all else failed that was all she had.

Both sides looking the same, she headed to the right side of the platform and took that tunnel. It curved with no indication of where it was headed. There weren't any signs on the grey walls, not even any old advertisements from an earlier era. In fact, the tunnels narrowed and sloped downward. How strange. She was not getting any closer to the surface. She checked her phone. Only ten minutes had passed. She kept walking, the thud of her boot steps and her steady breathing keeping her company. She wasn't afraid, just annoyed, and a little bit intrigued.

Then the lights placed high on the wall flicked off all at once, leaving her in complete darkness.

Her heart thudded, as the adrenaline kicked in. Fear edged closer.

She tapped her phone for some light and to check the time. For sure, she must have been down here for hours, her fear shouted at her.

Silly, she scolded herself. It had only been twenty or thirty minutes.

Her phone said otherwise. She'd been down in the tunnel for an hour. How had time passed so quickly?

Then without its usual warning, the light of her phone gave out. The battery was dying. She turned off the phone to conserve what little battery it had left and dug into her purse for her flashlight attached to her keys.

She swore. She'd left those in her suitcase. Back at the hotel. Who needs house keys when they're on vacation and away from home?

She could kick herself. She was always prepared. Well, usually. She always had the basics, and her flashlight was one of those items. Along with...she pawed through her purse, ignoring how her hands shook.

No matches or a lighter. What had she been thinking when she left her hotel room this morning?

Oh, yeah. Travel light with a small purse. Impress the potential boss. Well, she must have left too much of an impression and look where that had landed her—in the mysterious back tunnels of the Paris underground.

There was nothing usual about her situation.

Panic rose in her throat. "Hey!" she yelled. "Anybody there?"

How did she say that in French? She didn't know, so she continued to yell in English. Maybe Spanish spilled out too. She was a native Californian, after all. But her voice in either language fell flat against the narrow walls. Not even an echo.

All she could do was move forward. Or back. But her gut said to move forward. She blew out a breath. She could do this. She'd done survival training in Tehachapi Canyon for fun. She could find her way out of tunnel in a city. People were just above her. She had to keep going and find an exit.

She placed her hand on the wall. It was cool to the touch. Somehow that reassured her. Forward it was.

Even though there was a city of 2.2 million people above her, no one was waiting for her above ground. No one counted on her appearing at a certain time and would report her missing if she didn't show. At least not for another week. They didn't expect her back at the office until the following Monday. She was on vacation. There was no one to greet her and share a laugh about her adventures over an espresso or something stronger in one of Paris' cozy cafes while the rain drizzled.

Even her boss and her assistant, who was handling her work, didn't expect an email or text from her until next week.

A light flared ahead. Her heart sped up.

"Hey!" she shouted, but her voice fell flat again.

At least she had something to follow and head toward.

JOSH PUT UP HIS COLLAR against the rain that seemed to be coming down harder than earlier in the day. It was only lunchtime, but it felt like he'd lived a whole day, what with his short and intense conversations with fifteen, or was it twenty people, at the conference. He'd lost track. The breakfast meet and greet had been run by a high-powered New York trainer who'd kept them chatting away with each other for the last ninety minutes. He fingered the stack of business cards in his coat pocket, satisfied at the morning's work. He'd connected with a lot of interested potential clients that were waiting for him to follow up in the days to come. His business needed an infusion of cash, and short of applying for a business loan that he didn't want to strap his company with, or getting business partners that he didn't want, he needed clients to sign contracts by the end of the year.

He could and he would pull his business back up to pre-Melanie levels. He hadn't realized until she dumped him, just how much of his attention had been drained away from his company. He'd loved being in partnership, in collaboration, and in love with her. He'd felt on top of the world, like he could do anything he set his mind to. And Melanie was super smart, gorgeous, bold and gutsy. He'd loved those qualities about her. But she'd blindsided him. Even after all these months, he couldn't believe he'd been so oblivious to her true colors. How had she been able to deceive him and practically ruin his company?

The best answer he'd been able to come up with was that love made him blind.

But that was all months ago.

This was now.

Time for lunch and to stretch his legs. If he'd been back home in Oakland, he'd have changed into his running gear and had a good long run to Lake Merritt and back before lunch. But this was Paris and people didn't run in the streets in their running clothes and trainers, as the French called them, especially in the rain, or in any weather.

So he headed down the Saint-Germain Boulevard for the warren of streets near the Seine where he knew he could find the best shawarma sandwich in all of the universe.

While he couldn't get rid of his past the way a snake shed its skin, he could keep his mind on the present. That was where all the action was. He smiled. That was what his dad always said.

He peeled off from the big boulevard and took the small side streets, zigzagging his way to the Saint-Michel fountain. From there, he just had to cross the wide Boulevard St.-Michel to get to the cobblestone pedestrian-only neighborhood that had once been populated by mostly students back in the twelfth century when the cathedral Notre Dame was first being built. He stepped from the sidewalk to cross the street when a car coming too fast through what was supposed to be a red light splashed him from head to toe with water.

"Hey!" he shouted in English, then followed that with a strong dose of French swear words.

His heart pumped. His breath kicked up a few notches.

When the traffic finally stilled, he hustled across the street with the rest of the crowd without further incident.

Moments later he tread carefully across the cobblestones to a tiny restaurant for lunch.

"Excuse me."

He was finishing off his delightful shawarma sandwich with extra cucumber sauce when he heard the bird-like chirp of a voice.

He looked up. A bent gypsy woman hovered beside his table, eyeing him expectantly.

Probably wanted spare change.

Instead, she said in English, "I read your fortune for you, young man. Much is in store for you."

She pivoted away. Then she glanced at him over her shoulder and winked.

He blinked. For a moment she appeared taller, lean, with long brown hair and emerald eyes, laughing at him, as if he was funny and cute and she held a delicious secret, but in a good way.

He blinked again.

The gypsy woman grinned, her lack of a few teeth proudly prominent. "Love must be renewed and revealed by seven bells." She held out her palm as if she expected payment.

Josh stared at her, then handed her a one-euro coin. She sniffed the coin and frowned. She turned to leave, mumbling something in French about "see if I ever deliver your messages again, ungrateful beast."

Horns blared. The smells of the street assailed him, bringing him back.

That was weird.

He checked the time. He had to head back. No wait, he flipped through the conference program. There was another special conference tour he wanted to attend—a change of pace from the sessions and a good way to connect with his fellow conference attendees. He had to hurry if he didn't want to be late.

He hustled down the steps into the Saint-Michel metro station, one of the systems' largest, and navigated the crowded hallways to the tour starting place. He nodded to his colleagues, waiting at a grey door. No time to strike up a chat as they were being ushered in to an office behind a ticket booth.

The presenter started her spiel as she led them through back corridors of offices and control booths. Josh stifled a yawn. It was another behind the scenes tour of the Paris metro for transportation experts. He thought this one would be different from the last one from the other day. In fact, it was a repeat. The guide droned on about how many people worked behind the scenes, how they were trained for their different jobs, how the shift changes worked, etc. He'd heard it all the other day. She was repeating the lecture he'd already heard from a different tour guide. He checked his program. This one was supposed to be the next level of conversation, on safety issues, his specialty.

But now that he was down here, he may as well enjoy it. Perhaps chit-chat with the other attendees, more than he usually did on such tours. But everyone's attention was on the tour guide. So Josh only half listened to all the stats and details, and soon he was straggling behind the group.

A blast of warm air shot from a wall panel, bringing with it the rich aroma of chestnuts. So familiar. But why?

He glanced up, but the group was nowhere in sight. They must have been further ahead of him than he thought. He trotted to catch up, but first one turn then another, and he still didn't see them. In fact, nothing looked familiar.

Instead of the well-lit wide hallway with side doors leading to offices, meeting rooms, and control booths, ahead of him was a shorter and smaller tunnel with grey walls and no doors. The ceiling was maybe seven feet high, barely, and if he stretched his arms out, his fingers would surely touch the walls. That meant the tunnel was only a bit over six feet—the length of his arm span.

But there was the smell of roasting chestnuts—a rich aroma that reminded him of cozy nights at home with his parents and grandparents, before everything in his life had upended. Maybe he'd been unconsciously following the aroma instead of the group.

He could go back, but the scent pulled him forward. He turned a corner to another grey passage, same as the last.

A high-pitch keening sounded.

With horror he realized that it was his own voice, expressing a grief far beyond his own loss.

Waves and waves of sadness hit him. He felt for the walls. Something had to keep him up or he would fall over, the ache in his heart was so great.

What was happening to him?

Whispers of love lost and crazy anger flooded him, as if he were a pebble being tossed in the sea of massive wave of feelings too great for any one human to handle.

He had to sit down. The tsunami of emotion threatened to squash his very essence.

Words in his head, whispered:

A love so great can't be lost
But lost it has into the sands of time
Find me my love
Nourish
Replenish
Do the impossible and bring her back to me
Before the seven bells

The strange words rumbled through his mind. Josh blinked through the tears and examined his clenched fists, ready to batter the walls.

This couldn't be his grief, couldn't be, he reminded himself. Or his love lost.

But it felt so real.

Then the dim lights overhead shut off with a click.

Completely in the dark, he heard only his breath and his staccato heartbeat. He rubbed his hands over his face and stood, using the wall at his back as his guide.

The awesome and terrible grief abated, finally, and he was left with the realization that he'd never loved as much and grieved as much as what he'd just felt.

His life was empty of such love—except for what he had for his friends and his dog.

He couldn't and shouldn't trust his heart to love. He almost destroyed his livelihood because of his blind love for Melanie.

The words of the gypsy came back to him, something about love needing to be renewed and revealed by seven bells. Whatever that meant.

How could love be revealed and renewed if he never really experienced true love?

What he'd had with Melanie was just some kind of sham, though he'd thought he'd loved her at the time.

Josh trudged down the black tunnel, feeling his way one hand on the wall.

A light blinked in the distance. A way out.

He picked up the pace to a jog, one hand still on the wall.

There had to be a way out of here.

THE LIGHT FLICKED OFF. SARAH froze. Then put her hand out and found the wall again. Like before, its cool and smooth texture reassured her that despite the strange environment and occurrences something was solid around her—even if it was mysterious. She'd been in worse situations, she reminded herself, but for the moment couldn't remember what they were.

She continued forward for some time, then froze again when she heard an odd noise. She stilled and tried to quiet her breathing to hear better. It sounded like someone mumbling, a low voice, a man's voice. It was probably a tunnel rat—people who played and partied in the hidden tunnels of Paris. She heard that they prided themselves on knowing the few coveted secret underground entrances and had crazy parties down here.

Still, she didn't want to take any chances. She fished in her purse for a potential weapon and settled for the plastic metro pass holder. If she held it properly, it had sharp edges that cut into her hand. Something ironic about carrying a metro pass as weapon deep underground.

Who knew who was ahead of her? Assumptions were the mother of accidents.

Her hand brushing the cool surface, she followed the curved wall. The mumbling amplified to almost shouting, as if he were just a few feet in front of her. She gripped her plastic cardholder, sharp edge out. But she still couldn't make out the words.

As she approached closer, his voice rumbled on and changed from loud to a soothing coo.

She took another step, then another.

She turned another corner. Suddenly she had to squint against the light. When her eyes finally adjusted to a phone's screen glow, she could see a man hunched over his phone pressing buttons and muttering. His face was lit up by the phone's bright screen. His brown hair was curved slightly over his ears, his lean muscular body tense and agitated.

Her body responded.

Her heart sped up and anticipation for him flooded her belly. She wanted him.

Then her brain kicked in and she recognized him—the man from the cafe.

How could she feel such attraction so quickly?

It was probably just relief at seeing another person and one she recognized, she rationalized.

He didn't seem to notice her, but continued to talk at his phone. He was speaking French, she realized. No wonder she hadn't understood him.

"Hey," she said.

Then the lights clicked back on.

She blinked against the brightness. When her eyes adjusted, he was staring at her, as if in a daze.

Then he seemed to focus on her and his face lit up with recognition, and something else that made her body heat up even more—desire and joy, as if she were his long lost love.

He looked away. When he glanced back, she just saw a friendly smile, his desire banked, if it was really there.

She had to find her words. "Uh, hi, fancy meeting you here. Do you know the way out?"

"No," he said. "Got any ideas?" He angled his head. "I know you, right? From the cafe, this morning. Wait. And the bridge—last night." His eyes widened with surprise.

"You tried to come to my rescue this morning."

"Seems like you managed just fine on your own."

"Thank you," she said softly.

"For what?"

"For stepping in. Trying to do the right thing."

He nodded.

She said nothing.

Finally he spoke. "Weird, us running into each other down here."

"What are the odds?" She glanced around them, trying to get her bearings.

"Not great, from what little I know about odds."

She felt his stare on her. She looked up and felt caught in his hazel eyes. Her cheeks burned. Images of them entwined on silk sheets in a Paris hotel somewhere flashed before her eyes. She wanted to explore the feel of his wavy brown hair through her fingers and touch his chest and more. She couldn't deny the attraction, but they had more important things to do than explore her feelings or his body.

So she spoke. "Let's figure out where we are, so we can find our way out. My phone's compass won't work down here, but surely there are signs we can follow to get us out of here. Two heads are better than one." She stopped talking. She was babbling.

"Good, at least one person has the skills we need to get out of here."

"I don't know about that. I've been down here awhile without finding an exit. I'm not even sure how I ended up here."

"I'm with you there, but—" He shrugged. "I haven't any luck and I've been down here for—" he looked at his phone again. "A good two hours." He looked up at her. "Weird. Feels more like thirty minutes."

"I had the same feeling, like time is passing by quicker down here." She puffed out a breath and held out her hand. "Can I see your phone?"

"Sure." Without hesitation he handed it over.

Their fingers touched.

Sarah startled at the zing of electricity that traveled up her arm.

"Whoa!" he said.

"What was that?" Sarah said, at the same time.

They stared at each other.

Nothing, she wanted to say, but instead peered down at the phone.

He had cell reception. His phone was definitely better than hers. Looked like it was the latest model, in fact. Sleeker, lighter, and clearly more powerful than hers because it was working and got cell reception.

"Where'd you get this?" she said in awe, glancing up at him.

He grinned. "Just came out last week. In Singapore." He shrugged. "A friend got it for me."

"Hmmm." She studied it some more and was able to call up a GPS map. "According to this, we're... in front of the Notre Dame Cathedral."

"Weird. How did you get it to work?" He stepped closer to her, so his shoulders were beside hers. But he didn't touch her.

His body heat washed over her and she inhaled. Could she get any hotter? He smelled of man and earth. She had the crazy urge to jump into his arms and—and what?

She stepped away and handed him the phone. Their fingers brushed. She sucked in breath. He stared at her and gulped, then stared at the cell phone screen.

"What? I don't see anything. Just an error message."

"Let me see."

He gingerly handed her the phone, careful not to touch her this time.

The phone's screen was white with black lettering in French, then the view flipped to the navigation screen.

"That is strange," she said. "But I have heard of people affecting electrical equipment like this, shorting it out."

"That's never happened to me before," he whispered in such a sad voice that Sarah reached out and placed a hand on his shoulder.

He looked at her, startled.

"What's wrong?" she asked. She couldn't help asking.

He held her gaze, but blinked away whatever grief flashed there. "I don't know." Then he smiled, as if nothing were wrong. "Let's get out of here, shall we? I have people to see, things to do, you know stuff above ground." He crossed his arms and dropped the smile. "Do your magic."

"My magic?"

"Yeah, whatever it is that you do to get my phone to work."

She dropped her hand to mess with the screen view. But she couldn't find out anything more. "I suppose there's no special app we could download of the Paris tunnels."

He shrugged. "You got the tool. Make it work."

He was playing it cool, pretending like things were normal, as if being stuck underground in some strange Paris tunnel was normal.

Well, we all had our coping mechanisms, she knew.

Her coping method was to use the tools on hand. An image of him flashed in her mind, all naked. I'd like to play with him, play with his tool, she thought. She brushed the thought away.

She tapped more buttons on the phone, more like a tiny supercomputer, what with all the gizmos and apps. Her heart thudded and her core heated, yet she ignored her body's need to be wrapped around his.

After a few minutes of searching, she couldn't find anything remotely useful on his phone, besides the map. She looked up at him to speak and found him gazing at her again, as if she were the most amazing thing, like a marvel or the dawn of a new day.

Her throat closed up on her, and she blinked back the unexplainable tears.

She had to do something, anything, to shift away from these feelings of unexplained sadness that washed through her, reminding her of something.

"Hi." She stuck out her hand. "I haven't introduced myself. I'm Sarah Redman, nice to meet you."

He stared at her hand.

"Hi Sarah." He kept his hand in his coat pocket. "I'm Josh Kleine. Nice to meet you, too." He smiled politely then looked away. "You found a way out of here? I think we need to leave now. This place is doing funny things to my head."

"Is that what's going on?" She dropped her hand.

"Sarah, I don't know what's going on," he said, the anger strong in his voice.

She held out his phone. "Here, I've done all I can. No cool app for what we need."

He took back his phone for the second time. "Lead on," Josh said.

She stifled the urge to make sure he touched her. He obviously wasn't feeling the attraction or wanted to pretend it wasn't there. Or lived in denial.

JOSH RUBBED HIS PALMS OVER his face, and then snuck a peek at her.

She stared at him as if he had two heads. Then she peered up the tunnel the way he came and turned around the way she came.

"What are you doing?"

"Trying to figure out which way to go. You and I came from opposite directions. How did you get here?"

He shook his head. "I don't know."

"How could you not know?" she sounded more confused than upset. "Think. Retrace your steps."

"Why don't we just go back the way you came?" he asked.

"Won't work. There was no exit. So give me some clues."

Instead of answering, Josh paced the width of the tunnel, four steps to the wall and four steps back, back and forth, to blow off some steam.

"Will you stop that? We need to pool our resources and find a way out of here."

"I know." Josh rubbed his breastbone at the pressure building at his chest.

"Well?"

She was waiting for an answer, the beautiful Sarah. She made him nervous, her presence too close to him. If she stepped closer to him, he'd reach out and grab her and bury his face in her hair, and breathe deep her essence of woman. All he could think about was *her*. Not a solution.

He started up his pacing. *Think—think.*

He always got in trouble when he was so quickly attracted to a woman. He made rash decisions that nearly ruined his life last time he'd been attracted to a woman. He let Melanie move into his apartment after they'd been dating a week.

He had to bury the feelings swirling in his body. No good ever came from his passion for women. Melanie had left what he thought was a wonderful and passionate relationship. After they'd been together six months, she'd left him without warning.

Forever alone.

A wave of sadness crushed him. He fell against the wall. Good thing it was right there.

"What's wrong?" Sarah said softly, her warm voice washing over him like a silk sheet. She was at his side.

He shook his head to clear the vision of them tangled in sheets, sweaty and panting. He managed to stand and step away from her. "Nothing."

He scrubbed his face again and paced the tunnel again. He clenched and unclenched his hands. He blew out a breath and glanced up at her.

She stood in the middle of the tunnel, a square florescent light behind her and above, giving her a ghostly look. A specter from a beloved past. His heart sped up at that strange thought.

"I entered at Saint-Michel, the metro station." He blew out a breath. That calmed his racing heart a little. And not at all did it curb the desire to drink up her gaze, crush her body against his, and feel her soft curves against him. The desire he felt for her scared him. He didn't even know her, he cautioned himself.

She nodded as if that were helpful, seeming so oblivious to his attraction for her. "I was supposed to get off at Odeon but ended up at a station called Marronniers."

"Never heard of it."

"Me neither. But I was there. I'm guessing it was one of those abandoned stations. From the 1930s, from the looks of the decor, and lack of posters."

"So where are we?"

She brushed a wall. "These tunnels are too smooth and in too good of a condition to be in the ancient catacombs. They seem like abandoned administrative tunnels."

"Yes, they are. The things you learn at behind-the-scenes tours."

"Why didn't you say so before?"

He gazed at her. "Because I'm not in my right mind. Something is affecting me down here." Maybe something is affecting the whole city, like the smell of chestnuts and the hot steam at odd locations. But he couldn't share those details with her. She might think he was crazy and then leave him.

"I've been experiencing strange things, too." She shook her head and shrugged.

"Like getting lost and finding a ghost station," he said and took a deep breath, smiling.

He didn't smell the chestnuts now. Instead he just smelled her, her sweet perfume, something floral, and her womanly smell, indescribable but delicious.

She smiled, a small smile, but it was enough to show off her beauty even more. A little happiness lit up her green eyes so they seemed to sparkle. He could gaze at her all day.

"You're staring," she said, jolting him.

"Sorry." He looked away.

"It's kind of nice. It's been a long time..."

"For what?"

"For a guy to look at me the way you've been doing."

"You're beautiful." He blurted. And I want you so bad it hurts, he thought but didn't say.

"And we're still lost." She smoothed her hands on the pale grey walls. "You said these are administrative tunnels. How do you know?"

He told her how he'd been on a behind-the-scenes tour of the Paris metro and had seen tunnels similar to these, but wider and with doorways and offices beyond. And how he'd gotten separated from the group and probably taken some wrong turns.

"How far underground are we?" she asked.

He rattled off the facts that he'd learned on the tour. "Probably as deep as 112 feet or 34.13 meters or the equivalent of ten stories. Does that help us?"

"I don't know. But I'm pretty sure I've been following this one tunnel. I haven't seen any forks. Have you?"

"No." He shook his head, pretending not to feel helpless at the blackout he must have had since he separated from the tour group.

"I think we should go back the way you came." She looked up at him expectantly.

"I think I got lost to be able to find you," he blurted.

"What?" Her eyes widened.

"You don't believe me."

"I don't know what to believe." She didn't look at him, then she huffed out a breath. "I do know this is a hard place to be lost in without a guide." Then she said, more to herself, "I need to use what I have."

"You mean what we have," he said.

She peered at him oddly. "Oh, right. I'm so used to being on my own—

"Maybe that's part of the problem."

"What problem? You don't know me at all."

"It's true. I don't know you. But we're here together. And we need to solve this, together." He gestured between them. "Then when we get above ground, you never have to see me again, and you can go your merry way, all by yourself."

She pursed her lips. "Let's go back the way you came then." She pivoted and marched away.

Josh scrubbed his face one more time, as if that would help, and followed her. He caught up within a pace. "Since we're down here together, we may as well get to know each other better, to pass the time." She acted like she didn't need anyone. That bugged him. People needed people. Life worked better that way. He had his dog, Sally, and his housemate and best friend, Liam, and good friend, Brett, and their other fraternity brother from their college days.

"We need to pay attention to where we are." She waved at the grey walls.

"Everything looks the same to me. That's probably why I got so turned around."

He glanced sideways at her. She had her lips pursed again. He was seeing she did that when she was upset, but didn't want to voice it. He let her stew for a moment as they kept walking in the direction in which he'd come.

At least he assumed it was. He couldn't remember much. But now that he was beside the beautiful Sarah, he felt calm and alert. But the walls were still grey with the evenly spaced lighting placed about seven feet above their heads. Little florescent squares. Suddenly they flickered and went off.

He froze. Not again.

Then the earth shook. He reached out for Sarah as she grabbed for him.

"What's happening" she whispered, fear in her voice.

"An earthquake. I think."

"WHAT? IN PARIS?" IT TOOK a few minutes, but finally her heart slowed, and she could think a little more clearly. But could see nothing. Not a thing.

"I didn't know Paris was known for earthquakes. Back home, yes, but not here." She willed her nerves to still, but couldn't stop the shaking in her voice. Perfectly natural response to stress, she reminded herself.

So was holding on to a man, apparently. She extricated herself from him. Even though her body protested at leaving his warmth, his strength, and the feel of his firm, muscled back under her hands—that may have roamed just a little. She couldn't help it. She winced at the cool air that slipped between them.

She swore. Josh chuckled.

She smiled reflexively. If he could be calm in these circumstances... she let the thought trail off. She didn't want to think about more, more of him, more of them, at all.

But of course, her heart sped up at the thought of what that more could be. And heat flared from her core. She was burning up. In the dark, she slipped off her coat, careful to keep Josh by her side, her shoulder rubbing against his arm. His strong capable arm. She brushed the thought aside, trying to keep still. Breathe, she reminded herself. There was a way out.

"Are you okay?" Josh asked. "You're muttering."

"Yes, of course. I'm fine. More than fine."

"We need to keep going." He brushed her hand with his and gripped it. "And we have to stay connected."

She nodded, finding his palm easily in the darkness, and then said yes out loud, when she realized he couldn't see her.

They continued forward.

He was right about needing to stay touching. She held on. As if they were meant to find each other. Reassuring. She didn't have to be in a panic. Perfectly natural to feel a little heart flutter and the irrational urge to crawl into his arms and stay there forever, where it was safe and warm, so warm.

"I can't see anything," she said in a whisper.

Josh cleared his throat as if to speak. She waited a beat, but he said nothing.

The tunnel was blacker than night. At least above ground, there'd be stars, or the moon, or ambient light reflecting off shining surfaces. Not here. Here was as black as some of the mountain caves she'd explored. She waved her hand in front of her face and saw nothing. Not even pinpricks of light the eye sometimes creates in pitch blackness.

"Me neither. But I smell something. Chestnuts. Can't you? Come on." He tugged on her hand, his footfalls pounding loudly ahead of her.

She shook her head, even though he couldn't see her, and took longer steps to keep up. She didn't smell chestnuts.

Warm air brushed against her cheeks. That had to mean there was vent ahead of them. They were heading in the right direction.

She didn't believe in fate, but in making your own luck. But maybe she'd been playing it safe in her life. The perfect job. Nice friends. Organized and structured adventures that tested her, yes, but since when had she even gone into something unprepared? She couldn't remember when. She didn't particularly like not being prepared, though.

"Hey," he said softly. "Euro penny for your thoughts?"

She squeezed his palm, reassured by the squeeze back. Just the squeeze made her feel warm in her chest. Warm all over.

"Yeah, I'm fine." She swallowed to get past the sudden stiffness of too much emotion welling up in her throat.

"Good," Josh said. "Let's keep one hand on the wall. That way we can sense if there is a curve."

"Right." She reached out. Under her fingertips, the smooth and cool surface of the wall calmed her.

They continued forward for a while in silence.

"Tell me about yourself," he said, his deep voice a soothing rumble through her body.

"I live in San Francisco."

"No kidding. I live in Oakland."

"Nice," she said inanely. Nerves jittered up and down her body, unsettling her.

Underground, alone with a man she wanted like crazy, unprepared for this moment, in a city she didn't know well, far from home and all that was safe and familiar.

"Tell me more," she said.

So he did. His warm voice relaxed her as he shared with her about his life in Oakland, his thriving yet struggling business, his love for Sally, his Bernese Mountain dog, and about his good buddies from college, fraternity brothers all, including Liam, his best friend and housemate.

She let his words flow over her like the warm ocean in Marina del Rey in Southern California where she liked to visit and relax. Her nerves and her breathing settled.

Her fingers bumped against something. She stopped. Even though it was still pitch black, she could swear she could see some faint light around her, like a light echo.

"Wait," she said. "There's something on the wall. There's some light too. But it's not helping."

"That doesn't make sense. I can't see anything. What is it?"

Warm air brushed her cheeks, confirming they were heading toward an air intake fan or grate. Which had to mean that they were nearing an exit, hopefully.

"Some kind of raised bumps. Like Braille. Wish we had a light. It's here, at about shoulder level." She tugged on his hand. "Give me your hand. I'll show you."

In a twist of arms and limbs, he ended up with an arm over her shoulder. She traced the bumps with his fingertips.

"What is it?" he said, his voice a rumble against her back. A shot of electricity speared straight to her core. Light headed, all she wanted to do was turn and pour herself into his arms, like a wild cat in heat.

"A code or a language or a short hand of some kind." She had to stay focused on getting out of here, right? Even though being right here with him felt good, like an itch to scratch, in a good way.

He hummed as he considered his words, the vibration of his hum rumbling straight to her center.

Heat flamed from her core. She gasped.

"Are you okay?" he whispered.

She needed some air. "Yeah." She slipped from under his arm, tracing the wall and the raised bumps. They felt directional and reminded her of something but she couldn't remember what. Something to do with a dream she had just before coming to Paris.

Josh gripped her shoulder. "Hey, don't get too far ahead."

"Keep up." Sarah felt pulled ahead by the message, a message saying essentially "Follow me. Come here." How could she know that? She didn't know Braille. She didn't think the raised bumps were Braille. There were lines and curves under her fingertips.

"Where are we going?"

"Can't you feel that warm air? There's got to be some kind of exit up ahead."

"Lead on, fair guide." Josh said, with a smile in his voice. "Hopefully there's light, a shot of something warm and alcoholic, a bed up ahead. I'm getting sleepy." He yawned.

"Sleepy? Wha—?" She yawned too. "Can't be more than the afternoon. Check your phone. Maybe we can get signal and time, and why didn't I think of it before?"

"I don't know." Josh's voice sounded slurred. The pressure on her shoulder from his hand was heavier than before.

"Josh?" she turned around just as his body slipped into her arms. He didn't answer her. She took a step back to catch his weight and stumbled on something.

Down she went, Josh on top of her.

"Josh!" she yawned again. Whatever overtook Josh got her too, as she slipped into the blackness of sleep.

"SARAH! WAKE UP!" JOSH sounded urgent.

"I'm awake." Sarah sat up, rubbing her eyes. Her hip hurt. She rubbed that too. But scrambled to her feet as soon as her gaze focused on the room, more like, cavern around her. Her heart pattered. "Where the hell are we?" she whispered. She wanted to keep her voice down because the cavern looked like some kind of temple, right out of one her girlfriend's Tarot cards—part Egyptian, part art deco, lots of gold embossing.

"I don't know," Josh whispered too. He turned in a slow circle, eyeing the room, and reached for her hand.

Just the warmth of his grip soothed and calmed her, like he was her elixir, making everything instantly better. Even though he looked like a mess, like she must. His hair was disheveled, his shirt pulled out of his pants, and tie undone and askew. His coat was off but his shoes were still on.

"Done taking inventory?" he said.

"Yes. You look okay, none worse for wear." Heat crept up her cheeks but she didn't break eye contact. A giddy swirl of emotion burst in her chest.

Then her stomach grumbled.

"And you don't look too bad yourself. "

"Stop staring at me."

"What you can dish it out but you can't take it?" he smiled.

"Yeah. Not until I've had my morning coffee. Why do I feel like I slept a full night? Weird."

Josh shrugged. "I do too. I feel fully rested. Yay, weird. Do you smell chestnuts? I don't ever want to leave here."

"You're babbling. We have to."

"Why?"

She ticked on the reasons on her fingers. "No shower. No food. No espresso. No toilet. And, oh yay, something made us sleep what feels like the whole night."

"There's that. And no cell reception."

"What?"

Josh was frowning at his cell phone.

"Then we really have to get out of here if we can't get cell reception."

He eyed her then finally cracked a smile at her joke. "I really go into withdrawal if I can't play my tower defense games, check my email, or get messages about my dog."

"So we're agreed."

"But don't you want to explore this room, cave-like place?"

"It's a cavern."

"And what do these symbols mean?"

She shrugged. "I don't know. But last night, or whenever that was when we fell asleep—"

"That was weird, right?"

"Yeah—"

"We didn't—" he gestured between them.

"What?"

"You know...sex."

Heat bloomed on her face. She glanced away, but really wanted to cozy up to him and stay there, like a cat curled up against its companion. Ever since she'd awakened in this cavern imbued with magical symbols that spoke to her out of the edge of her awareness, she wanted to unlock the space's secrets and just be with Josh. She wasn't worried or scared, even though maybe she should be.

"I take it by your silence that you're embarrassed by the idea of ever being with me, so just forget it. Forget I said anything."

"No. I can't," she said a little too quickly.

He gazed at her with a look of yearning and hope. She stepped toward him, eyeing his lips. Suddenly she tripped on something, her ankle twisting a little. She sucked in her breath.

He was there to catch her before she hit the mosaic floor and did more damage to her ankle. "What is that?"

"What?" she pivoted on her good foot.

He stared at the ground.

She looked down at the outline of a huge paw print, three front claws and one back one, at least seven feet square. "Impossible," she whispered.

"What?"

"Nothing can be that big."

"A footprint."

"It's got to be a hoax, a piece of art."

"What do you think it was? The thing that went with that footprint."

Sarah scanned the cavern, letting herself take in the imagery on the walls, the ceiling, and the floor. The patterns, swirls and curves, a tree of life symbol she recognized, those dots she'd felt on the wall, sorted themselves into words, floating before her eyes. She shook her head. "Can't be."

"What?"

"I can understand it."

"And I can smell chestnuts and want us to stay like this." He stepped to her until his body was inches from hers. "What do you understand?" Urgency laced his voice.

"We're in a dragon's lair." She swiveled to survey the mysterious cavern. She could read the walls. With awe, she read what she saw. "It says, 'A love so great can't be lost. Do the impossible and bring her back to me.' "

Josh gasped.

She turned to him. He was pale.

"We have to get out of here," he said.

"But you just said—"

He gripped her arms. "I know. I think this place is making me crazy."

"So you don't want me like crazy," she tried to say in a joking voice.

"No, I do. It's just..." He gazed at her.

"The grief is too much," she whispered, drawn to him. "I feel it too, hovering on the edge."

"Come on." Josh grabbed her hand and headed toward a wall, as if that would somehow find him a door.

"No, this way." Sarah stopped him. "I can read the walls, remember?"

"I remember. Lead on, Pocahontas."

She pulled him in the opposite direction where the signs spoke of the heart of the city and of Our Lady of Blue. That made her think of Notre Dame, the cathedral at the center of the city. She'd read somewhere that Lady of Blue was another name for Mother Mary, Our Lady, or Notre Dame, in French.

That had to be her way out, her strange knowledge of the room told her. She had to trust the impossible, at least for now, especially if it led them out.

She led Josh into a darkened corridor that smelled musty and dry, like sandstone or heated vents, very different from the hallways they'd traveled in the night before, where, she realized, she hadn't smelled anything. "I think we're close."

"To what?"

"An exit."

Just as they arrived at an old barred gate and swung it open, the ground shook and something crashed behind them. It sounded like thunder.

She hugged Josh and he was right there hugging her back. She pulled away.

"Up ahead..." she said. "Come on."

She let go of Josh's hand and took the lead. The corridor was only wide enough to go single file. She pushed through another metal barred gate, this one shiny and new looking, up a series of cement stairs and into a low-ceilinged room that faded into shadow. Or was it a hallway? Glass paneling covered one wall, grey stone on the other.

"The archaeological crypt near the cathedral," Josh said. "You got us to a place I know." He hugged her again.

She hugged back, so glad to be in the real world.

"Josh?"

"Mmmm?"

"You can let go now."

"Why? Oh." He stepped back and gazed into her eyes, as if he wanted to devour her.

She gulped.

"Want to get—" He looked at his phone, and then smiled broadly at her. "Breakfast? I know a great place that serves excellent croissants and espresso at this lovely hour of 7 am."

"Only every good cafe in Paris."

"But this one is really good and it's only across the street. And not in a crazy tunnel under the city."

"Can't bear to be apart from me, huh?" She smirked.

"That's right. Come on." He winked.

Sarah hesitated, but only for a split second. She didn't want to be apart from him and wanted to understand what the hell had happened to them. Was it even real?

"Lead on," she said. "I'm not letting you out of my sight."

"Promise?" she thought she heard him say as they jogged up the steps and into the pouring rain.

JOSH TAPPED ON HIS smart phone. "Nothing, I got nothing."

Even out of the tunnels, just sitting in the cafe, he wanted her, and not just for a wonderful turn in the sheets. He wanted more. Well, that would lead to nothing good.

"What do you mean?" she asked.

He gazed up at her, her eyes wide with curiosity. Was all that interest in him or their mystery? Wish it were him. But he couldn't be sure.

She bit into her croissant, chewed, and sighed with delight. The she leaned toward him over the round marble table, licking at the crumbs on her lips.

He reached over and swiped a crumb off the side of her mouth and ate it.

"Hey, I wanted that," she said, frowning.

"Well, it's mine now."

She quirked her mouth up in a half-smile.

His heart thudded in his chest and he shifted in his seat to try to make room in his pants for his rising desire for her. He fought the urge to reach out and grab her hand. He remembered how warm and firm her grip was when they were in the tunnels. That, he did remember. But there were gaps in his memory from his time in the grey underground.

"So what do you mean? Looking for secrets on your super duper smart phone?" Sarah's words jolted him out of his ruminations.

"Yeah, I was searching for info about the cavern and the tunnel and found nothing. Except—it's weird—"

"Well. What? You've been staring at your screen for ages not talking."

"Oh." He sipped his espresso. It was cold. Guess he had zoned out there for a second. So many weird things. He blew out a breath and had the urge to pace. "I found someone who could maybe help us."

"In the city?"

"Yeah, in the Montmartre neighborhood. Big white cathedral."

"I know where that is." Sarah shot to her feet and slipped on her coat. "Let's go. But first I need to stop by my hotel and pick up a few things. Maybe you should go to your hotel. You know, take a shower..."

"Wait. Yeah. A shower. Hey, are you saying I smell? What about you? Maybe we can take a shower together."

"That's an idea," she said and smiled at him, but didn't sit.

He needed to adjust himself again. Good thing he still was sitting.

Josh tapped on his phone to distract himself. "I have to check my email and see if there is any meeting follow ups. Plus I have to give a presentation later today. I'm ready. I just need to review my notes one more time."

"I need to go, Josh."

Her voice had sadness in it.

He gazed up at her. "What's wrong?"

"Nothing. I just need to figure out what I'm doing for the rest of my week in Paris. I want to work here, I think. I just have some thinking to do." She smiled in a bright but polite way. She was hiding her true self from him. She wasn't the warm, intense woman he'd come to enjoy while being lost in the tunnels.

Nothing, my ass. Something was going on with her and he wanted to know what. He wanted to know everything about her.

He was falling hard. No good could come of it.

But then he blurted, "Come to my presentation at 4 pm."

What was said was said. He couldn't take it back. He didn't want to take it back.

She gazed outside at the pouring rain that seemed to be coming down harder than just five minutes ago. "Sure." She finally nodded.

Relief settled in his chest. He breathed out. "Oh, what about this place in Montmartre?" he checked his phone. "It's a museum. Doesn't open until 10 am."

"I'll meet you there," she said quickly and stepped out into the rain.

Through the pounding rain, he hustled back to his room for a shower—alone—and a change of clothes.

He could just be himself with her. She wasn't trying to control his career or his every move, as he realized Melanie had.

Being with Sarah brought constant surprise and adventure.

He'd let Melanie run his life. Well, he was in charge now. Eyes wide open.

Together he and Sarah would get to the bottom of the mystery of the tunnels.

He could give Sarah and him a chance, if she would.

SARAH RUSHED ACROSS THE bridges from the Left Bank to Right Bank, and clipped the blocks to her hotel, nestled behind the church St. Eustache at Les Halles. The rain pelted her. Her coat, hat, and boats were completely waterlogged. Not many people were out on the streets, but those that were had their shoulders hunched and heads down. It was brutal weather.

What was happening between her and Josh? Even as she let herself into her hotel room on the second floor, third floor in the French way of counting, she wanted to be with him. A pull on her whole body and an inner voice pleading with her that she shouldn't let that man out of her sight. That he was the best thing that ever happened to her.

She stripped out of wet things and hopped in the shower. Couldn't be. He couldn't be the best thing that had ever happened to her. No man could. She was an independent woman who thought for herself. She didn't need a man to be happy. Her mother had cried herself to sleep for weeks and weeks after her father had left them. That would never be her. All that grief. For what?

In fifteen minutes, she was out of the shower, dressed in her sensible clothes, and stuffing her bag with the practical items one might need walking across the city. She checked the time. It was only 8 am.

There were still two hours until she agreed to meet Josh. Her heart sped up at the thought of seeing him again.

She hadn't gotten this giddy over a man since—never. The last time she'd seriously crushed on a guy was Tony Azevdo her senior year of high school. But she'd broken it off before she went to college at USC in Los Angeles and he went to the community college in Vallejo.

This wasn't a crush. No, it was something much more. But when she saw him again, she'd let him know—just as she had all those other guys—that their lives were going in two separate directions. She would let him down easy. Politely. Like she'd done with all the others. Satisfied with her decision, she opened her laptop to check her email.

She clicked on the one from her assistant, Molly, who was covering her job while she was on vacation. And sat back in shock as she reread the note:

> *So sorry, Sarah, about what happened. Mr. R*
> *leaving a voicemail like that. Call me if you need*
> *to talk.*

What message? With shaking hands, she used her phone card to call and check her voicemail. Mr. Rodriguez gruff voice rumbled on her voicemail:

> *Ms. Redman, we're sorry to inform you that you*
> *have been let go. The corporate office wanted me*
> *to let you know. I'm sure the severance package*
> *the company has offered will suit your needs. It's*
> *on your desk and emailed to your intranet*

account. No need to call while you are away.
Please visit my office first thing Monday morning
next week to sign the paperwork. Good-bye.

That was it. No personal message. No "good luck" and a repeat of "we're so sorry. I'm so sorry." An about-face from the man she'd called her boss for the last 3 years. He'd always been cordial and friendly to her, always asking after her well being in an old-world avuncular way. What was going on? Why was she so suddenly fired? She racked her brain, but could come up with no explanation.

She closed her phone and sat on the hotel bed in a daze, not moving for many minutes. The pounding of the rain on the window startled her out of her daze. Then there was a loud boom, like a cannon going off. She jumped before she realized it was probably thunder quite close. A flash of light blinded her for a second. She could swear the lightning strike was right outside her hotel.

She rushed to the window, but couldn't see much through the sheeted rain. Another boom sounded. The ground shook.

Bizarre violent weather. She opened her laptop and searched for news of Paris weather on the English news sites. She scanned the headlines. They reported the massive storm, but no mentions of earthquakes.

She breathed out, waiting for her nerves to calm. Maybe she imagined the quake.

Her thoughts went to Josh. Stupid, she knew. But if there was going to be a massive storm, and she was stranded in a city where she knew no one, then she wanted to be with Josh.

She scolded herself for that schoolgirl desire. It would be a smarter move to hunker down and set up job interviews, since now she really needed a job. She shoved Josh out of her mind, the rain too, and tapped away online. She had some contacts in the banking industry—she'd just refreshed her resume, after all. She sent out some emails and resumes in San Francisco. But because of the time difference, it was nighttime in the city by the bay, so she'd have to wait until the evening to see if there were any responses. She had some banking contacts in Paris and London. That was how she'd found the first job that fell through. She sent off a few resumes to the international branches she knew. Now that the shock had worn off a little, she sent an email off to Molly and a super polite one to her boss, or former boss, now. Then she repacked her day backpack. And checked her email again. No replies from anyone.

If she wanted to walk to Montmartre, she had to get an umbrella and get started. According to her estimate, the walk would take an hour. She shut her laptop, straightened up her hotel room, and left.

That would be enough time to figure out her life, she thought. Not.

Sarah stepped outside of the hotel and got drenched. She hailed a cab.

She arrived at the museum in thirty minutes. She was early, so slipped into a small brasserie bar across the street to wait. She ordered an espresso and sat at a table by the window. The small museum entrance was shuttered. It sat between a patisserie and a small clothing boutique.

So no Josh. She was disappointed, even though she was early, and there was no reason to have any hopes of anything real happening between them. What they had between them couldn't be real. It seemed as if they were being influenced by things they couldn't see. Then there was the intense storm that only seemed to get worse. She didn't mind the elements, liked the storm even, but the weather was extreme. There had to be a reason. Cause and effect. She'd always believed that.

She didn't believe in omens. Or magic.

She tapped her fingers on the table. What was she going to do with her life? No job. No love. At loose ends. In a foreign country, far away from all that was familiar. The adventure she wanted, right?

She couldn't believe that she'd been let go from her job. She'd have to call Molly when it was morning there—in nine hours—and find out what happened. She clenched her fists. She'd always done good work. Her vacation had been scheduled for months.

"Hey."

She startled. Her heart sped up. She gazed up, frozen for a split second by her instant desire for him. Then she found her voice. "Josh. Finally."

He sat and ordered in French from the waiter who was suddenly there.

The brasserie was quiet. Only two people sat hunched over their espressos at the bar. She and Josh were the only other customers.

"You ready to get to the bottom of this," Josh asked.

"What?" she asked inanely.

Josh leaned toward her. "The mystery in the tunnels."

"Oh." She was hoping he'd say that he wanted to get to the bottom of their relationship.

He crossed his arms and leaned back, checking his watch. "I need to get something to warm me up, then we'll go into that museum and learn what we can." He didn't make eye contact with her, his jaw set hard.

"Look," she softened her tone. "I—I—don't know what to say."

"Then don't say anything." Josh tapped on his smart phone for a while and drank his coffee without looking up at her.

"Tell me about this museum," Sarah said gently. She wanted to break this odd tension between them. "We may as well work together at least."

"FINE," JOSH BIT OUT, more angry at himself than her.

It wasn't her fault that he fell hard and fast for women, this woman in particular, harder and faster than he could remember.

He couldn't afford to be distracted from his company for too long, even though Sarah was nothing like Melanie. She wasn't trying to get into his business and yet still showed an interest in him.

He felt her piercing focused gaze on him, as if she took in all of him. There she was with her ready-to-go attitude and her sheer presence of being. And her body too. He puffed out a breath.

"Well?" she prompted.

He glared at his phone one more time as if it could absorb his frustration, set the phone down, and met her gaze neutrally. "It's called La Musée des Petites Choses—the museum of little things—and focuses on the tales, legends, and hearsay about Paris and other parts of France. But mostly Paris."

She nodded and stared across the street. "That's interesting. Local lore can reveal a lot about a place and also the culture that comes up with the tales."

"Sounds like you know what you're talking about." He studied her profile, her smooth skin, her lips ready for kissing. His crotch tightened.

"Only indirectly. I studied folklore and sayings in college doing my psychology degree."

"Hmmm. You're more than meets the eye, Sarah Redman," he said softly.

She smiled at him, her cheeks reddening. "I know."

He glanced at his phone, so he wouldn't be caught staring at her pretty blush. "It says here that the curator, a Monsieur Lefevre, has been running the museum for over fifty years."

"We should go." Sarah stood and shouldered into her coat, before he had a chance to help her into it.

He was surprised at the strong urge to help her, to be there for her. With Melanie, she'd expected to be served, so he had, like an idiot. But that was over.

With Sarah he wanted to take care of her, show her he was there for her, in any way she needed. Her mix of strength and self-sufficiency and her passion for adventure drew him in.

Merde, as the French liked to say. He'd fallen for her in less than a day.

He slipped into his coat and followed her outside.

The rain still hadn't let up. He stood beside Sarah, shoulder to shoulder, feeling her body warmth.

"Ready?" he asked.

"Yeah, okay. Sure." She just stood there, gazing across the street. Finally she spoke. "This visit will tell us about what we saw in the tunnels, explain that cavern, right?"

"If anyone can, Monsieur Lefevre should be able to. If not him, we'll keep searching. We'll get to the bottom of what happened to us in the tunnels and to what we saw in the cavern. But we need to hurry it up because I have to give my presentation this afternoon, and need to get there by 4 o'clock. That's in—" He checked his phone for the time. "Six hours. We should have enough time."

We'd better, he thought. But deep down, he knew he'd be there, with Sarah, for however long it took. Was he crazy?

She didn't move or smile, just gazed straight ahead.

"You alright?"

"I just lost my job," she blurted out.

"I am so sorry." Josh turned to her, wanting to comfort her.

But she stood tall, shoulders back, staring across the street toward the museum. She didn't look like she needed any comforting. He kept his hands in his pockets.

She said nothing.

He grabbed her umbrella from her and opened the monstrous thing. The rain pounded the sidewalks and the street. He had to break this stalemate and get them moving. He slipped his arm in hers. She didn't protest.

"Let's go," he said and led her across the crosswalk and to the front of museum.

Cars rushed by. Lots of taxis. Lots of honking.

Even though it was few minutes after 10 am, the closed sign hung behind the glass door. He peeked through the windows, barred and dusty. Nobody moved about within. No lights were on, but he could make out display cases filled with small objects hidden in shadow.

"Call the museum," Sarah said.

"Good idea." He unhooked his arm from hers and missed her warmth instantly.

Maybe with her he could find lasting happiness. He didn't want to be single for the rest of his life—he wanted love, partnership, and maybe one day, a family.

He shoved that thought aside and punched in the numbers displayed on the door sign. After a few rings, a recording picked up stating the hours. According to those hours, the museum should be open. He frowned and was about to hang up, when a male voice came on the line with a quick, "Bonjour."

Josh quickly replied in French, asking to speak to Monsieur Lefevre.

"Yes, it is I," the man replied in French.

"We're out front and would like to visit the museum," Josh said.

"That is you with the beautiful woman out front?"

He must be looking out his window.

"Yes."

"Good. I will let you in."

"Thank you."

"But first you must do something for me. A quest, if you will."

"A quest?"

"Yes."

"What is it?" Sarah whispered.

"He wants us to go on a quest," Josh whispered to Sarah in English.

"What? Why?" She whispered back.

"I don't know. Hold on. I'll ask him." Josh spoke back into the phone. "Monsieur Lefevre, why do you want us to go on this quest? The beautiful woman beside me wants to know." He smiled.

"Good that you think she's beautiful. That is the first step," Monsieur Lefevre said.

"First step of what?" Josh asked.

"Now what kind of question is that, young man? It's a quest. And in quests you must do what you must. That's how it works. That is how quests always work. Taking this quest is the second step. Now here is what you must do."

"Steps to what?" Josh asked, but Monsieur Lefevre rattled off what the quest involved, then hung up without an answer or a good-bye.

"HE WANTS US TO BUY him fruit and croissants, a baguette, a pâté spread, and salad?" Sarah asked. "Why?"

"He wouldn't tell me why. Except to say that is how quests work. I guess he means in the fairy tales. Doing tasks—"

"As if we are in a fairy tale." She snorted, interrupting Josh. "Life is not a fairy tale. There's no such thing as happily ever after."

"For you, you mean. I want mine." He smirked and winked at her, as if this was all some big game. "Come on." Josh headed down the street.

Sarah followed. What else was she going to do? And since when did she sound like such a sour puss? She never thought she would have a loveless and single life. Now she was single, jobless, and had the hots for a guy she barely knew, racing around the most romantic city on earth, turning shopping for food into a quest. But right now the city had to be the soggiest. With no fairy tale ending in sight. She didn't believe in one anyway. Never had.

They gathered the requested provisions at the boulangerie—the bread shop, then to the pâtisserie, a kind of store just for pastries. She had to pull Josh away from the place. He wanted to ooh and ahh over the éclairs. They headed for the meat shop, the charcuterie, where they got the duck pâté, and the salad, a kind of celery root salad, apparently. At a little corner grocery store, they picked up some winter fruit—small apples and dried figs.

"If it wasn't such horrible weather, we could have a picnic on the steps of the Sacré-Cœur Basilica and forget all this nonsense about underground caverns and strange tunnels," Josh said with a smile.

"But we need to solve this mystery."

"Which one?"

"What do you mean?" She shook her head. "The tunnels. How we got lost. And that amazing cavern. That footprint. And how I could read the walls..." Her dreams too about the crying dragon. "And the weird sleepiness too we both seemed to experience."

"Not the mystery of us?" he asked, with a laugh in his voice.

She glanced at him as they walked up the hill back toward the museum, protecting their wares under her umbrella. She heated up at the thought of them, but shook her head and spoke. "Josh, there can be no us."

AS THEY APPROACHED THE museum, Josh grabbed the groceries from her. "I'll carry those."

"I'm perfectly capable."

"I know you are. I'm not questioning your capability." He moved his arms out of the way as she reached for the groceries.

She stalked ahead of him, carrying the large umbrella with her.

He hurried to catch up to stay out of the rain. Then they were at the museum entrance. The signage had change to show the "*ouvert*" or open sign. He pushed his way in.

As he stepped into the museum, Sarah right behind him, a bell tinkled.

"Monsieur Lefevre," Josh called out, when no one appeared right away.

The small space smelled of dust and cleanser and something else. He inhaled deeply but couldn't name the last odor. Silence pressed heavily in the one-room museum. He didn't even see signage about prices, but pulled out a ten-euro bill and placed it on the counter nearest him. The waist-high glass counters held knick-knacks on faded cushions. A glass case on the far wall displayed photographs, books, and statuary the size of sports trophies.

"Come on," he said. "Let's look around."

But Sarah was already strolling around the room, examining objects in the cases.

He was about to follow her and set down the groceries on the glass case when a voice boomed out in French ordering him to not put the bag on the case.

He pivoted. There was a white-haired old man standing at a doorway across the room. He looked a bit like Einstein with his big hair sticking outward in every direction. He was a petite man, dressed in a bright red fancy vest, a watch fob looping from a button into a pocket. Finishing the bright costume were green suspenders over a blue shirt, pressed grey slacks, and shiny black shoes, and a black bow tie at the neck.

Josh held out his hand. "Monsieur Lefevre, I presume."

The museum proprietor nodded curtly. "Bring your young woman, the provisions, and follow me." With that he turned, letting a curtain fall.

"Sarah—" He turned to her.

"You think he's harmless?" she asked.

"With that getup, and us having pastries for weapons, I think we're fine."

She smiled and waved him forward.

Josh carried the bag of provisions, brushed past a curtain, and stepped into a foyer. A wooden staircase led upwards and also downwards. In the few minutes he'd delayed, he'd lost the old man.

Sarah folded the umbrella and stuck it in the corner to drip, then trotted up the stairs. "Maybe this way."

"How do you know?" he asked, following her.

"I don't know." She stopped at the top of the stairs. "But it seems familiar to me."

He took the stairs up. Three doors led off the carpeted first-floor landing.

A door opened and Monsieur Lefevre stuck his head out. "Come on then. It's about time." He shook his head and stepped away from the door.

Sarah headed into the apartment without hesitation and introduced herself in clumsy French. "Je m'appelle Sarah Redman."

Monsieur Lefevre nodded, grasped her outstretched hand, and bowed over it, as if he were about to kiss it.

Got to admire her guts. Sarah wasn't afraid to step into new adventures. He liked that about her. Maybe there was hope for them, after all. Maybe she'd put up with how much he worked to keep his tiny company afloat. Maybe she'd go on more adventures with him. Josh followed her and stood in a tiny entryway. He was ready to give them a chance.

"Close the door, young man," Monsieur Lefevre said in French. Then to himself he muttered. "Where have manners fled to of today's youth?"

"Where would you like me to put these?" Josh asked in French, gesturing with the bag of goods.

Monsieur Lefevre called out, "In the kitchen."

From the entryway of the apartment, Josh took three steps and arrived in a tiny box kitchen. He left the bag on the small counter space.

"Very good, young man." Monsieur Lefevre bustled in. "Now go sit with your young woman while I get lunch ready. Or is it breakfast? I can never tell these days. One bleeds into the other." But he wasn't looking to Josh for an answer, so Josh did as he was requested and left the kitchen to find Sarah.

She was seated at a small—like everything else—round table, cleared except for a bowl of chestnuts. He sat and immediately picked up a chestnut. It was smooth and reassuring to the touch. Deep brown, it spoke of winter nights and warm fires. He inhaled and sat up with a start. He felt a little dizzy. Fragments of being lost in the tunnels, grief coursing through him, and the strong smell of roasting chestnuts flashed through him. The same strong smell of chestnuts he smelled now.

"What is it?" Sarah asked.

He'd felt her gaze on him, but hadn't wanted to look up at her until now.

"Are you okay?" she asked.

"Yes, why?"

"You gasped and—" She glanced away as if she were embarrassed to have caught him in something. "You look pale, and—I don't know—the only word that comes to me is 'stricken,' like with a loss ... of the heart." She spoke haltingly. Then waved the air, as if waving away all her silly words.

"Can you smell it?" he whispered, keeping himself still.

"What?"

"Chestnuts roasting. These—" He held up the chestnut. "Roasting on the fire." He looked around but saw no fireplace. "Ever since I walked into the museum. But I just realized it. Same as in the tunnels..."

Sarah shook her head. "I don't smell anything." She eyed him with concern. "I remember you said something about chestnuts when we were in the tunnels. I wonder how it's related. If it's related."

Josh shrugged. She was leaning in to him across the table, her hands clasped.

He reached out and touched her hands. "So glad you're here with me." Just touching her lessened the sadness some, brought him back to reality, with her. But he still smelled a faint wisp roasting chestnuts.

She nodded and didn't move her hands from his. Thank goodness.

"We need to find out what's going on. Do you think Monsieur Lefevre can help us? I know I already asked this—"

Before he could reassure her, the man himself bustled in carrying a full tray. Josh jumped up to help him, but it looked like the old man didn't need his help because he set the tray down on the table without a wobble.

"Sit," Monsieur Lefevre ordered.

He waited until Josh sat, then served Sarah first, then served Josh a plate with a bit of everything: pastries, salad, pâté, fruit, and cheese. A pungent Brie by the smell of it.

Josh nodded his thanks.

Lastly, Monsieur Lefevre served himself and sat.

"Eat," he said in French, and motioned to Sarah the universal gesture of eating.

"*Monsieur, je voudrais*—" Sarah started to say, "I would like" in French. She turned to Josh. "How do I say 'I'd like to know the story of the cavern in the tunnels'?"

Josh said the phrase in French and Sarah tried it in stumbling French, but Monsieur Lefevre ignored her. In fact, he stood and bustled back to the kitchen. He returned a moment later with a coffee, its strong aroma filling the room, almost nudging out the chestnuts Josh still smelled. Monsieur Lefevre poured for them into tiny cups and set them in the middle of the small table. Then he sat and resumed eating.

Sarah asked again in her clumsy French that she would like to know the story of the cavern. This time Monsieur Lefevre put a finger to his lips and mimed eating.

"Oh. You want us to eat first. Okay." She nodded.

For a few moments, everyone ate and drank in silence. Both Sarah and Josh were finished before their host. Sarah crossed her legs, and then crossed them the other way, examining the small dining area combined with a living room. Josh rubbed the chestnut and stared out the window into the driving rain. The heavens must be crying, he thought.

He didn't realize he'd spoken aloud until Sarah said, "What?"

"What?" Josh said.

"You said something in French. You sounded so sad."

"You are right, young man," Monsieur Lefevre interjected. "The heavens are crying, but that is not all. I presume you are here about the tale."

"What is he saying?" Sarah asked. So Josh translated.

"Yes, if the tale explains our experience," Sarah said to Monsieur Lefevre.

Monsieur Lefevre grabbed her hand in his and peered into her eyes. She stilled and let him look.

After a moment, he smiled. "*Vous êtes très belle, ma chère. Oui, je vais raconter l'histoire.*"

"What did he say?" she asked.

"Just say, thanks," Josh said. "He says that you are very beautiful and that he'll tell you the story."

"Merci, Monsieur Lefevre," Sarah said, nodding her head respectfully.

The museum curator kissed the back of Sarah's hand and sat. He patted his lips with a handkerchief, folded the cloth carefully, and replaced it back into his vest pocket.

THE STORY WAS FANTASTICAL, a tale so beyond her life experience as to exist only in the world of children's tales and dreams. But the tale was fascinating, so she leaned in and listened as Josh's voice rumbled in English between Monsieur Lefevre's pauses.

The story tugged at her heart, as the rain poured all over the city, and while she was holed up in a cozy Parisian apartment at the top of the Montmartre with a man she barely knew, but wanted, badly.

She snuck a glance at Josh. Smart, talented, driven, fun—she liked him too. Her heart sped up. Oh dear. She tore her gaze from him and put her attention on Monsieur Lefevre.

As Sarah watched Monsieur Lefevre tell the story in a sort of singsong French, she realized the man looked at once very old and also ageless, timeless, like one of the gnomes in the big gnome book she pored over as a child.

Monsieur Lefevre told of a young man who harvested chestnuts in the orchards beyond the city walls, roasted them, and then sold them as a peddler throughout the city.

Josh inhaled a sharp breath at this.

Monsieur Lefevre paused and nodded to Josh.

Sarah reached out for Josh's hand across the table and squeezed. The chestnut connection. He clasped her hand in his. Tingles of desire shivered up her arm and through her body. She breathed out to relieve some of the pressure of desire mounting inside and focused on Josh's words as he interpreted Monsieur Lefevre's tale.

Monsieur Lefevre smiled at her knowingly, as if he knew the secrets of her heart even better than she did, and continued. He shared about how one day this young man had met a lovely young woman outside an impressive gate, and the two began to court each other. She would not reveal her true name, and so neither did he. Instead they made up silly names for each other and changed them occasionally as the mood suited.

They fell deeper and deeper in love with each other with each passing day, spending all their spare time together, usually at the young man's humble abode, outside the city walls, in the chestnut grove.

One day the young maiden didn't show up. After a sleepless and restless night, the young lover went looking for her. The first place he went was the impressive gate where he'd met her. The gate belonged to a powerful baron, a member of the landed class. The young man asked at the gate and found out that his girl was indeed the daughter of the powerful baron who lived there. He wanted to storm inside and demand to see his love, but the servants at the gate convinced him that they could only pass a message to her for him. So he made the servant memorize the message to come meet him the next day at the special place they always met. He didn't want to reveal specifics. He was sure she would know the place.

That night he waited in the chestnut grove, roasting chestnuts and waiting for his ladylove.

But she never came.

The next morning he disguised himself the best he could into a person of means and got announced into the baron's estate. He used one of the silly names he'd made up with his love and the ruse worked.

He was announced into the hall and requested to see the young mistress of the house, that he'd heard of her beauty in his faraway land and wanted to marry this fair maiden.

The powerful baron was pleased and called for his daughter, calling her by her real name in front of her disguised lover.

The young man took that as a good sign that all would work out for him and his ladylove.

Finally, the daughter descended the staircase, regally, head held high, a shine in her eyes. By luck and by love, the two lovers would be reunited after all, she thought.

There in front of the powerful baron's court, the two lovers were reunited, at least in their gaze. A rosy bloom of excitement jumped into her cheeks. The young lover puffed his chest out in pride.

But the powerful baron was wily as a fox and saw how the two young people acted already in love, and he grew suspicious. He demanded to know the truth of their connection.

The two lovers denied ever meeting each other before, but their denials were forced. Anyone who was there could see that the two young people were drawn to each other like the bee to the rose.

The more the baron pressed, the more they denied it, until the powerful baron threatened the pain of death upon the young man, and the threat of banishment to a faraway kingdom and marriage to another baron's son for his daughter, unless the truth be revealed.

Then the two lovers knew the hoax was up. They flew into each other's arms, in grief and in pain, at the truth that lay just under the surface.

Because no matter what they did or what they said, the powerful baron would always keep them apart because he would not, could not, allow their love, once the baron knew the truth of the young man's circumstances—that he was just a lowly chestnut seller.

The old man paused again in his story telling and gazed out the window. The rain pounded against the small dining room window.

Sarah followed his gazed. The grey rooftops of the city spread out beneath them, barely visible through the sheets and sheets of rain.

When Monsieur Lefevre didn't resume the story right away, Sarah lifted an eyebrow at Josh in question. Josh shook his head, apparently not wanting to interrupt the elderly man's reverie.

The quiet of the room pressed on her. She wanted to know what happened. She wanted to relieve the sadness that pressed on her chest, a sadness that was as palpable as it was unexplainable. She slipped her hands from Josh's and was about to stand to meander the room when Monsieur Lefevre finally spoke.

Sarah sat at his next words in heavily accented English.

"A love so great can't be lost."

She stared at the old man, then at Josh.

Josh was pale and spoke in French to Monsieur Lefevre.

The old man shook his head and replied in rapid French.

Sarah shot Josh a questioning look for a translation, then turned to Monsieur Lefevre and asked, "So, you do speak English?"

"No, he doesn't," Josh said. "Just that line. Not sure why."

"Can you ask him to continue?"

"I just did." Josh reached his hand out to hers across the table and whispered. "This is all too strange. I don't know what to think."

Sarah took his hand. His palm's warmth was calming. "What I wonder is what does his story have to do with us? With the tunnels? With the cavern?"

Monsieur Lefevre patted their joined hands and nodded, smiling and spoke.

"He says his job here is done," Josh said, eyebrows raised in confusion. "But there's more—"

"What do you mean 'done'? Are you sure? But what happened to the man? And what about the cavern and getting lost in the tunnels? What do you mean, 'there's more'?" Sarah asked, tugging her hand away from Josh's. She stood, impatient.

"Sit down," Josh said.

Monsieur Lefevre ignored her outburst and scurried off without a word. He returned a minute later with a big book in his hands. Then rattled off in French in an excited tone, regarding them with shiny eyes.

Josh replied, frowning, and shook his head.

"What?" Sarah asked.

"He thinks you can read this."

Monsieur Lefevre didn't reply, but handed the large book to Sarah, glaring at her. He stalked to the kitchen.

"What did I do? What was that about?"

"He thinks we're meant to be together and we have to recite some words to stop the curse and fall in love before the week's end. Or else. I think that's what he said." Josh shook his head and frowned.

"Or else what?" She set the book in her lap, so that it wouldn't get any food crumbs on it.

"Or the city will self-destruct under the dragon's sorrow," Josh said softly and gazed out the window, his shoulders slumped.

The rain pounding against the windows increased.

"Oh."

Magic or no magic, fairy tale ending or not, she didn't expect to hear that.

As if to underscore the gravity of Josh's words, lightning flashed and thunder boomed in quick succession. Then the building shook. High-pitched alarms went off outside, eerie screaming wails that got her heart pumping.

Monsieur Lefevre spoke calmly from the kitchen, as if he was used to the sirens. Josh turned to her and said, "He says those are old air raid sirens, located throughout the city, leftover from World War II."

"We've got to turn on the news," Sarah said. "Ask him. To turn on the radio. Or the TV."

Josh asked Monsieur Lefevre, but the elderly man shook his head and said a few words.

"He says that it's the curse."

The sirens ended.

JOSH PULLED OUT HIS smart phone and checked his go-to sources for news, some in English and some in French. All he saw were reports of flooding, odd alarms, and the strange reports of isolated earthquakes in Paris that weren't actually quakes as far as the scientists could tell.

He reported his findings to Sarah who was staring at the large book in her hands.

Monsieur Lefevre must have bustled off somewhere while he was checking his phone.

Sarah seemed lost in thought, frozen in her own world. How could he reach her, touch her heart, draw her out? He did want that—so much.

It was time he gave love another chance—eyes wide open, this time.

He held his hands out to her. "Give me the book. There has to be something in there that can help us."

Sarah handed it over without a word and gazed out the window. He wanted to know what was going through her mind, but she seemed distant, unreachable. Would she ever truly let him in?

He placed the tome in his lap and made to open it, but the cover wouldn't budge. It was as if the book was glued shut. He examined the jagged edges of the pages. It looked like a real book. He sniffed it. It smelled musty and like old paper.

"What are you doing?" Sarah asked.

"I can't get the book open."

"Weird. Let me try."

Josh handed her the book.

Sarah flipped open the cover without a hitch. "Weird." She shut it again and sucked in a breath.

"What is it?"

"The cover. I can read it."

He glanced at it but couldn't decipher the language or the lettering. "Well, what does it say?"

"It says, 'The Retellings of the Dragon Elsevier and How He Became and His Undoing, as reported to the jester of the realm in the year of our Lord—' " She peered at him and then down at the book. "This can't be right."

"What?"

"It says in the year of our Lord, 952."

"952? How could that be?"

"I don't know." She stood and handed him the book. "Josh, I don't have any idea what's going on. But I need to get out of here." She gazed around the quaint apartment wide-eyed.

He stood, hugging the book at his chest. "You okay?"

"No." Sarah padded to the other side of the living room and returned, stopping here and there to examine the objects on the bookcases and shelves. Monsieur Lefevre still hadn't come back.

He waited. Maybe she'd open up if he were quiet and open to her. Her restlessness reminded him of his own need to run when he was frustrated or needed time to think.

So he waited and watched her wander through the small space, her gorgeous dark hair swaying with her steps. Her hips swaying too. He wanted to mold his hands on her body and pull her close and feel his lips against his again. So soft, so kissable, as if the world's answer could be found in their passion. In their connection.

A whiff of chestnuts flared. He gulped. Some sort of magic was at play here. Okay, he could roll with it. Much was unexplainable in the world today. Fine by him. Made life interesting and always new, with something to discover all the time. He was okay with not knowing or understanding, but he realized he was not okay with sitting in the sorrow of being alone and pushing away love. Without Sarah.

He set the book on his chair and stalked toward her.

"Hey," he said softly when she was heading toward him, her gaze pulled down to the floor and no doubt inward.

She started and looked up at him, her gaze pained.

"You don't have to be alone in your thoughts. Tell me what's going on." He touched her cheek. "I'm here."

Her cheeks reddened, but she held his gaze. "That's what I'm afraid of."

"Of me?"

"No. Of us."

"What's holding you back?"

"This can't be real."

"What do you mean?"

"Our feelings. The attraction. It's all just weird, like a spell. Even though I don't believe in any of that magic stuff."

"So a skeptic, eh?" He smiled at her. Her lips were just inches away.

"Don't make fun of me."

"I'm not. Just teasing you." He erased his smile and got serious. She deserved that and so much more. "So what if it is a spell? Why can't what we have be real anyway?"

Her emerald eyes widened. Her gaze dropped to his lips. "Because..." she blinked and stepped back out of his reach. "Because love isn't a fairytale or a spell. What we have isn't real. Just a factor of circumstance. Just coincidence."

"It is no coincidence," Monsieur Lefevre said in French. Ah, so the wily old man understood English.

"What? What'd he say?" Sarah peered at Monsieur Lefevre suspiciously, as if she too understood more French than she let on. Or maybe she was picking up on Monsieur Lefevre's tone of confidence.

Josh translated. "He says that it's no coincidence."

"Of course, it is. It can't be magic. Magic isn't real. What we have isn't real. This is all—all some kind of prank. That's what it is."

Josh grabbed her hands. "Hey, wait, what's got you so upset?"

"You don't know. You don't know what I'm going through." Sarah grabbed her coat and hat.

"Wait!" Josh stepped toward her.

She stormed toward the kitchen.

Monsieur Lefevre's words trailed behind him, laughter in his voice, "Yes, go after her. Go after love."

He followed, and then it was just the two of them in the tiny kitchen.

She was staring out the window at the pounding rain and slate grey sky, her long hair waving like fine silk down her back, almost reaching her fine assets.

He knew it in his gut that they together were the key to the storm and somehow ending it. But how could he convince her of that?

SARAH WAS SHAKING. SHE puffed out a few breaths to calm herself. She had to get back to reality. Find a job. Her savings wouldn't last forever.

She'd heard Josh follow her into the kitchen, but she didn't want to look at him. Her body betrayed her anyway, getting all warm and tingly at the thought of him. She inhaled his scent of rain and male essence. Her libido wanted to run the show. She wouldn't let it.

"Don't you want to want to know what happens next?" Josh said quietly, his voice a warm rumble, revving her libido and her desire to just let herself relax a little and lean into his quiet strength. And that maybe things would work out all right.

"About what?"

"The story Monsieur Lefevre's was telling."

"What good would it do?" Sarah shook her head and squeezed her eyes shut. She was hyperventilating.

"Whoa, what's wrong?" Josh's arm came around her shoulders and she let him pull her close. His warmth felt good.

She didn't know why. She'd let go of love a long time ago. Must be all the newness in her life in the last twenty-four hours for her to even consider opening the door of her heart to love

But here was love and connection and coziness standing behind her, ready for her—tears squeezed out the sides of her eyes. She shook her head and couldn't find the words. She thought she'd been all cried out years ago. She felt right in his arms, despite arguing with herself. She relaxed, felt her shoulders drop, and let him hold her for a moment.

The she pulled back. "I'm not good with this love stuff. Never have been." She puffed out a breath. "I don't do relationships. They never last. The men always leave."

He brushed a strand of hair behind her ears. So tender. "Well, I don't leave."

She shrugged and glanced away, eyeing the ceiling as if it had the answers. "I can't believe that. Love leads to heartbreak. Always does."

Josh said nothing for a moment and pulled his arm away. "Look at me, Sarah."

"What?" She didn't look at him. "I need to go. Alone."

"So, you're going to let your past dictate you love life?"

She shook her head, not trusting her voice, and stepped toward the apartment front door, but Josh blocked her way.

"Sarah, look at me," Josh said softly. More a request this time than a command.

He stood only inches from her. His smell, his presence, drew her. She wanted to lean into his strength, his courage, his willingness to go there, and this time not protest and pull away. His willingness to believe in love. Then she wouldn't have to be so alone.

She'd been so alone for so long, and hadn't even realized just how much.

She finally did look at him, tilting her face up so she could look him in the eye. Such warmth, such compassion in his gaze. He didn't even touch her, but she felt enveloped by him, by his care for her.

It couldn't last though. Relationships never did. "You don't even know me." She stepped away from him.

"And you don't know me. I'm not going anywhere." He stepped closer. "Give us a chance."

"What if you don't like what you see?" she whispered so low he had to lean closer to hear her. She wasn't able to break eye contact, but it hurt to say those words.

"What's not to like?" he said, edging even closer to her. "You're bright, beautiful, and adventurous when you let yourself be. You're resourceful, and did I say, sexy? I forgot to say, sexy." He eyed her lips.

"But I'm also stubborn and obstinate. Did I say, stubborn?"

"And funny."

"Am not."

"Yes. You. Are." Now he stepped right against her body and pulled her close, still eyeing her lips.

"Josh?"

"Hmmm."

She waited until he lifted his eyes to hers. "I don't know you. You could be anybody, a crazy person, unstable, ready to leave at any minute."

"I'm a dog person."

"Uh?"

"A dog person." He repeated. "We're loyal. Maybe too loyal."

"Oh." Sarah felt the last bit of her resistance melting. "But—
" She stepped out of the circle of his arms, but not the warmth
of his gaze. He let her go.

"What is it?" His tone was patient.

She shook her head. "It's nothing. I'm just super sensitive
right now. Being in a foreign country. The storm. The night in
the tunnels and the cavern."

"Come here," Josh said. And this time she let herself be
pulled into his arms. "Oh, Sarah, of the guarded heart."

She let his warmth wash away some of the past loneliness.
"Since when did you get so wise?"

"Since I found someone I want to be wise for." He pulled
back. "I think we need to hear the rest of Monsieur Lefevre's
story. Are you willing?"

Sarah realized she'd always been so willing to take physical
risks but not emotional ones.

Maybe it was time to risk her heart. With Josh.

"Yes, I'm willing." She leaned in and kissed him.

JOSH POURED ALL THE love he had for her into the kiss.
When he pulled back, her cheeks were flushed and her eyes
glazed. She smiled. He smiled back, grabbed her hand, and
stepped back into the living room.

Monsieur Lefevre was not there, but before he could call out
for the elderly man, he appeared, a cryptic smile on his lips.

"Please, Monsieur Lefevre, you have to tell us the rest of the
story. I think the key is there," Josh said.

"Does she love you yet?"

"I don't know. I think she's coming around."

Beth Barany

"But she doesn't quite believe. I can see that. But you do, young man." Monsieur Lefevre nodded thoughtfully.

"Sure, yes, I believe. Of course. Our world is full of magical tales of romance and adventure ripe for the enjoying and living and believing in." He smiled.

"Indeed." Monsieur Lefevre sat at the table. "Come. Sit."

Josh followed Monsieur Lefevre to the table where they'd sat at earlier. The book he couldn't open was in the center of the table, closed. Nothing else was there, not even the chestnuts.

Sarah had followed him, releasing his hand when she saw the book. She picked up the large tome and caressed the cover. Without looking at them, she sat and opened the book.

Monsieur Lefevre whispered, "She can open it. That's a good sign." Then he shook his head. "But it's not enough." Then he hustled off back toward the kitchen.

Josh didn't know what to do with himself. Now he felt the need to pace, more like run. But the weather wouldn't permit that.

As if in reply, thunder boomed. Then a flash of lightning snapped across the darkened sky.

He gave a sad, silent laugh. What was he thinking? But that was what he needed to do—think. And be patient. She had to come around. His gut told him she needed to, or else. Or else what?

Monsieur Lefevre came back in with a tray and coffee and cookies before he could run farther with that thought.

"Are those speculoos?" Josh asked. "My favorite kind of cookies. Coffee smells great too."

Monsieur Lefevre smiled. "Sit down, young man, and let me do what I do best."

"What's that, Monsieur Lefevre?"

"Serve." He smiled so beautifully, as if his life's work and passion was encapsulated in that word.

Monsieur Lefevre winked at him and served the coffee in tiny espresso cups made from delicate china that looked older than their host.

SARAH GULPED DOWN THE coffee at her elbow, even though it was cool. She felt like she'd been deep diving into a world she'd never imagined. And it felt so real. Guess that was the power of fiction.

She gazed around. The sky was black, the rain still pounding the city.

Night had fallen, which it did early this far north and in the winter.

She'd heard the murmuring in French around her, but the noise had sounded as if she'd been under water, all muffled.

She carefully put the book down on her seat and circumnavigated the tiny living room slash dining room combination.

Josh and Monsieur Lefevre were watching her. Josh with warmth and Monsieur Lefevre with some sort of question.

"What?" she said. Her voice came out as a croak. She cleared her throat and repeated herself.

"Well," Josh said, finally, a question in his voice. "What did you discover?"

Sarah blinked. "It's bunch of esoteric stuff." She puffed out a breath. "Weird, I don't remember exactly. Just that I was so engrossed, and—" Unbidden tears came to her eyes. "I don't know why I want to cry." She shrugged and sat down.

Monsieur Lefevre chattered away for a moment.

She glanced at Josh for the translation.

"He say he knows why you're—" Josh waved to her. "Crying, or want to cry." He looked a little embarrassed. Why?

"So?"

"He wants to finish telling the story."

"That will explain it? Explain everything?"

"He says it will."

Monsieur Lefevre spoke, shaking his head and frowning.

Josh translated. "He says that we have less time than he thought. By tonight we have to resolve this, or our the city will be—" Josh paled.

"What?" Sarah stopped nibbling the sweet cookie. Her heart thumped in her chest.

"The city will be destroyed."

"That's not possible. Is it? Check what's going on. Oh, I wish I could understand French."

She must have been reading for a few hours. Or was it a few minutes? She checked her phone. They'd only been in the old man's apartment for—

It had been seven hours. How could that be? Her sense of time was completely skewed. Just like it had been in the tunnels.

The time. Something about the time...

Josh pulled out his smart phone and started tapping away, shaking his head whenever he stopped to read.

Monsieur Lefevre spoke in rapid fire French, his words sounding like hammers pounding against nails, hard and insistent.

"Sarah, the Seine has flooded. All of the center of Paris is cordoned off. No one in or out." Josh checked his watch. "Oh, damn."

"What?"

"My presentation was supposed to be an hour ago. Damn, how could I have totally forgotten?" He gazed at her.

"Hey, don't look at me," she snapped, then immediately apologized.

"It's okay. No, I wasn't. Looking. I mean I—no. It's not— well, it kind of is. But there were lots of things going on. I guess I got turned around. And—" He shrugged and frowned, a pained look in his eyes. "It doesn't matter anyway. That area has probably been shut down." But his frown let her know that it did matter. A lot.

"You sure there's nothing we can do. Call someone?"

"No. That part of Paris is starting to flood." Josh tapped away on his cell phone, then looked up. "According the conference news feed, the venue was shut down hours ago and all the talks and events have been cancelled indefinitely."

"I'm so sorry."

He waved that away. "This storm is affecting way more that me—us. Hundreds of thousands of people, maybe millions affected by it..." He eyed the unrelenting rain.

This man had set aside everything to be with her, to solve the mystery with her. That had to mean something. He hadn't left. He'd stuck by her during this whole crazy episode. Her heart pounded. That hurt. She realized not only had she not believed in love, she had purposely not let love in.

Josh was saying something. "What? Sorry," she said.

"You okay?"

She shook her head without thinking, tears at corner of her eyes. She waved at nothing.

"Come sit down. Monsieur Lefevre wants to finish the story," Josh said.

She did sit and let Josh take her hand, his warm one warming her cold one, like he warmed her heart. Could she give them a chance?

If she believed Monsieur Lefevre, the city's fate perhaps rested on it somehow. She didn't understand the how.

She nodded to Monsieur Lefevre, hoping he'd see that as an apology for her outburst and stubbornness. She needed to learn how to apologize properly in French.

Monsieur Lefevre smiled kindly at her, as if all was forgiven, and re-filled their tiny cups, with fluid and graceful movements, then re-started the story. His voice took on the sing-song quality again.

Josh interpreted smoothly for Monsieur Lefevre, and Sarah could see the story unfold like a storybook animation.

ONCE THE POWERFUL BARON father pried the truth out of the two lovers, he condemned to death the young chestnut seller, to be executed the next morning. The young man was thrown into the castle dungeons. After much weeping and heart break, late that night, the daughter appealed to her father, offering to deliver herself to the farthest convent, if only her lover's life would be spared.

Her father finally consented. She asked to see her lover one last time before they would be separated forever. At least she was heartened to know that he would live.

With a saddened heart, she prepared for her travels late that night with her ladies' maid. Her ladies maid was related through her husband's family to the old healer of their native village. Late at night, she scurried home to tell her husband and the old healer of the fate of the poor young lovers. She knew if anybody could help it would be the healer. Hadn't the village healer helped her and her husband with their children's cuts and bruises throughout the years? The healer knew of things beyond their understanding, but she'd always been kind and exuded a wisdom of the earth.

With her loving husband at her side, the ladies maid rushed into the healer's hut and relayed the story.

The crone healer calmed her and assured her that she knew just what to do, but only if the lovers were willing to pay the price.

Early the next morning, even before the crows had risen, the village healer met the young lovers in the dungeon.

"What can you do for us?" the young man asked. "I must stay here the rest of my life, never to see my love again."

"At least I know that you live and that will glad my heart a little," the young woman said.

"I can help you both live forever, together," the old crone healer said.

The young woman wept. "I would settle for one lifetime."

"I will take whatever you can give us," the young man said.

"But there is a price," the healer said.

"There always is," the young man said sadly. "I will gladly pay it. Name it."

But the young woman was afraid and could not vow to pay the price. "Haven't I already forfeited so much?" she cried.

"Do not be afraid, my love. Whatever the cost for our love to live, for us to be together in eternity," he said.

The young woman cried as the old healer told them the price. They had to transform into creatures that lived in mythic time, existing in that space between. No one would ever see them again. Everything they ever loved except each other would be gone from them, but at least they would have each other.

"Can you pay that price?" the old healer asked. "You have to decide now. The sun rises soon and then the guards will be here to take you away, young miss."

"Yes." The young woman clasped her love's hands through the bars. Then she turned to the old woman. "But please, dear healer, may I have a few days to get my affairs in order? I must fool my father and the convent. I don't want there to be complications." She turned back to her young man and smiled bravely. "That way I can be with you and no one will be the wiser."

"You have five days," the healer intoned. "Now, we must leave, before we are discovered down here."

With that the ladies maid escorted the old healer and her charge out of the dungeon through the secret passage in which they entered. For a moment, the ladies maid and the crone conferred out of earshot of the young woman, then the ladies maid brought her charge back into the castle to make preparations.

The young woman appealed to her father to give her five days to prepare her next life big change to convent, by telling him she had to pray and make ready her heart for her new life.

He consented and left her be, while she sent a flurry of secret letters to various convents saying she'd be going to different convent. She hoped her messages would keep everyone confused and looking for her, only to determine that she'd been waylaid or lost or otherwise mysteriously accosted. All this she did with the help of her ladies maid and far from her father's prying eyes.

To finalize the plan, she worked it out to sneak down into the dungeon early on the fifth day, before the sun rose, where the old crone would transform her and her lover into mythic creatures to be with each other in the in-between forever.

She tried to wear her sadness like a cloak, so no one else would suspect a thing, but someone must have found out. For on the morning of the fifth day, when she slipped out of room, a guard was posted outside. Her story of needing to see her sick horse did not shake the guard. Stone-faced and with clipped words, he marched her to her father's study, where he sat surrounded by his books and scrolls the nearby monks had created for him.

He sat there regarding her with anger in his eyes and a frown of displeasure on his face. "You have deceived me," he finally said. "I will accompany you myself to the convent I have chosen. You will not leave my sight until I deliver you to the nuns myself."

"Father, no," she sobbed. "I want to be with my one true love."

"Never. You shall know no love of this world, except for what is ordained by the Church and the nuns. Is that clear young lady?"

The powerful baron would not allow any words or tears by his wayward daughter to sway him. Even appeals to the love he had for his daughter's mother, who had long since died, could not move him. His heart was hardened never to crack open in this life.

The young woman was isolated from all who knew and loved her, even separated from her ladies maid whom she had known her whole life. Straightaway she was escorted out of the castle into a waiting carriage, her father at her side every step of the way.

While this was occurring, the crone had slipped into the dungeon with the help of the ladies maid. As they awaited the appointed hour, and the young woman didn't show, the young man was distraught and beside himself with anguish.

"We must move forward with the ritual of transformation," said the crone sadly. "This is the appointed hour or else the change will not work."

"If I stay in this dungeon, I will never see my love again. But if I transform, is there a chance she will come back to me? She may find you and transform at a later time, no?" The young man didn't want to give up hope just yet.

"Who knows what the future holds, but those who live in that moment?" the crone intoned. "But you must decide now. Time is up."

"Please give me time to find her. She was supposed to be here," the ladies maid said.

The crone frowned, checked out the small window at the coming dawn, then she shook her head. "I am truly sorry."

A nearby churched chimed seven bells.

The ladies maid ignored the despair, flew out of the dungeon, and searched high and low for her charge. But she was nowhere to be found. The guards finally revealed what had happened. In her sorrow and through her tears, the ladies maid raced back down to the dungeon, but the crone was gone and so was the young man.

In their place were symbols scrawled all over the walls and floor, strange and arcane, unlike anything she'd ever seen.

But someone had seen the crone do her work and passed on this story from generation to generation until I am telling it to you today.

JOSH STOPPED.

Over the pounding rain, a nearby church chimed six bells.

"Is that it? What happened to the young man? To the young woman?" Sarah asked. "I want to know what happens next." She was drawn in despite herself, even though it was a made up fairy tale.

Monsieur Lefevre shook his head, frowning, and spoke softly.

Josh said, "He wants for you to see with your own eyes, and—" He paused and eyed Monsieur Lefevre.

Monsieur Lefevre rattled off something in an urgent voice and pointed to the book.

"He wants you to open the book again. He says the six bells have sounded. We much not let it get to seven bells." Josh paled.

"You okay?" she asked.

"I'm fine. Just read. We need to resolve this now."

She squirmed in her seat, her heart pounding like a drum. "I already looked at it and read it. I can't remember what it says."

Josh and Monsieur Lefevre were watching her expectantly. Really, it was just an old book. What did she have to be afraid of?

Her mind provided no answer, though her hands shook as she opened the book.

The symbols danced in front of her eyes then reformed themselves into understandable English. How was that possible?

Like in a vivid dream, the hand-drawn words and beautifully illuminated art spoke to her, drew her in, and she began to read.

"Aloud," Josh said. "Read aloud."

"How am I able to read this?" she asked, looking first at Josh and then at Monsieur Lefevre. "How is this right where Monsieur Lefevre left off? How is that possible?"

Monsieur Lefevre spoke in rapid French, a kind smile on his face.

"He says you must be related to the old crone's family. That magic runs deep in you, but that you never listened to it before."

At her skeptical look, Josh shrugged, as if he didn't believe it either.

She almost said aloud, "There's no such thing as magic." But after all she'd experienced with Josh in the tunnels and how she'd been able to read the symbols on the cavern walls, she couldn't say it. It didn't feel true anymore.

But maybe they'd been hallucinating and something affected her so she could read the symbols in the cavern and now in the old book.

Maybe magic was another name for a science that hadn't been explained yet.

Sarah read the story aloud.

A YOUNG PAGE HAD followed the ladies maid down to the dungeon, and stayed hidden in the shadows, even after the ladies maid ran out of there. He saw it all.

The crone gave a flacon to the sad young man behind bars.

"Drink it all down in one gulp, young man," she said to him. "It's nasty tasting, but it has to be done that way."

The young man bravely took the potion and drank it all. He immediately fell to the stone floor clutching his belly. He cried out in pain and writhed there like a fish out of water. Or like an immense snake, or wild big cat, or huge eagle. The page couldn't be sure because he saw all those creatures before his eyes, as if at once. In a blinding flash of light, the young man had turned into a dragon—an enormous dragon folded over itself to fit into the cell.

The dragon bellowed in tremendous sadness. Just then thunder boomed. A storm must have risen suddenly, because earlier the day had started clear skied and bitter winter cold. The page kept to his dark corner and cowered, but couldn't keep his eyes off the spectacle before him.

Then one moment the dragon was there, taking up the whole cell, and in a blink of an eye, he was gone.

The crone grabbed the page by the ear, pulled him out of his corner, and dragged out of there.

When they were far from the castle on the pathway to the village, the page asked the crone, "Where did he go?"

The crone was actually his grandmother, or great grandmother—he wasn't sure.

"Into the space in-between."

"Will we ever see him again?"

"Only when he searches for his love."

"When will that be? Maybe I can see him again."

"Not in this lifetime or the next, but some hundreds of years hence, and every few hundred years after that, he will emerge to call for his lady love. May that she come to him, or all will be lost."

"What do you mean, Grandma?" the page asked. He was only supposed to call her that when they were at the village. They didn't want anyone knowing they were related whenever she came to the castle.

"It couldn't be helped, but the young man's sorrow and his love are a powerful force—for good—but also a destructive force that can tear cities apart," she said sadly. "It couldn't be helped. Such is the power of love combined with a broken heart."

"But what about the young woman? How will she ever find him again? She isn't a creature like he is now, is she?"

"Right you are, young man." She nodded and picked herbs on their walk home, as she always did. "I have sent one of your brothers out to search for them and divert the convoy through magic to the convent north across the water, where my sisters will watch out over her and teach her the ways, so that she may one day find him. I hope." She said that last bit quietly and with a great deal of sadness.

Even though the page was young, all of nine years of age, he knew the ways of the world they lived in. "So there is a slim hope of them reuniting," he said, matter-of-factly, shaking his head.

"Yes, my child. That is the truth of it."

So from this day to that, every few hundred years the dragon searches for his love, and if he can't find her, he calls forth with his considerable powers for love to find its way.

But love must be recognized and seized, for this life is short, and not everyone is as immortal as the Dragon of Paris.

SARAH STOPPED AND WIPED the tears from her eyes. Again, those unexplained tears. But she felt for the lost lovers.

If she believed in love...

Never to see your love again, to have him ripped from you by the cruelty and hard heart of others was awful. She looked up.

Josh watched her, waiting.

Monsieur Lefevre grabbed the coffee tray and bustled off to the kitchen, leaving them alone, together.

"Well, what did you think of the story?" Josh asked, keeping his voice low.

She closed the book carefully and placed it in her lap. She wanted to keep it close, at least for a little while longer.

"I don't believe in magic," she said matching his quiet tone. But her conviction wasn't in her words.

He said nothing.

"And I don't believe in happily ever afters. Haven't seen any of those." The tears wanted to come. She swallowed to push them back.

Josh placed his hands on the table, palms open. "How about happily for now?"

She blew out a breath and placed her hands in his. "I'd like that." Her breastbone hurt, like it needed to make more room for her growing heart.

Josh leaned toward her and she met him halfway, her lips on his soft ones. She angled her mouth for a better kiss and gave to him her heart.

For now. For this time.

She could let love in.

She could find the love to give in return.

His kiss broke through the clouds in her heart and melted them straight through her core. Her heart raced.

Josh pulled back and smiled. He turned to the window. "The rain stopped."

Sarah sighed at their kiss, stood, and peered out the window. He was right. The clouds didn't seem as dark and ominous as they had been all day. In fact, she could swear she could see a tiny piece of blue sky peeking through.

He came around the table and hugged her, both of them eyeing the sky. Before their eyes, the clouds parted. She squinted against the brightness.

"Where's Monsieur Lefevre? I want to thank him and give him back his—" Sarah glanced around the room. "Josh. Um, everything's changed."

What had been an antique-filled apartment was now an art deco slash sleek modern tiny apartment. The book was gone where she'd placed it on the table. No longer a round mahogany one, but a square, metal one with a glass top.

Together Josh and Sarah searched the place, but saw no Monsieur Lefevre. There were no pictures of people either, only photographs of mountain peaks, wooded valleys, and river ways. No knick-knacks and no bookshelves.

"We did it," Josh said, awe in his voice. "We broke the spell."

"I can't believe it." Sarah rushed to the kitchen. It was tiny as ever, filled with modern stainless steel appliances, instead of Monsieur Lefevre's porcelain and crockery. She grabbed her coat. At least that was still there. "Let's go."

She clattered down the stairs, her heart pounding. Was it excitement? Fear? Her whole body was vibrating. She felt as if she'd just climbed a rock face and was about to look out over a stunning vista.

They stepped out on the sidewalk. A church chimed seven bells and a flock of pigeons fluttered and wheeled overhead. The cold air struck her cheeks, refreshing and bracing. She inhaled deeply. Parisians were outdoors enjoying the crisp winter weather. Every restaurant on the street was full of patrons laughing, eating, and drinking.

"Wow," Josh said. "The Parisians sure do recover in style, and fast."

"Wait." Sarah spun around.

"What is it?"

"This doesn't look like Monsieur Lefevre's museum."

What had been a dusty window with a small sign was now a chic clothing boutique called Le Dragon & La Princesse and featured recycled clothing with fantasy elements that looked like they were from all historical periods, but heavy on the frills. The shop was closed, but a cute young woman was straightening inside. When Sarah pressed her face against the glass, the young woman, maybe about twenty-five, waved at Sarah.

Sarah smiled and waved back.

"I think everything worked out," Sarah whispered.

Josh wrapped his arms around her. "I'm so glad." He bent to kiss her.

They were interrupted by a musical chuckle and words in French. The young woman had opened the shop door and stood in the doorway.

"So sorry, I don't speak French," Sarah managed to say in stumbling French.

The young woman smiled and gave her musical laugh again. "That is okay. I don't speak well the English. Did you want to see clothes?"

"No thanks," Sarah said. "Just looking."

The young woman smiled, stepped out of the shop, locking the door behind her. She peered up at the sky. "The dragon must have found his love."

"What?" Sarah gripped Josh's arm.

"Oh." The stylish young woman chuckled. "It's just an old— how do you say?—*une expression* we have in French for the rain storm has stopped."

"Yes, an expression," Josh said. "Never heard of it."

The young woman shrugged in that Gallic way, smiled and said, "*Bonne nuit.*" She waved, and walked off, calling something out over her shoulder in French.

"What did she say?" Sarah asked Josh.

"She said, 'A love so great cannot be lost.' "

She hugged Josh. "I hope that's true. Now that I've found love I'm not letting it or you out of my sight." She smiled into his hazel eyes that sparkled golden in the streetlights.

"I'm not going anywhere," Josh said and kissed her.

AUTHOR'S NOTE

This is a work of fiction. While Paris is real, of course, and does have many underground tunnels, I made up the tunnels in the story. Also invented are Credit Paris and the Musée des Petites Choses.

A Labyrinth of Love and Roses

(A Fairytale Paranormal Romance)

Novella Book 4 of the *Touchstone Series*

Summary:

Lily Grenault needs to succeed at her last pitch meeting to fund her international green tech business. She wants sexy investor Brett Barnaby to help her, but her grandmother's dire warning of ensuing chaos forces her to drop everything. Brett Barnaby's search for his great-grandfather's gravesite in Amiens may unlock far more than the treasure that family legends predict. Can the two of them work together to prevent chaos from triumphing and find love in the labyrinth of roses?

Chapter One

APRIL 25

AMIENS, FRANCE

LILI SET OUT THE tea and the mismatched fine china they both liked. Her hand shook. Something about Gramma's voice over the phone an hour earlier made her nervous. Gramma or Gra-mere in French, said, "We need to talk" in her serious voice.

She set out some speculoos cookies from the cupboard and some croissants she'd run to get fresh at the corner boulangerie.

She spun in her tiny but tidy apartment, really more like a studio, her bedroom separated by a curtain. It was all she could afford from her savings and her summer jobs from being a migrant fruit picker in the south of France, outlandish and as horrifying as it was to her upper class French family. She didn't want to take any money from them.

She wiped down the kitchen counters and glanced around again. Oh, her laptop. She shut it and draped a cloth over it. Her grandmother wouldn't want her to be distracted by it when she came over, and distracted she was. She'd been working for months on her prospectus for the investor pitch the next day. Despite the gorgeous spring weather in Amiens and the smells of the island gardens calling to her, she'd been holed up with her computer for days—chatting with her team via Skype and instant messaging, exchanging documents, getting everything ready for the big day tomorrow.

She had to get her business funded so she could go international. Her team spread around the world was counting on her. If she didn't get this funding from the international group of investors in town for the special World War I commemoration, she didn't know when she'd have another chance like this. She'd have to start at square one. When would there be another chance like this, where people who wanted to invest in local talent and clean tech software companies would be coming around again? She was born and raised in Amiens, well, Paris too. But that city was second in her heart to the river-wound city of Amiens with its gorgeous ancient cathedral and many, tiny farming islands.

A knock at her door interrupted her ruminations. Lili opened the door and smiled at her petite grandmother, shorter than her own five foot five inches. Gra-mere Leonora squinted up at her. "You've been worrying, dear," and brushed past her to step into Lili's apartment. Lili couldn't deny it. If she did, Gra-mere would know. She always knew when Lili was lying.

So she shut the door and said, "I have my big presentation tomorrow morning, Gra-mere. I told you." She set the kettle to boiling, so her back was to her grandmother for the moment. She just had to ask. "Gra-mere, what was so important that it couldn't wait until after my pitch?"

She heard the chair scrape against the wood floor and her grandmother sit. When Gra-mere or Gramma, depending on which language Lili was speaking, didn't answer, Lili turned around. Gra-mere eyed her intently.

"Sit down, child."

"But the water—"

"Forget about that. The water takes care of itself and so must you."

Lili wanted to cross her arms across her chest, but resisted the urge. She pulled out the chair and sat. Gra-mere often spoke in riddles. That was one of the things Lili always loved about her. She was so unlike the rest of the stuffed-up family—well, mostly her parents.

Gra-mere watched her intently. Lili squirmed, then jumped up when the kettle whistled. She poured hot water into the teapot. The rich aroma of tarragon and rose hips filled the room. Still Gra-mere said nothing.

She tried again. "Gra-mere, what was so urgent—?"

"Shh. I'm listening."

"To what?"

"The tea."

Lili sat back, amused but still antsy. She really needed to do one more pass, check some numbers on her slide deck.

Finally Gra-mere poured the tea into their cups, then spoke. "I came by to tell you about your legacy, dear Lili of mine."

Lili sputtered her tea that she was sipping. "What legacy, Gra-mere?"

"The one handed down from my mother, and her mother, and all the mothers before, since the time of the Great Calamity."

"What about Mom? And, what Great Calamity?"

Gra-mere waved her hand. "We're not discussing your mother. We're discussing you. And I think you're ready."

"For what?"

"For the truth. In seven days, by Beltane, you must go through your Rite of Initiation on the island to formally accept your legacy and find your one true love, not necessarily in that order. Magic finds magic. And yours is to be the Bringer of the Rose and protect the earth and all who live on it, but not with gadgets. With your heart."

"Gra-mere, what do you mean?" Lili jumped up. "This—this is farfetched even for you."

"Sit down, dear, and let me tell you what's at stake."

But Lili couldn't sit. She circled her studio, chewing on her fingernails. When she realized what she was doing, she stuffed her hands in her jeans pockets. She stopped by her laptop and put her hand on the cloth that covered it. "But Gra-mere, you realize how important this presentation is to me tomorrow, don't you?"

Gra-mere watched her with a small frown on her face, looking more like a disapproving matron than the high-spirited, artsy, young-at-heart woman she usually was around Lili. Lili plowed ahead. "With this funding, my water purification technology and app can go forward and get into the hands of anyone in the world who needs it. After a bit more testing and getting a factory set up in China or India—not sure yet. Ideally, Africa, but we haven't found the place with the right infrastructure—"

"Your legacy is more noble than that," Gra-mere interrupted her.

"What can be more noble than making sure everyone on the planet has drinking water?"

"Making sure that everyone will be alive to enjoy that drinking water."

Lili's gaze snapped to her grandmother's. "What? What are you talking about?" She squared her reports, slapped her pens back in their jar, and shoved books back on the shelf above her computer. Her hands were shaking. Lili turned to face her grandmother.

"The fate of the world, dear child. Well, your world. Your life." Gra-mere waved her hand as if it was all quite ordinary.

"Gra-mere, you can't be serious."

Her eagle gaze on Lili, she frowned. "Oh, but I am. Sit. You must learn of the consequences." She gestured to Lili. "Your project is nothing compared to the consequences of not obeying the magic."

Lili sat, shivering for no reason. She sipped her tea, but the normally soothing brew didn't calm the shaking in her body. She kept her mouth shut as Gra-mere spoke of a coming storm that would destroy all life on the planet unless the new generation of the Bringers of the Rose did their part. Their job was to make ready for the warriors to defend the Earth's population. Lili was to go to one of the river islands in the River Somme here in Amiens, read the signs, and accept her legacy, all by May first, Beltane in the Celtic Earth traditions.

"The signs will be very clear. I have taught and prepared you well." Her grandmother paused and sipped her tea, gazing at Lili as if taking in all of her. She clinked the cup on the saucer. "Do you understand?"

"No, I understand nothing." Lili huffed out a breath. "All that playing with tea leaves, tarot cards, and foraging. That was you teaching me, preparing me? I thought was just grandmother-granddaughter bonding."

"It was of course that, Lili dear."

"What am I supposed to do, Gra-mere? I am just one person. I don't feel prepared for what you're talking about. I don't even understand it. Besides I have a company to get off the ground. I've been working so hard on it for months, years really. Can't you ask one of my sisters?"

"There is only one Bringer in every generation of each chosen family. You are the one in this family, my dear. Not only have I taught you well, preparing you for now, you have learned well, too."

Lili glanced around her apartment without seeing anything. "I have? What? I'm supposed to do a Beltane ritual, fall in love, and do something to welcome some warriors? Who? How?"

Lili reached for a speculoos cookie and crumbled it into bits.

"You'll know him when you see him. Magic knows magic. Once you do your part, the Order of the Rose warriors will do their part to protect the wisdoms."

Lili shook her head and opened her mouth to speak.

Gra-mere raised her hand in a "stop" gesture. "If you don't do this, Lili my dear, if you don't accept your legacy, chaos in your life will reign, affecting others, getting things out of balance. Mark my words." She leaned forward and said more softly, "Power will shift to the dark side. Those who want all of earth's resources for themselves will dominate and millions will die. And there won't be anything you can do about it. Your project won't work." She waved her hand as if to erase her words. "But you must claim your legacy and let go of your project. You have more important matters to deal with. Small steps lead to big gains. And you must take your small yet important steps. It all counts." Gra-mere sat back with a firm look at Lili. She'd said her piece.

Lili sat back in her chair, hands gripped in her lap. She didn't want to chew her fingernails down to the raw. "Gra-mere, your timing is awful." She wanted to swear, but even her laid-back grandmother frowned on that. "This is too much. I want to work on a global scale, but this is all too much."

"You'll get used to it. You have seven days, dear. You will know him when you see him. Your heart will know." She stood and headed for the door.

Lili stood too and followed her grandmother. "That's it? That's all you have to say? I can't—I have questions. Why me, Gra-mere? What's the Great Calamity?"

Gra-mere opened the door, turned, and gave Lili a big hug. "It's your legacy. I know you can do this, Lili dear," she whispered. "I faced what you're facing and I survived." With that, she trotted down the hallway and out the building.

Lili stood there and watched her go. Gra-mere hadn't answered her question about the Great Calamity.

She didn't know what to do or say for a good long minute.

Then she shut the door with a definitive bang, cleaned up the afternoon tea in a daze, and sat down in front of her computer.

Whatever her grandmother was talking about could wait one more day.

Had to. She had a deadline. She opened her computer. For a second her screen was black and didn't respond to her key commands to wake up. She swore. She didn't need delays. Legacy or not, chaos or not, she needed to get to work. She hit the control and C keys together, and finally the computer responded. She blew out a breath. "Thank God," she said and got to work, tapping away on her laptop.

After a few more hours perfecting and checking with her team on last minute details—everything was in order—Lili stood and stretched. Night had fallen.

It all came crashing back to her. She couldn't do what her grandmother asked. Everything in her small apartment looked the same, but she didn't feel the same—not with her grandmother's words echoing in her mind—finding her one true love and accepting her magical legacy. Yah, right. Not yet. No room for that yet, despite her parent's pressure to settle down.

It was too much.

She flicked back the curtain and stepped into her tiny bedroom. She cast off her jeans and tank top and shimmied into her short, black dress with 1920s flapper fringes high on her thighs. She slipped on spiky heels, dashed on her favorite red Chanel lipstick, *Cambon*, and threw her keys and cash into her black, thin travel pouch that she strapped against her body while dancing. Lili was going to get her night on the town.

 The next day after her presentation she'd tell her grandma that she picked the wrong granddaughter. Her legacy lay in her successful pitch for investment funds tomorrow morning.

But now she was going to blow off some pent-up frustration and let go of all obligations, for just a little while. She was going dancing.

Chapter Two

THE CLUB WAS FULL even though it was a Tuesday night, or maybe because it was a Tuesday night. Lili didn't care for the reasons. She was only happy to have other sweaty bodies to dance with. The music was loud and pounding, rock verging on punk with intense guitar riffs and powerful vocals, reminiscent of Florence and the Machine mashed with Evanescence. That it was pounding enough was all she cared about. The music compelled her to move and forget her work and her grandmother's words.

She danced with her friends, she danced with strangers. She hopped and jumped when the music called for it, shimmied and swayed when it slowed down. One man danced with her more than the rest. He was delicious in his sweaty, practically see-through white tee shirt with the words "Surf Bum" on the back. His muscled chest was right in front of her. His jeans hugged his hips. He moved sinuously against her in the slow dances. She gripped his muscled shoulders. Her hands roamed his sweaty, muscular back. In the thumping songs, he jumped along with her with a big, kid-like grin on his face. Messy blond hair swept into his bright blue eyes, and he beamed at her because he knew she was watching him.

He flirted with his smile and how he put his hands on her back as he held her close. She flirted back with how she pressed against him, pelvis to pelvis. For some songs, he danced away from her to shimmy with other women, then danced back to her mid-way through the song with his smile quirked up, like he couldn't stay away for long. In a half-minute pause between songs, reality snuck into her thoughts. She didn't want to abandon her burgeoning business that could help so many to embrace a legacy her grandmother just dropped in her lap.

The music slowed down again, and the man shouted something in her ear. She couldn't hear him, so she shrugged and shook her head.

He mimed drinking and she nodded. He grabbed her hand and led her toward the bar.

He ordered for them. The bartender brought two short glasses. She sniffed hers—a whiskey sour. Lili smiled, clinked glasses with him as a thanks, and downed her drink. She coughed. She usually didn't inhale her beverages so quickly, but tonight was different. Tonight she wanted to forget the hard and confusing choice in front of her—just for a little while.

She felt his attention on her and met his gaze in the mirror behind the bar. She studied him a bit more, open-eyed, not caring if he saw her blatant, hungry gaze through the mirror. Her business had been her main focus for months.

Her hunger for him astounded her. It'd been a long time since she'd felt so strongly attracted to anyone. He had shaggy blond hair styled with studied carelessness. His blue eyes, the color of the Mediterranean off the coast of Crete, watched her. His square jaw spoke of stubbornness and determination. She had seen his body already and felt it against hers—hot and hard. He looked like a Southern California surfer she'd met many times in her trips and stays in the U.S.

A Labyrinth of Love and Roses

He put his lips up against her ear and said in halting French, "Vous êtes très belle." And then in smooth English, "You're gorgeous, like an angry pixie."

He pulled back and smirked at her again. Maybe he thought she didn't understand. Well, she'd show him—an invitation if there ever was one. She mouthed in unaccented English, "Thank you." She leaned against his ear and said, "You dance like a madman!" She lingered at the side of his neck and inhaled.

He smelled of the woods and salty and something all male.

She grabbed his hand and led him to a dark corner away from the dance floor and bar. She didn't normally make out with the first cute guy she met dancing, but tonight was different. He was different. And her life was suddenly different.

Her desire took on an urgency that had her hands shaking as she stopped with her back against the wall, and still with his hand in hers, pulled him against her body. She inhaled with surprise and smiled up at him. He was hard for her. She wanted him even more.

He didn't waste any time showing her how much he wanted her too. His hands roved over her breasts, squeezing with just the right amount of pressure. She moaned and kissed him hard, not waiting for any kind of invitation. Tonight she wanted this—this connection—this all-male hardness against her body. She wanted to feel the life in this moment. She wanted him. Her hands explored his muscled neck and back. She ran her fingers through his hair, then gripped it as he kissed her fiercely, meeting her desire with possession and passion. After a time, she came up for air. He looked as dazed as she felt.

He whispered loudly into her ear to be heard over the intense rock music. "Let's get out of here."

Beth Barany

She kissed him as a reply. He met her passion, angling his mouth over hers, his tongue dancing with hers, giving, taking. He was her lifeline, for the moment. She pulled him closer and danced flush against his body, swaying while the music was pounding.

He pulled back this time, panting.

The music downshifted to something slow and rhythmic, haunting and melodic—reminding her of her duties and responsibilities, at least to her business. Enough avoidance for one night.

"I have to go," she said loudly and shook her head.

He said nothing, just kept hold of her waist.

She kissed him hard and stepped around him. He let her go. For a moment, she felt as if she'd been torn in half. But she shook it off and hurried for the exit without looking back. It'd been a long time since she'd felt such passion for a man, like he was an essential part of her that she had to cleave to. Actually she'd never felt such passion for a man. God, he was sexy.

But hell, one-night stands weren't her style. Not even for a man as hot as he was.

Chapter Three

BRETT BARNABY WATCHED THE redheaded pixie make a beeline for the exit. He almost followed her, but that would be stupid. Although she was hot, so hot he wanted her right then and there in the dark corner of the raucous dance club, sweaty and hard for her, something held him back. Maybe it was the way she didn't look back and walked with her shoulders back and spine tall. She was quite something.

He leaned against the wall and watched the crowd swallow her up. The music was cranked up now, a hard rock number, but not hard enough for him. He wanted harder, badder, faster, sexier. He wanted her. His redheaded pixie.

Well, if he couldn't have her, he could always have another. There were lots of sexy women on the dance floor. They'd been eyeing him all night.

He stomped to the dance floor and got himself into the mix. But after a couple of hard songs and slow ones he didn't want to dance with any of the beauties shimmying around him. He just wanted *her*. That was so unlike him.

Hours before the club shut down, he left and stepped out into the cool night. He hoofed it back to his hotel. Amiens was a small town, he could go everywhere on foot. He had to burn off some steam, so he ran. The red-haired pixie dominated his thoughts, occupied his body. How she looked in that short, strapless, black number with the sexy fringes. She drove him crazy all night. Back home in San Francisco, he'd have gotten over her quickly with another beauty in his bed. There was always another willing lovely to romp around between the sheets. They were consenting adults. It was all fun.

But something had changed in him recently. Maybe it was his father's recent illness that made him realize that life was more than investing in yet another company with his inheritance and jet setting to dance clubs around the world with gorgeous women on each arm.

Life was short. That was why he was in Amiens searching for something no one in his family had been able to find. The gravesite and gravestone of his great-grandfather who'd fought and died on this soil in World War I.

The rumor or legend in his family was that his Australian great-grandfather had died in the war protecting some big secret, and that the secret, once uncovered, would unlock the family's true mission and purpose. Some said riches. Some said a higher calling. No one knew. He hoped it was a purpose bigger than just investing in companies as he did, or investing in movies, as his parents did. His family had riches enough. There had to be something greater he was put on this earth for.

He didn't know what that was, but it had to better than what he had—making money and partying. He let himself into his hotel room, took a quick shower, and slipped into bed, thinking, then dreaming of the red-haired pixie.

Chapter Four

F ATED TO BE MATED," that was what she was. Everyone always told her that—everyone being her parents and older siblings and aunts and uncles. She didn't want to believe it. Oh, they said it in different words. And now there was her grandmother's warning slash command that she would know him when she saw him and magic knew magic. She told herself she wanted adventure, freedom to travel the world and do good work. But deep down she wanted someone to love her, care for her, look at her with passion and devotion, a lot like the surfer beach bum from last night at the club. A lot like that. She shoved him out of her mind. Her parents looked at each other that way when they thought the children weren't watching, as if their love was something only they shared. If they caught the children watching they always put on their masks of sternness and propriety.

Lili didn't believe in fate or having a legacy. She believed in making her own luck and making her own way in the world. Even if she did have a leg up due to the circumstances of her birth, being born into a well-off banking family, not on par with the Rothschilds but close to it.

Her thoughts were straying as she clipped along in her sensible low heels, hurrying for the presentation. She'd made time to arrive early, but she'd planned to drive—even though the hotel was three kilometers away from her place. But her car wouldn't start. Then she hurried to catch the bus and it was late. She gave up trying to arrive in a pristine, unmussed state and hurried down the hotel hallway. Even with all the strange mishaps, she'd still be early. She pushed a stray red hair back into her bun. She thought her light green summer suit was professional and offset her fair complexion and red hair. Just the way she liked it. All those weird delays better not be the start of the chaos Gra-mere was talking about. When this morning presentation was over and she had firm offers in hand, she'd take them to her grandmother and show her where her legacy was.

She stepped into the conference room, expecting it to be empty. She was hoping to set up in peace and quiet and rehearse her opening one more time. She wanted some quiet to gather her thoughts and make sure everything was ready to be cued up on her laptop. Instead, it was half-full of mostly elderly men in tweed watching a slide presentation about the island gardens of Amiens.

She froze and blew out a breath in frustration.

She turned to leave and brushed past a man who was entering the room. "Excuse me," she said in French, and sucked in a breath. His smell was so familiar. She looked up in time to see a familiar and sexy smile.

He said in a Texas drawl in American English, "Sorry, ma'am." He hadn't sounded like that last night. Or maybe she hadn't been able to hear his drawl over the loud music.

If she thought he looked good in a sweaty tee-shirt and low cut jeans, he looked just as good in a tailor-made jacket and slacks, button down linen shirt and tasteful tie. He scanned her up and down. He winked when she met his gaze.

"Join me for coffee?" he asked and waved toward the extensive Continental breakfast service in the back of the large room.

She glanced to the front of the room where the crowd was still watching the slide show. She checked her watch. She had twenty minutes to spare. "This is the room for the international investment pitches. Is it not?" She said in English.

"I assume you're here to pitch?" A new look was in his gaze. Was that disappointment? It was gone in a flash. His face was a mask of politeness. Gone was the sexy heat in his gaze.

"I am." She felt deflated, but shoved that aside.

"Good. Then you're in the right place." He stepped to the coffee service and poured coffee into an espresso cup. "Cream and sugar?"

She shook her head. "Black. Thank you." She set her briefcase at her feet and took the tiny cup and saucer he extended toward her. Their fingers brushed. She gasped and pulled her hand away, spilling the coffee onto the saucer, and luckily none on her suit. He flustered her. She stepped back. "I need to get ready."

She scurried toward the back row of empty chairs with the coffee in one hand and her briefcase in another. She gulped her coffee, set aside the empty cup and saucer, and sat down. She had to get ready. What was he doing here? She hadn't even asked him. She didn't get his name, but he surely knew hers if he was an investor. Was he an investor? He looked too young to be one, at least in comparison with the other people in the room. He couldn't be more than thirty years old. He had a youthful, vibrant, hungry look about him, and was sexy as hell.

She dragged her thoughts away from him and put them back squarely on her notes. She had to nail this presentation, secure the international funding, and serve her company's mission of bringing her water purification technology and software app to all who needed it, mostly in Africa, but also in other parts of the world.

Polite applause broke her out of reviewing her notes. The slide show was over. She was next. Everyone was counting on her.

Chapter Five

AFTER HER DRAMATIC OPENING about the statistics of water usage in the first world compared to the third world and her slides juxtaposing children in Europe and North America with children in the southern hemisphere and equatorial regions, she felt good. Her audience was nodding. Everything was sailing along nicely.

Then the projector made an odd clicking noise she'd never heard before and stalled. The light on the machine went out. This better not be more chaos. But she'd prepared for this, prepared for every contingency, in fact. She pulled out a bulb from her briefcase and handed it to the hotel tech who'd helped her set up. While he was working on the machine, she smoothly segued. "Just like our technology doesn't always work as planned, it pays to have built in redundant systems. My water purification technology does just that and works under even the harshest weather, drought, or extreme rain, using the latest technology in fog reclamation and redundant back-up systems. This technology allows for—"

Somebody coughed in the back, drawing her attention there. The beach blond, sexy as all get-out, man who cleaned up very nicely in a suit leaned against the side wall and smirked at her. She pulled her gaze from his and continued. "This technology allows for all weather conditions and is affordable to build. Once we have our prototype in place, we can go to full production."

With your help of course, she thought. But that was implied. That they would help fund her company so they could move to production and distribution was why she was here. "We have a large-scale proof of concept project ready to roll out as soon as we have enough units." The projector's lights popped on, and she continued rattling though the numbers that appeared on the slide.

Her audience seemed engaged—their gazes were on her. But they seemed also a little restless, shifting in their seats and whispering to each other. An elderly man in front with a long, trimmed, white beard frowned at her and shook his head, like he disagreed with everything she said. She pulled her attention back to her presentation and clicked to show the next slide on the win-win-win profit potential. It was a blank. For a moment, she froze. That wasn't supposed to be there. She'd gone through the slides hundreds of time. More chaos. She puffed out a breath and clicked to the next slide and continued about the triple win of profit, people, and planet.

By the time she was done, she received polite applause, instead of—well, she expected more profuse praise. Her project was cutting-edge and could revolutionize how water was distributed. The leader stood and thanked her, saying they'd be in touch with any follow up questions in the next twenty-four hours. That wasn't the response she wanted. She wanted to hear how they were so excited to bring her an offer in the next day. He nodded to someone over her shoulder. Another man came up to her as she stuffed her laptop and notes into her briefcase. "I'll escort you out," he said. "We have another presentation starting soon."

Lili nodded and followed him out. The blond guy was nowhere in sight.

If she couldn't get funded by this group, she was out of options and would have to start at square zero for her funding strategy. She had exhausted the rest of her potential funders list.

Chapter Six

BRETT SLIPPED OUT OF the decent presentation by his redheaded pixie and walked to Amien's cathedral. He was a few minutes early. She couldn't be his, he reminded himself. No mixing business with pleasure. It had always been his rule and had kept his life simple.

As soon as the cathedral was open at 10 a.m. for visitors, Brett slipped in with a small crowd of tourists. His reading about Amiens led him here as the starting point to find his great-grandfather's gravestone. He checked the brochure and studied the map of the vast interior—the cathedral could hold ten thousand people, the population of the town in the Middle Ages—then headed for the columns near the front of the cathedral. Many memorial plaques were there, commemorating the fallen soldiers from England, America, and Australia. But he didn't see any mention of his ancestor or of the phrase that was one of the few clues to the legend, handed down through the generations in his family. He needed help. He approached an older woman dressed all in black, who was placing candles into the offering holders. He tried his French, asking if she knew where in the cathedral he could find the phrase, "*Fidelis, fortis, verus.*"

She backed away from him, frowning and shaking her head, no. She made the sign of the cross above her ample matronly bosom.

Was that no to his question or to something else? He didn't feel capable of asking that clarifying question in French. He needed a new approach.

He walked toward the center of the enormous cathedral. A priest stood in the middle of the empty worship area in the cathedral, reading a small, thick book—the bible most likely.

"Excuse me, Father," Brett said in French.

The man turned to him with a kind smile and replied in French. "Yes? Can I help you?"

Brett said haltingly in French, "I am looking for a gravestone of my great-grandfather. I think it's here."

"What was his name? We have records of that kind of thing."

"William Branford Barnaby."

"Australian? American?"

"Australian."

The priest pulled another small fat book out of his pocket, thumbed through it, and looked up at him, and spoke in heavily accented English, "No, so sorry, we have no one by that name on the rolls. Do you have any other clues or telling markers you know about?"

Brett told him the Latin phrase. The priest frowned and also made the sign of the cross. "Do you know where you're standing?" Then the priest shook his head. "I'm sorry. I can't help you, young man." He hurried away.

Brett was stunned. It was just a Latin phrase that also happened to be the motto of his college fraternity, Psi Alpha Omega Chi, at UC Berkeley. Cool coincidence, Brett always thought.

Where was he standing? He looked down. He was in the center of the cathedral's tiled labyrinth. He shivered. The symbol of his fraternity had a labyrinth, too. But their circular pattern had a rose, mason's square, and chisel at the center. The center of the labyrinth here in the cathedral was a cross white on black tile with four robed figures and four birds. He looked around for someone else to ask. He didn't know what to make of everyone's behavior, but he couldn't give up.

He headed toward the front of cathedral for an office or something official, beyond what a tourist usually sought. He'd learned in his world of investing that you sometimes had to look for the unusual situation. Perhaps a different priest or another church employee could explain the reactions. He found a locked door with the words *Bureaux* on the door.

The door opened. A nun stepped out.

"Can I help you?" she asked in English tinged with a lilting accent.

Brett explained what he was looking for—a gravesite or gravestone—and offered the name of his great-grandfather and the Latin phrase. "You best not be asking about with that Latin phrase." She pursed her lips and gripped the rosary hanging from her belt. "It's associated with the Green Man and considered allied with the devil in these here parts," she said in a definite Irish brogue. "Now I'm made of tougher stuff than most, so you can't scare me off that easily. What you're looking for surely isn't here." She shook a long finger at him. "Green Man belongs to the islands, the wilds. Go look out there, young man, but be careful. It's not stuff to be mucking about in. 'Tis powerful devilish magic, if you be asking me." She fixed her jaw at him and bustled off in long strides.

Green Man, devilish? What had he stumbled into? All he wanted was to find his great-grandfather's gravestone and unlock his family's true mission and give his life a purpose again.

Chapter Seven

O VER THE LAST TWO days—if she counted from the moment she finished her pitch—Lili had been driving herself crazy with waiting for an answer from the investors. They hadn't followed up in the twenty-four hours as promised. She'd debriefed with her team for hours over Skype, gone for a run along the river three times over the two days, and definitely stayed away from the clubs. But it was April 28, and if she didn't hear from the investors today, she'd have to assume the worst—that she wouldn't be funded and would have to find another deep pocket investor group or individual. This international group had been her twentieth pitch. She'd exhausted her A, B, and C list, and would have to start working on the Z list. Or make a new A list. That took time. Instead of ramping up her company this summer. She'd just gone on her morning run in the dawn hour and hopped out of the shower when there was a knock at the door. She threw on her bathrobe, rushed to the door, and peeked through the peephole. She pulled back. "Oh!"

"Hello? Ms. Grenault, is that you?"

"Just a minute!" Lili said and rushed behind her bedroom curtain to change into jeans, bra, and tank top. What was he doing here?

She rushed back to the door and opened up a crack. "Yes? Can I help you?" she said politely and blinked up at him. So tall. His blue eyes smiled at her.

"You do remember me, don't you?" He smiled and scanned her from head to toe and back up again.

She nodded, her voice lost somewhere crumpled amongst her bedding and clothes all piled in heap on her bed.

Don't think about your bed. Or him in it.

Like that worked.

Her heart fluttered.

How could I forget you? she thought.

He stuck out his hand, half-smile notched up further. "Brett Barnaby, investor, surfer, general layabout. We haven't been properly introduced." He scanned her more slowly from head to toe and back again.

Her core clenched. Her breath came short. She wanted to lean into him, but held back.

When his gaze reached her eyes, his smile faltered for a half-second, then he regained his devil-may-care attitude. She shook his hand, but he wouldn't let hers go. He stood there, frozen, his smile gone from his face. He opened his mouth then shut it.

A spark flooded up her arm from his grip. She shivered, then managed to pull her hand from his, missing his firm warm grip. This man did more than look pretty and spread money around, her bed sheets whispered at her. His grip was firm and warm, full of strength.

"Pleased to meet you, formally," she finally managed to say. "Lili Grenault. *Enchantée.*" She licked her lips and eyed his, drawn to them like a bee to a rose, a very delicious rose.

Rose. Bringer of the Rose. She sucked in a breath, frozen to the spot.

Time seemed to slow to stillness.

She stood in the doorway, the hard wood of her apartment door at her back. Brett stood in the hallway of the apartment building, gazing at her like she was the most interesting thing in the world.

"Can I come in?" Brett asked leaning forward, breaking the stillness.

She glanced over her shoulder. Her place was a mess, her sweats on a chair and papers on her desk, table, and floor. Dirty dishes were piled high in the small sink. Finally there was half-eaten Chinese take out on the table. The bed was unmade, sheets and blankets all tangled.

"No. Sorry."

She scanned him, slowly, giving him the same treatment he'd given her. He was wearing polished Salvatore Ferragamo plain toe grey boots, Armani grey slacks, and an Armani sky-blue button-up shirt that made his blue eyes bluer. His very nice business attire didn't come out of a catalog or off any rack—all tailored and made to fit his surely six-foot swimmers build frame.

She bit back a sigh and looked at him directly. "You're here on official business about my presentation, aren't you?"

He nodded, a thoughtful look on his face. What had chased that away? She wanted to know, wanted to know what made him tick. The image of them making out at the club flashed in her mind, and her body heated. She wanted more than to just understand him.

"Can we talk at a cafe?" he asked. "Or grab lunch somewhere?" His voice was modulated, polite.

"Uh, sure. Let me just grab my things." She shut the door in his face. She opened it again. "Sorry, but I can't let you in." She waved her hands and shrugged. "You'll just have to wait out here." She shut the door again.

"Oh, don't mind me. The hall is just fine. I always liked the hallway."

She smiled, despite her jumping nerves. Here she was mooning over him when she needed to keep her mind on the business and get their funding. She couldn't tell from anything he'd said or done about the investment group's position on investing in her, only that he wanted her too, or had before the cold politeness slid back into his voice. She grabbed her leather jacket, shoved her laptop and purse into her briefcase, and swung open the door. "So is it good news or bad?" she asked.

Chapter Eight

H E HATED TO DIM her bright hopeful gaze, but he couldn't lie to her either. "That depends how you feel about hard work."

"I'm fine with hard work." She lifted her chin like he'd just issued a personal challenge.

She led the way down the hall. He followed, admiring her ass in her tight jeans. He could look, but just not touch anymore. They stepped out of the building and headed down the street.

She glanced at him. "Well, lay it on me."

"You speak like an American."

She shrugged. "I spent a lot of time there."

He waited, but she didn't say more about herself or about why she'd been in the States, or spoke like a native.

"Your accent sounds Californian."

She hummed in reply.

Her professional bio hadn't explained either, just listed her impressive degrees and work experience. She'd been an undergraduate at the Sorbonne, with a degree in history, did graduate work both at Stanford in water engineering and at the INSEAD, the premier French business school. She'd also done work paid and unpaid with various overseas agencies in Africa, Asia, and South America, all on water projects. She knew her stuff.

He followed her in silence to the cafe. Once they sat at a table and ordered lunch, she said again, "Lay it on me."

She sat straight, hands folded in her lap.

Her light was dimmed. Brett wanted to see the light flare again in her aqua eyes. He wanted to see that light flare for him, and only him. He pushed that thought aside. He'd convinced the group that he was the best man for the job, and so it was on him. And her light wasn't probably going to brighten much anytime soon after she heard what he had to say.

He opened the folder he'd been carrying and eyed his notes. More a prop than he really needed the notes. The prop anchored him to reality. This was a professional relationship now and could be nothing more. And he didn't mix business with personal.

She sipped some water and set the glass down with a clack. "Well?" she said.

"Right." He gave her a tight smile and glanced at his notes without really seeing them. "They want more numbers, especially for the plant in Africa, projections for the next five and ten years. Also, they want to know how you're going to source your plastic components to keep within your ethical labor standards since, mostly likely, India and China are out, and the US and Europe are too expensive. Once they get those figures, they're happy to reconsider you and will reschedule a new presentation. And all this needs to be done in the next two days." He finally looked up at her.

She sat back. "All those figures and in two days? Is that all?"

He laughed. She looked so serious, but she had a glint in her eye, like she was challenging him to throw even more at her.

The waiter delivered their food. Lili tore into her salad like she had not a care in the world. She had a hearty appetite—for food, for dancing, for running her business. He liked how she embraced life.

There was no liking, he reminded himself.

"I need your help with something too." What made him say that? He knew. He stared at her red lips. They were fresh and ripe, like strawberries, unmarred by that hot red lipstick that he'd kissed off her in the club.

"Brett?"

"Hmmm?"

"You're staring."

"So I am." He set aside his notes and dug into his salad. Lili had ordered a salad niçoise for them both. "Delicious." He nodded.

"Glad you like my choice. So what is it you want me to help you with, and can it wait until after my second pitch?"

"Well, I suppose it can. But not really. I'm leaving in four days and don't want to leave it to the last minute."

"What?"

"The gravestone of my great-grandfather who died here in World War I."

She eyed him, her gaze unreadable.

"Will you help me?"

"Only if you help me."

"You need my help gathering the data?"

"No. I have a team for that, but I need you to look everything over. Make sure it's what the group wants and that it's presented the way they want."

"You're not just using me to get what you want, are you?"

She shrugged. "Maybe." She eyed his lips.

"What?"

"You have a little something here." She pointed to the side of her lips.

"Oh." He wiped at his lips with his napkin, Lili watching hungrily.

This whole separating business from pleasure was going to be hard.

Chapter Nine

LILI SIGHED WITH CONTENTMENT and put her fork and knife length-wise across her plate. She signaled the waiter. "*Deux cafés, s'il vous plait.*"

The waiter nodded and retreated.

"You got us some coffee?" Brett asked.

"Yep! So you speak some French."

"Some."

"So why do you need my help, then?"

Brett gazed out the window and then back to her. "Something strange happened when I was at the cathedral looking for the gravesite. Or clues to where to find it."

"Wait. How come you don't know where it is?"

"No one in my family has been able to find it, yet there's family legend that says it's here, in Amiens."

"So a quest."

"Of sorts."

"Hmmm." She sipped at her espresso. He wasn't just sexy, her meal ticket, he also had a mystery to unravel. Like she did. She didn't want to think about her mystery. It was more fun to think about his. "Okay. I'll help you."

"Great." He gulped his espresso in one go, like he had the drink at the club, that first night. What would it be like to make out with him again, but in broad daylight? Her heart accelerated and her breathing sped up. She looked out the window to the bustle of the day and sighed. His next words jolted her back to the moment. "Let's go."

"Now?"

"Yes."

"But I have my numbers to get moving on."

"You said you have a team for that."

"I do."

He slipped more than enough euros out of his fine leather billfold and tucked them under his espresso cup. Then he stood and held out his hand to her. "Then let's go a'hunting."

Her heart skipped a beat. She ignored his hand and stood too. "You know where to look? I thought you said you needed help with that."

"I do. I think the gravesite is on one of the islands. Somebody, this nun at the church, mentioned about starting there. But I need your help pinpointing which one. I gathered from your bio that you grew up here and would know."

The thought of the river islands made her nervous. Her grandmother's words ran through her mind. "In three days, by Beltane, you must go through your Rite of Initiation on the islands to formally accept your legacy and find your one true love, but not in that order."

"You know what?" She gazed up at him. "I can't—"

He eyed her lips, then met her gaze. He stepped toward her, so that there was just inches between them. He brushed a crumb from the side of her lips. "You have something there," he whispered.

"Oh," she said softly.

"You were saying?"

She felt an inexplicable tug toward him from the moment she'd met him on the crowded dance floor. She couldn't turn him down.

Magic finds magic, her grandmother said. Was he her one true love?

She shook her head. She didn't believe in fate. But her grandmother was so fervent. She shrugged and then nodded, a little light-headed.

"Having an internal committee meeting?" he stepped back to grab his notes still on the table, breaking the moment.

She breathed a little better.

"And the verdict is?" he asked.

"I could really use your eyes on my presentation."

"Good." He stepped toward the door.

She opened an email on her smart phone. "I'll call my team and get them rolling." She looked up at him, feeling a little dazed. "We'll explore the islands. I think I might know where to start. And—" she smiled. "You buy me breakfast tomorrow to go over my presentation. I need to get my funding."

"I like a woman who knows what she wants."

Chapter Ten

IN THE SPRING AFTERNOON, Lili led the way to the river quay where she got them a ride on a tourist boat that made stops at several different garden islands. In no time, they were stepping on a tiny jetty and walking into what looked like to be an English garden, full of manicured shrubs, statuary, and stone fountains. They were the only ones who disembarked.

Because the quiet and intimate environment called for it, Brett took her hand. Together they strolled through the garden in the bright and warm afternoon. He inhaled the fresh smell of earth and plants. Soon he felt like he'd stepped away from modern life and entered another time and place. They didn't speak for a while.

They wandered and soon found a bench, a polished wooden bench with a plaque in the back.

Lili rubbed her fingers over the plaque. "Dedicated to the British III Corps, under Lieutenant General Sir Richard Butler, its 18th (Eastern) Division, part of the K2 Army Group." She read aloud.

"Hmmm."

"Not a clue?"

"No, my great-grandfather was Australian."

"I assumed he was English."

"Lot of people do, with the last name Barnaby."

"Give me more clues." Lili sat back. "I thought this garden would be a starting point because, as you can see, it was created in honor of this division. It was the only island I knew of that did that. There's more, the boat tour guide said." She opened a map of the river islands and studied it.

He brushed back the streak of blue in her flaming red hair. She looked up at him, startled.

"I don't usually mix business with pleasure," he said, leaning toward her.

She eyed his lips. "Then don't," she whispered and leaned in to kiss him.

Her lips were delicious, soft and warm. They opened for her. She reached for him, circling his shoulder with her arms, map forgotten, and climbed on his lap. He was hard for her in an instant. Oh god. She filled his vision. Her sweet smell enveloped him. He kissed her hard and she met him, her passion flamed on, matching his.

And there they made out, on the bench, in the sun and warmth and flowers and bees. She finally came up for air and smiled broadly. "I so wanted this since back at the cafe."

"And you left me waiting?!" he said in mock anger.

"I left me waiting!" she said.

"So it's all about you."

"Of course." And she leaned in to devour his mouth all over again.

He roved his hands all over her back and her butt. What a glorious ass. He slipped his hands under her shirt and covered her breasts with his hands. They fit so perfectly in his palms. She wasn't wearing a bra. Where had that gone? He was sure she had it on earlier. He noticed those sorts of things in a woman, especially this woman. "So lovely," he whispered.

She squirmed over him like she wanted to crawl inside him. He wanted that. He wanted her. He reached for her jeans button and unhooked it.

She groaned and pulled back again. "Brett?"

"What?" He slowly pulled down the zipper.

She jumped off his lap. "I can't."

"Okay."

"Okay?"

"Yes, of course. Okay."

"Don't you want me?"

"You know I do."

She zipped up her fly and buttoned her jeans, then stomped in a circle around the fountain. She was muttering to herself. He throbbed for her, but he didn't need to run after her. She was right there, haggling with herself again, no doubt. He adjusted himself and waited.

She spun to him and stomped back. "I need time to think."

"Okay."

"Stop being so agreeable."

"Okay. What would you like me to be?"

"Argumentative."

He stepped over to her. "Sorry. I can't help you there."

"Oooh." She stomped off toward the hedges behind them.

"What's the deal?" he asked softly—his promise to himself blown to bits. "You want me and, I for some crazy reason, can't resist you."

"It's too soon."

"There's some rule?"

"Yes, my rule. First date is just a first date. No sleeping together."

"Well, technically it's our second or third. Or is it the fourth? Depends on how you count."

Lili shook her head, her back to him.

"Lili, come sit down. Talk to me."

She shook her head. "I gotta take a walk."

"Let me know what the committee decides," he shouted after her.

But she didn't laugh at his lame joke. He wished he could take a cold shower. He wanted her so bad it hurt.

He circled the fountain. Should he go after her? What was he doing mixing his passion for her with his business obligations?

He splashed some water from the birdbath on his face to cool off and clear his mind. His hand disturbed some leaves. Words at the shallow bottom of the bath caught his eye. He scooped off the leaves to see the lettering better. Chiseled into the bottom of the grey stone birdbath were the birth and death dates of a lieutenant in the UK division. His heart quickened. Maybe his great-grandfather has a gravestone commemorating him too. He rushed to the map that Lili left beside the bench and studied it. Luckily it was in English. He realized that the island actually was quite large and had several parts, split into sort of wedges like a pie. They were in the English section. He sucked in breath when he saw that two sections over was the Australian section. According to the map, she'd gone off into the Irish direction.

He considered going after her, but the Australian garden section pulled him, and she needed to blow off some steam. She'd come around. They'd eventually end up together. He felt it. It was only their first official date. That meant there would be more. He smiled and headed through an opening in the trimmed hedges.

Chapter Eleven

S HE WANTED HIM SO BAD.

And that scared her.

What if he was the one?

Did that mean her grandmother was right and she had to pursue her legacy?

As if she had a choice.

But what about her company? She'd worked so hard on it for months and years. Since graduate school she'd been working toward this goal.

No fair.

But life wasn't fair. As her grandmother often had said to her as a child.

In fact her grandmother had said many such pieces of advice to her, her whole life.

A thorn snagged her jacket, slowing her forward movement.

Lili finally noticed where she was. She'd walked blindly through the tall hedges and now stood at the mouth of a raised-earth labyrinth that was lined with hundreds of shoulder-high tiny pink rose bushes, all the tight buds popping open.

Prickles shivered from head to toe. The heady scent of all those roses overwhelmed her. She felt dizzy, and yet she felt drawn toward the center of the labyrinth. She always loved walking the one on the Amiens cathedral floor. She'd never walked an earthen one. The closer she got to the center, the taller the earthen mounds and the rose bushes got. The path narrowed. The thorns snagged on her jackets and her hair.

The center was her inevitable destination. Something urged her forward, not a voice, but more like a pull from her gut, urging her to take step after step. After another turn, there she was. A small clearing was just a step away. But first she had to pass under a bower covered with pink and orange roses, filling her with their heady scent. She stepped into the clearing and gasped. A man clothed only in green leaves, clearly naked underneath, stood in the grass. His hair was matted and full of leaves. His manhood jutted up at her, also covered. His eyes were open wide so that the whites showed all around his dilated pupils. He stared at her wild-eyed, mouth open, a long beard of green leaves trailing down his front.

"You!" he boomed and pointed a scythe at her. "You must cut to the truth and claim your legacy. Or else!"

He cut the scythe through the air, once, then twice, as if to emphasize his point.

Fear froze her in place. Then she found her voice. "But why?! I want my life the way I want it." And who the hell are you? She wanted to voice, but that seemed overly rude.

"The magic has chosen you," he said and swiped the scythe through the air between them again.

"I don't want it to have chosen me. I want to choose my life."

"It has always chosen you. Through all time. And this is your time."

Lili opened her mouth to protest.

But the man covered in all shades of green leaves interrupted her in a deep booming voice that sounded familiar. "Do not turn away from this, Lili of the Green, or else the very ones you wish to help will perish."

She gulped. "What does that mean?"

But the green man just glared at her and swung his scythe in a wide sweeping motion in front of them, again and again, and slowly stalked toward her. She had to get out of here, out of the way of that scary scythe. She turned and stumbled across the earth-mounds, breaking all respect for the labyrinth—her grandmother would kill her—and ignoring the thorns tugging at her clothing and skin. Was she going crazy? Was this the magical initiation her grandmother had insisted on? She so didn't want a part of any of it—especially if a crazy leaf-covered man was part of it.

Chapter Twelve

T HE MEADOW WAS TINY, hemmed in by the forest that surrounded it, all pine by the look it. How strange! He was in a tiny, postage stamp-size meadow in the middle of a river island. But he couldn't even see the river from where he stood. He couldn't see anything except the meadow and tall trees all around, hemming him in. There had to be a pathway somewhere. He spun, but didn't see the pathway that led him to this spot. He'd just have to cut through the forest. The river must be beyond. All the islands were small, no more than one hundred feet long and wide, by the scale on the map. But the map hadn't been accurate so far.

Brett had followed the map. Well, he thought he was following the map. But the pathway, instead of leading him through the next section then the next in short order, led him to a little lake, then a pavilion, then a little meadow. He hadn't seen any more commemorative plaques or fountains.

He stared at the map and turned it this way and that. The sun was high in the sky. He didn't know which way was true north. Nothing on the map seemed to match what he'd just passed through. What the he—?

He stepped forward and stumbled on something. It was a farm tool. He picked it up. A scythe, perhaps. He'd never seen one up close. He touched the sharp edge and yanked his finger back. The scythe's blade had cut him, only a little, but enough to draw blood. He sucked on his finger for a second.

He tried to set the scythe down, but it wouldn't detach from his hand. A jolt flooded his body, a powerful, electric shot. He sucked in a breath and glanced around. Not a cloud in the blue sky. It couldn't be lightning. A boom like a thunderclap sounded. Another jolt rushed from his feet to the top of his head and back down again. In an instant, his chest burned, from the inside. The power of the earth rushed through him a hundred times, no, a thousand million times more powerful than he'd ever felt before—a lot like the rush of playing racquetball, or surfing, or having sex, or all of those all at once. He couldn't stand, so he fell to his knees, one hand still gripping the smooth wooden handle of the scythe. The power—it was so immense, so huge—he fell the rest of the way to the ground and blacked out.

Chapter Thirteen

LILI BENT OVER TO catch her breath, putting her hands on her knees. The wind cooled the sweat on her brow. All she could hear was her labored breathing and the pounding of her heart in her ears. She finally paid attention to her surroundings. The vegetable garden was unfamiliar.

She pulled out her cell phone. No bars. The sun was on her right, in the west setting, so she turned around and headed north, because that was where the dock was.

Where was Brett? She checked her cell phone again. Still no service. She must be in a weird pocket where cell reception didn't reach.

She walked for about ten minutes and slipped through some hedges. In front of her were the bench and the fountain where she and Brett had kissed.

She didn't know what to think about him, about them. But she yearned for him anyway.

She kept walking north. And there he was, staring off into the sky, like he was bird watching or something. In fact a flock of white birds flapped overhead in a wave of color and sound, like coordinated confetti.

"Brett," she called out.

He didn't turn around.

She stepped closer and touched his arm.

He jumped at her touch.

She gulped when he turned to gaze at her. He seemed wild, his eyes narrowed and intent, like he'd been thinking about hunting those birds. She gulped. Then she stiffened her spine and gripped his shoulders with both hands.

"Are you all right?" she asked firmly.

Brett nodded, slowly focusing on her. She knew he was back with her when he gazed at her lips hungrily.

She was hungry for his lips too and leaned into him.

His body was warm and hard against hers. They kissed, short and passionate. She pulled back in a burst of breath.

"Better?"

"Mmm." He kissed her hard, again, like she was his lifeline. Passion burst from her core. She had to have him, too, but not here and now. She pulled back with effort. "What happened?" she asked.

He shook his head, confusion in his eyes, then shrugged. "Where were you?" he asked. "I went looking, but couldn't find you."

"I got lost. It was strange." She glanced away. "Come on, let's go." She grabbed his hand and headed toward the dock. He'd surely think she was strange if she told him that she saw a man covered in green leaves. "Sorry we didn't find your great-grandfather's gravesite."

Brett looked back the way they came. "It has to be here somewhere. No other islands have such memorial gardens, right?"

"Pretty sure. I'll ask my—"

"Who?" he asked when she snapped her mouth shut.

Lili sighed. "My grandmother. She grew up here, too. Like me. But maybe she knows things I don't. In fact, I know she knows things I don't."

They stepped on the boat that arrived as they did and didn't speak as they headed back. Lili held his hand, and that felt good. She even let him put his arm around her for a little while. Then she pulled away and checked her phone. It was finally working. She got absorbed in checking her email and tapping out messages to her team. Maybe by the time she got back to work tonight, she'd be prepared for the new presentation Brett's group wanted. She looked up at him to ask him a question about the numbers and caught him staring at her.

"What?" Heat crept up her neck and face.

"You are so beautiful."

"Don't let it fool you. Inside, I'm as rough and edgy as they come."

"Mmm. I want to see your edges." He reached for her. But the boat was docking so she hopped ashore, out of his reach.

"Work to do!" she laughed and danced away, glancing over her shoulder to make sure he was following her.

He hopped easily to the dock and wove through the other disembarking passengers, his easy jocularity back. He grabbed her hand and swung their hands between them as they walked down the broad sidewalk. He tried to grab her phone out of her hand when she tapped on it to check her email.

"But I have to work today," she protested.

"You can wait, can't you, until we get back to the hotel."

"I need to get to my place."

"Let's grab a bite to eat first. You gotta eat, right?" He gazed at her hungrily.

"I do."

Oh, he wanted more than to share a meal with her.

"Then there's no issue."

"Brett—"

"We all need to eat." He jutted his chin toward the hotel a block away.

Her stomach grumbled and she smiled. "I do like to eat."

Chapter Fourteen

BOUT AN HOUR LATER at the hotel restaurant, as the coffee after dinner was being served, Lili's cell phone rang. "*Oui, allo?*" she answered without paying attention to the caller ID.

"Lili, my dear, is he the one?"

Heat spread up her neck into her cheeks, again. She looked around frantically.

Her grandmother was at the bar. She lifted a glass of wine in her direction as a salute.

"Gra-mere," Lili switched into rapid French. "What are you doing? Stop interfering. It's just a guy I met at the investment group. He's helping me."

"I bet he is. I see the way he looks at you. Are those grass smudges on your jacket?"

Lili felt the blush all the way up to her red roots. She glanced at Brett. He smiled his lazy surfer smile.

She shrugged and waved her hand to convey her helplessness in the face of her spying grandmother.

Brett grabbed the phone out of her hands and said in clumsy but clear French, "Grandmother, why don't you join us?"

Lili shook her head fervently. "What are you doing?" she hissed.

"You didn't understand my French?"

"I understood perfectly well. You and I need to talk shop and she doesn't—"

"I don't what, dear," he grandmother said in British-accented English.

Lili stared wide-eyed at her grandmother.

Gra-mere winked at her and turned to Brett. "Hello, young man. Are you the one?" She reached out a hand to shake his. Brett shook her hand, sucked in a breath, and swore.

Lili shot to her feet. "Excuse me, Brett." She grabbed her grandmother's arm. "Gra-mere, may I have a word?"

Gra-mere nodded regally and let herself be dragged away toward the bar, looking over her shoulder at Brett.

Lili crossed her arms and glared at her dear, sweet, ever so innocent-looking grandmother. "What are you doing interfering?"

"I wanted to see if he is the one, and I'm not sure. He could be. I got something there when we shook hands. Something powerful."

"He's just an investor."

"But you like him." Gra-mere narrowed her eyes at Lili.

Lili sighed and resisted the urge to look at him. "I do. But he's leaving soon, and I have work to do."

"Excuses, all of them. You need to do the Ritual of Initiation on seven days or all will be lost." Gra-mere shook her long, bejeweled finger at Lili.

"So you've told me."

"You still don't believe me, young lady."

"Gra-mere, please. Don't young lady me. That's what Mom does."

Gra-mere reached out and touched Lili's cheek. "I know, Lili dear." She sucked in breath. "You saw him." It was a statement, not a question.

"Saw who?"

"The Wild Man." She clapped her hands. "You are most blessed. Not many have seen him."

"Gra-mere, what are you talking about?"

She remembered everything about her encounter in the center of the labyrinth, but a girl could be in denial just a little while longer, couldn't she?

She turned to glance at Brett, but their table was empty.

She left her grandmother in mid-frown and rushed to her table.

A note in a fine cursive handwriting sat at her plate. "Had to run for an unexpected meeting. Breakfast here at 8 a.m. to go over your presentation. Promise. I owe you an extra coffee." He signed it with a flourish with his first name and an x and o, for a kiss and a hug. She smiled, despite her disappointment. She turned back to stomp to her grandmother, but Gra-mere had quietly moved to her side. Gra-mere shook her head and tsked. "Maybe he isn't the one."

Lili wanted to say he was, to defend him, and forgive him for cutting out before their evening was formally finished. But she couldn't say he was the one. She couldn't defend him. She hardly knew him. But she supposed she could forgive him for leaving the way he did. Gra-mere was a force of nature.

"Gra-mere, you scared him away. Why do you always scare my men away?"

She sniffed. "If they're scared of me, then too bad for them. One day you'll be as formidable as I am, and if they can't deal with that, then they don't deserve you." Then she squinted at Brett's seat, as if she was still examining him. "But he was a strange one. He may still be the one. I can't tell. And that is odd."

"Gra-mere, you are odd. You owe me a digestif."

"Only if you do the ritual as planned."

"Tonight?"

Gra-mere patted her hand. "No, I suppose, not tonight."

"Whew! I'm off the hook."

"For now."

"I know."

She hadn't wanted to believe the ritual of initiation and her magical legacy was real, but after this afternoon's run in with the leafy man, she knew she couldn't deny the possibility.

Chapter Fifteen

THE NEXT MORNING, LILI rushed through her morning routine to get to the hotel cafe by the early morning hour. She was running late. Gra-mere had filled her ear with ritual preparations and gotten a little tipsy, then stern with Lili, when Lili didn't take her all that seriously. How could she? Gra-mere was tipsy, a glass of whiskey at her elbow, and Lili really didn't want to hear it.

Gra-mere also wouldn't stop asking her questions about Brett. Where was he from? What was he doing in Amiens, really? Lili told her about his search for his great-grandfather's gravesite, but held back from what had happened that day. She gazed at her grandmother's hazel eyes, then shook her head.

"You like him, don't you?" Gra-mere teased.

"I told you already." Lili shrugged and felt the flush flame her cheeks. She smiled, remembering their make-out session at the club and again on the bench.

Gra-mere leaned in so her rich whiskey breath was in her face. "I think he's the one. Pretty sure. But I can't test him, if you know what I mean?" Gra-mere winked.

Lili flushed even more. "Gra-mere, I need a break from all that. I don't have time to think about relationships right now. I have a company to run and a successful pitch to deliver."

Gra-mere had shaken her head, tsked again, and called for another whisky neat. When the drink came, Gra-mere raised it to Lili, "For courage," she saluted, and chugged it down in two gulps. Then she stood and sauntered off without a weave in her step, her back straight, shoulders back.

What a woman, Lili had thought. She wanted that class when she was her grandmother's age.

Gra-mere had called again in the wee hours of the morning to remind her once again of her deadline—that the ritual of initiation was in five days. She sounded wide-awake. Lili could imagine her grandmother clipping fragrant roses from her garden and snipping pungent herbs for her morning tea.

"Yes, Gra-mere," was all she said and tried to go back to sleep. It wouldn't do any good to get mad.

A few hours later, she was up and tapping away at her computer. The sun peeked through her kitchen window. The coffee, third cup, was at her elbow. Her team had come through with the new numbers, but her printer jammed when she tried to print out the final reports. She cursed.

She'd just have to take her laptop to show Brett the numbers. Her heart fluttered. His blue eyes and those oh-so-kissable lips, his arms wrapped around her, securing her against him. What was she going to do about him? About her feelings for him? Which were?

She couldn't sort them out now. She jumped in the shower to clear her head of Brett and her grandmother's words. The pounding hot water did the trick for the moment. Refreshed, she dressed in her favorite black slacks and slightly off-the-shoulder blouse. But when she went to dry her hair, her hair dryer didn't work. She shook the dryer and fiddled with some buttons, but the damn thing wouldn't turn on. She swore in English. She wrapped her hair in a tight bun and glanced at her watch. She jammed her foot into her favorite low-heel pumps. The strap broke. She cursed a third time, this time in French.

Threes. Trouble came in threes. Her grandmother's singsong chant from childhood ran through her mind.

She didn't have time for this. Grandmother warned her of dire consequences if she didn't follow through with the ritual of initiation, but these tech issues couldn't be a part of stopping her from doing what she loved, could they? They weren't dire, yet.

She didn't know what to think. She glanced at her watch. She was fifteen minutes late. She swore a fourth time, in German. Nothing was better, but nothing was worse, either.

Chapter Sixteen

BRETT EYED HIS WATCH for what seemed like the tenth time. Lili was so far only twenty minutes late. He checked his email on his smart phone, checked his texts. There was no message from her. He drummed his fingers on the table, on top of his notes for Lili.

He had three days to find his great-grandfather's gravesite, and all he wanted to think about was Lili. All he wanted was her. She was the key to unlocking the mystery, his heart told him, though he had no idea how that could be true.

He did know that he couldn't have her, not if he wanted to be one of the investors in her company.

"Hi."

He looked up. Lili, lovely as ever, wore a soft blousy thing, tendrils of her curly red hair escaping the tight bun other head.

"You're late," he said.

"I know. I'm sorry."

"You should have called. I was worried."

"Really?" she sat down and ordered an espresso from the waiter who'd silently approached.

Brett crossed his arms.

Lili took out her laptop, opened it, and turned it so he could see the presentation. She moved her chair next to his, so her leg and shoulder touched him, and began her revised presentation.

He leaned away slightly.

She paused in her detailed analysis of the factory readiness in Africa and said, "I don't have cooties," in perfect American English.

"Where did you learn about cooties?"

"Stanford. Now can we get back to my presentation? You said you'd help me. Are you going to follow through?"

"Of course."

"Good." Lili rattled off more numbers and analyses. He had to keep from touching her, her smooth skin, the column of her neck, a perfectly kissable place, right where her neck met her shoulder.

Lili paused. Then cleared her throat.

He lifted his gaze to hers.

"Can we stay focused, please?"

"Only if you go back to that island with me. I have to find my great-grandfather's gravesite. I leave in three days."

Lili frowned. "We looked all over."

"Did we?"

"What's so important about finding it?"

"What's so important about funding your company?"

"What do you mean? It's everything to me."

"Exactly." Brett eyed her lips then looked away. He gritted his teeth at what he was about to say next. "And we can't be together. At all."

Chapter Seventeen

L ILI GULPED AND HELD out her hand, for Brett to shake. "Friends, then."

He shook her hand but didn't look happy about it. In fact, he didn't look happy at all. Ever since she'd arrived late, he looked jumpy, drumming his fingers on the table, fidgeting, frowning at her. All the while, he was staring at her when she wasn't looking at him. She could feel his gaze on her face, her neck, her lips. In response, her core beat with heat and desire.

And then he dropped the friends bombshell on her. Fine. She could roll with that.

Maybe he wasn't the one. Maybe he was and she just missed out on the chance of a lifetime.

She'd never know because, magical legacy or not, her company came first. How could she look at herself in the mirror if she didn't try her all to get her very worthwhile project off the ground?

So friends it was.

Brett shook her hand firmly and looked away.

She puffed out a breath and dove back into the new numbers and analyses. He asked her hard questions and found flaws in her reasoning. Part of her was shocked at how could she have missed those things, but another part of her was impressed that Brett had the insight and the guts, *cochones, cueilles,* to not shy away from the hard questions.

After an hour, Lili had gone through the entire slide show presentation and had a ream of notes to integrate. She was discouraged. She had lots to do in the next little while. But she was also grateful. Her presentation would be better for his insight and hard questions, and she'd get the funding when she presented again in the next day. She was sure of it.

Then she wouldn't see Brett again. She shut her computer and shoved it in her bag to cover up the sinking feeling in her gut, like someone just punched her there. That was the price of a successful business. All work and no play makes Lili a sad, sexless, relationship-less woman, she thought. Then she pushed that thought aside. Founders always had to make sacrifices to build their companies. She knew that. All founders knew that. Later, she'd build a love relationship. With someone with sparkly blue eyes, sandy blond hair, a dangerous smile, and a hard body in all the right places.

She pushed that desire away into the little corner of her mind and her heart and sat up smiling, maybe a little too brightly. "Let me take you to lunch. As a thank you," she said. "I know just the place."

Brett checked his watch. "Okay, but I have another meeting in an hour."

"So we'll make it quick. It's just around the corner." She hoped the meeting wasn't with another investor he was helping, like he'd been helping her. But she kept that thought and question to herself and brought him to her favorite brasserie a few blocks from the hotel. A lot of her friends who were still in the business school nearby ate there around this time. Then she'd go home and work on her presentation.

She stepped into the noisy bar restaurant, an open plan with tables and wicker chairs, in the *bon vivante* style of Paris's wide boulevard cafes. She loved the place. She sighed, relieving some of the tension coiled up low in her belly, all that pent-up desire for Brett.

She glanced at him. He smiled at the place. He seemed more relaxed too. She'd made a good choice.

Five of her friends greeted her with loud hellos and kisses, *les bises*, on both cheeks all around. They each shook Brett's hand soberly. They were kind and didn't pepper him with impolite questions. Brett kept quiet while everyone jabbered in rapid French around him. After their salads niçoise, they all sat around the table with their espressos and joked about the good old days last year when Lili was still in class with them all.

Finally one of them turned to her and said in French, "You really like him, don't you?"

Her damn pale skin. She could feel a blush creep up her neck all the way to her hairline. Brett was watching her from across the table. She could feel his gaze on her without even looking, without even touching him.

Brett's phone beside his coffee buzzed. He glanced at it and frowned. He looked up at her. "They want your numbers this afternoon and your presentation has been moved to tomorrow at 9 am."

Lili squirmed then nodded. "Sooner than expected. But that's okay. Thanks."

The table of five friends all took that moment to be quiet. Then the teasing started again. "He likes you. You like him. Ooh."

"What is this, primary school?" Lili snapped.

Her friends just laughed at her, paid their tabs, and wandered off chuckling.

Brett set down his phone he'd been texting on. "I know you have a lot to do, but I'm leaving in three days..."

"You want my help, I know." Lili felt a sadness descend over her. "Can't you get someone else to help you? I have to prepare. Get the numbers in." She shrugged helplessly and fiddled with her spoon.

"Lili—"

She looked at him. "What?"

He grabbed her hand from across the table. "Come with me. It'll only take a little while. I know it."

His touch was warm, comforting. Then he rubbed his thumb pad across her skin and she felt electric from that simple touch.

"Give me one, no, two hours, to get my team in motion, with all these questions you gave me, get the numbers to the investment committee, and I'll meet you at the historical society near the cathedral. They should have some information in their archives about the islands, so we can find the right one."

He squeezed her hand, set down some euros, eyed her lips, and opened his mouth to say something. Then snapped his mouth shut, nodded at her, his expression unreadable, and stalked off.

Lili shuddered. Her inexplicable draw toward him was a constant low-level ache in her core. And she'd just said yes to meet him for yet another jaunt to the mysterious and mostly likely enchanted island where weird things had happened to her. She couldn't refuse him. She just couldn't.

Chapter Eighteen

LILI RUSHED HOME AND tapped furiously on her computer, sending out emails and requests and detailed notes to her team. Luckily, John was getting up in Silicon Valley, and Sarat liked to burn the midnight oil in South Africa. Wei was already into the middle of her day in Hong Kong, and Leo was a workaholic in London and would be finishing his afternoon tea right about now and be refueled for work.

They didn't know anything about her grandmother's deadline on her and she wanted to keep it that way. Her company was going to get funded. That was all that mattered. It was her job as founder to keep them inspired and motivated. They were skilled enough in their respective fields to do what she requested and well. They were already motivated by a desire to make the world a better place, same as she was.

She set the alarm on her phone and one on her computer to remind her of the hour so she could meet Brett on time, unlike the morning meeting, and hustled through her notes.

By the time the second alarm sounded, in case the first one wasn't enough, she changed into her favorite jeans and walking shoes, and into a more practical cotton top, this one pink, and her lined leather jacket and pink scarf. She sprayed on her favorite scent, which just happened to be l'eau de rose and hurried out of the apartment.

When she got to the historical society near the cathedral ten
minutes away on foot, Brett wasn't outside. She called his cell.
He didn't answer. She peeked inside and asked if an American
man matching his description had come in, but they said, no one
had.

She thought of going to the quay but nixed that idea. That
hadn't been the plan. Maybe he was still at his hotel for his
meeting. She rushed there on foot, but he wasn't in the lobby
cafe. She asked the front desk to call his room, but he didn't
answer the hotel's call.

She frowned and tapped out a text: *Where are you?* No
answer.

On a whim, she went back to the lunch cafe. If he wasn't
there, she'd go back home and get back to work. Disappointed
and getting a little angry with him, she rushed into the lunch
cafe. And there he was, his back to her, talking to an old man—a
man with a long trimmed white beard. He wore a dark grey
waistcoat and coat and snappy bowtie, as if he was from another
era. She recognized the older gentleman from the presentation a
few days ago. She hustled up to the table, ready to greet the
man politely and give Brett a stern eye.

Brett glanced up at her, wiping away what looked like tears.
He glanced away, frowning. She didn't get a chance to give him
a stern gaze, she was too shocked by his apparent sadness. She
turned to greet the elderly man but he was gone.

Deflated, she sat where the elderly man had been. Her anger
whooshed out of her. "What's going on?"

Brett looked up from his cell phone, all trace of any tears
gone. Had she imagined them? "I was doing research."

"With him?"

"With who?"

"The old guy with the beard."

"Who?"

Lili sat back and shivered. "You didn't see him."

He eyed her and wrinkled his brow. "No. Who?" he asked again.

"I saw him at the presentation. Elderly man, hunched in the shoulders, a long but neat white beard. A double-breasted suit. Bowtie. Old-fashioned grey in a herring bone pattern, I'm pretty sure."

He shrugged. "No. I don't know who you're talking about."

"Weird," she said quietly and glanced away. She was about to ask him why he wasn't at the agreed upon meeting spot when he placed his hands on her clasped hands on the table and said fervently, "Lili, I need your help. I need you to come with me. Right now."

Warmth and tingles flooded up her arms, down her body and settled in her core. "Yah, okay. I said I would," she managed to say, her voice a little breathy.

Magic recognizes magic, her grandmother's words echoed in her mind. She shook off the words, slipped her hands from his and stood, immediately missing the warmth and the spark. "But why me? You could ask anyone in this town. Many of us know the river islands quite well. My grandmother does, for example."

"Your grandmother isn't nearly as cute as you are."

"Not to you, anyway. My grandfather likes her just fine."

"I'm sure he does." He stood and grabbed her hand. "Let's go. I think we were on the wrong island."

"How do you figure?"

"Just a hunch from my research."

Then why do you need me, she wanted to ask, but didn't. Then, I need you, whispered in her mind.

Her phone pinged in her pocket. "I have to get that." She pulled her hand from his and checked. It was a text from Sarat in South Africa, asking her to check her figures in an email.

"We only a few more hours of daylight," Brett said. "Can it wait?"

"Hmmm." She tapped on the email and read it over.

Brett snatched the phone from her hands. "It can probably wait. For just a few hours."

She snatched her phone back and checked the time. It was 5pm. "We have four hours until sundown."

"How do you know?"

"I'm from here. I know."

In twenty minutes, they'd walked back to the quay and were waiting in line for the tourist boat. Fifteen minutes later, Brett motioned for her to get off at the island they paused at while the boat master droned on about the vegetable and flower crops grown on this island garden.

"What are you doing?" she hissed at him as she followed him onto the tiny jetty.

He reached out a hand for her. She gasped at the electricity that passed into her as they touched. His eyes widened but he said nothing in response to anything he felt. "The name of this island is Prince William Island."

"Yeah, so?"

"William was my great-grandfather's first name."

"That's your only clue?"

"Yes." He beamed at her. "Come on."

He turned and strode down the path, lined with lavender and rose bushes. She breathed in the heady peppery scent of lavender. These roses hadn't bloomed yet. It was only the end of April.

The rite of initiation she was supposed to do by May first, two days from now.

Her phone beeped, three beeps in sequence. She pulled it out of her pocket again. It was texts from the rest of team, all requesting her to check their work in emails and on the group online project board.

Brett was fifty feet in front of her. He called over his shoulder. "Put that thing away. Come on! Daylight burns."

She clicked on an email but it was empty. In fact, all the emails her three teammates sent her were empty. She sent them a group text to tell them that, then pocketed the phone again. "It's put away. I'm coming. Geez."

He chuckled and kept up his striding down the path, now lined with tall hedges. The path curved and Brett disappeared from view.

She hurried after him, took the curve, but didn't see him.

Instead, she saw a woman dressed in a gauzy white sheath, her black hair floating around her head. The garden shimmered behind her. Her body and dress were translucent.

The woman gazed at her sternly and pointed down the path, where Brett must have gone, but didn't speak. In the middle of the woman's chest was a red rose in full bloom embroidered on the white fabric above her heart. The woman pointed and glared at her, like Lili had done something wrong, or maybe that she was supposed to hurry. So she hurried. She had to ask her grandmother about this woman, who she was, what she meant.

Gra-mere hadn't said anything about ghosts appearing and glaring at her with roses embroidered on her chest. Gra-mere hadn't told her many things. Or maybe Lili hadn't been paying attention.

By the time she made it to the path where the woman would have been, there was no one. But there was a gap in the hedges.

Lili glanced ahead. Even though it was a straightaway, she didn't see Brett. She could continue forward or she could step through the gap in the hedges, like he must have done. So she did too.

She blinked. There was the green-leafed man, covered as before head to toe, his manhood jutting prominently forward toward her. He beckoned with one hand, his gaze impassive, and cut the air with his scythe with the other. He stood in the center of a clearing.

Lili blinked again, and the green man was gone.

It was Brett calling to her and waving his hand to bring her toward him.

She couldn't hear his words. She could only hear the sound of waves steadily beating on a shore and rhythmic two-step pounding of a deep drum.

Chapter Twenty

BRETT HAD STEPPED THROUGH the entrance. The path curved and turned. He rushed forward, calling to Lili over his shoulder, but she didn't answer. She wasn't behind him, but he felt drawn forward.

He wanted her to be here. She was instrumental in helping him uncover his family's true purpose. Without her he wouldn't have known where to start his search on the islands. He couldn't stop to see how far back she was. The answers had to be there. He was certain. Then he could uncover the secret his great-grandfather had kept for so long and uncover the family's true purpose and give greater meaning to his life.

He heard some talking and turned to look. Lili was staring at him. He waved her forward. "This way!" he said excitedly. She looked without seeing him, frozen, her mouth open in a small "o."

He waved at her again. "Come on!" He turned to follow the path. In short order, he was at the center of the labyrinth. A low stone blocked his path. He knelt to examine it. The writing was too faded to make out. He couldn't tell if he was looking at numbers or letters. He rubbed his fingers across the stone, as if that could get him closer to deciphering what was there. But no luck. He stood disappointed and blew out a breath.

In the center of the clearing covered in clover was a fountain, or maybe a birdbath, like the one they'd seen—was that only yesterday? It was, but it felt like eons had passed since he'd made out with Lili on the bench in the afternoon sun. He ached to have her in his arms again.

He approached the birdbath and leaned over it. Shallow water filled the basin, clear this time, with no leaves for him to pick out. He couldn't believe it. There were words etched in the bottom of the basin. They read *"Fidelis, Fortis, Verus"* or "Loyal, Steadfast and True." Etched also at the bottom of the fountain was the symbol of a rose and the drafting compass and chisel—the symbols Brett saw all over their fraternity but were never explained. Those were the symbols of the fraternity he joined in college and where he'd met Liam and Josh, his best friends.

Below the rose and chisel was his grandfather's name, William Branford Barnaby, and his birth and death dates, 1885-1918. The name of his regiment, the Australian 31st Battalion, 5th Division, was listed with the symbol of a sword and musket crossed. *Fidelis, fortis, verus* was repeated under that.

The family legend was that his great-grandfather had started the fraternity in Australia, but that story wasn't in the official records of the U.S. fraternity. Brett had always thought it was a coincidence and never put much thought into the connection between his fraternity and his great-grandfather until now.

How could a man born at the end of the nineteenth century start a fraternity that was supposedly founded in the eighteenth century? William Branford Barnaby had died at the too-early age of twenty-nine years, leaving behind a young wife and two little boys.

He'd found it. He stared at the fountain. His purpose and destiny was at hand. He heard footsteps behind him and pivoted.

There was Lili, her red hair undone and flying around her head in the breeze. Her eyes were wide.

"Lili, are you okay?" he asked.

She gazed at him, but she didn't seem to see him.

Her cheeks were flushed. She stood with her shoulders back, in a regal fashion, or like those ballet dancers he'd dated. They seemed so delicate and insubstantial to him, compared to Lili. She seemed solid, connected to the earth, and wild, with her hair flying all around her head.

He stepped to her side and touched her arm. For a second, he felt dizzy. Then it passed.

"Lili," he said again.

She gave no indication she noticed him and gazed at the fountain. She stepped forward, pointing her hand at the fountain, and swayed. She mumbled something.

"What did you say?" he asked and stepped to her side. Her words sounded like Latin or medieval French. He couldn't tell and wasn't well schooled in either to be able to decipher anything specific. Whatever it was she was saying she was repeating it over and over again. She stopped swaying and gazed off to a faraway point. Finally he could hear the separate words, something like "*amor, fiducia, communitas,*" clearly now. He didn't know why he couldn't hear the words before.

He clasped her hands.

Dizziness washed over him again.

She didn't acknowledge him and chanted those three words over and over again, her arms held out in front of her. She squeezed his hands. A jolt of electricity burned through his entire body, like a lightning burst. At once he felt naked and seen and held by some invisible force.

"Lili," he breathed. He wanted to hold more than her hands, but didn't want to upset her trance. He didn't know what would happen if he did. He didn't know how to bring her back to him.

Was this part of his purpose?

Her eyes were wide as she chanted. Maybe he had to join her somehow to bring her back. So he said the words with her—at first stumbling, then in rhythm with her, and finally in synch with her, so he couldn't hear her voice or his. Together they sounded as one voice.

He didn't know how long their chanting went. He had the strong sense that he had to stay with her or lose her. He stepped toward her when her grip loosened on his hands.

She swayed. He was there to catch her in a hug against his body. "Lili, my love, are you okay?"

Her eyes were shut. "Brett?"

"Yes."

"What happened?"

He sat on the soft clover with her in his arms. "I don't know. You were chanting over and over—"

"I saw the green man again. I think it was you."

He shook his head, but she couldn't see him. Her eyes were still closed. "No, don't think so."

"Yes, I saw you, like yesterday. It was you. You want me."

"I do want you." He bent to kiss her, a whisper of a kiss on her lips. "I always want you."

Chapter Twenty

LILI LEANED INTO THE kiss, deepening it. If she didn't have him, she'd explode into a million little pieces. She wrapped her tired arms around his neck and pulled him toward her. She wasn't sure why her arms were so tired. She remembered holding them out and she remembered Brett gripping her hands in his.

She came up for air and squinted at the sky. It was dark. "Brett—"

"Mmm." He nuzzled her neck.

She scrambled to her feet. "I need to get back. My presentation—tomorrow morning." She scrubbed her face and shivered. It felt like she'd been in a dream, a lovely dream, but so separate from reality.

In the starlight, Brett stood, looking as dazed as she felt.

He grabbed her hand. "Look! We found it." He led her to the stone birdbath a few feet away, at the center of the clearing.

"The birdbath is your great-grandfather's gravestone." She traced the edge of the limestone fountain. "Does it say something? I can't see it by only the stars."

He gripped around the waist. "Yes, it has the Latin saying and my great, grandfather's birth and death dates, the name of his regiment. And the carved symbol of the rose and the drafting compass and chisel."

"Why do you sound so disappointed?"

"I thought I'd feel different, once I found it."

"Like all would be clear? And your life problems all resolved?"

"Yes, something like that."

She turned in his arms and kissed him gently on the lips. "Does this help?"

"It does." He kissed her back, passion flaring between their tightly pressed bodies.

"Brett—" She pulled back, wishing she could see his eyes. He was staring at her lips. "So you've decided to mix business with pleasure?"

He said nothing.

She pulled and waited a beat. "Well?"

"Lili, I want to..."

"But what?" She dropped her arms, stepped away, and shivered. Nights were cold in Amiens at the end of April, and more so on the islands.

He shook his head. "I don't know."

"I can't do this right now." Lili stomped away from him and back toward the boat pick up. She heard him following her out of the labyrinth. Thorns caught on her coat and scarf, but she didn't care.

They didn't speak all the way back to her apartment. She pretended like she didn't care. But she did.

They stood under the front light of the building. She was glaring at his shoes.

"Lili," he said softly.

"What?" A yearning in his voice had her peering up at him.

"Come here." He opened his arms and she let herself be wrapped in them.

"I—I just need some time. I thought things would be different when I found his gravestone," Brett said.

"I wish things were different too." She kissed him on the cheek. "You'll be there tomorrow?"

He looked pained and shrugged.

"Well, you clearly have some decisions to make." She reached out and he took her hand. "I'm not going anywhere."

He pulled her back against his firm body. "Ah, Lili." He gave her quick, fierce kiss on the lips. "You're the best." He turned and strode away in the cold spring night.

She shivered. Why couldn't he stay and warm her bed?

She let herself into her apartment and busied herself with preparing for the next day's presentation. Brett's advice had been quite helpful. But her computer kept crashing and no amount of swearing in multiple languages did any good. Was the chaos her grandmother spoke of getting worse? She went to bed not sure. But it didn't matter. She had investment funds to raise for her company.

She woke up early, before her alarm, panic in her gut.

She made coffee and relaxed for a moment. Her place smelled liked sweet, spring roses. Then she realized she smelled like roses. An ache rose in her belly. An image of Brett and her wrapped in each other's arms in the labyrinth flooded her. She wanted him in her laugh. He made her smile and remember to have fun.

She hummed and jumped in the shower.

She rehearsed her new opener in the shower out loud. It sounded good to her.

Soap got in her eyes. That hadn't happened since she was a little girl. She threw the soap, swore and banged her wrist on the tile. That brought on more swearing. Her alarm blared and she hurried to finish in the bathroom to turn off the annoying repetitive shrill. She slipped on the floor and almost fell, but caught herself in time on the corner of her desk. Her palm stung. She must have cut it.

She quickly bandaged her palm with a Band-Aid and shimmied into her powder blue skirt. She slipped into a cream silk camisole top and powder blue blazer, careful with her hand. She turned this way and that in the full-length mirror. She thought she looked feminine, calm, and professional, as long as she didn't wave her bandaged hand in front over everyone. Luckily, her hair dryer worked after the second try, and so did her printer after a few false starts.

Nothing she couldn't handle, she told herself. She'd power through this morning and succeed. She had to.

She carefully slipped on her shoes, a pair of Louis Vuitton *Oh Really Pump* cream-colored heels and wobbled for a second dizzy. Everything had to work out.

She slid her laptop and her printed presentation into her slim briefcase and let herself out of the apartment. She caught a taxi to the hotel to save time. She read her team's text of Good Luck and well wishes and wiped tears from the corner of her eyes. She normally wasn't ever weepy. Lili put a hand on her belly to calm herself. She took a few deep breaths before stepping into the hotel and pasted on a brave smile. She could do this.

Would Brett be there to cheer her on? She wished things were certain between them.

Then she had to push those thoughts from her mind and step into the whirlwind. As the conference room filled up, Lili smiled and nodded hello to the men and few women that filed in for her

9 a.m. pitch. By the time she was about to start, Brett still hadn't arrived. He hadn't said he would, but she'd assumed he'd be there to support her, even if he didn't want to mix business with pleasure and hadn't chosen her over business. Or had he? She wasn't sure.

She took a deep breath and began with her introduction on the key importance of access to water for everyone as an international civil right and how it would be to the benefit of all communities and nation states. She had everyone's attention all the way through, but when she ended her pitch exactly on time, the applause was polite, and there were no questions. The elderly man with the trimmed but long white beard smiled at her and gave her a little wave. She didn't know what to make of that.

The leader stood, shook her hand, and said he'd be in touch the next day. And that was that. She was ushered off the platform quickly. They had another pitch in ten minutes, she overhead someone say. Of course. She left the conference room, puzzled, not sure if her second pitch was any better than the first.

Still, she thought it went well overall. At least, she didn't have any technical mishaps. That had to be a good sign, right? She wanted to find Brett and tell him what happened. He may be able to figure out what the end results would be. To save time, she flagged down a taxi and headed home to change out of her suit and back into her favorite jeans. In the taxi, she emailed and texted her team about how the pitch went. She promised they'd do a group video call the next day and let them know she was taking the rest of the day off to celebrate.

In her apartment, she called Brett. He didn't pick up his cell or answer her text. Not this again. She called the hotel and the cafe, but he wasn't at either place. That left only one place he could be—at the Prince William Island.

In thirty minutes, she was on a boat, mostly empty of tourists and landed at the island. She ran the path to the labyrinth. She didn't see the lady in white this time and found the proper entrance to the labyrinth. She hadn't noticed yesterday how high the hedges were—they came up to her shoulders—or that they'd been laced with open pink tea roses woven along the top.

She called out Brett's name, but heard no answer.

She rushed through the curves and double-backs until she arrived at the clover clearing. She spotted the fountain they'd discovered the day before, but no Brett.

Then out of the hedges stepped the man covered in green leaves, as if he had been a part of the hedges and now was separating himself out into human form.

She ran up to him, certain now of who he was. "Brett!"

He gave no response and stared at her wide-eyed, the whites of his eyes scarily showing. He smelled of earth, leaves, and the sweat of a man. Her man. She recognized Brett's smell. She called his name again, and again he gave no indication he recognized her.

He spoke. At first she didn't recognize the words. They were sing-song-y and lilting, sounding like a combination of French and Irish.

He shoved a cup in front of her and spoke in gibberish.

Finally the words formed themselves in coherent phrases that she could understand.

"You must repeat after me, 'I pledge myself to the community of the Bringers of the Rose.' " He presented the cup to her again. She didn't take it. He wasn't looking at her, but through her. She turned around to ensure there was no one behind. But there was. It was the woman in white, nodding at her, smiling, her long, dark brown hair floating in the air all around her head.

Lili glanced again at Brett, the Green Man. He bowed to the lady in white.

"What is going on?" Lili asked the lady in white. But the lady pointed at Brett and then shimmered, fading into nothingness.

Lili turned back to Brett, and this time he gazed at her, actually looked at her. "Brett!"

He held out the cup, again, more like a goblet, gold-colored with etchings along the rim. She reached out and took the goblet. Inside was a clear liquid. She sniffed. It was odorless. Hopefully it was water and nothing harmful.

"Repeat after me," Brett intoned in a deep voice, deeper than his normal speaking voice. "I pledge myself to the community of the Bringers of the Rose."

"But what does that really mean? How can I commit to something when I don't know what I'll be doing? I can't give up my business. I just can't. I've devoted years of my life to it. You can't be serious." That last bit came out weakly. Her modern expression sounded funny against her ears.

Brett frowned. "You form a community with others. You are not alone. But if you don't take the pledge, the circle will be broken, and many millions will die. The very people you want to help, and those who want to help them, will die. The fate of millions is in your hands and in your heart."

He gazed at her as he said those words, but it wasn't Brett talking. It was as if some greater force of nature was speaking through him in an ancient language.

"Brett, or Green Man, or whoever you are, what about my business? I can't just abandon it. What will happen if I take this pledge? Gra-mere said I had to put my commitment to being a Bringer above everything."

"Yes, you do."

"To even love?"

"Love is the glue that holds it all together."

"That's sufficiently cryptic," Lili grumbled.

"Today is the day you must pledge or all will be lost." He gestured to the goblet in her hands. "Say the words 'I pledge myself to the community of the Bringers of the Rose,' then drink from the goblet of life. Your love will seal the pledge."

The sun slipped lower in the sky, at the edge of the Western horizon. How long had she been in the labyrinth with Brett?

She opened her mouth to protest one last time. Her scientific, numbers mind wanted to protest loudly. Where was the proof, it screamed. You're being led by folly, it yelled. She felt the soft clover against her feet. At some point she'd taken off her shoes. When had that happened? The wind caressed her body. She wasn't in her jeans and t-shirt anymore, but a white shimmery dress, just like the lady in white. She had no memory of changing. The clover circle they were in felt safe, but there was no trace of her clothes.

"Pledge," he intoned.

Lili leapt into the unknown and said the pledge. "I pledge myself to the community of the Bringers of the Rose."

"Now drink," Brett, the Green Man, said. "And let your love seal the pledge." His low voice caressed her, but still he gazed at her with no recognition in his eyes. Brett had to be somewhere in there.

"Only if you drink too," Lili said. Maybe that would bring Brett out.

He nodded slowly, acquiescing to her order.

So she drank. It was water, the sweetest water she had ever tasted. She felt woozy and handed him the goblet. "Drink," she said in slurred speech.

He took the goblet from her, drank deeply, and said, "*Fidelis, fortis, verus.*" Then he slipped to the ground.

"Brett!" She rushed to him and held him in her arms.

In an instant, the leaves vanished, and there was Brett, naked and asleep.

She kissed his cheeks, his lips, his forehead, and whispered his name, and didn't notice when rose petals and leaves covered them like a soft blanket.

Brett murmured something about purpose and legends, but didn't wake. She spooned him because it felt right. They were lying on sweet clover or *Casse Lunettes*—good for thinning the blood and healing bruises—her busy mind whispered. How did she know that? Oh, it was the magic of the land. What did she do with that?

Then Brett's sweet kisses pushed all thought from her mind. She let her hands roam over his body. In her mind's eye, he was covered in leaves, but her hands felt only the soft fabric of his silk shirt. She found the buttons, undid them with urgent yanks, all the while kissing his sweet lips, so hungry for his taste. She couldn't get enough.

"I have to touch you," she breathed. His chest was firm in all the right places, his shoulders muscled and strong. His soft chest hair tingled under her palms.

"This isn't our first date anymore, is it?" he smiled into her mouth, then sprinkled kisses down her neck. He found the sweet spot at the edge of her shoulder. She squirmed with delight as a fire of desire shot straight to her core.

"Brett," she sighed.

Chapter Twenty-One

"MM." HE TOOK THAT as agreement.

"More," she half-sighed, half-moaned.

He took that as full assent. He roamed his hands over her chest, stopping to kiss her nipples under her shirt. She pressed them against his mouth. He nipped and sucked and she sighed and squirmed.

To hell with not mixing business with pleasure. Lili was more than that. Lili was everything to him. In just a few days, she had become all he wanted. All he ever wanted. His heart felt like it could burst out of his chest, it was expanding so much.

She shoved his shirt off him and caressed his skin like she was drinking him up through her hands. She undid his belt buckle. He reached for her pants. In minutes they were both undressed and kissing and caressing.

She was his entire world. Love expanded his heart and focused him at the same time.

He froze. *My one true love*, he thought.

"What is it?" she whispered.

"I—all—I—" He smiled and reached for her jeans. "All I want is you. Only you."

She beamed and leaned in for a kiss.

My one true love, he thought again and kissed her back.

Chapter Twenty-Two

"WHAT?" SHE WHISPERED.

He kissed her deeply, hungrily.

When they came up for air, he said. "I didn't say anything."

You're my one true love, he thought again, and nipped and kissed the side of her neck.

She squirmed with delight and smiled. "You did. I heard you. You just said it again."

"What? While I was kissing you? My mouth was busy."

"You said, 'My one true love.' "

Brett shook his head. "I only thought it."

"I heard you, Brett. I heard you." She hugged him so tight she couldn't tell where her body ended and his began.

He hugged her in return, like he'd never let go.

Somewhere between the dance floor five nights ago and now, she'd given her heart to him and hadn't even realized it until this moment. "And you are my one true love," she said and opened herself to him fully. "Forever and a day."

"Forever and a day." He kissed her, and they made love under the stars on the eve of May first, Beltane eve.

Chapter Twenty-Three

AT SOME POINT IN the night, Lili awoke. She was curled up against Brett, warm and satiated. But she still wanted him, again. By the light of the moon and the stars, she could see that their naked bodies were entirely covered in leaves and rose petals. She wasn't cold. But how would they get off the island and into a proper bed, preferably in a bed together?

"Brett," she whispered and touched his shoulder.

He stirred but didn't open his eyes. "What, love?"

"We need to get home."

"We are home."

"I mean off the island."

"Why?"

"Well, work, for one. Presentation follow up. Be ready when they call. That sort of thing."

He made kissing noises, so she chuckled and kissed him. The kiss deepened to steamy, and she was ready for another round with him, when a horn sounded in the distance. She pulled away from his willing and delicious mouth.

"We have to get going. That's the last call horn."

"How do you know? It could be the mating call of the loon, for all I know."

"I know what it is because I grew up here, remember? That horn means it's 2 a.m."

"But you've never done this here on an island, have you?" He gestured between them.

"Why? Jealous?" She wiggled her eyebrows at him.

"Maybe. But you're mine now."

"Yes, I am." She stood and held out her hand to him. "And no, I never did romp on the islands during Beltane. You're my first Beltane boy, and I want a bed."

He stood, leaves plastered over his body. "Me too."

She pulled a leaf off his chest. "I think we need to get dressed first."

He chuckled and tugged a leaf off her breast. "Right away?"

She swatted his hand away. "If we want to catch the last boat."

He hugged her. She inhaled his musky scent and smiled.

It was May first. She had taken the pledge, but she didn't feel any different. She didn't know what she was expecting. She did notice though that the hedges were whispering and so were the roses.

If she listened closer, she could hear them singing to the stars, a most beautiful song that made her heart ache with joy and wonder.

"Brett," she whispered. They were covered in roses and leaves, a warm blanket on a cool night.

"Good evening," he whispered. "I had the weirdest dream."

"It wasn't a dream."

He sat up. "What happened to my clothes?"

She chuckled. "I was wondering the same thing. The hedges told me they have our clothes safe and sound."

"The hedges told you?"

"Yah, the plants can talk to me and I understand."

He eyed her sideways. "Can you talk back?"

"I don't know. I haven't tried it yet. But I think they understand me. I think they've always understood humans. It's just that humans don't understand them. Or don't listen." The roses woven into the hedges chuckled kindly at her. She smiled.

Brett hugged her and made understanding noises.

My Lili, she heard him think.

"I can hear your thoughts too," she said.

"That's a wonderful benefit of—of—what do I call it?"

"You mean my initiation?"

"Yes." He rubbed his head. "Did I really say all those things, do all those things? Wearing only leaves?" He opened and closed his hand. "I remember holding the scythe and the goblet and saying things..." He looked around. "How did I get back here?"

"You don't remember?"

"Not exactly."

"Well, maybe it will come back to you." She stood. "We'd better go, unless we want to swim home."

"A swim sounds like a great idea."

She swatted his shoulder. "A bed sounds like an even better one."

"Are we going to end up here every night?"

"Depends."

"On what?"

"Not sure. I think we have to complete whatever it is we've been given. Do you feel any different?"

He shrugged. "Yes, no. Actually I do." He spun in a circle. "So where are our clothes?"

Lili heard then saw the branches move to create a little opening. She pointed to it. "There they are!"

"Impressive," Brett said.

They hurried to dress and followed the path that seemed to form into a straight line for them. They made it to the jetty just as the little boat pulled up, full of Beltane party goers wrapped in blankets and giggling, with bottles of wine at their feet or sticking out of wicker baskets.

Lili huddled close to Brett. "Tell me, what's different for you?"

He nuzzled her ear. "I have you in my life, and I want it to stay that way."

She giggled. "So you do mix business with pleasure!" She shifted in her seat. "I feel energized. Like I can take on anything. But I'm worried about my business. What if I don't get the funding? I'll have to start all over again."

He kissed her. "Shh. It will all work out."

"How can you be sure? You missed my second pitch. I wanted to talk to you about it. That's why I came to find you yesterday."

"I know." He kissed her again. "I had to spend some time at my great-grandfather's grave site, to unlock the mystery."

"Did you?"

Brett puffed out a breath. "I think so." He grabbed her hands, his grip warm and strong. "I dropped out of the funding group."

Lili tugged her hands from his. "Why?"

"To not have a conflict of interest."

"Can't say I'm not disappointed."

"But it makes sense."

Lili nodded.

Brett held out his hands. "Lili, I finally found it."

"What?"

"My purpose."

The boat docked. The partygoers hopped out. The boat rocked. The guide and pilot said, "*Allez.*" Go.

Brett stood, hopped out, and lifted Lili onto the quay. The balmy air caressed her cheeks. She reached for his hand. "Tell me about your purpose."

They took the street past the park beside the cathedral. Even though it was closed, Lili wanted to be in nature. They hopped the low gate and found a bench hidden from the entrance. "I don't want to go indoors just yet," Lili explained.

"We're not going to go naked and get clothed in leaves again, are we?" Brett asked and hugged her against him.

She sat on his lap and nipped his neck. "I think we've passed that phase. Besides, I think we need to be in the labyrinth for that to happen."

He chuckled. "Darn."

"You like that part?"

He shrugged. "It was scary, having all that energy coursing through my body. But I survived it." He sighed.

"And?" she prompted him.

"Well, I always wanted the cool and the prestigious."

"And expensive tailored clothes."

"That too."

"But..." He blew out a breath. "That stuff is fun. Great, even. But not enough. I came here looking for answers to my family's secrets. I don't understand my great-grandfather's reasons. But I think he left, or had his fraternity brothers leave the fountain for him for someone in the family to find. It sounds weird, but the journey of searching connected me not only to him, but to nature. To my desire to take care of our home, the earth in a more direct way."

"So no more investing?" She tried to hide her disappointment from her voice. "I was hoping you could be a part of my company."

"Lili, I want to be more than that. Come back with me to San Francisco."

"But—"

"You can work from anywhere."

"I know, but..."

The wind whispered to her, *Follow love, follow your one true love.*

"What is it?" he asked.

"The wind is speaking to me."

"And what does she say?"

"She. Something as changeable as the wind has to be female." She smiled. "She says to follow love."

Chapter Twenty-Four

A T DAWN, LILI LED Brett to her apartment. Her place was on the way to the hotel and it was time to let him in. A momentous occasion. Was it only six days ago that she'd met him at the club? So much had happened.

Leaning up against the door were two packages. One was a plain white envelope labeled from the investment group. The other was an unmarked plain brown paper package, tied with a brown hemp string. Stuck in the knot was a single pink tea rose. It had to be from her grandmother. The string was her grandmother's preferred packing string, and the rose, well, the rose was clear.

She set the packages on the table and gave Brett the grand tour, waving in direction of the bathroom, bedroom behind the curtain, and the obvious kitchen and dining area.

"Nice!" He gazed around. Then he grabbed her around the waist. "Let's take a shower."

She kissed him, then stepped out of his arms. "Rain check. I want to—" she waved around her messy place. "Pick up."

"It's fine. Looks lived in and cozy." He kissed her neck.

She smiled. "Go ahead. Clean towels are in there. I'll join you in a second."

Brett kissed on the lips. "I like your place. It's colorful and inspiring, like you." He padded into the bathroom. In moments, the shower was on and Brett was humming a tune she'd recognized from the dance club.

She gazed around her apartment and saw it through his eyes: the green herbs in the kitchen window, contrasted by the red-orange curtains and by the bright blue crockery on open shelves. And that was just the kitchen. She smiled again and sat at the table to open the packages.

After a moment of hesitation—she really wanted to know the fate of her company, but she wasn't ready to dive back into work just yet—she opened her grandmother's package first. Wrapped in white tissue, she uncovered a silver chain necklace. She lifted it. A pendant of a rose in a full bloom spun. She examined it. On the reverse had been engraved a drafting compass and chisel. Below that was written in the Latin words for Bringers of the Rose: Love, Faith, Community: *Luciferi Rosa: Amor, Fiducia, Communitas.*

She gripped it in her palm. The medallion warmed her hand. Electricity shot up her arm. She jumped up from her chair and set the necklace on the table.

Her heart thudded.

She picked up the medallion again and again it zapped her.

Gra-mere, what have you given me?

Was she up to the task? What was her task? She'd said, "Yes," at the labyrinth, but she really had no idea what was in store for her.

Chapter Twenty-Five

BRETT DRIED OFF FROM his shower, wrapped a towel around his waist, and padded into Lili's main and only room.

Lili was sitting at her table staring off into space, her curly red hair mussed, her t-shirt off one shoulder. He kissed her shoulder and Lili sighed.

"What do you have there?" He lifted the necklace from the table.

The silver pendant caught the light and seemed to glow.

"Hold it," Lili said. "In your palm."

Brett captured the medallion. "Okay."

"Does it tingle? Shoot electricity up your arm?"

"No. But it glows." He looked at it and said the Latin phrase aloud. "It's similar to *fidelis, fortis, verus.*"

"Yes, how strange."

"Or how cool! Let me put it on you," Brett said.

Lili lifted her hair and he just had to kiss the back of her neck.

She sighed again and he clasped the necklace around her neck.

"Let me see," he said.

Lili stood and twirled.

He clasped her around the waist and pulled her to him. "Lovely, my love. Who's it from?"

"My grandmother."

"Oh. The woman I met at the restaurant the other night?"

"The one and the same."

A white envelope lay unopened on the table, the investment group name and logo stamped on front. "Aren't you going to open it?" he asked.

"Scared to." She eyed it. "What if we don't get funded?"

"What if you do?"

"I'm not sure my company is the right path for me anymore."

"What? But you've worked so hard on it."

"I know. Wait. Don't you know what they decided?"

"No. I was with you. Remember? And then I recused myself. Didn't seem right."

"Not mixing business with pleasure and all that?"

"Yes. Something like that."

"What do you mean?"

"I was trying to tell you on our way back. But why don't you open it and we can talk about me later."

Lili eyed the white envelope. Then there was a knock on the door.

"I'll get that," Lili said.

"I better get dressed," Brett said at the same time.

"I like you like that, but whoever is at the door may not."

He chuckled and headed for the bathroom.

Chapter Twenty-Six

LILI OPENED THE DOOR. "Gra-mere, what a surprise!" she said in French.

Gra-mere beamed at Lili. "You did it! I'm so proud of you!" She pushed past Lili and stepped into her apartment. "Where is he?"

"Who?"

"Your man. I can smell him."

"Gra-mere!"

"No need to be coy with me, Lili dear, I've been there and done that, as you young people say. Now, where is he? I have something to say to you both."

"He's in the bathroom, getting dressed."

"Oh good. Put on some tea, Lili dear," Gra-mere said and sat at the table, neatly folding the brown paper wrapping and pushing aside the white envelope with a slight frown.

Lili set the hot water to boil and set out their favorite tea bags of tarragon and rose hips on the table. She grabbed the gingery speculoos cookies for good measure.

She loved the ginger-flavored sweet biscuits combined with the aromatic and slightly bitter and tangy tea. Would Brett like the cookies and tea too? Nerves shimmied in her belly. She was sharing an important, homey, silly, little ritual with him. Would he accept that about her? What would become of them?

"Well, look who we have here!" Gra-mere said.

She turned and smiled at Brett, who was turning for her grandmother. Of course.

Brett sat and folded his hands on the table.

"Give me your hands, young man."

Brett did.

"Turn them over so I can see your palms."

Gra-mere had read her palms many times when Lili was young.

Would Brett think this practice was strange?

He turned his hands over and let Gra-mere peer over them. He caught Lili's gaze and quirked an eyebrow.

Lili shrugged. "She does this," she said in English.

"I get that." He smiled. "I'm from California. This kind of thing is normal over there."

"Right." Lili relaxed her shoulders. "Good."

The kettle on the stove whistled and Lili poured them all some tea. The rich and pungent aroma filled the room.

Full circle from a week ago.

My man, my legacy, and what about my work. That still felt uncertain.

She reached for the white envelope.

"Can you let that wait a bit longer, Lili dear?" Gra-mere said without looking up at her.

"Why?" Lili touched the white envelope. No zing zapped up her arm.

Gra-mere peered at her, her gaze full of wisdom and warmth. "What does your heart say?"

Lili looked at Brett. Her heart thudded. All she wanted was to be flush against him. "Desire and passion isn't everything, Gra-mere."

"I know that, dear, and so does your young man, by the look of his hands and the glow around him."

"I have a glow?" Brett grinned. "I always knew I had a magnetic personality."

"I'm the one with the electricity zapping him," Lili said.

"Actually I felt that too, when I picked up the scythe," Brett said.

"You remember that?" Lili leaned forward and wrapped her hands around her cup.

"I do. I remember everything, all of a sudden." Brett flexed his hands and stared at them as if they contained the answers to his memory return.

"Children, please stand." Gra-mere ordered. "Come here." She waved to Lili.

Lili stood and came around the table to stand beside Brett.

"What's going on?" Brett stage-whispered.

"I don't know," Lili whispered back.

Gra-mere smiled. "Good. Brett, is it?"

"Yes, Brett Barnaby, the Second."

"The Second?" Lili chuckled.

Brett shrugged.

"Brett Barnaby, the Second, hold out your right hand."

Brett did as instructed.

"Lili Grenault, my dear granddaughter, hold out your left hand."

Lili did.

"Now clasp each other's hands so that your palms and forearms touch."

Lili smiled up at Brett. He gazed at her with love and something more.

Gra-mere was wrapping something around their hands and forearms.

Panic rose in her throat. "You're hand fasting us, Gra-mere."

"What's hand fasting?" Brett asked. He moved closer to Lili so their shoulders and legs were touching, as if he were trying to protect her.

"It's a benediction, Lili dear. Not to worry," Gra-mere said and stepped back. "A blessing." She smiled at her handiwork.

The twine wasn't tight, yet it felt snug on Lili's skin.

"Repeat after me—"

"Gra-mere, this feels too soon. We didn't ask for this."

"It's okay, Lili," Brett said. "I want to be with you."

"I want to be with you too, but my company needs me. This legacy...There's so much I don't know, don't understand." Lili shrugged and turned to Gra-mere. "Please, Gra-mere, give me some time. You're rushing me."

Gra-mere frowned. "But you took the vow. In the gardens. With the Green Man. You've decided already."

Lili dropped their bounds hands and forearm. Brett offered no resistance. "I know I did. I felt that was the right thing to do. But I have no idea what I'm getting into." She spoke to Brett. "And neither do you, by being with me."

"I do," Brett said. "It will be wonderful, magical, unexpected, and full of heart and global vision. That's what I want. I want you. Whatever you do. Wherever you go."

"Oh, Brett." She turned and awkwardly hugged him.

"There's more," he said and pulled back.

"Oh?"

"Yes, I decided to quit my investment business and come work for you."

"But you said no mixing business and pleasure."

"I'm not mixing it. I'm putting you first and business second."

"But I want your business expertise."

"As long as it's in the service of love and the greater good," Brett said. "Will you have me, the complete package?"

"Even if the future is uncertain?" Lili asked, gazing into his deep sky-blue eyes.

"The future is never certain until you decide," Gra-mere said. "Now turn and face me."

Lili stood on tiptoe and kissed Brett, just a little peck, but the kiss edged deeper until Gra-mere cleared her throat.

Lili broke off the kiss, smiling.

"There'll be time enough for that later," Gra-mere said.

Lili turned to face her grandmother again. And so did Brett.

"Now where was I?" Gra-mere said. "Oh yes, by the powers invested in me by the Elders of the Bringers of the Rose, I hereby bless you—" She nodded to Brett, "the Green Man of the Labyrinth."

"You knew?" Lili sucked in a breath.

Gra-mere nodded.

"With new Bringer of the Rose." Gra-mere nodded to Lili. "And I bless the magic that you create together. And may it serve the Earth and all her peoples, for the good of all."

She beamed at them.

"That's it?" Lili asked.

"Yes! Let's have tea." Gra-mere bustled to the stove and set the kettle to boil again.

Brett turned to Lili. "You haven't answered my question."

"Which one?"

"Will you come with me to California?"

"Can I see what's in the envelope first?"

"Will it matter?"

"Well..." Lili considered.

"You can run your company from anywhere, and there are great tech and funding contacts in the Silicon Valley."

"I know. It's just that... this magical legacy. I feel I need to stay near the land, here, in France."

"Gra-mere," Brett said. "May I call you Gra-mere?"

"Yes, or Lenora, as you prefer, my dear young man."

"Gra-mere, Lenora, does Lili need to stay here to do her work, for you?"

"She needs to follow the call of her heart," Gra-mere said. She spoke to Lili. "You know that, Lili dear."

"I do." Lili nodded. "Gra-mere, can we take this off?" She waved their joined hands.

Gra-mere smiled and shrugged, then turned to attend to the whistling kettle.

Lili laughed and undid the twine.

Brett kept his hand clasped in hers and pulled her to him, their bodies flush against each other. He smelled of her lavender and rose soap and of man, her man.

She wrapped her arms around him. "I want to go with you."

"I hear a 'but' coming." He patted her behind.

"I need to come back here often."

"Of course." He leaned in to kiss her. This time she did deepen the kiss. He sighed. Gra-mere chuckled.

Lili heard the door open and shut. She smiled into the kiss.

"I love your grandmother, but I thought she'd never leave."

"She'll always meddle in my life."

"I know. But I get you all to myself. In your home."

"Yes, in my home."

"Wherever you are, I am home, with you, Lili."

Lili smiled and back-walked to her bed, flipping the curtain aside.

"And I am home with you, Brett, wherever you are, my love," she said and fell backwards onto her soft bed, pulling Brett with her.

He laughed and kissed her. "Always."

Falling in Love Again

(Paranormal Time Travel Romance)

A short story in the *Touchstone Series*

SUMMARY:

Sexy Medieval stonemason Julien has to rely on his fiancée Rose to adapt to a 21st century life, to learn English, and find his place in a modern world. Software expert Rose has no time to spare with two jobs to support her and her fiancé Julien in expensive San Francisco. Will a weekend getaway rekindle the spark so these two time-crossed lovers can fall in love again?

For EB, who inspires me to fall in love again with him every day.

Special thanks to my critique partner Kay Keppler for her sparkling story insight and to Ezra Barany for his physics help.

Rose clomped up the stairs to her apartment, her legs heavy with fatigue. She felt out of shape. She missed her long runs with Julien though the park. She missed spending time with him, visiting the neighborhoods of San Francisco, eating in the quaint neighborhood restaurants, or hiking in the Marin Headlands. When had work overtaken her life? When had her love for Julien seemed more like a memory than a lived experience? She frowned and sighed. She had to do something about it. Julien deserved better. Their relationship deserved better.

Almost a year ago, she'd fallen back in time to thirteenth century France while on a business trip and had then miraculously returned to her own modern time. The best part about her strange five-day stay in the medieval village of Beauvais was meeting Julien, her hunky stonemason.

When he had surprised her by following her back to her time, she'd been overjoyed and had spent every waking moment with him. They'd traveled, kissed a lot, and spent lazy mornings in bed together.

Then real life had reared its head, and she'd had to go back to work, and he to school to learn English and settle into modern life.

She didn't know if he would mysteriously fall back into the thirteenth century. She didn't see how. So she needed to make the most of each day. She hadn't done that though, had she? Not lately anyway.

Love had brought them together, but the daily grind of living a modern life had torn them apart with its mundane busyness. Short of leaving modern life, she had to find a way to bring them back together.

She shifted her computer bag with her groceries. She'd made an extra stop on her way home, thinking of them, of how they could spend more time together.

Only one more flight to go. She needed the exercise today after having to cut her lunchtime walk short. Her boss had handed her a new project that needed her immediate attention. And like a good worker, she'd jumped when he called. That had to stop.

What was she going to do? Work was no longer fun. And her love life certainly had been suffering for these last few months. She'd taken on new consulting gigs so Julien wouldn't feel the pressure to work so much in his furniture repair and landscape jobs. She wanted him to take his time integrating into her time and world.

She landed at her floor and puffed out a breath. Maybe she could suggest that she and Julien go running together again. She needed the exercise, and more importantly, she needed to spend time with him. He needed her help and words of comfort—he'd been crankier than usual at her lately, more impatient with himself and with modern technology. She wanted to do what she could to help him adjust. This was his home now.

She shoved her key into the lock, but the door was already unlocked. That wasn't safe. They lived in the city, not the wide, open country that he was familiar with. She frowned. Keeping the front door locked was a modern city habit Julien really didn't like.

She stepped into the apartment and felt her shoulders relax at the smell of cooked tomatoes and baked garlic.

"You left the door unlocked," she called out.

"Yes, I know," Julien shouted back in medieval French, his first language.

"English, remember?" She smiled and deposited her bags beside the coat tree. She slipped the bottle of wine from the grocery bag. Julien liked the dark reds from Sonoma. Hopefully he'd like this one.

"Yes, I know," he said again, this time in English.

"Thanks!" she said, slipped off her heels in the bedroom, and placed her bags of goodies by her bedside table. Just a little something to reignite their connection, she hoped.

She padded into the kitchen with the wine, kissed him on the cheek, and set the wine on the counter. "I got you another dark red."

Julien nodded absently and set down the knife on the cutting board beside the chopped carrots. "Wait." He washed his hands at the sink. "Come here."

She stepped into his arms and gave him the kiss he was leaning in for. "You're making me dinner? How nice!"

"Yes, as an apology, for getting mad at you about the dishwasher—"

"Don't worry about it. I can get it fixed or replace it."

He pulled back and grimaced. "I really don't like these—these machines."

"I know. I'll take care of it." She danced out of his arms, leaned over the stove, and inhaled the rich aroma of garlic and tomatoes. "Oh, Julien, how lovely. I accept your apology."

"That was easy. You haven't even tasted it yet."

"I will." She kissed him, a peck on the lips. "I'm going to take a bath, okay? Just a quick one."

He nodded, staring at the broken dishwasher that he'd yelled at her about the night before, as if it were her fault the modern machine broke.

She sighed and headed for the bathroom. They both needed a break and a positive distraction from the woes of their modern life.

JULIEN SPRINKLED SOME PARMESAN cheese on the bubbling tomato sauce. The timer rang. He jumped. Electric devices still freaked him out. He liked that odd phrase, "freaked him out." He rolled it around on his tongue as he pulled the garlic bread out of the oven. The pungent aroma of the French bread, butter, and garlic filled the small kitchen. He hummed a wordless tune he'd heard on Rose's iPod and spun to the counter and placed the bread to cool.

He hoped she'd like his "I am sorry" meal. He really had been an oaf to yell at her like that last night. The machine not working properly wasn't her fault. That he strongly disliked motor-operated machines also was not her fault.

When had he become more of a grumbler than a doer? It was as if he couldn't stay busy enough. The English class and busywork with furniture and people's yards and gardens wasn't enough.

He missed gazing at Rose with his artist's eye, chiseling stone, feeling its smooth coolness under his hand, as Rose gazed at him with sleepy, happy eyes, like he'd done in Beauvais. When was the last time he'd sketched her with that feeling of having all the time in the world? It had been months.

Back in Beauvais, back in his time in the thirteenth century—so strange to think of his home that way—he'd treasured every sweet moment Rose was in his arms.

He had to tell her how he felt. He headed for their small bathing room.

She was leaning over the bathtub in just a skirt and bra undergarment, setting the water running, some flowery scent filling the small room. He liked running water.

He came up behind her and caressed the soft skin of her waist.

Rose jumped and bumped her head on his nose.

"Ow!" he yelped.

"You scared me!" Rose touched his nose. "Sorry. You okay?"

"I'm okay." He pulled her to him and inhaled her scent. "You make it better dressed like that."

She smiled and pressed herself against him. But too soon she danced out of his arms. "What? A bra and a skirt?"

"Hmmm." He reached for her again, but she stepped out of the small bathroom.

"Just a second!" she said and giggled.

"Dinner will be ready soon."

"I know." She slipped back in, carrying a few candles. "Why don't you join me?" She brushed up against him and placed the candles alongside the tub filling with water.

He caressed her waist. "I want to, but—"

She straightened and turned to face him. "I can't tempt you..." She jutted out one hip and pouted.

"You're doing a good job," he said in French. "But the dinner—"

"I understand. You don't want to burn anything." She too slipped into French.

"Ah, Rose."

The damnable buzzer rang. He swore. "I don't want to leave it unattended."

She frowned. "Bad timing."

"I can get you a glass of wine though."

"That would be lovely." She smiled at him and unhooked her bra ceremoniously, without a backward glance.

"No fair," he said to himself, shook his head, and stepped to the kitchen to get her a glass of the Sonoma Cabernet Sauvignon, better than any wine he'd tasted back in Beauvais in 1240. He stirred the sauce and reset the timer for the next check.

When he came back to the bathroom, she was in the tub up to her neck in bubbles. Her eyes were closed. A small smiled played her lips. He set the wine glass on the floor and bent to kiss her. She looked divine.

Her eyes flew open. "Julien, come join me," she whispered.

"I—the dinner—like you say, timing."

"Next time?"

"Yes." He smiled. "Dinner will be ready in ten minutes, *mon amour.*"

He had to make more time for them and find a way to help her not work so much.

THAT NIGHT, DESPITE ALL of Rose's plans and good intentions, she fell into bed exhausted. She'd cleaned up after Julien's delicious apology dinner while he'd tinkered on his furniture repairs in the spare bedroom-turned-workshop. She'd slipped into bed, lit candles, and called for him. But he didn't arrive after ten or so minutes. Did he not hear her? Another time perhaps. She blew out the candles and pulled up the covers over her sexy negligee.

They needed to do something to get back in synch with each other.

JULIEN WASHED UP AND slipped into the bedroom. Rose was already asleep. She was working too hard. Going straight to sleep had nothing to do with him. Time was not on his side tonight. He kissed her cheek and changed into his running clothes. He still had energy to burn and didn't want to wake Rose. She had to get up early for work the next day.

AFTER A FEW BLOCKS, he was running in Golden Gate Park. Being amongst the trees and animals calmed him. Some of the tree leaves were turning red. Fog blanketed the park. He felt his muscles relax as he ran past the Hall of Flowers. He really wasn't a city person. Maybe if he could take Rose out of the city, they could make the time to recapture what they had together.

Tomorrow he'd ask his friend Abu Nalini in his English-language class if he had any recommendations. Abu had a large extended family all over the area and could help him find the right place for Rose and him to rekindle their love.

SOMETHING WOKE HER. SHE reached out, but Julien wasn't there. A key rattled the lock.

"Julien?"

The front door closed softly. In a moment, he brushed a kiss on her cheek. "I'm here."

"Where were you?" she said, eyes still closed, half in and half out of sleep.

"Running."

"Without me? Where?"

"In the park." He kissed her cheek again. In a second, the shower was running.

The bed felt cold without Julien at her side. She tried to wait up for him again, but sleep pulled her under.

A WEEK LATER, AT the first rain of the fall, Julien propped up a card with his invitation next to Rose's espresso maker and slipped out for his English class. He hoped she liked his invitation for a three-day weekend away at a hotel in Berkeley at a date of her choosing.

THAT NIGHT, ROSE SMILED as she found the apartment front door locked and used the key to let herself in. Julien remembered. So sweet. And so sweet was his invitation to stay at his friend's hotel. How resourceful! He had some income from his repair and gardening work in addition to what she gave him for groceries and other things he might want. But he never went on a shopping spree and only brought home groceries and tools.

"Julien!" she called out when she didn't see him in the kitchen.

Another note was propped up against her espresso maker. "Gone running," it said.

That was the third time this week.

No dinner was on the stove or in it, or even in the refrigerator.

She heated up some leftovers and sighed. Julien must be quite frustrated to avoid her like this. She hoped their weekend away would help.

She turned his note over and wrote on the back, "Yes! Let's go to Berkeley for the weekend and soon!" She noted a date a week away.

She'd already blocked off a Friday through Monday on her schedule and cleared it with her boss and private clients.

It was time to take a much-needed break.

On a Friday mid-morning the following week, Rose pulled her electric hybrid in front of a California craftsman bungalow. "This doesn't look like a hotel." She frowned. "But it's lovely."

Julien glanced at the piece of paper in his hand. "But this is the right address. Panoramic Way."

She turned off the engine. "Well, let's get this vacation started." She tried to smile, tried to relax, but it felt forced. She so needed to get away. So here she was. She prayed to whatever capricious gods were listening that she could recapture the magic with Julien and with her life. She'd been working too damn much.

Julien reached for her hand. She gave it to him. "It will all work out," he whispered in French.

"I hope so," she replied in French and squeezed his hand.

He leaned in for a kiss, but she was already moving in the other direction and his kiss landed on her cheek.

She thought she saw him frown as she got out of the car. She bit back a sigh. Bad timing again. "Shall we check in and then take a stroll? I don't know this part of Berkeley."

Julien nodded and grabbed their bags out of the back of the car.

The house was actually a cute bed & breakfast run by a member of the Nalini family, a relative of Julien's classmate. In no time, they were checked in and shown upstairs to their adorable room with a view of the Berkeley Hills. A big four-poster bed, homey furnishings done in soft mauves, browns, and burgundies. She felt her shoulders release some of their tension as she surveyed the room.

The view held nary a building—all chaparral and trees with dark red bark. Jays and wood thrushes whistled in the branches. A warm breeze blew through the open window.

Julien set down their luggage beside the bed and took off his short-brimmed sailor's cap.

She turned to him and smiled. "Let's go for a walk."

Julien put his hat back on, and in a few minutes, they made their way down to Prospect Way toward Piedmont Avenue that she knew ran the top of UC Berkeley's campus. Lots of students strolled or trotted up and down the hills toward the campus or back to their housing, back packs slung over their shoulders.

On the corner of Channing and Prospect, Julien stopped in front of a huge house with a wrap-around porch and a statue garden in the front yard. He was staring at the statues, his face pale.

"What's wrong?" Rose asked and touched his arm.

Beth Barany

"That's mine." He pointed to one of the four statues.

"Really?"

"Yes. But how could that be?"

"I don't know. Time travel is..." She didn't know what to say. Truth was no one she ever knew had had the kind of experience she'd had—of falling back into thirteenth century France, and then for no reason she could understand, bringing Julien, a man she'd fallen in love with from that time, with her.

"What is going on?" he whispered, his voice tight with tension.

"I don't know," she said again. "We can research. Ask someone." Her stomach clenched at the thought of talking to a professor. Silly phobia, she reminded herself for the millionth time.

Julien turned to her, his eyes bright with an intensity she loved. "Yes, let's ask someone. Today. Universities are always good for that, in my time and in yours, I assume."

She nodded. "Come on. Let's get some lunch at a place I know, and I'll research who to talk to."

She had an inkling of who to speak with, but wanted to warm herself up to the idea of actually holding such a conversation.

After a delicious lunch at the Durant Hotel on Durant Avenue, where she relaxed even more with a midday glass of wine and smiled at Julien's jokes in English, she was ready to do some research. She pulled out her smart phone. "Do you mind?" she asked him.

He shrugged and signaled the waiter. "Two espressos for us, please."

The waiter smiled, nodded, and scurried off.

"Your English is getting quite good." Rose smiled, something unwinding in her.

"Why are you surprised? You and I speak English a lot."

"I know. I—it's just that—" She felt the heat of embarrassment crawl up her face. "I feel silly...you and I don't go out, or haven't in months." She shrugged, feeling a little helpless.

Julien grabbed her hand, warmth and understanding in his chocolate brown eyes. "I know. We've been busy." He nodded at her phone. "Go. Do your research."

She blew out a breath, smiled, and leaned over to plant a quick kiss on his lips.

He looked surprised. She giggled, a little giddy at the sense of freedom bubbling up in her chest. Julien was getting at ease with her language and her time, and maybe a little with her gadgets, at least being okay that she used them in front of him. He still wouldn't touch an electric device of any kind if he could help it. It'd been weeks before he'd felt comfortable turning on a light switch in her apartment.

She bent over her phone and tapped in some keywords to the search engine, including "world-renowned expert on time travel." When she'd come back last year from France with Julien, after her mysterious jaunt to 1240 Beauvais, she'd done some research but had never talked to anyone.

Now was the time.

There it was, Professor Peter M. Einman, Emeritus, Physics Department. His office hours were—soon. There was even a way to book an appointment right from his web page. She clicked through.

"We can get an appointment in four hours."

"Let's do it." Julien sipped his espresso. "Maybe he can tell me why my statue is here in someone's garden in Berkeley."

"Maybe. But couldn't it have just withstood time, and someone found it and brought it here?"

"Rose, you don't understand. I never made this statue. Only dreamed of it. Before you came."

"Oh." Chills passed through her body. "I hope he can tell us how that could be."

R OSE PAID THEIR BILL. "Where to next?"

An email notification popped up on her phone.

"Let's go back to the hotel."

She nodded and tapped the notification to open it.

She read the email and sucked in a breath with surprise.

"What is it?" Julien asked.

She shook her head. "Good news for me."

Julien was quiet so she looked from her phone at him. He was eyeing her lips.

"Never mind." She smiled. "You want to go back to the B&B to nap?"

"Something like that," he said, slapped on his hat, and grabbed her hand. "Tell me about the good news for you."

"A client wants to cancel a project so that means less work for me."

"That's good news? That will mean less income for you."

She swung their hands between them. "I really don't need to work as much, I recently realized. What I need is to enjoy my life more. Like this. With you."

Julien stopped and pulled her against him. "Like this."

She laughed and kissed him. "Like this."

They resumed their walk up Durant Avenue for a few blocks, then zigged and zagged a little until they were in front of the bungalow again.

He shut the door to their room and turned to her with a secretive smile. "I'll be right back. Make yourself comfortable. You know that thing you had on when I first met you? Wear that."

"You mean naked?"

"Yes." He smiled broadly then slipped out of the room.

Julien was strong, valiant, always looking out for her in little gentlemanly ways that most men didn't know of anymore. What did he have in store for them?

Because she could and she was on vacation, Rose took a quick shower and wrapped herself in her robe. She brushed out her shoulder-length dark blond hair in front of the mirror, looking at herself but not really seeing. When was the last time they had really taken the time to make love? She couldn't remember. She squared her shoulders and smiled at herself in the mirror. The time was now to make things right and recapture the magic that had brought them together.

She rummaged in the drawers under the bathroom mirror and smiled. Some smart person had stocked the room with several dozen short candles of various scents, small glass candleholders to match the color palette of the room, and matches. She sniffed a handful before she picked out lavender, rose, and rosemary scents.

She was placing them around the room, on the windowsill, the bedside tables, and the desk, when Julien came back with a wicker basket.

"Oh, what's that?" Rose asked.

"You'll see." He gazed at her with a small smile and shut the door behind him.

"Why, Julien de Beauvais, are you trying to seduce me?" She stood by the bed, a little dizzy at the aromas from the candles and at the sight of Julien so intent for her.

"Could be, Madame. Could be." He stalked toward her.

She shivered, even in her robe.

He set down the basket on the bed. "Are you cold?" He reached for her, and she let herself be held by him, by his strong arms. His body felt warm and welcome and ready for her.

"Julien, I'm sorry for being so tired all the time..." She pulled back to gaze up at him.

"No, I'm the one that is sorry—my anger—at the machines." He stretched an arm behind himself. "I have something for you."

From behind him, he drew out a small bowl of ripe strawberries beside luscious-looking cream.

"You didn't have to."

"Oh, but I did. When was the last time someone fed you cream and berries like a queen?" He held up a strawberry, its tip lathered in cream. "Taste. Just a bite."

So she did and sighed. "Crème fraiche."

"*De mon pays.*" From my country. He set the bowl back into the basket behind him, all without turning away from her. "*C'est si bon.*" The French just slipped out. It was the language of luxury, after all. Her eyes teared up. "You're so sweet. And I've been so—busy, distracted—"

He kissed her. "Let me take care of you. We have good timing at last."

"Oh, Julien." She smiled. Tears of relief trickled down her cheeks as she leaned into the kiss. When was the last time she really relaxed and let herself disappear into Julien's embrace? She reached for the sweetness of the moment and released the "should haves" of the past.

JULIEN PUT HIS HEART into his kiss. Rose's sweet lips, made even sweeter from the cream and fruit, made him stir with desire. He wanted her to know how he felt, how much he desired her, how much he loved her, despite the whirlwind of his new life. All that didn't matter. What mattered was her, was them, was their love. He just needed to show her.

He slipped his hands between them to open the robe and slide the damned robe off, so he could feel her skin and show her with his hands and his lips how he felt.

With time and the help of the sweet treats he had prepared ahead of time, he hoped he could rekindle their magic, their love.

Rose smiled at him, tentatively at first, then more broadly, as her fingers found the buttons of his shirt, then his pants, and did away with his clothes.

He tumbled them onto the wide bed.

"Rose, my Rose," he breathed and lost himself in her.

SOMETHING WAS NUDGING HER shoulder and kissing her cheek. She peeked open an eye. "Julien, what time is it?"

"Time to get to the appointment with your professor."

"He's not mine." She sat up and grabbed her phone, checking the time. "Oh, dear. We have to hurry."

Julien nibbled her earlobe. "Call him and tell him we'll be late." His kisses made their way down the column of her neck.

She wanted to melt into them. "We can't. He's an emeritus."

"So?" Julien reached under the covers and caressed her belly.

"That means he's old."

"Then he knows the meaning of patience."

"No. We have to—" She hopped out of bed. "Hey, wait. You're already dressed." She threw a pillow at him. "You're playing with me."

"Just a little. Here." He handed her her clothes. "Let me help you dress."

She swatted away his hand that was caressing her shoulder.

"You're sending me mixed messages. I need to take a shower."

Julien chuckled as she walked into the small bathroom and turned on the shower.

She smiled. It was fun to see his playful side. They both had been so serious for far too long. How could they bring more playful and lovemaking time back into their day-to-day relationship? She'd had blinders on the past few months with barely any room for their relationship. Things needed to be different from now on.

"THANK YOU SO MUCH for agreeing to see us, Professor Einman," Rose said and broke eye contact with the elderly man, who looked like he enjoyed the good life—ruddy cheeks, a shock of white hair, a strong grip when he shook hands with her, and a nice tweed suit. He looked a lot different than the professor who'd failed her out of her Master's program.

"Ah, that is not a problem. Your message to me through the Internet said that you had some time travel questions and some first-hand experience. I'm intrigued." The professor crossed his legs in his leather chair and smiled kindly.

His smile relaxed her a little. She felt the tension drain from her shoulders. She examined the room. She and Julien sat in a love seat across from the professor. A small table between them was empty except for a bowl of marbles. Books lined the walls from waist-high to the ceiling. Posters hung behind his desk, showing telescope pictures of the stars and galaxies. This office was not her old professor's—she was not in the past. She relaxed her shoulders a little more.

"Yes," Julien said in accented-English and squeezed her hand. "I am a man out of this time. Not from this time. I don't know how it happened. But I am grateful that it did." Julien squeezed Rose's hand again.

She nodded. "It's strange. I fell back into thirteenth century France, met Julien, and somehow came back to my time—the day I left in fact—I'd been there five days. I've never told anyone who Julien really is or how we met—"

She interrupted herself to watch the professor's reaction. He didn't seem surprised or disbelieving in the least, just blinked at her with a cat-like calm. She had to ask. "This is unheard of, right? How did it happen? People say time travel can't happen. And yet—" She shrugged.

"And yet maybe it has," he finished for her. "Whether it happened or not, I can't say. But yes, time travel can happen according to the laws of physics." He steepled his long fingers and explained evidence of time travel to the future, something about muons, but there was no evidence of time travel to the past.

"But I was there," Rose blurted.

"When precisely?"

"1240."

"I see." He stared off into the middle distance past Rose's shoulder.

She held herself from squirming. "Is it even theoretically possible to time travel to the past?"

Professor Einman stroked his clean-shaven jaw and refocused on them. "Yes, there is another theory that could explain what happened—"

"And why my statue is here in someone's yard," Julien interrupted.

"Explain, young man."

"I-I am a sculptor." Julien said and seemed to sit up taller. "My statue has only been imagined. Back in Beauvais. When I left to follow Rose, the preparation for it was in my artist's shed."

"Someone could have completed it," the professor said.

"What I mean to say is that the stone was there, and I had only made a few marks on it. Nothing for anyone to know what I had in my designs."

"Anyone could have worked on it and made this statue," Rose said gently.

Julien shook his head. "No. I know my work. And this statute could have only been made by me. It is my design."

"Forgers perhaps," the professor said. "Happens in all time periods, I'm afraid."

"No, impossible. I know my work, my chisel stokes."

"Let's go by later to check closer, okay?" Rose said.

The professor nodded. "Good idea, and in the meantime, I can offer a hypothesis, if you would like."

"Yes, please," Rose said. She looked at Julien and reached for his hand.

Julien took it and nodded at the professor. "Thank you for your kindness in seeing us like this and on such short notice. I don't know if the professors of my time would have been so kind with such an odd story as ours."

Rose smiled. She had never heard Julien say so many words in English, or in Medieval French for that matter.

The professor leaned forward and grabbed a few marbles from the bowl in front of them. He handed them each two. "Some physicists describe our universe as a bubble floating through something larger, in which other universes float."

"Parallel universes?" Rose breathed, awed, and rolled the cool, colorful marbles between her palms. They clacked softly. "How do we get from one to the other?"

"Ah, yes, you're a step ahead of me, I see. Smart woman. You're sure you never studied physics before?"

"Just as I said in my email, humanities major all the way."

"Hmm, yes, well, as you guessed, some believe that there is a way to get from one universe to the next." The professor reached around to his desk for something and came back with a long narrow piece of what looked like a section of racetrack from a child's set. He placed that on the table. He held out his hand. "Your marbles please."

Rose handed hers over and so did Julien.

With little clicks, the professor placed their marbles, with a handful of others, along the track, so that they were lined up in a row, each touching the other.

"Imagine alternate realities lined up like this—"

"Touching at a point?" Rose leaned forward.

"Yes, and all similar, yet different."

"And something can pass from one glass ball to the other?" Julien asked.

"Perhaps," the professor said. "It is only an idea."

"How?" Rose clasped her hands together to keep them from fluttering about with excitement. She loved it when there were reasons and explanations for things. Some invisible weight was lifting from her shoulders to know there could possibly be a logical and scientific reason for what had happened to her and Julien.

The professor gave her a small smile. "Gravitons."

When he didn't continue but just watched her with a twinkle of mischief in his eyes, Rose felt compelled to speak, a little laugh behind her words. "What are those?" This process of discovery felt like a game, and she was eager to find out the answers. She would have loved to learn from this kind man.

"We physicists posit, that is guess, that gravitons are the one and only particle that can travel from one universe to the next."

Rose frowned. Julien was doing the same.

"I see I have confused you. Look at it this way." The professor went on to explain that all matter is believed to be made up of strings. String theory, he called it. "And these strings at the proper vibration can become tiny pieces of gravity."

"I am sorry, Professor, but what does this have to do with my statue in that yard?" Julien asked.

"Yes, I'm getting to that." Professor Einman nodded at Julien. "If one changes their vibration so that all their matter becomes gravitons, then it's possible they could pass from one universe to another."

"What would pull them through? And would they stay 'them'?" Rose asked. A fear bloomed in her chest of Julien leaving to go back to his time.

"All good questions, my dear."

"But you don't have the answers, Professor," Julien stated.

"Only hypotheses. Ones we can't prove. Yet." The professor stood. "I'm sorry to disappoint you, but there are no absolutes with time travel. It is only an idea to us."

Rose stood and slipped her purse over her shoulder; her excitement popped like a soap bubble. She sighed. She didn't know what she'd been hoping to find, except perhaps definitive answers. Physics didn't seem to have any.

Julien stood and held out his hand to the professor. "I understand, Professor. Thank you for your time."

The two men shook hands.

"To us, time travel is very real. I'm sorry to have wasted your time," Rose said.

"It was a pleasure, my dear. If you ever want to come and study physics, you let me know. You know where to find me. And take care of your man there. He looks like a keeper."

Rose eyed Julien who seemed out of place in a room full of books with his broad shoulders and strong hands created for making things. "He is a keeper."

ROSE LED JULIEN THROUGH LeConte Hall and onto the curving pathways of the UC Berkeley campus.

The sunlight had softened after the peak of the day and dappled through the pine and redwood trees that lined the pathways. The campanile clock tower struck the hour.

"It's later than I realized," Rose said.

"If I close my eyes, I can imagine myself back in Paris."

"You've been to Paris?"

"Yes, I went with the Master Stonemason to deliver stone for the new cathedral." He sighed. "It was new then."

"Do you miss it?"

Julien grasped her hand. "Enough about the past and strange theories. Let's get dinner. I made reservations."

"You did?"

He smiled. "I did. Through a friend of a friend of Abu Nalini."

"He's quite the resource."

"Yes." He gestured before them. "We walk this way downhill, and I will escort you to our dining establishment."

She paused, gazing up at him. "Thank you." She kissed him on the lips.

Julien smiled and seemed to stand taller. Near the bottom of campus, they crossed a stream. Julien stopped and stared.

"What is it?"

"Another one of my statues."

"Where?"

"At the edge of the bridge, there." Julien pointed to the creek bed. A squat, stone creature sat just under a bush beside the stone bridge. He let go of her hand and rushed through the branches, down to the creek side.

"Don't we have dinner reservations?"

Julien said nothing.

She had to see what he saw and followed him into the trees and down a short embankment.

It was a stone troll, no more than knee high.

"Look here. What are these markings?" Julien brushed leaves and pine needles from the base of the troll.

"Greek letters. I don't know my Greek alphabet." She snapped a picture with her smart phone. "I'll look them up. You sure this is yours?"

"Yes. Look." Julien brushed his fingers against the chest of the troll.

There was his imprimatur of the rose, the chisel, and mason's square.

"And here." He pointed to the back of the statue.

There was a rose carved in full bloom with a fancy *J* woven through it, as if the rose was nestled in its stem—just like on the plaque in Beauvais.

Julien stood staring at the little frowning man. "How can this be?" His voice sounded pained.

"I don't know. We'll figure it out."

"How? Even your smart professor couldn't give us a good answer. Not one that I could understand."

"Maybe we were asking questions to the wrong person."

"Or the wrong questions."

"That too." She put her hand on his arm, wishing there was some way she could bring him peace and comfort. "Let's get dinner. Then ask questions. Can't do that on an empty stomach, right?"

Julien nodded and led the way up the creek side and onto the path. In twenty minutes, they were seated in a quiet booth of a lovely Thai restaurant in downtown Berkeley down the street from more famous restaurants.

After being served some coconut milk chicken soup, Julien finally spoke. He'd been quiet except for ordering.

"I want to get a job working with stone. I am ready. My English is ready."

Rose set down her Thai iced tea. "I think your English is ready, too. But—"

"You are still worried for me."

Rose shook her head, then nodded. "Yes."

"I need good work."

"I have no argument with that. We all need good work."

"Stonework," Julien said.

"Okay." Rose nodded.

"But I don't know where to go. No cathedral building around here as far as I know."

"Ah. We need to do research." Rose tapped her phone which was face down on the table.

"Research. Your answer to everything." Julien frowned.

"Are you teasing me?"

"A little." He grabbed her hand. "I am not used to not working."

"That's why you have repaired every non-electrical item in our house."

"Yes. And for some friends too. But working with wood isn't the same as stone."

"I imagine." She squeezed his hand. "Want me to research possible places to work with stone?" She itched to search her phone to solve Julien's problems.

"No. Not right now. Right now I want to be with you."

"Me too." She smiled and took back her hand so she could eat. Over their next dish of ginger beef over rice, Rose set aside her desire to be a problem-solver. It was time to enjoy his company.

They ate in silence until Rose had to blurt out, asking again, "Do you miss it?" For a second, her heart revved up in fear at what he would say, that he might want to find a way to return to his time.

"What?"

"Beauvais. Your time."

Julien shrugged. "No. Not really. But I miss the open air and wide spaces."

She breathed out in relief. "That's why you run in the park."

"Yes. And to—" He waved in the air. "Move. Otherwise too much sitting."

"We do sit a lot in modern times. It's not good for us, they say."

"It's why I chose Berkeley for our weekend away from the city."

"What?"

"More open air here. More trees. Less cars." He grimaced.

"I didn't realize you've been to Berkeley. I didn't take you here." She swallowed, feeling the guilt press on her chest. "Julien, I'm sorry for not taking you to more places." She set her fork down and took a sip of water, looking away from him, damn tears threatening. "But that's going to change."

"I know it will. I could get a job at a place like the Crucible."

"At where?"

"The school of handiworks and arts in the west of Oakland. They teach classes there, handwork classes. But not stonework." Julien frowned.

"We'll find a place. Drive all over. In fact, I want to take you to some beautiful places here—Sonoma, Santa Barbara, Tahoe, Marin. The beaches. We haven't gone to the beaches. Except that one time at Ocean Beach. We have so much to catch up with."

"Catch up?"

"I mean, to do what I should have done, what we haven't done since you've been here."

"Should have?"

"Yes, I feel so bad. I had this great adventure and met you and then went back to life as normal, at least my normal. Well, more than my normal. Just working a lot, you know."

"Nothing has been normal for me." Julien held out his hand to her.

She gave her hand to him.

"When we arrived here, you did take me to many wonderful places. Delicious restaurants. Amazing views of the bay waters. Incredible art in the museums."

"I know, but...I could have done more. And it's been hard for you, adjusting. I want to give you more time, as much as you need. No need to rush into a job."

"Yes, it has been hard...as you say, adjusting."

Though he'd already answered her question, Rose had to be sure. "Do you want to go back?"

"Even if I could, I would not want to leave you, Rose Waldman." He leaned over the table to give her a small peck on the lips. He sat back in his chair and peered at her. "I just need to feel useful, and I need to work with my hands."

"I think I can find something for you to do with your hands." Rose smiled.

Julien smiled knowingly. "I'm the man for the job."

THEY WALKED BACK UP the hill toward their bed & breakfast, hand in hand, in silence for a while.

"We still haven't solved the mystery of your statues," Rose finally said.

"Not as important as having you at my side." Julien smiled at her.

"I'm not going anywhere," Rose said.

They crossed Piedmont Avenue at the top of the campus and turned up a side street. Julien stopped. They were in front of the large sprawling house with the wrap-around porch, with Julien's statue in the front yard. The lights were on in the house. Rose could hear laughter and loud music blaring. It was Friday night after all. Students partied. She'd done her fair share in her college days.

Julien strode up the front walk. He looked over his shoulder at her. "I'm sorry. I need to talk to them."

"No need to apologize. I'm right behind you." Rose smiled. "Need me to translate?" She hadn't done any so far in their little getaway.

"Perhaps," Julien said in French.

She hurried to catch up with him.

He knocked at the front door. A young man answered. He had on a Cal Berkeley sweatshirt and had the height and slender build of a swimmer.

"You two here for the party?" He looked Rose up and down and smiled.

Julien said in English, "I have some questions about the statue—"

The young man's eyes widened when he gazed at Julien.

He shouted over his shoulder, "Hey guys!"

The young man turned back to Rose and Julien and waved them to follow him down a wide hallway. "Come in."

Julien grabbed Rose's hand and together they followed the student into a game room where men were playing pool and sipping beers.

The students, all young men, gathered around them, staring at Julien and peppering him with questions over the music. *Are you Roman? Are you related to the Builder? What's this about a statue?*

Julien stood tall and nodded at their questions but didn't reply.

Someone turned down the blaring pop song, and all the questions faded away too.

"Hello," Julien said politely and looked at each young man. "I'm here to ask about the statue in your front garden."

"Garden?" one young man asked.

"Yard. He means, your front yard," Rose said. "Are you guys a fraternity?"

"Yes, the Psi Alpha Omega Chi fraternity," the swimmer who answered the door said, standing up a bit taller than his already tall six-foot-two frame.

"Yah, Psi-Alpha-O-Chi," another said, running the words together.

Then Rose noticed some of the fraternity brothers had t-shirts with Greek letters. The same Greek letters that Rose and Julien had seen on the troll statue.

Rose didn't know what to say. Julien seemed at a loss for words too. He was staring at the same student.

"Dude, I mean, sir, we know you," the swimmer said. "Or you look exactly like someone we know."

"What?" Julien shook his head as if in a daze.

"Or at least someone in your family tree." He gestured to another room. "Yah, you're, uh, hanging in our living room. Follow me."

All twelve young men filed out quietly, subdued even. Rose and Julien followed them into a wide living room with lots of couches and easy chairs.

Hanging above the stone fireplace was an immense portrait of a man who looked exactly like Julien, only he was wearing a Roman soldier's garb—same square jaw, strong cheekbones, and direct chocolate-eyed gaze.

Julien sat on the couch and stared at the painting. Rose recognized it as an oil painting reminiscent of many eighteenth century portraits she'd seen of Napoleon—that same military pride and bearing.

"An ancestor maybe," the swimmer said, apparently taking on the role of spokesperson for the group.

"How could this be possible?" Julien whispered.

"It's possible he's an ancestor, a Roman ancestor," Rose said.

Julien jumped up and strode to the fireplace. He stood on the brick ledge and leaned in to examine the painting. "What's that on his breast?" Julien asked, pointing at an emblem painted over the man's heart.

"Our fraternity symbol. The shield."

Julien shook his head. "Impossible."

She could see the symbol from where she sat and recognized it. Uncanny. Chills rippled through her body.

"Why?" a student asked.

"These are the same symbols I use on my work. My hat." He took off his short-brimmed sailor's cap. He pointed to the pin on the band. "I made this. The same design of the compass and chisel. The rose, chisel, and the mason's square are my—how do you say? Like this." Julien clenched one fist and pounded it into the palm of his other hand a few times.

"Your stamp," Rose said.

Julien nodded.

"Dude, no way," another student said. "I mean, sir, excuse me, sir."

"How could that be?" another said.

"Time travel, man," one young man said.

"No, couldn't be. Simply the hypothesis of multiple discovery," another student said.

"The symbol evolved long before he was born, that's all," another young man said.

"Parallel universes," shouted a fifth student. "Or, alternate realities. String theory."

The fraternity brothers weren't shy now and shouted out ideas one after another.

"Whoa, hold up, guys. Let the man talk," the swimmer said to the others.

"Yah, sure, Hank," said another student.

"Sorry, sir," the swimmer said. "It's not every day that the man who looks like our founder shows up at our doorstep."

"You'll have to explain," Rose said.

"And what about my statue in your front yard?" Julien asked, perched at the edge of the couch.

The swimmer nodded. "The legend is that our fraternity was founded by Flavius Aetius, a Roman general." He gestured to the painting. "Much of the history is shrouded in mystery, but we know that the fraternity was brought to the States by a member of the Barnaby family, the son of an Australian soldier who died in World War I. We're part of a larger order called Order of the Rose and are partnered with our sister organization, the Bringers of the Rose."

Rose shivered. "My name is Rose. Rose Waldman, and this is Julien de Beauvais."

"Hank Delore." The young man nodded.

Another student spoke up and gestured to the painting. "We call him the Builder. And you say you make statues."

"I do," Julien stated, sitting straight, his shoulders tense. "I am a stonemason."

"You are like him. He's probably your relative."

"Perhaps." Julien clasped his hands then unclasped them.

The room fell quiet until a student held out a brown glass bottle to Julien. "Beer?"

"Yes, thank you." Julien took a sip and examined the bottle. "Very nice." He lifted the bottle in a salute to the fraternity brothers. They lifted their bottles and drank.

Julien gulped beer too and set the bottle down on the table with a clack. "Yes, very good beer, men."

The students laughed.

Julien smiled and said, "I'd like to see the statue again to examine it more closely."

"Yes, sir." Hank stood.

Someone handed Rose a beer, and she followed the group out onto the front yard. Night had fallen. The outside lights were turned on, and the front yard illuminated.

"Which one is yours?" Hank asked.

Julien circled the four statues placed around a low fountain. All the statues were about four and half feet tall, she guessed, all of different white stones.

Julien stopped in front of one. It looked like the gargoyle he'd made for her. Only this one had wings folded around its back. He traced a symbol on its chest.

"Just like your pin, sir," one of the students said respectfully. "The symbol is why it's here. All the statues have at least one of the symbols from the Builder's painting."

Rose stepped to the fountain. Through the clear water there was a mosaic patterned into a green labyrinth with a pink rose at its center at the bottom of the shallow basin. Etched along the edge of the fountain, was a Latin saying. She read it aloud, "*Fidelis, Fortis, Verus.*" She looked up at Hank. "What does that mean?"

"That's our motto. It means—"

"Loyal, Steadfast and True," Julien said, interrupting Hank.

"How did you know that, sir?"

"I don't know. I must have heard it—back home." He eyed Rose.

She shivered. Back home for him in 1240 Beauvais, France.

"Okay. Spooky but cool," Hank said.

"Yah, spooky and cool," echoed the others. They gathered around Julien and smiled, slapping Julien's shoulders and back.

Julien nodded to Hank and the others. "Thanks."

Someone whispered in Hank's ear. Hank nodded and smiled, gesturing to go ahead.

"You could make a statue for us," one of the young men said.

"Yah." The others chimed in.

"Something like this. A gargoyle," Hank suggested.

"I-I—" Julien nodded, speechless. His eyes widened. He looked a little stunned. "Things move fast here."

"Yes, they do," Hank said.

"Then, I accept." Julien smiled.

The fraternity brothers surrounded him, reaching for his hand and shaking it, saying variations of, "It would be an honor." And "It would mean so much to us."

Rose watched him be love-bombed by the students, probably no more than ten years younger than him and smiled. Something settled within her. She'd been so worried about Julien finding his place here. She really wanted him to be happy and find a place where people valued him for him and where he didn't have to fit some twenty-first century mold. He couldn't anyway.

"Great. It's decided," Hank said. "You'll make another gargoyle for us. We'll commission you, and you can come by to start work on Monday."

"Monday?" Rose chuckled. "We haven't even discussed terms yet. Man has to eat."

"Are you his agent?" one of the students asked with attitude.

"No, she's my fiancée," Julien said and stepped toward the student, his hands gripped into fists.

"Same thing," another student said and smiled at her.

"You're right," Rose said. "Shall we go inside and settle the terms over a few more beers?"

Cheers and shouts of agreement from the fraternity brothers. Julien stood there and endured the claps on his back and the handshakes. A small smile played on his face while he nodded to the students.

After the rowdy group had shuffled back into the fraternity house, Rose asked, "You okay with this?" She stood beside the fountain. Someone turned off the front lights. The yard was quiet and dark.

Julien stalked toward her and wrapped her in his arms. He bent to kiss her. She leaned into the kiss and relaxed in his warm embrace.

When he pulled back, he smiled hungrily at her. "I am okay with this. It's work I love, after all."

"I'm so glad. I've been worried." She smiled up at him. "We need to go on weekend getaways more often, maybe every month."

"Or every week." He brushed her cheek. "You are happy when you travel."

"I am."

He kissed her cheek where his warm palm had been a moment earlier. "You're not worried now, are you? I could get more jobs like this and even perhaps teach stonework."

"Good idea." Rose offered up her other cheek to him.

He kissed it.

"We can work it out, right?" she whispered.

"Yes, we can." He kissed her on the lips again. "We've come this far. Our love can take us wherever we want to go."

Rose smiled. "I think I know how we traveled through time."

"How?"

"Well, as the wise professor said, gravitons."

Julien shook his head, not understanding.

"Gravitons, the one thing that can pull us from one universe to the next, that's love. Love pulled me to you and you to me."

"You're brilliant." Julien kissed her. "Then perhaps I did make my statues in an alternate reality." He kissed her again.

Rose smiled. "Anything can happen."

Julien pulled her closer. "My love of stonework brought them here, where I needed them most."

"I love that." Rose hugged him.

"And I love you." Julien kissed her.

When they finally came up for air, Rose said, "And I love you. Let's fall in love again every day."

"Yes, every day, my love."

ABOUT THE AUTHOR

Award-winning novelist *Beth Barany* writes magical tales of romance and adventure to worlds where anything is possible. In her off hours, Beth enjoys gardening, capoeira, and watching movies with her husband, award-winning bestselling author Ezra Barany. Together they live in Oakland, California, with their two cats and over 1,000 books.

You can sign up for Beth's newsletter at her site: http://author.bethbarany.com or follow her on Twitter or Facebook.

www.ingramcontent.com/pod-product-compliance
Lightning Source LLC
Chambersburg PA
CBHW030846030726
47495CB00005B/1401